Moon Wreck
Fleet Academy

Raymond L. Weil

DEDICATION

To my wife Debra for all of her patience while I sat in front of my computer typing. It has always been my dream to become an author. I also want to thank my children for their support and of course to the thousands of fans who have bought my books.

For updates on current writing projects and future publications go to my author website. Sign up for future notifications when new books come out on Amazon.

Website: http://raymondlweil.com/

Other Books by Raymond L. Weil
Available at Amazon
-

Dragon Dreams: Dragon Wars
Dragon Dreams: Gilmreth the Awakening
Dragon Dreams: Snowden the White Dragon
-

Star One: Tycho City: Discovery
Star One: Neutron Star
Star One: Dark Star
-

Moon Wreck:
Moon Wreck: Fleet Academy
The Slaver Wars: Alien Contact
The Slaver Wars: First Strike
The story continues in
The Slaver Wars: Retaliation
Coming January 2014
-

Star One: Tycho City: Survival
Coming December 2013
-

Dragon Dreams: Firestorm Mount
Coming 2014

Chapter One

Cadet Lieutenant Jeremy Strong was struggling to pay attention to the instructor in the front of the class. He stifled a yawn as he listened to the lecture. The older man in the dark blue fleet uniform was patiently explaining the basics of how a spaceship's sublight drive functioned. Without thinking, Jeremy let his thoughts stray; he found the lecture extremely boring. The man was rehashing an earlier lecture that a number of students had questions about. Jeremy was dark headed with hazel eyes and twenty-two years of age. This was his final year in the Fleet Academy located on the Moon. After graduation, he and his fellow classmates would be assigned a tour of duty on one of the fleet's four interplanetary exploration cruisers. Once the tour was complete, they would receive their official assignments and commissions.

Jeremy closed his eyes and thought back to the military exercise the day before. His group had spent six hours in spacesuits practicing grueling battle drills on the surface of the Moon. The drills were designed to improve decision making under extreme stress. Jeremy still marveled at the new lightweight spacesuits that were prevalent now. They were nothing like the old cumbersome spacesuits his dad had worn when the New Beginnings lunar lander crash-landed on the Moon twenty-four years ago.

His group of six won the final drill by taking advantage of the Moon's light gravity to move rapidly across the surface, shielded from their opponents by a small plateau. They managed to attack from an unexpected direction, taking the rival squad entirely by surprise. The other squad leader had been extremely aggravated at losing the drill to Jeremy and hadn't hesitated to voice his contempt at Jeremy's victory. Jeremy had listened patiently, and then reminded the other squad leader that his own shortsighted tactics had led to his squad's failure. Jeremy's squad had been exhausted, but the victory over the opposing squad had made it all worthwhile.

By winning the drill against the other squad, Jeremy's group had been allowed to sit at the commandant's table during the evening meal. Commandant Everson had spent part of the evening talking about the early days on the Moon before the academy had been built. Everson had described in detail what it had been like living on the crashed spaceship Avenger before the academy and the adjoining facilities had been constructed. He had gone on and described how the Avenger had been partially rebuilt to make it more habitable. They had spent months clearing wreckage and repairing what damage they could to the interstellar ship. Jeremy had heard Greg Johnson and his father speak of this a number of times, but it was interesting to hear someone else's perspective of those early days.

"Cadet Lieutenant Strong!" Instructor Branson's voice echoed loudly across the room. "Do you find this lecture so boring that you can't keep your eyes open?"

Jeremy's eyes snapped open, and he felt as if he should kick himself for losing his focus in class. This wouldn't look good considering who his father was, and especially being so close to graduation. "No, sir," responded Jeremy, trying to keep his voice level and respectful with his eyes focusing on the instructor.

"Is that so," Branson replied, doubtfully. His strict eyes cut into Jeremy like a knife as he thought about what he should do.

Jeremy was one of his top students, but this mental lapse on his part could not be allowed to go unpunished. He wished he could spare the young man the humiliation he was about to be put through. However, because Jeremy's father was Admiral Strong, he didn't dare. It might look as if he were showing favoritism toward the admiral's son.

In a strict voice, he said. "Why don't you come up here and describe to the class how the sublight drive core functions on our new ships. I want you to describe in detail the necessary core temperatures and the metal alloys used to contain the drive reaction."

Taking a deep breath, Jeremy stood up and walked to the front of the class. He knew that everyone's eyes were focused on him. Turning around, he looked at his fellow classmates. There was almost an even mix of male and females. His eyes fell on fellow Cadet Lieutenant Matt Barr. Barr had a particularly pleased smirk on his face. It was Matt's squad that Jeremy had beaten in the battle drill the previous day. The two had been constant competitors ever since they had started at the academy together four years ago. Jeremy also knew that the two of them would never be friends.

"The sublight core is powered by a fusion reaction," Jeremy began in an even tone.

He smiled inwardly to himself. Because of who is father was, he spent a lot of extra time studying. He wasn't near the top of the class for a lack of effort. He also spent a lot of extra time studying for another reason. Up above the Moon, docked to the recently completed spacedock, was the exploration cruiser New Horizon. It was the first ship to be equipped with an experimental FTL drive. Its full crew would be named in the coming month after academy graduation. The word being spread around campus was that part of the crew would be selected from this year's graduates, and Jeremy planned to be on that ship. He was currently ranked number three in the standings of the eighty-seven seniors in his class. After final exams in two more weeks, he hoped to be number one!

Instructor Branson kept a strict and disciplined look upon his face, but he felt relieved that Jeremy was obviously extremely familiar with the subject matter. The young man was doing an exceptional job of explaining the workings of the sublight drive in Earth's spaceships. He felt pleased that it would not be necessary to give Jeremy any demerits for his brief lapse in class.

After class, Jeremy was walking down a hallway in the main instruction building, preparing to take a connecting transit tube to the senior dorm. Jeremy still marveled at all the work that had been done in the crater where the Avenger had crashed so long ago. All the wreckage had been cleared, and a number of new buildings had been constructed. Underground transit tubes connected the buildings to one another for safety reasons. The primary and largest building in the crater was the large Fleet Academy, where the brightest students from Earth were brought for instruction. Each year, fifty thousand students were put through a strict interview process, with two hundred and fifty selected to attend the prestigious Fleet Academy on the Moon. If you wanted to be involved in the exploration of the solar system and possibly travel to other worlds someday, then the Fleet Academy was where you wanted to be.

"Jeremy," a familiar female voice spoke from behind him.

Coming to a stop and turning, Jeremy saw that Cadet Ensign Kelsey Grainger was the one who had called out to him. Kelsey was a cute blonde the same age he was and was studying astrogation. She was also currently ranked number two in the class. They had been friendly rivals and good friends for quite some time.

"I was so worried when Instructor Branson reprimanded you," she began, her deep blue eyes gazing at Jeremy. "I was afraid he might give you demerits for falling asleep in class. Jeremy, we're so close to graduation. How could you do that?"

"I wasn't asleep," Jeremy replied with a defensive smile. Kelsey was part of his squad and extremely easy to get along with. She was someone he had learned to depend on. "I have heard that lecture so many times that I can repeat it in my sleep. I guess I just let my thoughts stray for a moment."

"I'm glad you knew the information," Kelsey continued with a nod. "You did a great job explaining the workings of the sublight drive. I don't think Instructor Branson could have done any better. You need to be careful. We have finals and graduation coming up."

"Thanks, Kelsey," responded Jeremy, feeling pleased with her praise. He wouldn't let his thoughts stray like that again. Too much was at stake. "But I'm probably still going to hear about it from my dad when he finds out."

"Your father," Kelsey said, her deep blue eyes growing wide.

Sometimes she forgot who Jeremy's dad was. Admiral Jason Strong had been in charge of the Avenger Project and the Fleet Academy since its inception. Kelsey had never been allowed on the Avenger; none of the cadets had. Only research scientists and dignitaries from Earth were ever allowed upon the ancient, crashed spacecraft. Even Jeremy's access had been severely restricted since he had entered the academy.

Jeremy paused for a moment. He was supposed to eat with his parents later on. Greg Johnson and his wife Elizabeth were coming up from Earth on today's shuttle, and the two families and some close friends were going to get together. With a distasteful frown, Jeremy knew that meant the Johnson's daughter Katie would also be coming. Greg still worked as a government consultant on the Avenger Project, and he and his family came up to the Moon several times a year to discuss the current conditions down on Earth.

Katie was a royal pain and Jeremy wasn't looking forward to spending any time with the aggravating fifteen-year-old. She was constantly under foot. When he was younger and had been attending school down on Earth, he had stayed with the Johnsons. Katie had always followed him around everywhere. Now that she was older, it was becoming even worse. Looking over at Kelsey, he had a sudden inspiration. "Kelsey, what are your plans for tonight?"

Kelsey looked at Jeremy in surprise. She knew he didn't date. Jeremy spent most of his time studying. "Nothing yet," she replied cautiously. She didn't want to get her hopes up too high. When they did get together after class, it was usually to study together. They had always had a very friendly relationship, and Kelsey had been careful not to push it, even though at times she had fantasized about dating Jeremy.

"My parents have some friends coming up from Earth, and we're having a family meal in the private dining room at the academy cafeteria. Afterwards, they're going to go on a tour of the academy facilities. I'm allowed to bring a guest. Would you be interested in coming?"

Kelsey didn't want to sound too excited about Jeremy asking her out. "Sure," she responded, smiling and feeling her face flush slightly. "I could use a good meal." This didn't sound like a real date, but it was close enough.

Jeremy was in his dorm room getting ready for the evening meal with his family. Walking over to the large, heavily reinforced window that looked out over the bleak lunar landscape, his eyes wandered upward. His dorm room was on the third floor of the five-story building. His eyes stopped on two bright points of light that were touching one another. It was where the New Horizon spacecraft was docked to the orbiting spacedock at the Moon's Lagrange point. From here, all he could see were two bright dots in the night sky. He knew that the New Horizon was nearly 400 meters in length and was by far the largest spacecraft Earth had constructed up to this point. It had taken four years to build the large interstellar spaceship.

Earth had four other spacecraft, all of which were smaller than the New Horizon. The others were used for exploration missions in the solar system, including supplying the small science colony on Mars. The exploration cruisers were all 200 meters in length and easily capable of making the roundtrip to Mars in less than a week.

The New Horizon would be leaving on her first interstellar mission within another six months. Part of the crew were already on board familiarizing themselves with the ship's intricate systems. The final crew would consist of two hundred and forty highly trained men and women and possibly ten cadets from this year's class. The announcement of which cadets would get to go would be made immediately after graduation.

Stepping over to the full-length mirror in his room, Jeremy checked his uniform one last time to make sure everything was perfect. If he were one of the ten cadets selected for the New Horizon mission, he didn't want there to be any doubt that he deserved it.

On board the Avenger, Admiral Jason Strong stood in the Command Center with his long time friend Greg Johnson. They were talking to Ariel, and Greg was waiting patiently for the AI to send an FTL message to his son. His son was at New Tellus working on the large orbiting shipyard that had been constructed by the Federation survivors. Some of the top graduates from the academy occasionally were transferred to New Tellus or Ceres for additional and specialized training.

"Hard to believe we can send a message across twenty-seven light years of space," Greg commented as Ariel transmitted the message that Elizabeth and he had put together.

"With the new technology developed on Ceres, it will only take the message twenty minutes to get there. But it's still just a message. You and Elizabeth need to fly out to New Tellus to see Mathew," Jason commented with a friendly smile, looking over at Greg. Greg hadn't changed much over the years. He was a little heavier, and his hair was grayer. "It wouldn't be that hard to arrange."

"Elizabeth would never agree to it," responded Greg, shaking his head. "It scares her to death just to fly to the Moon. I can't imagine how she would react flying into a spatial vortex and going into hyperspace. No, as long as we can send Mathew a message occasionally, that will be fine. He has two week's leave coming in another four months and then will be coming home. Elizabeth's already making big plans for his return."

"Mathew is doing fine on the shipyard," Ariel spoke, her dark eyes seeming to sparkle as she gazed at Jason and Greg. She kept a very close watch on the children of these two men.

She could well remember how these two had first entered the Avenger, made their way cautiously through the wrecked ship, and eventually into the Command Center. Since that time, much had changed. She had named Jason as commander of the Avenger, and later Fleet Admiral Streth had promoted him to admiral. Fleet Admiral Streth had long since returned to cryosleep. Someday the venerated

Fleet Admiral would lead the humans of Earth and the Federation survivors of Ceres against the Hocklyns. However, that was still many years in the future.

"How is progress coming on the New Horizon?" Greg asked curiously. He knew the ship should be nearing completion. "Everyone on Earth is talking about the first interstellar flight. It's really big news."

"She's ready to go," spoke Jason, feeling pleased that the ship had been built by humans from Earth with just a small bit of help from Ceres.

"Has the crew been selected?" Greg asked. He knew that ten cadets were going to be included to fly on the mission.

"The majority of them," Jason answered with a nod. It had been a long process picking the crew. There were so many qualified candidates to choose from, and everyone wanted to go. "The Earth's brightest and best will be on the mission."

"What about the cadets, have they been chosen yet?"

"Not until after graduation," responded Jason, glancing around the Command Center and noticing that Ariel's eyes were still focused on them. "Once the cadets are finished with finals and the standings are posted, we will make a decision."

"Will Jeremy make it?" asked Greg, knowing there had been some discussion between the higher ups in the academy about this. Some were deeply concerned about how it would look if Jason's son went on the mission.

"If he keeps his grades up," Jason replied with a grin. He was very proud of what Jeremy had accomplished at the academy.

"Has a destination been chosen?" asked Greg, knowing that the Federation survivors had already explored all the nearer stars.

The Federation survivors had a robust exploration program and were constantly sending out exploratory missions. Greg knew there was another driving reason behind the numerous missions. The Federation survivors hoped to find other advanced civilizations that might be willing to help them in the future war against the Hocklyns.

Greg understood it was now time for the humans of Earth to learn what was out there. That was one of the primary reasons for the New Horizon mission. The humans of Earth needed to take the necessary steps to be able to embrace all the new technology that was being introduced. Only a few people on Earth even knew about the Federation survivors and Ceres. Even fewer knew about the Hocklyns and the threat they represented to Earth's future. These were closely guarded secrets. Everyone thought the new technology was coming from the computers on the Avenger and reverse engineering of some of the ship's advanced technology. What very few knew was that the majority of the new technology was actually coming from Ceres.

"Tau Ceti," responded Jason, recalling the numerous long discussions. "We have discussed it in detail, and it should be a good enough test for the new systems and the FTL drive the New Horizon is equipped with."

"Tau Ceti," repeated Greg, trying to recall what he knew about that star. "Isn't it about eleven light years distant?"

"Yes," answered Jason, nodding his head. "It's 11.9 to be exact. There are two habitable planets in the liquid water zone. They are both suitable for eventual colonization."

"Won't it take two jumps for the New Horizon to get there?"

"They will jump to Proxima Centauri first, take a few quick sensor scans, and check the ship's systems. If everything is working properly, they will then jump to Tau Ceti."

"I can still remember when I was young and dreamed about going to the stars," Greg spoke with a distant sigh. That seemed like so long ago. "That was before we found the Avenger and Ariel."

"You can travel to the stars anytime you want, Greg," Ariel spoke with a refreshing and innocent smile. Her black hair lay upon her shoulders, and she was wearing her customary dark blue fleet uniform. "Ships leave Ceres all the time. I can arrange for you to go to any of the explored star systems if you like."

Greg looked at the large viewscreen in front of the Command Center where Ariel's avatar was displayed. He knew she was serious in her offer.

"It's not the same now," he replied slowly. "However, going on the New Horizon would be fun."

Jason laughed and shook his head. "I think we're both getting too old for that. We can leave the exploration of the nearby stars to our children. At least we both got to go to New Tellus together with Admiral Streth in those early days."

"Speaking of our children, isn't it getting close to time to eat?" commented Greg, rubbing his stomach. He had gained a little weight as he had gotten older, but he was still in pretty good shape. "I'm starving."

"I think you're always starving," responded Jason with a chuckle. "Let's head on over to the cafeteria. I suspect our families are already waiting."

"Just keep a watch out for Katie," Greg warned with a heavy sigh. "That daughter of mine has been driving me crazy recently with all the questions she has been asking about the Avenger."

"She's a teenager, Greg," Jason said with an understanding smile. Then, looking over at his best friend, he continued, "What did you expect?"

Kelsey had just finished dressing and was looking at her reflection critically in the mirror. Adding just a little bit of makeup to her cheeks, she felt satisfied with her appearance. She felt nervous about the dinner tonight. Taking a deep breath, she looked at her reflection one more time. Her deep blue eyes gazed back, and while her blonde hair was cut short, it was still long enough to allow for a slight curl. She was dressed in a dark blue fleet uniform, open at the neck, which was allowed for informal meals.

Hearing a knock at her door, she knew that Jeremy had arrived. Kelsey wondered why she was feeling so nervous about this date. She had known Jeremy since her first day at the academy, and he had always been charming and polite. Not once had he ever acted inappropriately or tried to take advantage of his father being the admiral in charge of this facility on the Moon.

Opening the door, she found Jeremy standing there with one of those big, easy smiles that always seemed to be on his face. "Hello," she said hoping she didn't sound nervous.

"Hi Kelsey," Jeremy replied innocently. "Are you ready for this?"

"Sure," answered Kelsey, trying to sound as normal as possible. She could feel her heart fluttering. Perhaps she was expecting too much out of this. After all, it was only a meal, and he had been nice enough to ask her to accompany him.

"Then let's go," said Jeremy grinning. "This should be the best food we have had in a while. I'm hoping for a big juicy steak!"

Kelsey laughed, pleased that Jeremy seemed to be looking forward to this. "I could use a steak myself," she admitted, then glancing down at her figure she added, "A small one, anyway."

"You look great, Kelsey," said Jeremy, noticing that she had evidently spent some extra time on her hair and applying makeup. Jeremy realized something he had taken for granted, perhaps because he had always looked at Kelsey as a close friend and nothing beyond that. Kelsey was actually a very beautiful young woman.

"Thank you, Jeremy." Kelsey felt her face flush and hoped that Jeremy wouldn't notice. Damn! She felt so out of place in this situation.

The two walked down the corridor and toward the transit tube that would take them to the cafeteria and the private dining room. Neither suspected that after the events of tonight their lives would never be the same again.

They took several sets of stairs and walked down a long transit tube to the large building that contained the cafeteria. They passed several other cadets who gave them some questioning looks, probably wondering why they were so dressed up and where they were going. A few minutes later, they entered the private dining room. Jeremy took a moment to take stock of who all were there. He saw his father and mother and of course Greg Johnson and his wife Elizabeth. Commandant Everson was also there, as well as semi-retired General Greene and a few others.

"Jeremy!" a high-pitched voice screamed.

Jeremy turned just in time as Katie threw herself at him, trapping him in a tight, embarrassing hug. After a long moment, Katie let a flustered Jeremy go and then turned to look questionably at Kelsey.

"Who are you?" she asked in a voice tinged with jealousy.

What have I gotten myself into? Kelsey thought, looking at the young teenage girl with shoulder length blonde hair. She knew that this must be Greg and Elizabeth Johnson's daughter.

"I'm Cadet Ensign Kelsey Grainger," she answered in a calm voice and smiling at the young girl.

"Kelsey, huh?" Katie spoke sharply, her green eyes checking Kelsey out. Then turning back to Jeremy, she asked. "Is she your girlfriend?"

"We're just close friends," Jeremy responded, quickly feeling self-conscious He noticed that everyone in the room was staring at them. This wasn't how he had wanted the evening to go. Leave it to Katie to attract everyone's attention.

"You're sitting next to me," continued Katie looking at Kelsey challengingly. "Your girlfriend can sit on the other side of you."

"Go sit down, Katie," her father said in a firm voice, walking up and shaking Jeremy's hand. Greg knew that Jeremy needed rescuing. Katie had a way of doing that to people. "You sure are growing Jeremy. You remind me of your father when he was your age."

Jeremy nodded. He knew that his father and Greg had been friends even before the New Beginnings mission. "This is Cadet Ensign Kelsey Grainer," Jeremy said introducing Kelsey to Greg.

"Hello, Kelsey," Greg replied with an easy and disarming smile. "Don't let my daughter scare you."

"Hello Mr. Johnson," Kelsey replied, her eyes growing wide at actually talking to Greg Johnson, one of the two men on the New Beginnings mission. The other was, of course, Jeremy's father, Admiral Jason Strong. "I have heard and read so much about you."

"Don't believe everything you read," replied Greg, grinning. "The history books tend to exaggerate."

A few moments later, they were all seated and the meal began. Jeremy knew he was going to be in for a long evening with Katie sitting next to him. Kelsey seemed to be adapting to everything extremely well. She was like that and it was one of the reasons Jeremy enjoyed her company so much. Nothing seemed to take her by surprise.

"So, are you going on the New Horizon mission?" asked Katie, staring at Jeremy and pointedly ignoring Kelsey.

"The cadets haven't been chosen yet," answered Jeremy, uneasily. He knew that Katie was going to bombard him with unending questions the entire evening.

"The cadets will be chosen after graduation," Commandant Everson spoke from where he sat across the table. He had been watching Jeremy and Katie with amusement. His own daughter had been much like Katie when she was fifteen. Now she was grown and working on the shipyard at New Tellus. "Katie, I am sure you will be interested in knowing that both Cadet Lieutenant Strong and Cadet Ensign Grainger are at the top of their class."

Katie looked down the table at Kelsey with a frown. "So that means that both of you could be going on the New Horizon mission."

"Could be," Kelsey spoke with a friendly smile. It was so obvious to her that this young teenager had a crush on Jeremy. No wonder he had wanted her to come tonight. He needed some protection from this young adolescent girl. It didn't bother her that this was probably the reason he had asked her out. It made her feel good to know that he had turned to her for help. "What are you studying in school Katie?"

"Computers," Katie spoke, her face brightening. She loved to talk about computers. "I hope to be a programmer when I get older."

"We can certainly use some good programmers," Kelsey responded with a nod. "If we have time, perhaps later you can show me some of what you have learned in school."

"That would be great," responded Katie, deciding that maybe Kelsey wasn't so bad after all. She would reserve judgment until later.

"I have seen some of Katie's work with computers," Lisa spoke from where she was sitting next to Jason. "It's very good. If she keeps it up, she may find herself working up here at the academy someday."

"If she can stay out of trouble," added Elizabeth, eyeing her young daughter. She hoped Katie wasn't bothering Jeremy and his date too much. The young woman Jeremy was with was quite attractive. Lisa hadn't mentioned that Jeremy was dating. She would have to ask her about it later.

"I can stay out of trouble," Katie said defensively, glancing at her mother.

"Really?" Jeremy spoke quietly so only Katie could hear.

"Yes, I can!" replied Katie, giving Jeremy a threatening look.

"I'm sure she can behave if she needs to," added Kelsey, nodding at Katie. "Girls are just different than boys."

Katie nodded. She was beginning to like Kelsey better all the time.

Everyone continued to eat and make small talk. Kelsey began to feel more at ease and even allowed herself to be drawn into a conversation with Admiral Strong, Jeremy's dad.

"What are your future plans, Kelsey?" asked Jason, preferring to use first names in this informal setting. "I understand you're studying astrogation."

"I want to navigate a starship someday," replied Kelsey, her blue eyes taking on a faraway look.

"An ambitious goal," responded Jason, nodding his head approvingly. "If you qualify to be one of the cadets to go on the New Horizon mission, you might just get your wish sooner than you expect."

"I hope so," Kelsey responded, respectfully. It had sent chills down her back hearing Admiral Strong use her first name. She had already decided that she was going to like Jeremy's dad.

"Speaking of the New Horizon," Greg broke in as he used his steak knife to cut off a generous portion of the tantalizing steak on his plate. "You were saying earlier that the ship's ready?"

"She could leave tomorrow if she had to," responded Jason, recalling the latest status report from the spacedock. "Part of the crew is currently on board, and they're in the process of doing a final check of all the ship's control systems."

"When will they be checking the ship's drive systems?" Commandant Everson asked curiously. He knew the ship hadn't left the close vicinity of the spacedock yet.

"In another two weeks," responded Jason, recalling the schedule. "If everything is found to be working properly they will be taking the New Horizon on a sublight trip to Mars. The Columbia will be escorting her in case there are any problems."

Everson knew that the Columbia was one of the four smaller exploration cruisers that were being used to explore the solar system. The smaller ships were also used on a regular basis for further training of the cadets after graduation. A few cadets were placed on each of the exploration cruisers to complete their officer's training.

"What about the FTL drive?" asked Greg, laying his fork down and looking over at Jason. He knew this was the key to the ship's mission. The drive was not as efficient as a Federation drive, but they were trying to introduce Federation technology gradually.

"It's scheduled for testing a month after the sublight trip," responded Jason, recalling the FTL test schedule that Commander Tellson and he had come up with. "The ship will make fourteen micro-jumps in the system to check the drive. Once we're satisfied everything is working properly, Tellson will bring the ship back to the spacedock and we will begin making the final preparations for the actual mission."

"We have introduced so much in the last few years," Lisa said, looking over at her husband. Sometimes it feels as if we're moving too fast."

"I wish we could introduce the new technology even faster," Jason responded, looking around the table.

"How is Earth adapting to the new technologies that are being introduced?" asked Emerson, looking over at Greg. "I understand there have been a few problems."

Greg leaned back in his chair and nodded his head. "The medical technology has been the biggest problem. The new medical technology has allowed us to cure most forms of cancer. Several other serious diseases are also in the process of being eradicated. This has had a serious economic impact in the medical community, which has for years based its economy on long-term care. It's caused tens of thousands of people to be put out of work."

"That's why we're introducing the technology we found on the Avenger gradually," Jason added. He was being careful in what he said. Not even his son knew about Ariel and the Federation survivors on Ceres. Only a select group on the Moon and in the leading governments down on Earth knew about that closely guarded secret.

"Some of the Third World countries are resisting the introduction of some of the new technology," commented General Greene, picking up his glass and taking a sip of water. "There have even been some threats against companies that use some of the technology."

"I'm not surprised," spoke Emerson, nodding his head in acknowledgement. "People are always resistant to change."

"That's one of the reasons we have tried to be so careful with some of the technology we have been introducing in those countries," explained Greg, looking around the group. "We have been working very closely with those governments on what we thought would be safe to introduce. Even so, we have found some of the people in those countries to be very resistant to new ideas and technology."

"There have even been some threats made in our more advanced countries," added General Greene, showing some worry on his face. Over the years his hair had turned mostly gray, and there were more worry lines around his eyes. "Even a few against the New Horizon mission."

"Anything we should be concerned about?" asked Jason, frowning. He wasn't pleased to hear there had been threats against the New Horizon.

They were being so careful to introduce Federation technology slowly. The plans were to have Earth up to what was considered normal on the former Federation worlds within one hundred years. Once that was reached, the Federation survivors on Ceres would reveal themselves. It was also at that time that Earth and Ceres would begin focusing on preparing for the eventual war with the Hocklyns.

"We are watching several dissident groups down on Earth," General Greene responded in a serious tone of voice, leaning back in his chair. He was working as a security consultant to the government for anything that had to do with the Avenger and its technology. "We don't think they pose a serious danger as of yet, but they do bear watching. We have several people close to their organizations, so we will know shortly if there is a serious threat."

Jason nodded his head. He had a meeting scheduled later with General Greene and Greg, and he fully intended to get into more detail about this. It might also be necessary to involve some of the Federation people. There were a quite a few of them down on Earth, and he wanted to make sure that none of them were in danger.

"How are things going at the academy?" asked Elizabeth, looking at Commandant Everson.

She didn't like the men talking about things that might worry her. She was much more familiar with the academy since their son Mathew had graduated from here four years ago and preferred to talk about it. It had taken her a while to get used to the idea of flying to the Moon and Mathew joining the academy.

"Our current graduating class is by far the best yet," replied Emerson, glancing over approvingly at Jeremy and Kelsey. "Our freshman class is the largest up to now, and we expect to continue to increase enrollment over the coming years."

Jeremy and Kelsey listened with interest as the two talked. Every once in a while, Katie would ask one of them a question about the academy and its classes. She was highly curious about the Fleet Academy and what it was like to attend. Jeremy and Kelsey found themselves drawn into the conversation, explaining to Katie what life was like living on the Moon.

The meal finally ended, and Jeremy noticed his dad staring at him. He wants something, Jeremy realized. He just isn't sure how to ask it. Jeremy braced himself. He knew it probably had something to do with Katie. His dad probably wanted him to show her around the academy.

"Jeremy," began Jason, knowing that Jeremy wouldn't be pleased with what he was about to ask. Then his eyes fell on Kelsey, and he realized that perhaps this could work out. He knew that Kelsey had been wanting to go on board the Avenger for quite some time. Her advisor had mentioned that to Jason several weeks back when they had been discussing the academy's top students. "Would you and Kelsey mind doing us a big favor?"

"What kind of favor?" Jeremy asked with a sneaking suspicion, noticing that his mother and the Johnsons were staring at him.

"We need to attend a special meeting on some of the problems we're encountering with introducing the new technology down on

Earth. Would you and Kelsey mind staying with Katie in our quarters for a few hours?"

Jeremy looked over at Kelsey. Her eyes had brightened, and she had an excited look on her face. He knew she had been wanting to get on the Avenger for weeks now. Katie also had a pleased look upon her face. Letting out a long sigh, he looked back over at his father. "Sure, no problem."

Kelsey looked curiously around the admiral's quarters on the Avenger. They were quite large and spacious. "So this is where you were raised?"

"Not really," replied Jeremy, sitting down on a plush sofa and turning on the vid screen. He wondered if there was anything good on to watch. This night wasn't turning out quite as he had planned. "I spent a lot of my childhood going back and forth between the Moon and Earth. I stayed with the Johnsons and attended school down on Earth until I started attending the academy. During breaks, I would come up here and spend time with my parents."

"Were you close to Katie's brother, Mathew?" Kelsey knew that Mathew was currently in the fleet and had finished highly ranked at the academy.

"Mathew's four years older than I am," responded Jeremy, watching Kelsey. "We were close, but it's been a while since I've seen or talked to him.

Kelsey came over and sat down next to Jeremy with their legs almost touching. She didn't want to seem as if she were coming on too strong. She still wasn't quite sure what Jeremy wanted from this date. However, one thing she did want Jeremy to tell her was what life had been like being brought up on the Avenger. The Avenger and the mysteries surrounding it had always fascinated her. "So tell me what it was like living on the Avenger."

Jeremy took a deep breath. He knew Kelsey was fascinated by the Avenger, all the cadets were. "A lot of the areas on the Avenger are restricted, so I was only allowed in the more public areas. Even today, this ship has a lot of secrets. Sometimes, when I am on the ship, I feel as if someone is constantly watching me."

For the next hour, Jeremy spoke about his childhood and what it was like being the son of Admiral Jason Strong, who had discovered the Avenger. He told her about the early days before the academy had been built and how things had not been so glamorous then.

Katie listened to the two for a while and even asked a few questions. Some of what they were talking about she had heard from her father. During those early days, he had spent a lot of time on the Avenger. She finally excused herself, saying she needed to go to the restroom. Instead, after making sure that Kelsey and Jeremy weren't watching, she slipped down a short hallway and into Admiral Strong's office. Unbuttoning two buttons on her shirt, she pulled out a small handheld computer. It was the latest and best that money could buy. It also had several special programs on it that Katie had carefully written just for this occasion.

Taking a deep breath, Katie walked over to Admiral Strong's desk and laying her computer down, she activated a program that should interact with the ship's computer that was on the desk. It was time for her to find out just who this Ariel was she heard her mom and dad whispering about on occasion. She knew it had something to do with the Avenger. She just wasn't sure what, but she intended to find out.

Ariel was watching the three young people in the admiral's quarters. When Katie slipped into the admiral's private office, Ariel's interest intensified. What was the young girl up to? When Katie took out her small computer and activated a program, which instantly began to connect to her system, Ariel's interest peeked. With amazement, she watched as Katie's program began interacting with her security programs. She was surprised at how advanced it was. Ariel smiled to herself. She was quite pleased that Katie was showing such initiative. It promised a bright future for the young girl in computer programming. Ariel just wasn't sure what to do. She didn't want to get Katie in trouble with her parents, so she decided just to wait and let the situation develop.

After a few minutes, Katie began to feel nervous. If she couldn't break into the system soon, Jeremy and Kelsey would come looking for her. She didn't want them to find her in the admiral's office. Letting out a long breath, she activated a second program. This one would search out and find any files that mentioned the word Ariel. She watched as a small light on her small computer began blinking green. It seemed to be working.

Ariel almost panicked as the new program blew past several of her firewalls. This programming was truly advanced. It was almost as good as what Lisa could do. Not only that, but Katie was searching for any references to Ariel. How had the young girl found out? With resignation, Ariel knew what she had to do. She just hoped Jason wouldn't get too upset. Of course there was a slim chance that he would never have to know.

Katie was just about to give up when she heard a strange noise behind her. Slowly turning around, she noticed that the large viewscreen on the front wall of the office had come on. A beautiful dark headed young woman was pictured on the screen. What's this? Katie wondered nervously. Then the woman on the screen smiled.

"Hello Katie," Ariel spoke in a pleasant voice. "That's a very sophisticated set of programs you have written."

"Who are you?" stammered Katie, realizing that she had been caught. She noticed the woman was dressed in a dark blue fleet uniform. She was busted, and this was going to get her into a lot of trouble. This person must be someone in security.

The woman on the screen hesitated for a long moment. "I'm Ariel, the AI of the light cruiser Avenger. I'm the one you are looking for with those two computer programs."

"An AI," Katie breathed slowly scarcely believing what she had just heard. "How long have you been watching me?" asked Katie, wondering if this was a program that Lisa had developed. AIs had always fascinated her. "Did Lisa design your program?" With resignation, Katie knew that if this was Lisa's program then Lisa would be notified shortly about what she had just attempted.

"No," replied Ariel. "This all began a long time ago. I don't have time to explain it all to you now, but I was on the ship when Admiral Strong first stepped into the Command Center twenty-four years ago."

Katie turned pale and almost stopped breathing as she realized what Ariel was saying. "You were on the ship when it crashed?"

"Yes," Ariel replied, then in a more serious tone, "You can't tell anyone that we talked. You and I both could get into a lot of trouble over this. If you promise to stay quiet and behave, we can talk again and I will tell you more."

Katie was silent for a moment. Talking to Ariel was like talking to a real person. It was easy to make her mind up. "You have a deal Ariel, but I want to know everything."

"You will, Katie," Ariel promised solemnly. "But you need to put your computer away and go back into the main room. Jeremy and Kelsey are starting to wonder what's taking you so long."

Jeremy felt relieved when Katie came back into the main room. For a moment, he had been afraid that she had managed to sneak out. He didn't know how he would have explained to his dad that Katie was running around unsupervised on the Avenger.

"Hi," Katie said with a friendly smile, plopping down on the sofa next to Jeremy. "Anything on the vid?"

Later, Jeremy walked Kelsey back to her quarters. They were both quiet as they made their way through the transit tubes back to the senior dorm. Jeremy was still confused by Katie's behavior. She had been so polite most of the evening that he had a hard time believing that it was the same teenage girl.

"You know, Katie is extremely talented," Kelsey finally said as they came to a stop in front of her door. "Don't let her being so young hide the fact that she has a rare talent for computers."

"I know, but sometime she can be a real pain." Jeremy paused and looked at Kelsey.

He was unsure whether he should attempt to kiss her or not. He wasn't sure if this could be called a real date since they had ended up babysitting. He hoped Kelsey wasn't too disappointed in how the night had ended.

Kelsey solved the problem by leaning forward and giving Jeremy a quick kiss on the lips. "I did enjoy tonight, but we probably shouldn't do this too often. We have a lot of studying to do in the next few weeks if we want to qualify to go on the New Horizon mission."

"I know," Jeremy responded, fully in agreement and visibly relaxing. Now was not the time to get emotionally involved. He knew it would be best for the time being to keep their relationship at the friendship level. However, he had really enjoyed spending the evening with Kelsey. It made him realize just how special she was.

Kelsey turned to go into her quarters, then stopped and glanced back at Jeremy with a mischievous smile. "But if you have to babysit again, you'd better call me!"

"Sure," Jeremy replied with a grin. "I'll see you in class in the morning." He watched Kelsey go into her quarters and shut the door.

Turning, he started down the hallway to take the elevator to his own floor.

Back in her parent's guest quarters on the Avenger, Katie lay in bed deep in thought. Her discovery of just who Ariel was had been stunning. She was now more determined than ever to learn everything she could about the Avenger and the AI. She hoped she could become friends with Ariel. For a long time, she lay in bed thinking about what she had discovered.

In the Command Center, Ariel stared out across the quiet room. Only two people were currently on duty, and they were manning the communication and sensor consoles. The Avenger had the only working FTL communication gear outside of Ceres. The advanced sensors on the Avenger were also capable of monitoring the ship traffic in the entire solar system. Ariel hoped she had not made a mistake talking to Katie. The young girl showed so much promise. Ariel now had to decide how much to tell Katie. The families of Admiral Strong and Greg Johnson were very special to her, and for that reason alone she was willing to speak to Katie of things that were forbidden for most people on the Moon.

Chapter Two

Jeremy was on his way to class when he heard some loud, boisterous talking behind him. Stopping, he turned around and saw Cadet Lieutenant Matt Barr and two members of his squad.

"Hey daddy's boy!" Barr spoke contemptuously, looking at Jeremy. "I still haven't figured out how you cheated in that drill the other day, but I will."

"I didn't cheat," Jeremy replied calmly, refusing to be baited into a fight by Barr. "You were in a static defense that wasn't defendable from all directions."

"It doesn't matter," Barr continued with a gloating look on his face. "I'm still ranked number one in our class and will be going on the New Horizon mission. Even though you're ranked number three, they will never let you go!"

Jeremy didn't reply. He just turned around and started walking off, with Barr and his cronies still making insinuating comments behind his back. Jeremy felt anger but knew he couldn't afford to be drawn into a confrontation. He was determined more than ever to ace those final exams and take that top spot away from Barr in two more weeks. Sometimes he wondered how someone with Barr's attitude had even gotten into the academy. The interview process was lengthy and quite thorough.

Barr watched Jeremy walk away. He smiled arrogantly at the receding form of Cadet Lieutenant Strong. There was no doubt in Barr's mind that he would be on the New Horizon mission. That was the whole reason for him being at the Fleet Academy. The number one class ranking was his and would remain so. He would make certain of that.

"Want us to rough him up some?" asked Cadet Ensign Rafferty, watching Jeremy's retreating figure. "We can arrange for him to fall down a flight of stairs. It can be set up to look like an accident."

"No, leave him to me," replied Barr, shaking his head. "I will take care of the admiral's son later. We just need to stick with the plan."

On board the Avenger, Jason and Greg were in the Command Center. They had just finished talking to Admiral Anlon on Ceres. Admiral Anlon was currently the highest-ranking military officer on the asteroid and in charge of the base plus all military operations. Jason and Anlon tried to talk to each other daily whenever possible.

"Their new ship is finally finished," commented Greg, looking over at Jason with deep concern in his eyes. "Do you think it's wise to send that ship back to their old worlds to see what the Hocklyns are up to?" Greg knew this would be a hard sell to the involved governments down on Earth.

"I don't think we have a choice," replied Jason, thinking about the conversation he had just finished with the admiral. "Their new ship is a Monarch Two heavy cruiser. It's covered in a special composite material that makes the ship almost impossible to detect with sensors. It has better shields and weapons than any other ship they have ever built. If they would have had ships like this one when the Hocklyns attacked, the Federation might have been able to survive."

"It took them ten years to make enough of that material to cover the ship," added Greg, folding his arms across his chest and looking at Jason. "That's an exceptionally determined group of people. But this mission could still be extremely dangerous. Right now, the Hocklyns don't know we exist. They think all humans were killed when they destroyed the Federation. I would prefer to keep it that way. If they have to use those new and improved weapons, it will tell the Hocklyns that there are still some human survivors out in the galaxy somewhere. That could cause the Hocklyns to start looking for us. How do I explain that to the governments down on Earth?"

"We need to know, Greg," Jason responded in a serious tone, leaning back in the command chair and taking a deep breath. He knew Greg would have to do a lot of talking to convince the governments involved in the Avenger Project that this mission was necessary. "We have to know how far the Hocklyn Slave Empire has spread since they destroyed the Human Federation of Worlds. It will let us know if our timeline is still workable."

"It's still so hard to imagine what's in our future," continued Greg, letting out a long and deep breath. "We are preparing to fight an interstellar war some day. Most of the people down on Earth still don't know what's up here or ahead of us."

"It's either prepare or see Earth destroyed like the Federation worlds," replied Jason, arching his eyebrows and looking up at the main viewscreen and Ariel. Ariel in the past had shown both of them what had happened to the Federation. They had also seen videos on

Ceres that the Federation survivors had provided. The videos had been both frightening and eye opening.

"We can't allow Earth to be destroyed," Ariel said in a determined voice, looking at the two men who meant so much to her. "The Hocklyns and their masters will not show Earth any mercy. Once they learn of us, they will do everything within their power to destroy us. I agree with Admiral Anlon that we need to know what the Hocklyns have been doing since they destroyed the Federation worlds. Only by sending the new ship can we find out."

"This is just a necessary step in the war effort," continued Jason, thinking about all that had been done in recent years. "Their commander will be careful about not letting her ship be detected. The ship is equipped with a number of stealth scouts that will do most of the surveying of possible new Hocklyn controlled worlds as well as the old Federation ones."

"Who will command the mission?" asked Greg, knowing that there was probably nothing he could say or do that would stop the mission. He wondered what it would be like returning to those worlds that the Hocklyns had destroyed over one hundred years ago. Jason had said she, so it must be a woman.

"Colonel Amanda Sheen will be brought out of cryosleep in a few months," Jason answered. "She is very familiar with the Federation worlds."

"That name sounds familiar," commented Greg, trying to remember where he had heard it before.

"Colonel Sheen was Admiral Streth's second in command on the StarStrike," Ariel spoke, her dark eyes looking at the two men. "She is an extremely competent fleet officer and from Aquaria originally. Her parents were killed there when the Hocklyns attacked. She was also in command of the StarStrike when it destroyed the first Hocklyn warship above the moon of Stalor Four."

Greg was silent for a moment as he thought about the mission and what waited for Colonel Sheen back in the old Federation worlds. Greg wondered how difficult it had been for Colonel Sheen to make the decision to go into cryosleep to begin with. He understood why it had been done. When the war was finally here, it would be an asset to have a core cadre of officers available who had actually fought the Hocklyns and were familiar with their battle tactics. Currently there were sixty-eight people in cryosleep on Ceres. "When will the mission be launched?"

"About the same time the New Horizon sets out for Tau Ceti," Jason replied.

Greg nodded, looking around the Command Center. There was only a small crew currently on duty. All trusted personnel who knew about Ceres and the current state of affairs. In two more days, he would be taking his family back home to Earth. For today, he had other business set up he needed to take care of.

Jason and he had a meeting scheduled later that afternoon with Jarvin Sinclen. Jarvin was currently in charge of the Federation people that had been deployed down to Earth. In certain universities and research labs, Federation people were teaching young people new ideas and others were helping Earth to further develop its science. Nearly two hundred Federation people were working behind the scenes.

"I'm sure both missions will be successful," Ariel commented with the faint hint of a smile on her face. She was sure Jeremy would be on the New Horizon, and hoped she would get to talk to Colonel Sheen before she left on her mission. It had been over one hundred years since she had last spoken to the colonel.

Jason smiled back at Ariel. Over the years, they had become very close friends. "I hope so." Sometimes he tended to forget that she was an AI. She sounded so much like a real person when he was talking to her. "Once the New Horizon discovers the two habitable planets in the Tau Ceti system, we can rapidly expand our space program and begin colonizing those two worlds. It will give the people of Earth even more reasons to adopt the new technology we are trying to make available to them."

"It should," agreed Greg, hoping the lure of colonizing new worlds would give a boost to the introduction of the new technology. "There will be a lot of people who will want to go to those worlds. It's getting crowded down on Earth."

"That's one of the reasons we chose this time to launch the New Horizon mission," Jason added, fully in agreement with Greg. "We should have plenty of qualified volunteers for colonization as soon as we announce the two new planets are fit to live on."

Greg let out a long sigh. Things were getting ready to change a lot over the next year. It was time to head back to his quarters. He had promised Katie he would take her over to the main computer lab at the academy and show her around. Greg also felt uneasy. There was something about Katie that was bothering him. He couldn't quite put his finger on it, but she was acting different recently. He wondered what she was up to. He would have to talk to Elizabeth and see if she had any idea what was going on with their highly spirited daughter.

Ariel watched as the two men left the Command Center. Jason and Greg would always be special to her, just as their children were. It was one of the reasons she had decided to tell Katie the truth. The abilities that the young girl had revealed were amazing when it came to understanding computers and their operating systems. She had a knack for computers and Ariel strongly suspected that, in a few short years, Katie would be showing Lisa some new concepts in computer programming.

Ariel had talked to Katie briefly the previous night by appearing on the vid screen in her bedroom. Ariel had promised to reappear tonight and tell Katie what was going on. In some ways, Ariel was excited about the prospect of being able to confide in one of the special children. It was an opportunity that Jason had strictly forbidden her where Jeremy was concerned. Jason didn't want Jeremy to feel pressured to take on a military career. If he had known the truth from the very beginning, Jeremy might have felt that he didn't have a choice in joining the military. For this reason and others, Ariel was a little nervous. She knew that both Jason and Greg would be highly upset with her if they knew what she was doing. However, neither had specifically forbidden her to talk to Katie.

Later that evening, Katie was in her room sitting cross-legged on her bed with her handheld computer in front of her. The previous night, Ariel had appeared on the vid screen on the wall and promised to tell her more about what was going on tonight. Katie was trying her best not to look and act impatient. She tossed her head back, letting her blonde hair tumble across her shoulders. It really needed to be cut, but Katie had been hesitating. She was currently working on a new program that she thought would make her handheld computer run twice as fast.

Katie didn't know how long she had been sitting on the bed when she heard a quiet chuckle come from the vid screen. Looking up, she saw Ariel watching her.

"How long have you been there?" Katie asked, curiously. Sometimes she got so wrapped up in her programming that she literally lost track of the time.

"Only for a little while," replied Ariel, smiling. "What are you working on?"

Katie turned her computer off after saving her work and gazed intently at the vid screen. "Just a new program to help my computer run faster."

Ariel nodded and then spoke. "Katie, you are extremely talented. Most adults can't do some of the things you can do with computers. You should really talk to Lisa. I don't see any reason why you can't come up here during the summer and take some computer classes at the Fleet Academy. Lisa would have to recommend you."

"You really think so?" Katie asked, her face brightening at the idea. That would also allow her to stay close to Jeremy. She knew she had a schoolgirl crush on Jeremy and that it wasn't realistic to hope anything would ever come of it. There was just too big of an age difference. Jeremy had been special to her all of her life. He had spent a lot of time down on Earth at her parent's home when he had been attending school. She had been much younger then, and it seemed to her that Jeremy had always been around.

"Talk to Lisa," Ariel said encouragingly. "I will mention something to her also."

Katie nodded, but now she wanted to know more about the AI. "You said you would tell me more about the Avenger and how you came to be the ship's AI."

Ariel nodded. She knew that once she started talking about the Avenger and what had transpired in the Human Federation of Worlds, there would be no turning back. "You realize Katie that you can never reveal to anyone what I am about to tell you. You can't speak of this to your dad or to your mother."

Katie slid off her bed and, walking around it, grabbed a chair and sat down directly in front of the vid screen. "I promise," answered Katie in a very serious and solemn voice. She had been keeping secrets from her parents for quite some time. Her light green eyes stared raptly at the screen.

"Very well," Ariel replied, her eyes focusing on the young girl. Then, with a faraway look in her dark eyes, she began. "It all started over one hundred and twenty-five years ago back in the Human Federation of Worlds."

For the next two hours, Ariel gave Katie a brief summary of the events that had led to the Avenger crashing into the crater on the Moon. She went on to describe how Jason and Greg had found the ship and later her making her presence known to them. Without hesitation, she also described the base on Ceres and how the Federation survivors along with several Earth governments were trying to push Earth's technological development.

"They want to get Earth up to the same technological level that the Federation was when it was destroyed," Ariel finished. "Once that happens, the Federation survivors on Ceres will reveal themselves, and we can start preparing for the arrival of the Hocklyns."

"So there are people from Ceres teaching at some of the universities down on Earth?" Katie asked wide-eyed.

It was hard to believe that people from space were already down on Earth and no one suspected. It was even more frightening to realize that there were hostile aliens out in the universe bent on destroying all humans. She hadn't been expecting to hear anything like this from Ariel. It sounded so much like a sci-fi vid movie.

"Yes," Ariel replied with a nod. "There are a number here on the Moon as well teaching at the academy."

"Can you tell me who?" Katie asked with interest. She wanted to see if they looked different than Earth humans.

"No, Katie, I can't," Ariel replied, her dark eyes gazing at the young girl. "That is very secret, and only Admiral Strong, your dad, and a few others know who they are."

"I guess that's for the best," admitted Katie, sounding disappointed. Then, looking at Ariel with a serious look on her face, she asked another question. "What can you tell me about these Hocklyns?"

Ariel sighed to herself. She had to keep reminding herself that this girl was only a teenager. Katie was a very bright and intelligent girl, but a teenager nevertheless. Ariel suspected and hoped that this was only the first of many long conversations. Ariel truly wanted a close friend she could confide in, and she hoped Katie would become one.

Jeremy was in the cafeteria eating breakfast. Pancakes, sausage, toast, and two eggs were a good way to start the morning. One thing he could say about the academy, they definitely fed you well.

"More pancakes," a pleasant female voice spoke from behind him as Kelsey appeared. She was carrying a tray with what looked like half a grapefruit and some strawberries. "Don't you ever get tired of pancakes?"

Kelsey sat down across from him, and he noticed her companion Angela DeSota. Angela was studying advanced communications and hoping to be a communications officer on a starship some day. She was also a valuable member of his squad. All the seniors were divided into squads of six and were constantly put in stiff competition against one another. The drill the other day where his squad had beaten Barr's had been the final one. He knew that his squad stood atop the rankings. His squad had worked hard to get there, even working out together rather than taking recreation time some evenings. They had spent many long hours in the academy gym exercising and discussing tactics.

"Good morning, Kelsey," Jeremy spoke as he picked up his glass of orange juice and took a long drink. Setting it back down, he looked across the table at the other young woman. "Hello, Angela. How are your communication studies coming?"

"I'm ready for the final exams," the young brunette said with a charming smile. "Professor Galen also says that I'm ready."

"That's great," Jeremy replied with a huge smile as he took a bite of his pancakes. "You will make a good communications officer someday."

"I hear that you have a teenager that is smitten with you," Angela continued in a teasing voice and a twinkle in her eyes.

"Katie," replied Jeremy, shaking his head in annoyance. "Sometimes after I've been around her, I'm glad I don't have a sister."

"She wasn't that bad," Kelsey said as she took a bite of one of her strawberries. "She reminds me a lot of what I was like when I was her age."

"So you two got to babysit," Angela said with a chuckle. "I bet that was interesting. Sounds as if it was an intriguing first date."

Kelsey felt a slight blush color her face. "It wasn't actually a date," she said carefully. "I was just helping Jeremy out."

"Yeah, right," commented Angela with a grin.

The three continued to talk when Jeremy noticed that both Kelsey and Angela were looking behind him with looks of distaste on their faces. Feeling aggravated, he didn't even have to turn around to know who was standing behind him.

"Well well, what do we have here?" Matt Barr spoke in a mocking voice, gazing down at Jeremy. "I guess this must be the loser's table." Barr walked on around the table and stood behind the two girls. He looked challengingly at Jeremy as if daring him to say something.

"We kicked your ass in the drill the other day," Angela said defensively, her face showing annoyance. "You didn't seem to do so well out there on the Moon."

"You got lucky," Barr snarled, anger spreading across his face and gazing contemptuously at Angela. "You could never do that again!"

"Let's not argue," interjected Kelsey, turning her head and frowning at Barr. "Instructor Branson is watching us. You don't want to get any demerits, do you Matt?" Kelsey had noticed that Instructor Branson and several other instructors were watching them from where they sat at the head table.

Hesitating, Barr glanced over at the head table and noticed that Kelsey had spoken the truth. He knew he couldn't afford to get any demerits. There was too much riding on him finishing at the top of the class. A lot of time and effort had been expended to get him to where he was. He couldn't afford to blow it. The people he was working for wouldn't tolerate failure. Matt let out a deep breath and unclenched his fist. Now was not the time to provoke a confrontation with Jeremy, even though he badly wanted to do so. He wanted it so bad he could taste it. Someone had to put the admiral's son in his place, and he was determined to be that someone when the opportunity finally presented itself.

He had always disliked Jeremy. It seemed to him that the instructors always gave Jeremy the benefit of the doubt. There was no question in his mind that since Jeremy was the admiral's son he was being allowed to coast through the academy. It was just like down on Earth where corrupt politics favored certain individuals.

"Until later," Barr commented evenly, his eyes narrowing as he looked over at Jeremy. "This isn't over between us, Jeremy. Someday your protectors won't be around." Barr turned and strolled off, heading toward the exit.

"I wish he wasn't like that," muttered Angela, noticing that her appetite was gone.

"Matt is just being Matt," commented Kelsey, looking over at Jeremy. She picked up another strawberry and bit into it. This one tasted sour and for some reason that didn't surprise her. She was determined not to let this little incident with Matt ruin her breakfast.

"I don't understand how he got into the academy with that attitude," Angela said, her tone betraying her agitation. "I thought they were supposed to screen people out that had that type of mind-set."

"He doesn't act like that around the instructors," Jeremy explained as he took a bite of his eggs. He had watched Barr's actions for several years now. Barr was always careful in what he said or did around the instructors at the academy. "Eat your breakfast, Angela; don't let Matt get to you."

"I will just be glad when graduation is over," Angela said, picking up her fork and stabbing her grapefruit. "Maybe then we won't have to put up with Matt anymore."

Jeremy didn't reply. He knew there was a good chance it might not work out that way if they were all chosen for the New Horizon mission.

The three finished their breakfast and headed off toward their first class. Instructor Branson watched them leave. He wondered if it might be wise to mention this incident to Commandant Everson. There was something about Barr that didn't feel right. He couldn't quite put his fingers on it, but it was there. Branson felt that Barr was up to something, but he had no idea what it could possibly be. Other than his obvious dislike of Jeremy, he had been a model student. Perhaps it would be best if he just watched the situation for a while longer. Barr hadn't actually done anything wrong yet. It was just his attitude toward Jeremy that bothered Branson.

Katie was sitting in a Raven class shuttle waiting to return home. She looked over at her mom and dad, who were busy talking quietly about something. With resignation, Katie knew it would be quite some time before she got to return. Her best hope was that the long talk with Lisa earlier paid off. The two had spent a good part of the morning talking about computers. Katie had shown Lisa some of the programs she had written, including the one that she was currently working on to speed up her computer. Lisa seemed to be impressed and had promised Katie that she would talk to Commandant Everson and her parents about allowing Katie to come up to the Moon to study over the summer.

It was also going to be hard to leave Ariel. They wouldn't be able to communicate once she left the Moon. Katie felt as if she were leaving a close friend behind. It was strange; they had only talked a few hours over the vid screen but Katie felt as if she knew Ariel. In some ways, she felt as if they were kindred spirits.

"I don't know, Greg," Elizabeth spoke in a quiet voice so Katie couldn't hear. "I just don't feel comfortable with Katie being up here on the Moon for the summer."

"She will be fine," Greg responded in a soothing voice. "Jason and Lisa are both up here and so is Jeremy. She will be well looked after."

"Maybe," responded Elizabeth, looking doubtful. The Moon had always frightened her. Even today, she had to fortify herself to make these occasional trips to the academy to see Jason and Lisa. "Mathew is already gone and now Katie. I don't know if I want both of them in the fleet."

"Katie may not choose the fleet," spoke Greg, looking over at his young daughter. Katie had her handheld computer out and was working on something. "The summer computer courses at the academy are well structured. She will be supervised constantly, and another older cadet can be assigned to watch over her. There is no way she can get into any trouble."

"Lisa did say she would keep an eye on her," conceded Elizabeth, wondering if she were doing the right thing. She knew that Katie was gifted. Her teachers at school had been ecstatic when Katie had excelled in her aptitude tests. "Let's wait until we get home; we can discuss it in another week or two. That will give us both time to think this through."

"Sounds fine," said Greg, taking his wife's hand and squeezing it approvingly. "We just need to do what's best for Katie."

Jason watched from the Command Center as the shuttle carrying Greg and his family left the flight bay. Ariel kept it centered on the main viewscreen as the shuttle arrowed up into space and then vanished as it flew toward Earth. Jason let out a heavy sigh. He missed the days when Greg was constantly around. However, the need for someone to coordinate the implementation of the technology from the Avenger Project had fallen on Greg's broad shoulders. Jason wished Greg could come up more often, but his job down on Earth was extremely important. They did try to talk daily, but it wasn't the same.

Perhaps if Katie came up for the summer, Greg and Elizabeth would come up more often. Lisa and he had discussed Katie's request earlier about attending summer classes at the academy. Even Ariel had mentioned how advanced Katie's computer skills were. After listening to the two, Jason had contacted Commandant Everson with the request. Commandant Everson didn't seem to be too surprised. He had talked to Katie some the night of the dinner about computers. Commandant Everson had said that Katie would have to be well supervised, as she would be the youngest student attending the summer session. However, he thought adequate arrangements could be made.

"So is Katie going to be attending the academy over the summer?" Ariel asked in an even voice, not wanting Jason to know how interested she was in his answer.

"Probably,' Jason replied, his eyes still gazing at the now empty viewscreen as the shuttle was no longer visible. Ariel's avatar was on the viewscreen next to the large one. In some ways, he missed the old days. Everything had been so much simpler.

-

Up in lunar orbit at the Lagrange point, the starship New Horizon was docked to the large spacedock. It had taken years to build the spacedock, and then an additional four years to construct the New Horizon. It could have been done quicker with Federation construction technology, but Jason had insisted that they take things slowly for now so as not to disrupt the economy down on Earth. Jason felt that introducing highly advanced construction technology too quickly could cause immense economic problems.

Commander Tellson was in the Command Center of the New Horizon watching the main viewscreen as a supply shuttle from Earth was maneuvered into the ship's small flight bay. The flight bay had just enough room to hold two of the medium sized shuttles.

"The manifest shows the shuttle contains some basic supplies plus some of our food stores," Tellson said as he studied some information on a computer screen on his command console.

"I'll see to the unloading," his Executive Officer, Brent Maher, spoke with a nod.

"Make sure everything is stowed properly," ordered Commander Tellson, looking over at Major Maher. "We leave on our sublight trials in less than two weeks. I don't want any supplies or equipment stowed incorrectly in case there are problems."

"There won't be any problems," Maher promised with a confident smile. "The engineers have done an outstanding job on the ship."

"You're probably right," Tellson said, nodding his head in agreement. "Just make sure the crew handles everything correctly."

-

Maher watched as the crew diligently unloaded the boxes of supplies and some food stores. There was one small crate in particular that he was watching for. His people down on Earth had promised that it would be on this shuttle. It had been extremely difficult and expensive to smuggle this box on board with the other supplies. It was labeled emergency food supplies and when he saw it, he casually walked over and instructed the two men who were handling it to follow him.

After leaving the small flight bay, they walked through several corridors and took a small elevator up to the deck where the main mess hall was located. Just off to the side of the mess hall was a small storage room for emergency food supplies. The room was heavily shielded, and enough reserve supplies of food and water would be kept inside to feed the crew for several weeks. The box was stored and secured with several others on a large shelf. Once he was satisfied that the box was stored properly, he dismissed the two men and ordered them to return to the flight bay to help finish unloading the shuttle.

Once the two men were gone, Maher checked the corridor to make sure no one else was around. Satisfied he was alone; he went back to the small storage room and opened the heavy metal hatch. Stepping inside, he shut the hatch behind him. He approached the crate and gazed down at it. He knew what it was supposed to contain, and several inspectors down on Earth had been paid handsome sums of money to pass it through inspection. Maher also knew that those two inspectors would have fatal accidents sometime during the next week. His group couldn't afford to leave any loose ends.

The crate had a small lock on it that Maher had the only key to. Quickly unlocking it, he opened the lid and glanced inside. This was what he had requested from his people down on Earth. Inside the crate were half a dozen assault rifles and a number of pistols with plenty of ammunition. There were also a good number of stun grenades. If things worked out as planned, the New Horizon would be making a much longer trip than the one to Tau Ceti. Now he just needed Cadet Lieutenant Barr to get his group up to the ship.

Jason was flying up to the spacedock in one of the new Raven class shuttles. The new shuttles were built down on Earth at a special facility in the Arizona desert. What many people didn't know was that some of the special components, such as the miniature fusion reactor that powered the shuttle, were actually produced on Ceres and shipped to Earth. People working at the base were told that the reactors, as well as a few other specialized parts, were produced at another top-secret government facility. Jason was surprised that so far no suspected that the parts weren't actually produced on Earth.

They had modified the shuttles and they were now the main workhorse for travel between the Earth and the Moon. One version of the shuttle had been changed to accommodate passengers only. The seats were more comfortable, and there was even a flight attendant to help out the passengers. The other version of the shuttle was to haul cargo. One other thing that had been done was the removal of the FTL drive. The new shuttle designs had been done down on Earth by several engineers from Ceres who had been directing a special team made up of Earth scientists and technicians. Everyone assumed the shuttles had been reverse engineered by Earth scientists, which is what it was supposed to look like. The shuttles were capable of traveling anywhere in the solar system, but Jason and the participating governments had agreed to restrict them to the Earth-Moon system with occasional trips to Mars.

Looking out the cockpit window, Jason saw the spacedock rapidly growing larger. The New Horizon was also visible as it was still docked. Jason felt very pleased at what had been accomplished here. The spacedock was a combination of Earth and Federation technology. The entire space facility was 900 meters long, 200 meters wide, and 200 meters thick. It had a permanent crew of 800 and was capable of producing two types of spacecraft. In its large construction bay, the 200-meter in system exploration cruisers could be built, or they could build the 400-meter FTL capable cruisers like the New Horizon.

What no one knew but Jason and a few others was that, in a few more years, they would begin construction of Federation style destroyers. The New Horizon was very similar in size to a Federation destroyer. It would take only a few minor modifications and Earth could begin building its first warships. The current plans were to build ten in the guise of protecting the new colonies, such as the ones planned for Tau Ceti, from any unknown danger. There were already plans drawn up to expand the spacedock, adding several larger construction bays. This would give them the capability to produce Federation light cruisers as well as other ships. However, all of this was in the future. Right now Jason was more concerned with making sure the current expedition was a success.

A few moments later, the shuttle entered the spacedock's large flight bay and sat gently down on the landing pad. Jason waited patiently for the hatch to open and then walked down the extended ramp to be greeted by Captain Stinson, the officer currently in charge of the spacedock. Stinson was an engineer as well as a marine officer.

"Admiral Strong," Stinson spoke as he saluted. "Welcome aboard."

"At ease, Captain," spoke Jason, smiling. He had made numerous trips up to the spacedock during the construction phase as well as when they had been building the New Horizon. He was extremely familiar with the spacedock as well as the ship.

"I understand you want to make an inspection of the New Horizon today, sir."

"Yes, I do," replied Jason, evenly. Jason was looking forward to this. He just wished Greg could have come, but his duties down on Earth had prevented it. Jason knew that Greg would have loved to see the newly completed New Horizon first hand. "I haven't been on board the ship since she was completed. I am looking forward to seeing our first FTL capable ship."

"I think you will like what we have done with her," Stinson replied, confidently. "The crew has been checking the systems and becoming more familiar with her for the last several weeks. I believe the last time you were aboard there were still wires hanging in the corridors, as well as open panels all throughout the ship."

"How many of the crew are currently on board?" asked Jason, curiously. He knew more crewmembers had been reporting almost daily to the ship as they finished their training either on Earth or on the Moon.

"One hundred and twelve at the moment," replied Stinson, recalling the latest crew roster. "The civilian specialists that will be going on the Tau Ceti mission won't arrive for another two months. Not all of the crew, as you know, have been chosen yet. There are still a few important positions to fill."

"That should be completed in the next two to three weeks," responded Jason, recalling the latest crew assignments. "There are a lot of qualified people that want to go on this mission, and it's difficult to choose who gets to go and who doesn't."

"I can understand that," replied Stinson, nodding his head. "The first interstellar mission. I have to admit, I wouldn't mind going myself."

"I think a lot of us would," responded Jason, smiling.

A few minutes later, the two made their way through the spacedock to the New Horizon. The spacedock was kept at three quarters Earth gravity, and the wide, spacious corridors made it difficult to believe you were actually in space. Everything was immaculate and well ordered. They passed a few crew personnel and finally arrived at the large airlock that the New Horizon was docked to.

Commander Tellson and his executive officer Major Maher were waiting for them on the other side in the ship.

"Admiral Strong, I'm glad you could find the time in your busy schedule to come up," Commander Tellson said, greeting Jason.

"I'm afraid things will soon get hectic with the sublight trials and the rest of the crew arriving," Jason replied with a friendly nod. "Why don't you take me on a tour of the ship and let's see what we've built."

"The New Horizon is going to be a good ship, Admiral," Tellson commented as they began walking down a well-lighted corridor. "This ship makes our exploration cruisers look small."

Jason nodded and smiled. He wondered what the commander would think if he saw one of the larger Federation ships, such as a battle cruiser or a battle carrier. For now, those ships were kept out of sight of Earth. No Federation ships were allowed around the inner planets so as to reduce the accidental risk of premature discovery.

Their first stop was in Engineering. Jason looked around the large compartment at all the controls and consoles that operated the ship's two fusion reactors, as well as the ship's two main drive systems. The sublight drive, as well as the FTL drive, were all monitored from here and needed adjustments or repairs could be made by the men and women who manned the stations.

"How long will the drive core need to cool after a jump?" asked Jason, curiously. He knew that Federation warships needed about four hours.

"If our calculations are accurate we are estimating four to six hours," Commander Tellson answered. "It will depend partially on the length of the jump. When we make the mini-jumps around the solar system, we should know more about the necessary time needed."

The tour continued until they were in the Command Center. Jason looked around and smiled to himself, noticing the similarities between the Command Center on the Avenger and the Command Center on the New Horizon. The main difference between the two Command Centers was the one on the New Horizon was smaller with slightly fewer consoles, and there were no armed guards at the entry hatch.

After looking around for a moment, Jason turned to Commander Tellson. "One of the reasons I came up here today was to pass on some information that's been circulating around down on Earth."

"What type of information?" asked Tellson, curiously. He was so busy he didn't get to watch much news.

"Greg Johnson and General Greene were at the academy recently. Evidently there are rumors flying around Earth's Internet about threats to the New Horizon."

"Threats?" Tellson blurted out surprised, his eyes growing wide in disbelief. "Why would they be threatening us?"

"Change, we guess," replied Jason, arching his eyebrow and shaking his head. "Your trip represents our first real step outside our solar system, and I guess it frightens some."

"Are we taking any precautions?" asked Major Maher, trying to sound calm.

How the hell had word of their plan against the New Horizon gotten out? They had spent years putting this plan together. The other question was, how much did they know? Maher was doing his best not to look nervous. He needed to contact his people down on Earth and make these rumors go away. This could threaten everything!

"I have already ordered extra screening of all material coming up to the New Horizon," replied Jason, looking over at the major. "Who ever these people are, they don't have access to the space technology necessary to be a threat to us way out here. But our people down on Earth are going to be monitoring the situation and trying to find out where these threats are coming from."

"We will take extra precautions as well," replied Tellson, feeling agitated that someone would actually threaten the mission. Then turning to face Major Maher he continued. "Take part of the crew and begin inspecting all the cargo that has come up from Earth in the past week. I want every box opened and what's inside it compared to the ship's manifest."

"I'll get right on it," Maher promised with a nod. "We'll check everything, though I don't see how anything dangerous could have slipped on board."

"I don't believe it could have either," Jason said, agreeing with Maher. "But it doesn't hurt to be safe." It still bothered him immensely that there had been a threat against the mission. If something were to occur to the New Horizon, it could set their plans back by years.

A few hours later, the crew was busy checking all the supplies that had come up to the ship recently. Major Maher personally checked several of the supply lockers as well as the emergency supply room, signing off on them. His cache of weapons was still safe, but he needed to get a message to Earth. The plan must succeed. Nothing could be allowed to get in the way. If people down on Earth were talking, they would have to be eliminated. Maher smiled to himself. The only thing the admiral had to go on right now were rumors. There was no way the admiral or his people could suspect that plans had been made to hijack the New Horizon after she made her jump to Tau Ceti.

Chapter Three

Jeremy looked down at the computer pad in front of him. This was his final exam for the day. The past two days had been mentally exhausting as he had waded through exam after exam. This was his ninth exam in a succession of increasingly difficult tests from the instructors at the academy. He let out a deep sigh as he read the question in front of him one more time. This was an essay question. If he were the commander of a small exploration spacecraft with a crew of twelve, what skills would he expect each member of the crew to possess? Jeremy closed his eyes and thought. He was in officer's training, and this was the type of question he was expected to know.

Some of the skills were obvious. You would need at least one or two ship engineers, a navigator, a communications expert who could double as a scanner and sensor operator. You would also need a medical officer and a helm officer. The rest of the crew would need to possess the necessary skills and knowledge needed in the exploration of another solar system. Even the crewmembers such as the navigator and communications officer would be expected to possess a wide range of abilities.

For nearly two hours, Jeremy keyed in his answer on his computer pad. He listed each individual and the type of skills and mindset he would expect them to possess. When he was finally finished, he read over his work one more time, making a few minor corrections. Looking around the small classroom, he noticed that Matt Barr had already finished and turned in his computer pad. Jeremy hadn't even noticed when Matt had left.

Feeling satisfied with his answers, Jeremy stood up and handed his pad in to the instructor. The instructor nodded and told Jeremy he could leave. Walking out of the room, Jeremy felt relieved that the tests were finally over. As he stepped into the corridor, he found Kelsey and Angela waiting patiently for him.

"Was it tough?" asked Kelsey, looking at Jeremy. Some of her exams had been difficult but not any worse than she had expected. She knew Jeremy was studying to be a commanding officer one day. She just wanted to navigate a starship.

"Same as the other tests," replied Jeremy, forcing a smile on his face. "They were all hard, but I expected that. How were your tests?"

"I think I aced mine," Angela said with a contented grin. "I studied really hard for this and I think it paid off."

"Mine weren't too bad," Kelsey added with an understanding nod at Angela. "The astrogation tests were the hardest. There was a lot of math and some extremely intricate navigation problems, but I feel pretty sure I answered them correctly."

Jeremy looked at the two. The three of them had stuck together all through their four years at the academy. He hoped they could continue to do so in the future. "I guess now we wait and see where we end up in the final rankings."

"I think all three of us will be on the New Horizon," Angela said confidently with a hint of excitement in her eyes. "I can't imagine being on the ship without the two of you. I just hope all of us end up ranked higher than Matt."

"We'll see," replied Jeremy, hoping Angela was right. It would be deeply satisfying if all three of them finished ahead of Matt in the rankings, but Matt had in the past proven to be highly intelligent. It might prove difficult to knock him out of that top position.

"Let's keep our fingers crossed," Kelsey said, taking a deep breath. "We should know the results the day after tomorrow at our graduation ceremony."

"Let's go get something to eat," suggested Jeremy, feeling hungry. With the tests over it would be nice to unwind some, and the two girls were great company.

Later that evening, there was a knock on Jeremy's dorm room door. Getting up, Jeremy opened the door to find his mother standing there. "Mom," spoke Jeremy, gesturing for her to come in. His mother didn't come to the academy very often. She spent most of her time on the Avenger working with the ship's computer systems.

Lisa Strong walked into her son's dorm room. Glancing around, she saw with satisfaction that the room was immaculate. Jeremy had always kept his room clean even as a child. "How are things going with you and Kelsey?"

Jeremy felt his face flush. Leave it to his mother to ask a question like that. "We're just good friends for now. We didn't want anything to interfere with our studies and finals."

"Good decision, Jeremy," responded Lisa, sitting down in a comfortable chair at the small table in the room. "I wanted to come over and talk to you about Katie now that you are finished with your finals."

"Katie!" Jeremy exclaimed, his eyes narrowing. He couldn't imagine why his mother would want to talk about that impetuous teenager. "What has she done now?"

"Nothing," replied Lisa, trying hard not to laugh. "It's just that she has asked to come up during the summer and take part in the academy's summer computer program."

"The entire summer!" Jeremy blurted out with a shudder.

He couldn't imagine what it would be like for Katie to be around all the time now that she was a teenager. His life would be a nightmare. He could still remember vividly what it had been like living with the Johnsons down on Earth when he had been attending school. Katie had been underfoot the entire time.

"Don't worry, Jeremy," Lisa said with an understanding smile. "Your dad and I will watch her most of the time. We promised Greg and Elizabeth that we would make sure she is well supervised."

"I suppose," replied Jeremy, thinking it over. He didn't know if his parents really understood what they were getting into. "I know Katie is extremely good with computers, so I guess spending some time here at the academy would be good for her. But she has a knack for getting into trouble at times."

"I'm glad that you agree about the academy," responded Lisa, nodding her head in approval. "We managed to raise you, I'm sure your father and I can handle Katie. Now, the other reason I came over is that we will be having a party for you after graduation. We will be inviting some of your classmates, including Kelsey and Angela since their parents can't make it. Commander Tellson from the New Horizon will also be there."

"Commander Tellson," repeated Jeremy, intrigued. He had met the commander a couple of times when he had come down to the academy on official business.

In a more serious tone, Lisa looked at her son and then spoke. "Jeremy, you should finish high enough in the rankings to qualify for the New Horizon mission. So should Kelsey and Angela. Your father and I have talked it over. If you qualify, we won't stop you from going."

"Even if some people say the only reason I got on the ship is because my dad is the admiral?" asked Jeremy, knowing that some stubborn people would think exactly that.

"We aren't worried about that," responded Lisa, firmly. "If you make it, you will have earned it. We won't interfere, no matter what some people may think."

"Thanks, Mom," Jeremy replied, pleased that his parents would support him in this.

"Another thing," Lisa added with concern for Jeremy showing on her face. "Matt Barr will probably also qualify. Is that going to be a problem?"

"Not for me," Jeremy answered with a slight frown, wondering how his mother had found out about the problem with Matt. He suspected that one of the instructors from the academy had spoken to her. "It probably will be for Matt, and I will have to find some way to deal with it."

"Just be careful," Lisa cautioned, as she stood up and gave Jeremy a motherly hug. "We are very proud of you."

Jeremy walked his mother back to the door. He leaned forward and kissed her on the cheek. "Tell Dad thanks."

"I will," replied Lisa, smiling. "We will see you at graduation."

Jeremy shut the door and sat back down. He hadn't actually thought about how hard it would be to be on the New Horizon with Matt Barr. The ship was a large one, so it shouldn't be a problem as long as they weren't working together.

Lisa paused outside of Jeremy's door. Instructor Branson had told her about the problem between Jeremy and Matt. Branson was from Ceres and had been keeping an eye on the situation. Lisa let out a heavy sigh. So much had changed over the years since she had gone on the original mission to Ceres. Falling in love with Jason, getting married, and having Jeremy. Then of course there was Ariel and the Avenger. She still loved working with computers, and she had learned so much from Ariel.

It would be difficult letting Jeremy go on the New Horizon mission since he was their only child. Perhaps she should speak to Jason. She had always wanted a little girl. It still wasn't too late for that using the medical technology available from the Federation survivors on Ceres. Lisa smiled at the thought of having another child, and then her thoughts turned back to the New Horizon mission.

There would also be two Federation officers secretly on the New Horizon. Perhaps she should mention this issue between Jeremy and Matt to one of them. Jason would not approve, but he wasn't a mother.

Turning, she began walking down the corridor toward the elevator. She had a lot to think about.

It was graduation night, and Jeremy stood rigidly at attention as Commandant Everson looked over the two long lines of graduates. The commencement speech was over with, as well as speeches by several others, including Jeremy's dad.

Commandant Everson looked over the two lines of graduates. "It is my pleasure tonight to introduce a very important man. I speak of none other than the commander of our first interstellar mission, Commander Tellson of the New Horizon. He has a special announcement to make."

Commander Tellson walked out to the speaking platform and looked over the group of graduates and then he smiled. "This is a special year for the academy and for Earth. This year, the New Horizon will be leaving on the first interstellar flight. I am pleased to announce that the top ten cadets from this year's graduating class will be invited to go along on the mission."

Jeremy felt a sudden rush of adrenaline. He wondered if Commander Tellson was about to announce those ten. He wanted this so bad he could taste it. He had no idea what his final rankings were. They would be posted tomorrow. He hoped he was at the top, but he wasn't sure. He risked a quick glance at Kelsey who was just to his left. She had an excited and expectant look on her face as she listened to Commander Tellson.

"I am pleased to announce that the following cadets have been selected based on their grades, their attitude, the recommendations of the instructors, and their final rankings in the class." Commander Tellson paused as his eyes moved over the cadets. "I will announce the names in the order of their current and final class rankings."

"Cadet Lieutenant Matt Barr has the privilege of leading this year's class of graduates. I am also pleased to announce that we have two other students that are tied in rankings and finished just barely behind Cadet Lieutenant Barr. They are Cadet Lieutenant Jeremy Strong and Cadet Ensign Kelsey Grainger."

Jeremy let out a sigh of relief. He didn't realize he had been holding his breath. Both Kelsey and he had made it! They hadn't beaten Matt, but it sounded as if they had come extremely close. He looked over at Kelsey and saw her looking at him with a big satisfied smile on her face. He barely listened as Commander Tellson read the rest of the names. He did notice that Angela's name was called out as being ranked number six in the class. All Jeremy could think about was that Kelsey and he were going on the first interstellar mission.

Major Maher was also attending the graduation. He frowned heavily as he heard Jeremy Strong's name called out. The few connections he had at the academy had been unable to prevent Jeremy's name from being added to the ten cadets that would be going on the New Horizon mission. He was just ranked too damn high! If he had been lower or toward the bottom of the group of ten, it might have been possible to manipulate the grades on the finals to move him out of that elite group. Unfortunately, that didn't occur. This was another unfortunate problem he would have to deal with. The damn boy was just too smart. Fortunately, Barr had made it, as well as three others from his handpicked group.

He would use Barr to keep Strong under control. Taking a deep breath, he turned and left the graduation ceremony. Maher wanted to get back up to the New Horizon as soon as possible. There were a few things he needed to do while the commander was down at the academy. It was very seldom now that Commander Tellson left the New Horizon.

Jeremy, Kelsey, and Angela were all standing together in the private dining room next to the academy cafeteria. Jeremy's mother had reserved the room for their graduation party, and it was full of festive and laughing people.

"We all made it," Angela said with a satisfied and excited smile on her face. "We're going on the New Horizon mission!"

"Yes," replied Kelsey, nodding her head and smiling, then her look changed to a more serious one. "But so is Matt and three other members of his group. We will have to watch ourselves."

"I'm not too worried," replied Jeremy, seeing his dad and Greg heading over in their direction. Greg and Elizabeth had flown up for the graduation. "Commander Tellson is a good commander and will keep Matt and his group under control."

"Congratulations," Jason said to the three with a big approving smile on his face. "Commander Tellson was just telling me how pleased he is to have all three of you on the mission."

"That's great!" Angela spoke, her eyes glowing with excitement. "We can't wait to go on board the New Horizon and begin our new assignments."

"That will be another month yet," spoke Jason, understanding their youthful enthusiasm. "Once the sublight trials are finished and Commander Tellson feels the ship is ready for its full crew, then you can board. You will have two months to familiarize yourself with the ship before we test the FTL drive. When everyone is satisfied the drive is working properly then the mission to Tau Ceti will begin."

"Do you think there are any habitable planets in that system?" Angela asked, her eyes glowing with excitement at the prospect of doing some real exploration. She had always dreamed of traveling to the stars.

"It's a G class star, so there is a possibility," Jason replied evenly. "From the latest astronomical observations there are at least five planets in the system. Hopefully there are more in the liquid water zone. That's one of the reasons we're sending the New Horizon to Tau Ceti."

"What if we find an Earth-like planet?" Kelsey asked, her eyes gazing inquisitively at the admiral. "Will we colonize it someday?"

"I would hope so," replied Jason, smiling. "We are already talking about terraforming Mars, but the Earth's population is still growing. We need some empty space to move people to. A couple of new planets to colonize would be a big bonus for the mission."

"We would have to build some colony ships," spoke Jeremy, thoughtfully. "Probably a large number if we wanted to move a lot of people."

"The spacedock could be used for that," responded Jason, recalling the additional plans that had been made. "We will be starting construction of the second construction bay in a few more months."

He didn't want to reveal that the designs for the first colony ships were already finished. The colony ships would be 400 meters long and able to transport 1,000 colonists on each trip. Current plans called for the construction of ten of the large ships over the next five years. Construction of the first would begin as soon as the New Horizon returned.

"This mission is really important, isn't it," Angela commented as she realized what finding some habitable worlds would mean to Earth's steadily growing population. Her mother down on Earth was constantly complaining about how crowded it was becoming and how long she had to stand in lines to get everyday items.

"What if we don't find any habitable planets?" Kelsey asked. She knew that just because a star was the right size and type didn't necessarily mean it would have planets that people could live on.

"There are fifty-five stars within sixteen light years of Earth," responded Jason, looking at the three. "I suspect we will find some decent planets around a few of them. If the New Horizon doesn't find anything at Tau Ceti, she will return to Earth and, after a quick systems check, she will be sent out to explore some of those systems."

"Will we be allowed to stay on the New Horizon and be part of that?" asked Angela, wanting to experience the excitement of being on those future missions.

"That will be up to Commander Tellson," Jason answered, his eyes focusing on Angela. "If you do well on the mission to Tau Ceti there is a good chance you could be included on the others."

"Also keep in mind that even if we move people to new planets to colonize, that won't solve Earth's overcrowding," Greg broke in. "There will still be far more people being born everyday than we can safely move off the planet."

"My mother said the government is already talking about stricter population controls," commented Angela, recalling what her mother had told her the last time she had been able to return to Earth.

Her mother hadn't been able to come up for the graduation. Angela could hardly wait to call her mom and tell her the exciting news. She would be thrilled that Angela and the others had been selected for the New Horizon mission.

"The Earth can only support so many people," explained Greg, recalling one of his recent meetings. "Very soon we will reach the point where the Earth will not be able to support the human population. That's why we're terraforming Mars and trying to initiate some limited population controls."

"I know it's necessary," Angela responded with a nod of understanding. "We just have to find some new worlds to live on!"

"That's one of the reasons we built the New Horizon," Greg answered in a serious tone. "She represents our future."

The small group continued to talk about the mission and graduation. Jason wished that his brother and sister had been able to come up. However, both of them now had important jobs on Earth. Trevor was currently working in Europe helping to introduce new industrial technology. Jason knew that Katherine and her husband were still in the United States working with the health department to bring in more advanced medical technology.

What many people didn't know was that the Federation survivor's medical technology was capable of extending a person's lifespan by twenty to thirty years. Jason and a number of others crucial to the program had already been subjected to the advanced medical treatments since they were so heavily involved with the Avenger Project. Once news of these advanced medical treatments got out to the general public, there would be a huge demand for them. That would also cause additional problems due to Earth's growing population.

A few hours later, Major Maher was back on board the New Horizon. There was only a skeleton crew on board as many had been allowed to go down to the academy to attend the graduation ceremony. Maher was in his quarters when there was a knock on his door. Reaching forward, he pressed a button on his desk and the door to his quarters opened.

Four men came in, all with determined looks upon their faces. All four had been carefully chosen by Maher for the New Horizon mission.

"Sit down," spoke Maher, gesturing toward the four chairs in front of his desk.

"Everything is going according to plan," Lieutenant Reece Sandusky reported as he sat down and looked over at Major Maher. Reece was Maher's second in command of their small group.

"Barr and three other members of his team qualified for the trip," announced Maher, gazing at the others.

"That gives us eighteen that we can count on," Reece spoke not caring for the odds. He had hoped more of Matt's group would make it. Their plans had called for a total of twenty to be able to carry out the hijacking of the New Horizon.

"But we will have the only weapons," Maher pointed out. "Once the command crew is eliminated, the rest will do as we say. We will also have full control of the FTL drive once we upload the new computer program. Remember that a portion of the crew will be civilians wanting to explore Tau Ceti. They won't try to resist us. Actually, there are six or eight of them that might just join us with the right inducement. Our people down on Earth have paid a lot of money to the right people to ensure certain individuals who might be sympathetic to our cause are included on the mission."

"That would give us around twenty-five that we can count on," Reece spoke thoughtfully. "That should be enough."

"I'll be ready to take care of the FTL drive," Ensign Bates reported. "I have the necessary program disks ready. Once we make the jump to Tau Ceti, I won't have any problem downloading them into the computer core. That will give us complete control of the FTL drive."

"The hard part will be the Command Center officers," Maher reminded them all as he looked over the small group. "They all have to be eliminated. We can't leave anyone alive for the crew to rally around."

"What about the other cadets that are coming on board?" one of the other men asked.

"That might be a problem," Maher conceded. "One of them is Jeremy Strong, the admiral's son."

"A bargaining chip if something goes wrong," Lieutenant Sandusky suggested, his eyes narrowing. "If we have him as a hostage then the admiral won't be able to move against us."

"Perhaps," commented Maher, seeing the wisdom of using Jeremy as a hostage if necessary. "But let's make sure nothing goes wrong; too much is riding on this. Besides, once we reach Tau Ceti, what can they do? We will have control of the only ship with a working FTL drive. It will take them at least a month to equip one of the smaller exploration cruisers with a drive so they can come after us. By that time, we will be long on our way toward the galactic core where they will never be able to find us."

The next few weeks passed rapidly by. The New Horizon went out for her sublight trials escorted by the Columbia, and everything went as planned. The ship was brought back inside the spacedock for a complete systems check. This took an additional two weeks, with surprisingly few problems found. Once everyone was satisfied that the ship was ready, it was moved back outside the spacedock to its former position. It was now time for the rest of the crew, including the cadets, to be brought on board. Commander Tellson had two months of grueling drills planned.

Tellson sat in the Command Center thinking about what he had planned for the crew. He knew at the end of those two months that he would not be very popular. But the New Horizon was preparing to go out into the unknown on the first interstellar voyage. He expected the crew to be able to handle any emergency situation that might come up. If that meant waking them up in the middle of their sleep rotation, then that's what it meant. Emergencies or dangerous situations didn't wait conveniently to happen. They occurred when you least expected it.

Jeremy, Kelsey, and Angela stared out the viewports of their shuttle at the rapidly approaching spacedock. It seemed to be huge. Its entire structure was well lighted, and several small shuttles could be seen moving around it.

"I've never been to the spacedock before," spoke Angela quietly, her eyes glued to the viewport. "It's gigantic!"

Jeremy chuckled and looked over at Angela. "It's pretty big, but in a few years it will be even bigger. I have heard it's going to be expanded."

"If we expand and colonize other star systems we're going to need more ships," added Kelsey, thoughtfully. The spacedock was a miracle of modern engineering. She was surprised that Earth had been able to build it so quickly.

"I can see the New Horizon from here!" Angela called out excitedly.

Jeremy looked back out the viewport and sure enough, the New Horizon was visible. It was moored to one of the large docking ports on the side of the spacedock.

"Our new home," spoke Jeremy, starting to feel excited himself. This was what all the hard work at the academy had been for.

"I wonder what it will be like?" asked Angela, looking over at Jeremy. She supposed that Jeremy's father would have said a few things to him about the New Horizon and their schedule.

"Be prepared for a lot of drills," Jeremy warned in a more serious tone. "Sometime in the next four months we will be leaving for Tau Ceti, but not until Commander Tellson feels the crew and ship are ready."

"Drills," Angela spoke, her eyes narrowing at the thought. "I wonder what type of drills?"

"Everything you can imagine," replied Kelsey, glancing over at Angela. "Power failure, decompression, fire, emergency repairs to key systems, dealing with serious injuries and casualties, and everything else that Commander Tellson can think of. Remember, once we activate the

FTL drive and leave the solar system, we will be on our own. If something goes wrong, no one will be coming to rescue us."

"I guess we still have a lot to learn," admitted Angela, realizing that Jeremy and Kelsey were right. It wasn't going to be like a vid show. This was real life.

Looking back out the viewport, she saw that the shuttle was about to enter the large brightly lit flight bay inside the spacedock. Angela knew that shortly a new stage of her life would begin. She could hardly wait.

"We won't have to worry about what we eat," Kelsey added with a knowing laugh. "With all the running we will be doing in the emergency drills, we won't have to worry about gaining weight."

"Running," Angela groaned. She didn't mind a good work out, but she absolutely hated running.

The other two laughed. They were all glad that they would be together on the New Horizon. It would make the transition of moving from the academy to the ship so much easier knowing they had each other to count on.

It amazed Jeremy how girls always seemed to be so concerned about their figures. Both Angela and Kelsey had nice figures and didn't really need to worry. It still seemed to Jeremy that they were always watching what they ate and routinely working out. It had to be a girl thing, Jeremy had long ago decided.

A few minutes later, the three walked down the shuttle ramp to stand in the flight bay. They instantly noticed that the gravity field in the bay was less than what was maintained at the academy.

"Three quarters Earth normal," explained Jeremy, seeing the surprised look on Angela's face. "They keep it that way to make construction easier."

"I suppose," Angela commented with a frown. While she was used to moving around in the Moon's light gravity due to some of the drills she had participated in, she still preferred a full one gravity.

"Cadets, attention!" barked a voice in front of them.

Instantly all three snapped to attention with their eyes straight ahead. The other two cadets that were with them in the shuttle did the same thing.

Jeremy instantly saw a lieutenant in the dark blue uniform of the fleet standing in front of them. Jeremy hadn't noticed him when they had come down the ramp. I need to be more observant, he reminded himself. They weren't at the academy any longer.

50

"I am Lieutenant Devlin Nelson, the navigation officer for the New Horizon. I understand one of you has been studying astrogation at the academy?"

"I have been, sir," Kelsey answered smoothly and respectfully. She wondered if she would be working with Lieutenant Nelson.

"Think you can navigate this ship, cadet?" Nelson asked in an even voice, looking at Kelsey.

"Yes, sir," Kelsey responded without hesitation.

Nelson was quiet for a moment as he studied the young cadet in front of him. "We shall see. All of you follow me, and I will take you to your quarters. Inside your quarters, you will find your meal schedules as well as your work schedules. You are expected to show up to your work assignments ahead of time to be briefed by the person you are relieving. Don't be late!"

"Yes, sir!" responded all five cadets.

Lieutenant Nelson nodded his head in approval. "One more thing, cadets. You are going aboard a spacecraft. This is not the academy. Act accordingly."

Jeremy looked around the small set of quarters he had been assigned. He was sharing his quarters with Cadet Ensign Kevin Walters. Kevin had not been a member of either Jeremy or Barr's squads. Kevin was the same age as Jeremy but had red hair and a few freckles across his face. Their quarters had two small bunks, a desk with a computer, several comfortable chairs, and two lockers for their uniforms and other personal gear. There was also a small restroom with a shower in the back. On the front wall was a vid screen.

"Not too bad, I guess," spoke Kevin, tossing his bag on one of the bunks and looking over at Jeremy. Walking over to the desk, Kevin picked up two small folders. One had Jeremy's name on it, and the other had his. "I guess these are our orders." He handed one to Jeremy, sat back down on his bunk, and opened the folder with his name on it.

Jeremy opened the folder Kevin had handed him and read over the first few pages. It was a training schedule for the next two weeks and what he was expected to do. Meal times, work schedules, as well as additional studying. They were expected to learn how the other systems on the ship functioned, not just the ones they had been trained on.

"I have been studying how to operate a ship's sensors as well as its computers," Kevin commented as he read through his folder. "It looks as if we're going to be busy."

"There will also be emergency drills," added Jeremy, reading the last page of his folder. "For today, we're supposed to become familiar with the ship. The only areas that are off limits are the Command Center and Engineering."

Kevin stood back up and, opening his bag, started putting his gear in one of the lockers. Jeremy got up and began doing the same. In just a few minutes, they had everything properly stowed away.

"Let's go get the girls, then we can start checking out the ship," Jeremy suggested. "I have a feeling the sooner we become familiar with the layout of the New Horizon the better off we will be."

"Emergency drills," replied Kevin, nodding his head in understanding. "We better know where to go."

A few minutes later, they were standing in front of the door to the girl's quarters. Knocking, Jeremy smiled when Kelsey opened it. Glancing inside, he saw that the girl's quarters were identical to those that Kevin and he were sharing. "Have you read your folders yet?"

"Yes," replied Kelsey, nodding. It had been the first thing she had done after Lieutenant Nelson had shown them their quarters. "I guess we're supposed to become familiar with the ship."

"It's a large ship," Angela said, stepping up to stand next to Kelsey. "We're going to have a lot to learn and quickly."

"Do you want to come with us?" Jeremy asked. He thought for the time being it might be wise for the four of them to stick together. Particularly since Barr and three of his squad were also on board.

Jeremy had spent some time before they had come up to the ship looking over the schematics for the New Horizon. One of the schematics that he was allowed access to was a detailed description of each level of the ship. There were twenty levels on the ship. A big part of that was taken up by Engineering, which held the ship's two fusion reactors, the sublight drive, the FTL drive, and all the intricate control systems that made the ship work. Much of the rest of the space was taken up by food and parts storage, the medical bay, and two mess halls. One of the mess halls was close to the Command Center and was for the ship's officers. The other mess hall was quite a bit larger and served the rest of the crew. There were also half a dozen small labs to study any samples that were brought inside the ship. The rest of the ship consisted of crew quarters and some small recreational areas.

"I think that would be great," replied Kelsey ready to get started. "Where should we start?"

"Let's go check out the mess halls first," Jeremy suggested.

"Great idea," spoke Kevin, grinning. "Food is a big priority. We need to know where to eat."

Angela laughed and smiled at Kevin. "I hope the food on the New Horizon is as good as what we had at the academy." They all knew Kevin from the academy. He had a good sense of humor and was easy to get along with. While not a member of their squad, they all had spoken to him on occasion.

"Cadet Lieutenant Strong," a commanding voice spoke from behind Jeremy.

Turning around Jeremy found Lieutenant Nelson standing there. "Yes, sir!"

"Come with me. Commander Tellson wants to see you in the Command Center."

Jeremy felt a cold chill run down his back. Was he already in trouble? He turned back to his friends. "Go ahead without me. I'll catch up later."

Kelsey watched Jeremy go down the corridor with the lieutenant. She hoped nothing had happened.

"Let's go," said Kevin, motioning to the two girls. "We have a lot of ship to explore. I'm also feeling a little hungry."

Jeremy followed Lieutenant Nelson down several corridors and up several sets of stairs until they arrived at the Command Center. The hatch was open, and the two stepped inside. Jeremy looked around, taking it all in. There were eight people at various stations plus the commander standing at the center command console.

"Cadet Lieutenant Strong," spoke Commander Tellson, seeing that Jeremy and Lieutenant Nelson had made it to the Command Center.

Jeremy walked over to stand in front of Commander Tellson. He stood at attention curious as to why he had been called in front of the ship's commander.

"I have read your file from the academy. I understand you want to be a ship's officer someday?"

"Yes, sir," Jeremy responded, his eyes straight ahead.

"Do you think that someday you can command a starship?" Tellson asked, his eyes gazing intently at Jeremy. "Do you think that someday you can follow in your father's footsteps?"

"I hope so, sir," responded Jeremy, respectfully.

"We shall see," commented Tellson, nodding his head thoughtfully. "The Command Center is manned twenty-four hours a day with a full crew. I'm normally here on the first watch along with Major Maher, the ship's executive officer. I do drop in routinely on the other shifts to see how everything is operating. Lieutenant Nelson is in charge of the second watch, and that is where you will be doing your training. Matter of fact, the other four cadets that came up with you will be on the same shift. I want people who trust each other working together."

"You will be expected to continue your studies as well," Lieutenant Nelson added. "You may have graduated from the academy, but you still have a year to go as a cadet serving on a ship."

"At the end of that year, if you have proven yourself, the cadet status will be removed and you will be a ship's officer," Tellson said. "Understand one thing, Cadet Lieutenant Strong; this will not be easy! I run a tight ship, and I expect everyone to pull their own weight. Just because your father is the admiral, doesn't mean you will be given any special considerations."

"I don't expect any, sir," replied Jeremy, evenly. "I made it here on my own, and I expect to continue on my own."

"Very good," responded Tellson, nodding his head in approval. "You may return to the other cadets and work on familiarizing yourselves with the ship. You will begin your first duty shift in the Command Center tomorrow."

"Thank you, sir," Jeremy responded.

"You're dismissed," Commander Tellson said.

Jeremy turned and left the Command Center. Commander Tellson and Lieutenant Nelson watched him go.

"That boy has a lot of potential," Tellson commented to Nelson quietly. "I read over his files, and he did an outstanding job at the academy. He is definitely following in his father's footsteps. Work the boy hard, Lieutenant. Make him learn everything necessary to become a good commanding officer someday."

"Yes, sir," Nelson replied. "I will keep him busy. When I'm through, he will be able to find his way around this ship blindfolded."

Chapter Four

Jeremy was sound asleep after spending a long day becoming familiar with the New Horizon. He felt as if he had walked every corridor and gone up every single stairwell in the ship. The lights in the room suddenly flashed on and a loud alarm klaxon began sounding. Jeremy almost fell out of bed as he hastily threw back his blanket.

"What the hell is that?" Kevin yelled, his eyes wide standing next to his bunk in his underwear. "Is there something wrong with the ship?"

"Ship is now at Condition One," a commanding voice came over the speaker on the wall next to the vid screen and barked. "All crew report to their emergency stations!"

"Crap, where are we supposed to go?" spoke Kevin, grabbing his folder and frantically looking through it. He realized now it was one of those freaking emergency drills.

"Level eight, section twelve," responded Jeremy, recalling where they were supposed to go. They had different stations to report to depending upon the time of day.

"Where's that?" asked Kevin, looking over at Jeremy, relieved to know that at least one of them knew where they were supposed to go.

"The medical bay, or just outside of it," responded Jeremy, opening his locker and starting to get dressed. "We need to get there as rapidly as possible. I imagine that Commander Tellson is timing us."

Two minutes later, the two were in the corridor and hurrying toward a set of stairs that led upward. They were not allowed to use the small personnel elevators in emergencies or in drills. The reasoning was simple. What good were emergency personnel if they were trapped in an elevator?

It took them nearly twelve minutes to reach the medical bay. They made a wrong turn and had to backtrack to get on the correct deck. Jeremy felt his heart drop when they rounded a corner and he saw Lieutenant Nelson waiting impatiently in front of the Med Bay, staring at his watch. He knew Kevin and he were in for it.

"You're late!" Nelson snapped with a displeased look upon his face. "You should have been here five minutes ago. Show me the route you took to get here. The lives of some members of this crew might depend on you two getting to your emergency station on time."

"Yes, sir," Jeremy and Kevin both spoke. They had failed to get to their emergency station on time. This wouldn't look good on the Daily Report.

Jeremy and Kevin retraced their steps with Lieutenant Nelson following close behind. No one spoke until they reached their quarters.

"You made a common mistake by taking the main corridors to your station," Lieutenant Nelson informed them, his sharp eyes drilling into the two cadets. "There are two smaller auxiliary corridors that could have gotten you to your station on time. Follow me and I will show you which ones I am talking about."

Lieutenant Nelson took his time and showed them the two auxiliary corridors. They walked each one, eventually arriving at the medical bay. After reaching the Med Bay after walking the second corridor, Nelson turned around and looked at the two cadets. "Now use the first corridor and return to your quarters. Then use the second corridor to return." Glancing at his watch, he continued. "You have ten minutes to return to your quarters, touch the door and return here. If you're late, you will do it again. We have all night if necessary."

"Yes, sir!" Jeremy and Kevin shouted as they turned and sprinted down the corridor.

Lieutenant Nelson watched them and then smiled as they disappeared around a corner. This was a common mistake for cadets to make; they would get better with time. He could well remember his first few days on one of the smaller exploration cruisers. He had spent a lot of time running the corridors until he became familiar with the ship.

Jeremy was lying on his bunk staring at the vid screen. It was currently on a channel that was showing the New Horizon and giving a brief history of its construction. The vid show was showing scenes of the New Horizon at various stages of its construction. Letting out a deep sigh, Jeremy reached down and massaged the large muscle on the back of his leg. His entire body ached from all the running Kevin and he had done trying to reach the Med Bay in the time that Lieutenant Nelson had allotted. Jeremy had finally realized that it was not possible for them to reach the Med Bay in the time Lieutenant Nelson had set. This was their punishment for not being on time originally. After the sixth attempt, Lieutenant Nelson dismissed them and informed the two to be better prepared the next time.

When they had returned to their quarters, they had spent the next two hours walking various corridors to the other two emergency stations they were supposed to report to depending on ship's time. Once the two of them were satisfied that they were ready for the next surprise drill, they had both taken a quick shower and then collapsed onto their bunks.

"Are you ready for our shift in the Command Center?" Kevin asked from where he was sitting at the desk, studying some information he had been looking up on the computer screen.

Jeremy sat up and looked over at Kevin. "Has to be better than last night."

"You can say that again," replied Kevin, nodding his head in agreement. "I thought I was in good shape, but running up those flights of stairs changed my mind about that. I didn't realize this ship had so many stairs!"

"Might be a good idea for us to set up a regular exercise routine," Jeremy suggested. He liked to work out anyway, and the ship did have a good weight room.

"I wonder how the girls made out in the drill?"

"I haven't talked to either of them today," Jeremy replied. He had tried to contact them once earlier, but neither had answered the com line in their quarters. Jeremy lay back down and shut his eyes. "I'm going to get a few more minutes of sleep. It's going to be a long shift tonight."

Jeremy and Kevin entered the Command Center fifteen minutes ahead of schedule. Lieutenant Nelson was sitting at the center command console. He nodded his head toward them.

"Cadet Lieutenant Strong, you will work with Ensign Roberts at the sensor and scanner console. A good commander needs to know the capabilities of his ship and what might be coming his way. There are several shuttles coming up from Earth tonight going to the academy with the summer recruits. Ensign Roberts will show you how to use the scanner and sensors to track the incoming shuttles."

"Yes, sir," responded Jeremy, walking over to the scanner and sensor console where Ensign Roberts was waiting.

He was familiar with how the equipment worked from his studies at the academy, but this would be the first time he had tracked an actual shuttle. He also wondered if Katie was on board one of those shuttles coming up with the summer recruits. There was a good possibility she was since classes were due to begin in just a few more days at the academy. He just hoped his parents were ready for the young teenager. Jeremy was just glad he was on the New Horizon and wouldn't have to deal with her.

"Ensign Walters, I want you over at the environmental controls. The main computer has been acting up, and we're currently running on the backup. See if you can find out what's wrong." Nelson didn't mention that the computer had been intentionally disabled to see if Walters could find the problem. The problem should occupy him for several hours, assuming he could eventually figure it out.

Kevin walked over to the indicated console and sat down. In just a few moments, he was running a diagnostic program to see if it would reveal what the problem was. Kevin knew this might take a while.

"So you're Admiral Strong's son," commented Ensign Roberts, motioning for Jeremy to take a seat next to him. "He's done an amazing job with the academy and the Avenger Project."

"It's been his life," replied Jeremy, looking at the two large screens that were on the console. The one on the left was the short-range scanner screen, and the one on the right was for the long-range sensors.

"I hope I can meet him someday," Roberts continued as he pressed several buttons and turned a dial on the large console.

Instantly the two screens came on. Jeremy had studied how the sensor and scanner screens worked as had all the cadets that were in officer's training. They were required to become familiar with all the operating systems in a ship.

"What do you know about the ship's main sensors?" asked Roberts, wanting to know how much Jeremy had learned at the academy.

"The main sensors have a range of nearly one hundred million kilometers," Jeremy replied. "They are extremely sensitive and can detect planets, asteroids, comets, and other ships that are within that range."

"How detailed are they?" Roberts continued. Roberts knew that the academy instructors were extremely thorough. He was just trying to see how much Jeremy had learned from them.

"Not very," replied Jeremy, looking at the two screens. "For detailed information we need to use the scanners. They are good up to two hundred thousand kilometers and can give detailed information on anything larger than one hundred meters. Of course, the closer you can get the more detailed the scans become."

"Excellent," spoke Roberts, nodding his head in approval. At least Jeremy had paid attention in class. "Now let's see if we can spot those two shuttles." Roberts gestured toward the scanner screen and began adjusting it to focus more on Earth.

Lieutenant Nelson watched, satisfied that Jeremy at least knew his stuff. He seemed to be following what Ensign Roberts was doing without a problem. Every once in a while he would ask Roberts a question and Roberts would go back and explain some fine point about the ship's scanners again. Nelson hoped the young man was just as well versed in the other duty stations in the Command Center. Turning his attention back to the schedule for the night shift, Nelson saw that more supplies had arrived during the day and were supposed to be inventoried. He sent several crewmembers to check them and to make sure they had been stowed correctly.

He was under strict orders from Commander Tellson to double-check everything since Admiral Strong had mentioned the rumors going around down on Earth. Nelson had a hard time imagining there being any kind of legitimate threat against the New Horizon. He strongly suspected it was just a few locals letting off steam at the money being spent in lunar orbit instead of on more welfare programs.

Katie was in one of the shuttles that were just climbing out of Earth's thick protective atmosphere. She felt excited about returning to the Moon. For the next three months, she would be a student at the Fleet Academy studying computers. This was something she had dreamed about, now it was actually going to happen. She noticed several people were staring at her, probably wondering why such a young girl was on the shuttle without adult supervision. She smiled politely at them and nodded.

In just another few hours, she would be back on the Moon. One of the first things she wanted to do was speak with Ariel. In the few months Katie had been away from the Moon, she had come up with hundreds of questions she wanted to ask the AI. Looking out the viewport next to her, she noticed they were finally out of the Earth's protective atmosphere. Space had turned darker, with a sprinkling of stars. She reached into her backpack and took out her small handheld computer. Turning it on, she was soon engrossed in working on her newest program.

Several times the flight attendant came by to check on Katie. Katie had a strong suspicion that her mother had told the woman to keep a close eye on her. She smiled at the flight attendant and nodded her head in acknowledgment.

"Is there anything you need, dear?" the flight attendant asked.

"Water would be nice," Katie replied in her most polite voice.

The flight attendant nodded and soon returned with a bottle of slightly chilled water. "If you need anything else, just let me know."

"Thank you," Katie replied with a sweet smile. She watched as the flight attendant left. Katie shook her head and went back to working on her computer.

An hour later, the flight attendant picked up a microphone and began addressing the passengers. "We will be passing close by the spacedock shortly. The New Horizon is still docked to the station and you should be able to see two really bright points of light."

Katie turned her attention to outside the shuttle. In a few minutes, she saw two bright points of light that steadily grew brighter. She knew the light was from reflected sunlight. She let out a deep sigh of regret. Jeremy was on the New Horizon, and she wouldn't get to see him while she was on the Moon for the summer. That was her biggest disappointment. Then her light green eyes brightened. Perhaps she could talk Lisa or even Jason into taking her on a tour of the spacedock. Surely if they were on the spacedock, Jeremy would be allowed to come and see them. Maybe she could even talk one of them into showing her the New Horizon!

Katie watched as the shuttle quickly neared the Moon and began its descent toward the crater that held the Avenger and the academy. Looking out the viewport, she could see the rough and desolate lunar terrain passing by below them. The ground was dark and gray and covered with multiple impact craters. Without an atmosphere, the Moon had nothing to protect it from occasional meteor strikes. Katie knew there were bunkers beneath the academy buildings where the students could take refuge if a potential meteor strike were detected.

The shuttle reached the crater and landed inside a large flight bay that had been built over to one side of the crater. Over a dozen Raven class shuttles were parked inside. The hatch on the shuttle slid open, and the ramp was extended so the passengers could depart.

"You may now disembark the shuttle," the flight attendant informed everyone with a friendly smile. "If you are not sure where to go, you need to report to the new arrivals station. You will see signs posted outside directing you."

Katie stood up and grabbed her backpack. Walking down the ramp, she saw Lisa waiting for her with a friendly smile on her face.

"Hello Katie," Lisa said. "I hope you're ready to spend the summer here on the Moon."

"More than you can know," Katie responded with a big grin.

Ariel was waiting, and Katie could hardly wait to get checked into her dorm room so she could speak to her. She had a special program she had written on her handheld computer that should give her instant access to Ariel if she was close enough to a main computer terminal.

"Where's Jason?" asked Katie, looking around. She had expected Jason to be here to greet her along with Lisa.

"Jason had somewhere he had to go," replied Lisa, evenly. She couldn't tell Katie that Jason had left to go to Ceres to discuss the upcoming reconnaissance mission into Hocklyn space.

Jason watched from behind the pilot's seat as they neared Ceres. Since their original mission to the asteroid twenty-four years ago, a lot had changed. The number of defense platforms orbiting Ceres had doubled. Two Federation light cruisers were also patrolling farther out. Both cruisers had limited stealth shielding so as not to be accidentally picked up on the sensors of Earth's four interplanetary exploration cruisers. The two cruisers only showed up dimly on the short-range scanners, but Jason knew they were there.

From Ceres, the entire solar system was monitored. If anything unknown showed up on the sensors, the two cruisers could be sent instantly to investigate. The Hocklyns must not learn of Earth until far in the future. If more warships were required, there were two Conqueror class battle cruisers available as well as two fleet battle carriers if needed. All four were in the massive ship bays inside Ceres with partial crews on board.

"We are cleared to land," the copilot commented as he listened to instructions from Ceres base.

Approaching the asteroid two large hatches slid back, revealing a cavernous flight bay. Even as they landed, they saw four space fighters take off to conduct a routine patrol of the asteroid field around the base.

"Security is tighter than ever," the pilot commented, watching the fighters enviously. He wondered what it would be like to fly one of them.

The pilot normally made the run between the Moon and Ceres once a week. The shuttle he was flying did have an FTL drive installed, and they had used a micro-jump to reduce the flying time between Earth and Ceres to slightly less than four hours. Those four hours were the time the shuttle spent clearing the Earth and Moon's gravity well.

"We have a lot going on right now," commented Jason, knowing the reason for the increased security.

In the last few years, the Federation survivors on Ceres had been working hard about what to do if there were a Hocklyn incursion before the Earth was ready. Ceres and the ships hidden within were the solar system's first line of defense. It would be years before Earth had an armed space fleet of her own powerful enough to resist an invasion.

The biggest problem right now was a shortage of manpower. The population of Ceres was only 146,000. That just wasn't enough people to man all the ships. There was one battle cruiser and one battle carrier that were fully manned, but they were both in the New Tellus system. Hopefully, in a few more years, the academy on the Moon would start to furnish a big part of those badly needed crews. Plans were already being made to quadruple the size of the classes as well as increasing the size of the academy. It would be necessary so the new colony ships could be crewed.

For today, Jason had a meeting scheduled with Admiral Anlon to discuss the upcoming reconnaissance mission. Jason also wanted to see the new Monarch Two heavy cruiser. This was a completely new warship built by the Federation survivors in one of the large construction bays inside Ceres. Supposedly, the ship included a lot of new technical advancements, both in weapons and in its drive systems.

The pilot carefully maneuvered the shuttle inside the flight bay and landed it smoothly on the indicated landing pad. As he shut off the engine, he noticed a small group of people walking toward the shuttle. The welcoming committee, he assumed. The pilot knew that Admiral Strong didn't come out to Ceres very often. His busy schedule back on the Moon didn't allow it.

Stepping out of the shuttle, Jason smiled upon seeing Admiral Anlon and a younger woman with an air of authority about her. Looking closer, Jason saw she was a brunette with beautiful blue eyes. He didn't recognize her and was not sure who she was.

"Hello, Admiral," spoke Anlon, offering his hand. Then he turned to introduce the woman standing next to him. "This is Colonel Amanda Sheen, former executive officer of the StarStrike."

"Colonel Sheen," spoke Jason, nodding in recognition as he realized who this was. "I have heard a lot about you from Ariel on the Avenger."

"Ariel," spoke Colonel Sheen, recalling the AI. She had already spoken to Clarissa here on Ceres. It was hard to believe that both the AIs had managed to survive. She shivered slightly. Amanda didn't think she had fully gotten over being in cryosleep all of these years. Then, indicating the tall dark haired man standing next to her, she continued. "This is Major Richard Andrews, my husband."

Jason shook Richard's hand. He knew from the reports that Admiral Anlon had sent him that both Colonel Sheen and Major Andrews were intimately acquainted with the former worlds of the Federation. He knew that Colonel Sheen had spent a lot of time on Aquaria where her parents had lived, and Major Andrews had worked on the large shipyard above New Providence.

"I understand you have a new ship to show me," Jason said anxious to see the new warship. "Why don't we head over to the construction bay and we can discuss the mission as we tour it?"

"Good idea," Admiral Anlon commented. "I think you will be impressed by our new design. It's far more advanced than anything we have ever built before."

"I hope so," Colonel Sheen commented as they left the flight bay. "We will need every advantage possible if we're going deep into Hocklyn space to see what they have been up to for the last one hundred years."

"I still can't believe we've been asleep that long," commented Major Andrews, looking over at Amanda. There were only sixty-eight people who had chosen to go into cryosleep. When they had the time, Richard wanted to see what had happened to some of those that had chosen to live their lives out on Ceres.

The small group walked through the base, then took a recently installed transit tube to the construction bays. Once they arrived, Admiral Anlon led them through several connecting corridors until they stepped out onto a large platform that overlooked one of the bays.

"This is the Monarch Two heavy cruiser WarStorm," Admiral Anlon spoke with pride in his voice. "She is 900 meters long, 220 meters high and 210 meters wide."

"That's bigger than a normal Monarch heavy cruiser," commented Colonel Sheen, gazing at the large ship that rested in the construction bay. The composite armor on the hull was a dark gray, nearly black. Everything about the ship looked new.

"She's also much more powerful," continued Admiral Anlon, gesturing toward the front of the ship. "She has four primary lasers in the bow. The new lasers are four times more powerful than the old ones."

"Four times!" Major Andrews spoke, his face showing surprise. "How did you do that?" He had spent a lot of time with Amanda discussing the specifications for the large lasers that had been installed on the shipyard above New Providence. He knew that power for lasers was always an issue.

"You must remember that our fleet had never fought a war when we encountered the Hocklyns," Admiral Anlon explained. "We had never had the need for stronger and more capable weapons. Any type of energy weapon, including lasers, is an energy hog. We have a small fusion reactor that serves no other purpose than to power those lasers. These lasers are also a completely new design from the older ones. We also have plans for a future energy beam weapon to replace the lasers. But we have a number of technical issues that need to be solved before we can build one."

"Energy weapons," Colonel Sheen spoke, her eyes turning dark. "The Hocklyns have a type of energy beam weapon. It was much more powerful than our lasers."

"There's something that's always confused me," spoke Jason, gazing at the new ship and wondering how long it would be before Earth could build something like this. If they stayed on their current schedule, he knew it would be nearly another one hundred years. "Why aren't the Hocklyn ships more advanced? With all the worlds they have conquered, you would think they would have assimilated some of that technology."

"We have a theory about that," responded Admiral Anlon, glancing over at Jason. "When we get back to my office I will ask Telleck Simkens to come talk to us. He is one of our leading weapons scientists and has put forth an explanation as to why the Hocklyn technology is not more advanced than it is. I think you will find it interesting."

"What about railguns?" Colonel Sheen asked, still looking at the cruiser. "Does it have railguns?"

Admiral Anlon smiled. "Do you know why the Federation used railguns, Colonel Sheen?"

Amanda shook her head. She had just always taken them for granted. Every warship she had ever been aboard had them.

"They were cheap and easy to install and maintain," Anlon explained. "They're basically cannons that hurled large shells at very high velocities. The size of the shell and its speed at impact are what makes it deadly. However, the introduction of energy screens was bound to make them obsolete. Just before the Federation encountered the Hocklyns there was already research being done to replace them with something deadlier."

"So, no railguns," spoke Amanda, looking over at Admiral Anlon and wondering what they had been replaced with.

Admiral Anlon smiled and shook his head. "Not railguns per se. We have come up with something better. The ship is equipped with twenty-four HGs, or heavy gun turrets. The HGs fire one-meter explosive shells at a speed of 10,000 kilometers per second. At impact, they release an explosive force of one-kiloton."

"A kiloton," Richard repeated amazed at the destructive force these guns could bring to bear. "And you say the ship has twenty-four of these turrets?"

"Yes," Admiral Anlon replied, then turning back to Colonel Sheen. "The ship also has a full range of offensive and defensive missile tubes. The missiles the ship is equipped with are also much more advanced than what you are familiar with, both in speed and destructive capability."

"Let's go on board," Colonel Sheen spoke, her eyes gleaming with excitement. It sounded as if this ship had been built for one thing and one thing only, war! She wanted to see the inside of her new command.

A few minutes later, they were inside the ship. As they walked through the new warship, Jason marveled at how well built the ship was. Heavy bulkheads, armor, new improved energy shields, comfortable crew quarters. It was a ship designed for long-term deployment and to take out the enemy.

"How long will this mission last?" Jason asked as they stopped in Engineering and talked to the chief engineer about the new sublight drive and the FTL core.

"Six to eight months," Admiral Anlon replied. "The ship will be making six jumps per day of fifteen to twenty light years. We figure it

65

will take them three to four months to reach the area of space the Hocklyns are currently active in."

"How long for the FTL core to cool?" Colonel Sheen asked the chief engineer. Even on the StarStrike, it had taken nearly four hours. She was also impressed by how new everything looked.

"The new drive core can be cooled back down in two hours," Chief engineer Edwards replied. He smiled broadly gesturing toward the large sealed compartment that held the drive core. "We have added a specialized cooling system that can better handle the excess heat generated by an FTL jump."

"So many changes," spoke Amanda, gazing around Engineering. A multitude of things seemed different, while others seemed strangely familiar.

"That's why you will have six weeks to become familiar with the new design," Admiral Anlon explained. "The ship is ready to launch at your discretion. We have already taken her out on a shakedown cruise to New Tellus. You have six weeks to get the crew ready and request any additional supplies that you think you might need."

"Let's go up to the Command Center," Amanda suggested. She wanted to see what changes had been made there.

Jeremy was walking down the main corridor toward the mess hall. It had been a long duty shift. Fortunately, Ensign Roberts had been patient and had answered all of Jeremy's questions. Jeremy had even managed to spot both shuttles and track them as they landed in the crater containing the academy. Lieutenant Nelson had explained to Jeremy that he would be expected to be able to operate every station in the Command Center. Kevin had returned to their quarters to get some much needed sleep. He still hadn't recovered from the emergency drill.

Entering the mess hall, Jeremy saw that both the girls had already filled their trays and were sitting next to one of the walls talking. Seeing Jeremy, Kelsey waved and indicated for him to get his tray and join them. Jeremy knew that the two girls were not scheduled to begin their shifts in the Command Center until the following day.

"How was your day?" asked Jeremy, taking his seat and setting his tray on the table.

"We were in the Med Bay assisting Doctor Stevens with inventory," replied Angela, rolling her eyes. "Boring!"

Jeremy laughed. He took a bite of his food and found that it had a surprisingly good flavor. It looked and tasted like Salisbury steak.

"How's the food, daddy's boy?" an obnoxious voice spoke from behind him. Cadet Lieutenant Barr came to stand next to Jeremy, looking down at him with a smug look upon his face. Jeremy didn't know if his first twenty-four hours on the New Horizon could get any worse.

"Hear you got stuck on the night shift with Lieutenant Nelson. Guess that should tell you something. I'm on the day shift with the commander and executive officer."

"That's fine, Matt," Jeremy replied in a neutral voice. "I have no problem training under Lieutenant Nelson. He seems to be a very capable officer."

Barr stared at Jeremy speculatively for a moment, and then continued, "Stay out of my way on this ship, Jeremy. This isn't like the academy where the instructors can rush in to protect you. Your daddy isn't here either. You get in my way or cause me any problems and you will regret it. Stay on the shift you're on!" Matt turned and walked away.

"What was that all about?" Kelsey blurted out, feeling confused. Why was Matt so concerned about Jeremy? She had hoped all of this nonsense would stop once they got aboard the New Horizon and were not competing against one another.

"Who knows?" replied Jeremy, taking another bite of his food. He wasn't going to let Matt get underneath his skin. Jeremy suspected that was exactly what Matt had been trying to do. Why, Jeremy had no idea.

Katie was in her dorm room at the academy. She was staying in the senior dorm, and one of the older girls had been assigned to check up on her regularly. Lisa had told Katie it was to help her adjust since she was the youngest person attending the summer session. Sitting on her bed, Katie wondered what her time at the academy would be like. She could hardly wait to get started in the computer classes she had enrolled in. The computers at the academy were supposed to be the top of the line.

"Hello, Katie," a friendly female voice spoke.

Whirling around, Katie grinned when she saw Ariel on the vid screen. "How do you do that? Does anyone else know that you can appear anywhere there is a vid screen?"

A guilty look spread across Ariel's face, and she slowly shook her head. "No, I've never revealed that to anyone. It helps to pass the time if I can watch what people are doing. I don't invade their privacy or anything, but I do watch some of the games they play and other things they do for entertainment. They don't have any idea that I have modified the vid screen programs so I can watch people."

"Lisa doesn't even know?" asked Katie surprised. Lisa was one of the smartest people she knew. She didn't think anything could get past Lisa.

"Particularly not Lisa," Ariel answered in a more serious tone. "She's a good enough programmer that she could probably block my spying around. Besides, I like to keep track of what's going on in the academy."

"Why don't we start tonight by you telling me what you did down on Earth while you were gone?" Ariel spoke, her dark eyes brightening. Katie offered her something she had never had a chance to experience before. To hear what Earth was like from the viewpoint of a teenager should be fascinating.

Katie spent over two hours describing what she had done down on Earth. Ariel would interrupt her occasionally and ask Katie to explain some things in more detail. Finally, Katie became quiet and looked expectantly at Ariel. The dark haired young woman on the vid screen had a particularly pleased look upon her face.

"Thank you, Katie," responded Ariel immensely pleased with everything Katie had told her. She had really enjoyed listening to Katie describe Earth. Her descriptions were so different than listening to Lisa or Jason. "Now I understand you have some questions."

"Yes," replied Katie, leaning back on her bed and gazing at Ariel. "I want to know more about these Hocklyns and the AIs that rule over them."

"We don't know a lot about the AIs," Ariel began slowly. "Only that they are extremely advanced and their ships seem indestructible. But we do know quite a bit about the Hocklyns."

Jason, Colonel Sheen, Major Andrews, Admiral Anlon, and Telleck Simkens were all seated at a small conference table. They had finished their tour of the WarStorm and had been extremely impressed. The Federation survivors hadn't scrimped on the new ship. Every system and weapon were the top of the line. Admiral Anlon had claimed that the WarStorm had more firepower at her disposal than a Conqueror class battle cruiser.

"As I said earlier, we have wondered for quite some time why the Hocklyn's technological level isn't higher than it is," Admiral Anlon began. "At the time of the Federation's initial contact with the Hocklyns, it was quite evident that they held a significant technological advantage. However, after quickly updating our ships following that first disastrous encounter, the technological gap was quickly closed. Telleck here has an explanation as to why their technology is being held back."

Telleck Simkens stood up. He talked better when he was standing and could use hand gestures. "At the very end of the war between the Hocklyns and the Federation, there was already a growing suspicion that the Hocklyn's technology was being held back on purpose. Look at the viewscreen and I will show you what I mean."

On the viewscreen appeared a Hocklyn war cruiser battling a Federation Monarch cruiser. The two ships seemed evenly matched. Explosions covered both ship's shields and missile trails could be seen between the two.

"If you look closely, you will notice that both ships are using similar weapons," Simkens pointed out. "Railguns and missiles. The only real advantages the Hocklyns seemed to have at the end were their slightly stronger shields and the energy weapon they had on the bow of their ships. Now observe this."

On the viewscreen, an AI warship appeared. The fifteen hundred meter behemoth was attacking several Federation ships including a battle cruiser. Numerous explosions covered the AI ship's screen, including several large nuclear blasts.

"As you can see, the AI ship's screens are not even weakened," Simkens commented. "Even nuclear explosions seem to have little or no affect."

On the screen, the AI ship seemed to tire of the antics of the attacking Federation ships. Powerful energy beams blasted out at the offending ships. The beams cut right through the energy shields, spearing the ships with death and destruction. In just a matter of a few short minutes, the attacking Federation ships were eliminated.

The room was very quiet. For some, it was the first time they had seen this footage of an AI ship engaging Federation fleet forces. It made them realize exactly what they were facing sometime in the future. It left an uneasy silence in the room.

"As you can see, the AIs obviously have the advanced technology the Hocklyns don't have," explained Simkens, gesturing at the AI ship still being displayed on the viewscreen. "Their shields, weapons, space drive, all are a mystery to us."

"So why don't they share more of their technology with the Hocklyns?" Jason asked with a confused look. There had to be a reason. "With better technology they would be able to expand their empire much quicker."

"It's actually quite simple," Simkens commented evenly, looking at Jason. "They don't want the Hocklyns and their other three warrior races to become a threat to them. They give them just enough technology to defeat any race they come across. If any of the four proxy races encounter an advanced civilization, then the AIs step in and either level the playing field by destroying the other civilization's fleet, or they destroy the civilization completely as they did the Federation."

"Why don't the Hocklyns develop more advanced weapons on their own?" Colonel Sheen asked. "They should be able to."

"Out of fear," replied Simkens, pointing at the AI ship on the screen. "They don't want those ships to appear over their home worlds and do to them what has been done to so many others. As long as they are allowed to continue to grow their empire, the Hocklyns are satisfied to maintain the status quo."

Jason nodded his head. What Simkens had said made a lot of sense. If that was true and they could continue to advance the technological level of Earth and the Federation survivors, it might just give them the edge they would need when the conflict with the Hocklyns arrived in the future.

"How do we know for sure if your theory is accurate?" asked Amanda, gazing at Simkens. Those Hocklyn ships had been difficult enough to destroy as they were.

"It's simple," responded Simkens, turning his head to gaze directly at Amanda. "On your trip back to the Federation worlds, you need to find a Hocklyn ship and engage it. Then we will know if there has been any advancement in their ship designs and weapons in the past one hundred years."

The room was quiet. The only noise being the air blowing through the ventilation ducts. For several long moments, no one said anything. Then Admiral Anlon cleared his throat.

"That means, Colonel Sheen, that the Hocklyn ship will have to be destroyed and their communications jammed so they can't send out a distress signal."

"You agree with this?" asked Amanda, gazing at Admiral Anlon.

"It is vital information we need for our war planning," Anlon responded with a determined nod of his head. "Admiral Strong, do you agree that we should do this? You represent Earth. If you decide against this part of the mission, then I will instruct Colonel Sheen not to engage a Hocklyn vessel."

Jason was quiet as he mulled over the ramifications, then he finally spoke. "As long as the engagement is far enough away so the Hocklyns can not find their way back here. If the Hocklyns were to locate Earth or New Tellus now it would be a disaster."

"I think we can write some orders for the colonel that can accommodate your concerns," answered Anlon, agreeing with Jason. "There will be no engagement if there is even the remotest chance of the Hocklyn ship surviving or getting off a distress signal."

The meeting lasted for another hour. When they were done, Jason felt they had a good understanding of just what was expected of Colonel Sheen and the WarStorm. Now it would be necessary to return to the Moon and have Greg call a meeting of the special council he was responsible for. Greg chaired a government council of the five nations that knew about the base on Ceres and the Hocklyns.

Jason knew this might be a hard sell to those five governments. While the Federation survivors didn't really need the approval of the Earth council for the mission, they wanted it so as to keep good relations with the five governments. Over the next few years, several more governments were going to be invited to join the council. It was important for the council to feel that it had a pertinent voice in important policy decisions.

Chapter Five

Colonel Sheen sat behind the command console in the Monarch cruiser WarStorm. For four weeks, she had been busy familiarizing herself with the new ship and becoming acquainted with the crew. Looking at the sensor and scanner console, she felt comfort knowing that Lieutenant Benjamin Stalls was sitting there. At Communications, Lieutenant Angela Trask was busy talking to Ceres control as they were preparing to depart. Lieutenant Macy Ashton was at Navigation. All three of these crewmembers had been a part of First Fleet when it had journeyed to Earth over one hundred years ago. They had all been awakened from cryosleep for this mission due to their familiarity with the space they would be traveling through as well as their knowledge of the former Federation worlds.

Her husband, Major Andrews, would serve as her third in command. Richard and she had decided that in order to keep confusion in the chain of command to a minimum that she would continue to use her former last name. Major Martin Fields was the WarStorm's executive officer. He had been involved with the ship since its inception and was fundamentally familiar with all the ship's systems and its unique capabilities.

"Ready for departure, Colonel," Major Fields reported as all departments finished checking in and reporting their readiness.

"Request that the outer doors be opened," ordered Amanda, looking expectantly at the large viewscreen on the front wall of the Command Center. She had spent a lot of long hours familiarizing herself with the new ship. If they had to go into combat, she wanted to know what the WarStorm was capable of.

Lieutenant Trask quickly passed on the request to Ceres control and nodded her head when she received a quick response. "Doors are being opened," she replied. The communications system on the WarStorm was very similar to the one on the StarStrike, just a little more advanced and efficient.

The front wall of the Command Center was covered with numerous viewscreens. There was the large center screen with four others, only slightly smaller, next to it. Two additional banks of ten more on each side of the big screens displayed different views of the outside of the ship as well as the inside. Two ensigns sat in front of the screens, monitoring them as well as changing the views every few minutes. The views from any of the smaller screens could be placed on one of the larger screens if a potential problem needed to be brought to the commanding officer's attention.

On the large viewscreen, the massive metal doors at the end of the one thousand-meter tunnel slowly began sliding back, revealing space and a few beckoning stars. Amanda watched for a moment, drawing in a sharp breath. It would feel good to be back out in space again. For the last four weeks, she had run her crew through drill after drill until she felt satisfied they were melded together. Now it was time to test that with drills in open space.

"Take us out, Major Fields," ordered Amanda, glancing at her second in command.

Major Fields was standing next to the holographic plotting table. Reaching forward, he activated the holographic display. The air above the table began to glow, and then an image of the WarStorm and the tunnel appeared.

"Helm, activate maneuvering thrusters and move us out at ten percent thrust," ordered Major Fields, keeping his eyes focused on the holographic image. "Keep the WarStorm in the center of the tunnel and be prepared for emergency stop if necessary."

"Yes, sir," the helm officer replied as he activated his console.

Computers would handle the actual movement of the WarStorm. The helm officer knew that all he had to do was keep a close watch on their trajectory to ensure the computers were actually doing as instructed. His primary job was telling the navigation computers what to do and to initiate minor course corrections as needed.

The maneuvering thrusters fired, and the massive warship began moving slowly down the tunnel. The computers constantly scanned the distance between the ship and the tunnel walls, making instant adjustments to keep the large ship in the center. The helm officer watched his data screens closely as they showed the distance the WarStorm was from the tunnel walls. So far, the navigation system was performing flawlessly.

"How soon until we exit the tunnel?" asked Amanda, trying not to let her impatience show in her voice. She wanted to get back out into space.

"We will exit the tunnel in two minutes," the helm officer reported as he made some minor adjustments to his controls. One of the maneuvering thrusters seemed to be slightly out of balance. He reported the minor problem to Engineering knowing it should be an easy fix from there.

Amanda leaned back in her chair and smiled. It felt good to be exiting the construction bay. She felt alive and rejuvenated knowing that shortly their mission would begin. Watching the main viewscreen, she could see the tunnel exit gradually growing wider as they got nearer.

"One hundred and twenty meters and we will exit the tunnel," Major Fields reported as he watched his holographic display intently. He didn't want the WarStorm to accidentally graze the tunnel walls. He knew that numerous people, including Admiral Anlon, were watching the ship depart.

The ship continued down the tunnel and then exited out into open space. Several fighters appeared and, after making a close pass of the ship, began wagging their wings. The Federation's newest warship was now officially in service.

"Forty percent thrusters," ordered Major Fields. "Let's put some distance between us and Ceres. Lieutenant Trask warn those fighters to keep their distance. I know they're excited about seeing the WarStorm, but I don't want to accidentally slam into one of them."

"Yes, sir," Angela replied as she switched over to the fighter's com channel so she could contact them.

The ship seemed to move forward a little faster, even though the highest thruster speed was far less than the minimum speed the sublight drive was capable of. On the main viewscreen, which was now focused on Ceres, the asteroid could be seen gradually receding.

After several minutes, Major Fields was satisfied and turned toward Colonel Sheen. "Ship is ready to initiate sublight drive Colonel."

"Very well," Amanda nodded with an expectant smile. "Take us out at ten percent sublight until we clear the asteroid field, then go to forty percent until we clear the field's gravity well."

"Yes, Colonel," Fields responded as he passed on the order.

The WarStorm seemed to leap forward as her sublight drive was activated. A light blue glow came from her engines as she gained speed, and the helm control officer guided the warship out of the asteroid field.

Forty minutes later, Major Fields studied his holographic display, which showed the WarStorm was finally clear of the asteroid field's gravity well. "We can jump at any time," he reported, looking toward Colonel Sheen.

"Plot a micro-jump to just outside the orbit of Neptune," ordered Amanda, noting how smooth everything was functioning. The Command Center reminded her a lot of the StarStrike. Glancing at the crew, they all looked to be professional and adept in their jobs. "I want to plot three long-range jumps to New Tellus."

Major Fields passed on the order and Lieutenant Ashton began plotting the jumps. The new computer systems made everything easier. They were much more advanced than the ones used on the StarStrike or on the Victory. It didn't take long for Lieutenant Ashton to have the first jump plotted.

"Jump plotted," Fields reported as Lieutenant Ashton keyed in the first set of jump coordinates.

"Initiate jump," Amanda ordered, her eyes focusing on the main viewscreen.

A swirling blue-white vortex suddenly formed in front of the WarStorm. The helm officer quickly guided the ship into its center. Moments later, the WarStorm and the vortex vanished.

Amanda felt a sudden queasiness as the WarStorm jumped into hyperspace. They were on their way to New Tellus. Amanda closed her eyes for a moment. Another few weeks of trials and they would start the long journey back to the former Federation worlds. Letting out a deep breath, she wondered what they would find. She hoped she could take a shuttle down to the surface of Aquaria, and visit Krall Island to see if there was anything left of their old vacation home. She would also like to discover the fate of her parents. The not knowing had bothered her for months after they had left Federation space. This mission might offer her the chance to put that guilt to rest.

In the Command Center of the Avenger, Jason watched the long-range sensor screen as the friendly green icon representing the WarStorm vanished. He let out a deep breath as he thought about the consequences of this mission. This was the first step in finding out what the Hocklyns were up to and if their timeline was still workable. It was hard to believe they were planning a future interstellar war that very few people on Earth even knew about.

"They're gone," reported Ariel, seeing the WarStorm vanish from her sensors. "They should arrive at New Tellus in ten hours."

In some ways, Ariel missed not being able to travel in space. She knew the Avenger would never take to space again. However, the Fleet Academy took up a lot of her time now, and she enjoyed watching the Earth humans and being able to interact with some of them. Perhaps sometime in the future she would return to space in a new warship.

"That's fast," Jason commented, amazed at the speed the new warship was capable of. It was far faster than anything else they currently had. Jason knew that it had a lot to do with the extended range of its jump drive, as well as reduced cooling time for the jump core.

"They could have cut the time even more by only using two jumps instead of three," commented Ariel, feeling a little jealous over the WarStorm's new drive systems. "However, Colonel Sheen wanted to do the extra jump to further test the ship's systems."

Jason sat down in the command chair behind the command console. He folded his arms across his chest and gazed speculatively at Ariel. Her avatar was prominently displayed on the main viewscreen as it usually was. She was wearing her dark blue fleet uniform, and her black hair lay upon her shoulders with a slight hint of a curl.

"Ariel, what is Katie currently doing?" asked Jason, curiously.

He had been so busy with everything recently that he hadn't taken the time to check on how Katie was. He felt guilty in some ways since he knew that Greg was counting on him and Lisa to keep a careful watch over their teenage daughter. Jason knew he had left too much of the burden of watching the young teenager to his wife. Lisa was a fabulous wife and had done a tremendous job raising Jeremy, but now they had another teenager to take care of.

Jason had asked Ariel to help keep track of the young teenager to ensure that she stayed out of trouble. He knew that Lisa had quickly found out that Katie was a handful. She had so much energy and always seemed to be full of hundreds of questions. She was also tearing through the academy's computer courses as if they were elementary science. Her instructors had been highly impressed and had placed her in even higher-level classes.

Ariel always kept track of Katie. She was amazed at how rapidly Katie was absorbing the information being taught in the academy's computer classes. Ariel didn't want to admit that she watched the young teenager almost constantly through the vid system that she was tapped into. Jason had no idea that she could do that. As far as Jason knew, the only cameras Ariel had access to were the security ones scattered throughout the Avenger and the academy complex.

"Katie is currently in Professor Style's class," reported Ariel, putting Katie's class schedule up on one of the smaller viewscreens. "He teaches advanced computer programming."

"Yes, I know Professor Style," Jason replied with a nod. "He is an excellent instructor." Jason didn't go on to add that Professor Style was also from Ceres and knew more about computer programming than almost anyone in the solar system.

Jason knew that Katie had really been studying hard trying to take advantage of her short time at the academy. She only had another four weeks left before she would have to return home. Jason supposed it would be a good idea to invite her over to the Avenger for a meal with just Lisa and him. He would like to discuss an idea he was toying with and see what Katie and Lisa thought about it.

Aboard the New Horizon, Jeremy was sitting in the commander's chair behind the command console. Reaching forward, he adjusted several of the small viewscreens to show additional information on the ship's current status. For the last two weeks, Lieutenant Nelson had been allowing Jeremy to command the night shift operation under his watchful guidance.

Lieutenant Nelson was currently sitting at the navigation console plotting potential jump points. Tomorrow, the New Horizon would leave the spacedock and begin a series of fourteen planned mini-jumps within the solar system. Once they were satisfied the jump drive was working properly, they would start on their mission and jump to Proxima Centauri. From there it would be on to Tau Ceti.

Jeremy looked around the Command Center. Over the long weeks of intense drills, he had become extremely familiar with all of the duty stations. Angela was currently at Communications talking to someone on the spacedock. Kelsey was at Navigation talking to Lieutenant Nelson and watching him plot jump coordinates. Every once in a while, she would stop him and ask a question or point to a mathematical formula on one of the computer screens. Kevin was at the scanner and sensor controls tracking an incoming shuttle that was bringing up more food supplies.

The hatch to the Command Center suddenly opened and Commander Tellson stepped in. Jeremy instantly stood up and snapped to attention. "Commander on deck!" he called out.

"At ease," spoke Tellson, gesturing for everyone to continue as they were. He walked over to Jeremy and stood looking at him. "You seem to be doing extremely well, Cadet Lieutenant Strong. Are you ready for our jump trials?"

"Yes, sir," Jeremy replied evenly. "The ship will perform well, sir."

"I believe you're right," replied Tellson, allowing a slight smile to cross his face. "If everything goes according to plan, we will be leaving for Proxima Centauri in two more weeks. How do you feel about leaving our solar system?"

"It's the right choice, sir," Jeremy replied with a slight nod of his head. "Our future is out there in the stars. New worlds for us to colonize and who knows; perhaps even other civilizations for us to contact."

"Do you believe in aliens?" Tellson asked curiously, his eyes focusing on Jeremy.

"It's a big galaxy, sir," Jeremy replied carefully, not certain where the commander was going with this question. "There has to be other life out there somewhere."

"Good answer," responded Tellson, nodding his head satisfied. "It shows you realize we're going out into the unknown. Do you agree that this ship should be going off exploring and not armed with any weapons?"

"I don't know, sir," Jeremy replied honestly. "You would like to think that if a race is advanced enough to have space travel they should be peaceful. But look at our own world. There is still a lot of violence on the planet every day. Not everyone out in the galaxy may be friendly."

"Yes, there is a lot of violence on our world," replied Tellson, fully in agreement. "But by the New Horizon not being armed, we avoid the risk of there being an incident if we were to encounter an alien race. It was a tough decision, but I believe it is the right one. If there were aliens close by, they would have contacted us by now. I doubt if we will find anything dangerous in any of the nearby star systems."

Commander Tellson stepped away from Jeremy and walked over to Lieutenant Nelson. The two talked for several minutes before the commander left the Command Center.

Later, Jeremy and the other cadets were in the mess hall eating a quick meal. They were all excited about the upcoming jump trials.

"Just think," Kevin said excitedly. "We could be on our way to Tau Ceti in two more weeks!"

"Do you think we might find aliens at Tau Ceti?" Angela asked her eyes wide. "It's possible isn't it?"

"I doubt it," replied Jeremy, smiling at Angela who was seated across the table. "It's more than likely we won't find any habitable planets in the system. It might take a long search before we find another world like Earth. We don't know how common Earth-like planets are. That's why we need to go out there and explore."

"They may be more common than you think," Kelsey spoke as she buttered a warm roll. "Earth-like planets may be very common. Almost every star has a habitable zone where liquid water can exist."

"But in some of the multiple star systems that zone may change due to the orbits of the companion stars," spoke Jeremy, shaking his head in doubt. "I just don't think Earth-like planets are that common."

"Depends on the distance between the stars and how they might affect the liquid water zone," Angela spoke thoughtfully as she used her knife to cut her chicken sandwich in half. "I guess we will find out shortly."

"Eating again, daddy's boy?" spoke Matt Barr, walking up to the table with a smirk on his face. This time he was with two other members of his former squad that had qualified to come on the New Horizon mission. "I heard the commander made a visit to your shift. Probably had to go and straighten up some of your screw ups."

"More than likely you're the one screwing up," retorted Kevin, glaring at Matt. Kevin had decided that Matt was someone he didn't really care for. He didn't understand what the problem was that Matt had with Jeremy, but he knew it had started at the academy and now had carried over to the ship. "Why don't you go mind your own business instead of bothering us?"

"Think you're big enough to make me, freckles?" taunted Matt, stepping closer.

Kevin stood up his right hand making a fist. He was tempted to see if he could knock that smirk off Matt's face.

Jeremy quickly stood up, placing himself between the two. "Cut it out Matt," Jeremy warned in a determined voice giving Matt a cold and disapproving look. "We're not going to have a fight in here."

"Is there a problem cadets?" a powerful voice cut through the room.

Jeremy looked toward the door and saw Lieutenant Nelson standing there. The lieutenant quickly walked over to the table, frowning at the group. "Care to explain to me what's going on?"

"Nothing, sir," Jeremy responded quickly. "Just a minor disagreement. It's been settled."

"Is that correct?" asked Nelson, looking directly at Matt.

"Yeah, it's settled," replied Matt evenly. "We were just leaving."

"Then I suggest you do so before you find yourself on report," Nelson warned.

Matt nodded and turned to leave, followed closely by his two supporters. A few moments later, they were gone.

Lieutenant Nelson watched the three leave and then turned toward Jeremy. "A word," Nelson said, indicating for Jeremy to follow him. They stepped over to one side of the room where they could not be overheard.

"Watch out for Cadet Lieutenant Barr," Nelson warned in a steady voice. "He doesn't like you."

"I'm well aware of that, sir," responded Jeremy, wondering how Lieutenant Nelson had found out. "There won't be another problem."

Nelson was quiet for a moment. He had been warned by Instructor Branson about the problem between Matt and Jeremy. Branson and Nelson had been friends for quite some time.

"We leave for our FTL trials in less than twenty-four hours," Nelson continued in a serious tone. "Don't do anything to get kicked off the ship because of Barr. I will be watching both of you."

"Yes, sir," replied Jeremy, wishing this conversation wasn't occurring.

When Jeremy returned to his table to finish his meal, the others didn't say anything. They figured if Jeremy wanted them to know what Lieutenant Nelson had said, he would tell them.

"We leave spacedock tomorrow," Jeremy said, looking around the table at his friends. "I think we should all get a good night's sleep. We're going to need it."

"I agree," Kelsey said completely in agreement. For a moment, she had been afraid there was going to be a fight. She was relieved that Lieutenant Nelson had showed up in time. This interstellar trip was important to her, and she wanted Jeremy to be a part of it.

"A good night's sleep," Angela said doubtfully, rolling her eyes. "I'm so excited I don't think I will be able to sleep!"

"Lieutenant Nelson said he might let me plot one of the jumps," Kelsey commented casually as if it wasn't big news.

"Really?" said Angela, grinning. "That's great!"

"Sure is," added Jeremy with a nod. "Now let's finish our meal and go turn in."

Jeremy and Kevin were sitting in their quarters watching the vid screen. It was currently showing the same view as seen on the main viewscreen in the Command Center. They could also hear Commander Tellson's voice as he gave orders to initiate the first jump. It had been a tense morning as the New Horizon had moved away from the spacedock and then accelerated out of the Moon and Earth's gravity well so they could attempt the first of fourteen planned micro-jumps. The first jump would be to just outside the gravity well of Mars. Then the New Horizon would fly into the planet's gravity well and orbit the planet. The Columbia was currently in orbit around Mars and would be ready to assist if there were any problems.

"I wish we were in the Command Center," Kevin mumbled with disappointment in his voice as he watched the screen.

"We will get our chance," Jeremy responded. But he also agreed with Kevin. This experience would be so much more exciting if they were right where the action was occurring.

"Let's listen to Commander Tellson," spoke Jeremy, gazing intently at the vid screen. He reached over, picking up a control, and turned up the sound.

In the Command Center, Commander Tellson knew it was time. "Standby for first micro-jump. Major Maher, enter the first set of coordinates."

Maher nodded at the navigation officer who quickly complied. "Jump coordinates entered," Maher reported.

"Activate FTL drive," ordered Commander Tellson, gripping the command console tightly, not sure what to expect.

In front of the New Horizon, a blue-white vortex formed. It seemed to beckon to the waiting ship, knowing that this was its first time.

"Take us in," Tellson said tightly.

"Helm, enter the vortex using our maneuvering thrusters. Set forward thrust at twenty percent."

The New Horizon moved slowly toward the vortex that seemed to have acquired a life of its own. The ship neared the vortex and then entered it. Moments later, the vortex vanished, leaving no trace of the New Horizon.

Commander Tellson felt a slight feeling of nausea and vertigo, and then everything steadied. Looking at the main viewscreen, he saw a multitude of swirling colors dominated by deep purple. Then the nausea feeling came back and the ship came out of hyperspace, exiting the vortex. Moments later, the New Horizon was alone in space, and the vortex was gone.

"Status," Tellson barked. If they were where they were supposed to be, the New Horizon was now twenty-five point seven million kilometers from Mars.

Major Maher conferred with the navigation officer as the ship's sensors began scanning the surrounding space.

"I have Mars on the sensors," the navigation officer reported jubilantly. The view on the main viewscreen changed to show the red disk of Mars. The image was greatly magnified, but there was no doubt that it was indeed the red planet.

"Twenty-six million kilometers," confirmed Major Maher, smiling. "Engineering reports the drive core is cooling down and should be ready for its next jump in six hours."

"Just as we hoped," Commander Tellson said with satisfaction in his voice. "Take us in to Mars, we will do a couple of orbits and say hello to the Columbia."

"Helm, set speed at twenty percent sublight," Major Maher ordered then, turning to the commander "We will achieve Mars orbit in two hours and twenty minutes."

"Excellent," Tellson responded with a nod. "We will make two orbits and then accelerate back out. We should be well clear of the red planet's gravity field by the time we're ready to jump again."

Jeremy and Kevin had watched the whole thing spellbound. Both had felt a strange sensation when the New Horizon had entered the vortex and jumped into hyperspace.

"That was fantastic," spoke Kevin excitedly, his face still flush from the adrenaline that was rushing through his body.

"Not as bad as I was expecting," Jeremy said, looking at the vid screen, which was still showing Mars. "If things go as planned, we will do at least one jump later during our duty shift."

"We're supposed to jump out just beyond the asteroid field," responded Kevin, recalling the briefing that Lieutenant Nelson had given them on their last shift. "Do you think Commander Tellson will be in the Command Center when we jump?"

"I imagine so," replied Jeremy, looking over at Kevin. He knew that if it were his ship, he would be in the Command Center for every one of these jumps.

Back in the Command Center of the Avenger, Jason let out a deep sigh of relief as he saw the New Horizon appear on the long-range sensors. He had known that the jump drive on the New Horizon would function properly. However, because Jeremy was on the ship it had made him feel apprehensive. After all, the New Horizon was a new ship and things could go wrong.

"Long-range sensors have picked up the New Horizon almost exactly where the jump was planned," Ariel reported. She had been using her sensors to watch the New Horizon very closely, particularly since Jeremy was on board. "They are off by less than two percent from their planned exit point."

"That's a pretty significant margin," Jason commented with concern in his voice. His eyes narrowed as he spoke to Ariel. "If that were an interstellar jump they would be off by tens of millions of kilometers or more."

"It's nothing to be concerned about," Ariel responded, her dark eyes seeming to sparkle. "They're not calculating their jump calculations with enough decimal points. If they were to add four more, the jump would have been dead on. They will do that on their interstellar jumps. As a matter of fact, they are supposed to do that on the next micro-jump they have scheduled."

Jason looked at Ariel and smiled. They had been friends for years. He knew that she had always wanted to talk to Jeremy, but due to security reasons Jason had not allowed it. Sometimes he wondered if he had made a mistake in not introducing Jeremy to Ariel.

Katie had watched the New Horizon's FTL jump with interest. Ariel had transmitted everything to the vid screen in her dorm room, giving Katie a running commentary on what was happening. Katie knew that Jeremy had to be thrilled to be on the New Horizon and taking part in the interstellar mission. The prospect of exploring new worlds was an exciting attraction even to Katie as she thought about what they might discover. She wished she were going on the New Horizon mission. Thinking about the impending mission, a sudden thought occurred to her. Katie's eyes grew wide as she thought about the possibilities and the ramifications.

What if there was a way for her to go on the New Horizon mission. Forget it, she thought to herself. If she tried what she was thinking, she would get into tons of trouble. But again, she was the daughter of one of the discoverers of the Avenger. She was also under the watch and care of the admiral. What could they do to her? Katie sat down on her bed and pulled out her handheld computer. For the next hour, she hatched out a plan. It would be daring and require her to write an entire series of new computer programs, but she felt sure it could be done. She would also have to keep this hidden from Ariel.

Jeremy was in the Command Center standing next to Commander Tellson. Lieutenant Nelson was manning the navigation console along with Kelsey.

"Well, Cadet Lieutenant Strong, what did you think of our jump earlier today?" asked Commander Tellson curious to hear the young lieutenant's response.

"It was fantastic, sir," replied Jeremy, allowing some excitement to creep into his voice. "It wasn't quite what I had been expecting."

"No, it wasn't," responded Commander Tellson, allowing a slight smile to cover his face. "From what I understand, we had several crewmembers get sick from the jump."

Jeremy saw Kelsey's face turn red. He would have to ask her later what that was about. He wondered if she was one of those that Commander Tellson was talking about.

"Are the next set of jump coordinates set?" asked Tellson loud enough for Lieutenant Nelson to hear.

Lieutenant Nelson bent his head closer to Kelsey and whispered a few words to her. She nodded back keeping her eyes glued to the navigation screen.

"Yes, sir," replied Nelson, glancing quickly back at the commander. "The coordinates are set, and we have extrapolated them out six more decimal places. That should put us dead on the exit coordinates we have plotted."

"We shall see," replied Commander Tellson, sitting down in the command chair behind the center console. "If you can put us within two hundred kilometers of our planned exit point, I will buy you a steak when we get back to the Moon."

"Sounds good to me," replied Nelson, grinning. "I can already taste that steak."

"Stand by to jump," ordered Tellson, turning his head so he could watch the big viewscreen on the front wall of the Command Center.

"Ready to jump at your command," Nelson replied with confidence in his voice. He glanced over at Kelsey and noticed the nervous look upon her face. "Everything will be fine," he whispered.

"But I plotted this jump," Kelsey whispered back, afraid the commander would overhear her. "What if it's wrong?"

"Only one way to find out," Nelson replied with a twinkle in his eyes.

"Initiate jump!" Tellson called out. "Helm, take us into the vortex."

Instantly a blue-white vortex formed in front of the New Horizon. For a moment, everyone in the Command Center gazed spellbound at the phenomenon. Then the helm officer accelerated the New Horizon and the vortex seemed to leap at them on the screen. An instant later, everyone felt the queasy sensation they were beginning to associate with hyperspace travel.

Moments later, the New Horizon exited hyperspace and stars once more covered the main viewscreen. Everything looked just as it had before they jumped.

Kelsey let out a deep breath and began running numbers on the navigation computer. Lieutenant Nelson watched her closely, but he had already been extremely impressed by her ability to compute jump coordinates. He could already taste that steak.

"Sensors, where are we?" asked Tellson, looking around the Command Center. Everyone seemed to be doing their jobs as if traveling in hyperspace was an everyday occurrence.

Ensign Roberts and Kevin were both busy trying to determine their current location. The sensors were reaching out and scanning everything within one hundred million kilometers. It took a minute, but soon the computers began to map familiar objects in the asteroid field.

"We're ten million kilometers from the asteroid Vesta," Ensign Roberts reported as more information flowed across one of the screens he was watching. "Preliminary position estimates place us within two kilometers of our planned exit point."

Lieutenant Nelson looked back at the commander and licked his lips. "I prefer my steak cooked medium with a loaded baked potato."

"And you and Cadet Ensign Grainger will have it," Tellson spoke back smiling. "And yes, Cadet Ensign Grainger, I am aware that you plotted the jump. Good work."

Kelsey turned red and nodded. She wondered how the commander could have known that.

"I had his permission," Nelson confided in her. "I told him you were ready. You're going to make a fine navigation officer someday."

Ariel flashed her dark eyes at Jason. "I told you this one would be more accurate. They're almost dead center in their exit coordinates. All they need to do is refine their jump equations slightly, and they will nail the next one."

"You were right," admitted Jason, smiling back at the AI. "This is a good learning process for them."

"It's a shame we couldn't give them more help," Lisa spoke. She was standing next to the command console watching her husband and Ariel.

"We have to develop some of this technology on our own," Jason commented with a sigh. "We are already introducing so much new tech down on Earth that we're causing some economic problems. We don't dare crash the entire planet's economy. The experts on Ceres, as well as our own people, have decided on the path we need to take. They're constantly reviewing the situation and being careful not to move forward too quickly."

"It just seems odd some of the things we are having to do," replied Lisa, gazing at the sensor screen above the plotting table, which showed the friendly green icon that represented the New Horizon. Jeremy was on that ship. It was the main reason she had come to the Command Center, so she could watch the jump.

Sometimes, like today, she really missed her son. Due to their jobs on the Avenger Project, Jeremy had been shipped back and forth between Earth and the Moon most of his life. Lisa was just thankful that Greg and Elizabeth had been there to help out.

"How many more jumps?" Lisa asked. She knew the new ship's FTL drive had to be tested.

Lisa knew that the New Horizon was being watched from the Avenger as well as from Ceres. If there were any problems, help would only be a few minutes away. The Federation survivors had a light cruiser standing by if it was needed.

"Twelve more," replied Jason, looking at his wife. "There is no need to worry. One of the assistant engineers is from Ceres and could repair the FTL drive blindfolded."

"How many Federation people are on the New Horizon?" Lisa asked curiously.

"Only two," Jason replied. He had met both of them, and they were each excellent officers. "This exploration mission is for Earth. They're only along as a safety precaution."

Ariel listened to the two with interest, but she was also focused on Katie. The young teenager had been busy on her small computer entering information furiously now for hours. Ariel wondered what Katie was up to. Since the small computer was not part of her network and the wireless connection was shut down, she couldn't see what Katie was doing. She would have to ask her later. It was probably another new program to show to her instructors at the academy.

Katie had been busy for several hours now making a list of what she would have to do in order to sneak aboard the New Horizon. It wasn't going to be as easy as she had thought. One of her biggest obstacles was going to be Ariel. Katie knew that the AI kept a constant watch on her. There was also some vital information she was going to need from the AI in order for her plan to have any real chance of succeeding. Katie laid her handheld computer down on her bed and let out a heavy sigh. She stood up and stretched. The muscles in her neck were feeling tight, and she took a moment to loosen them up.

Walking over to the small refrigerator in her room, she took out a diet soda and, popping the top, sat back down to think everything over. All of her life she had been different. Computers and how they functioned were second nature to her. She didn't have a lot of friends. Most of the kids her age considered her to be odd and not part of the group. Katie had never fit in. While other kids were playing sports or the girls her age were talking about boys, she was playing with computers instead. The only boy she had ever found herself interested in was Jeremy, and he was too old for her. Not only that, now he seemed to have a girlfriend. Kelsey seemed nice, but Katie couldn't help but feel jealous.

Looking at her watch, she saw it was nearly time to eat. At least the cafeteria here at the academy had much better food than the school cafeterias back on Earth. Turning off her computer and putting it in a drawer, she walked over to the door. Waving at the vid screen, she stepped outside into the corridor. She knew that Ariel had been watching her the entire time.

Ariel saw that Katie was going to eat her evening meal. The young teenager seemed to be doing exceptionally well at the academy. Ariel was pleased that she had made the suggestion for Katie to attend the summer classes.

"Katie is going to eat now," Ariel reported to Lisa who was still standing next to Jason talking. She knew that Jason and Lisa would assume she had gotten that information from one of the security cameras.

"I think I will go over to the cafeteria and eat with her, Jason," spoke Lisa, placing her hand on Jason's arm. She had been trying to spend as much time as possible with Katie but not so much as to intrude into her space. Elizabeth called every night checking on Katie, wanting to hear everything that her daughter had done for the day.

"I'm going to stay here for another hour or so," replied Jason, leaning over and kissing Lisa on the lips.

"I'll bring you a plate," promised Lisa, smiling.

Her marriage to Jason had worked out exceptionally well. They had worked so closely together in the first few years of the Avenger Project that they had fallen in love and gotten married. She knew that Greg and Elizabeth had been ecstatic when the two of them had finally joined together. Those two were still talking about possibly having another child. With the advanced medical technology from Ceres, it was definitely feasible. Both Jason and she had taken advantage of the treatments, which would extend their life spans by several decades. They both looked as if they were in their early to mid forties.

Jason watched Lisa leave the Command Center. He didn't know what he had done to deserve such a loving and caring wife. Life now was a lot different than back in his test pilot days or during the time of the New Beginnings mission.

Jason's gaze returned to the main viewscreen. "Ariel, what do you think of Katie?"

Ariel paused as she gazed back in surprise at Jason. She had not expected this question. "She seems very bright for her age," responded Ariel, trying to keep all traces of emotion out of her computerized voice. "Katie is doing extremely well in all of her classes and, from what I understand, continues to amaze her instructors with the speed she comprehends computer programming."

"Yes, she does," admitted Jason thoughtfully. He had spoken to Greg the day before mentioning that Katie's instructors were very impressed with her.

"I have looked at some of Katie's programming, and it is very good; almost as good as Lisa's," Ariel ventured. "It is my opinion that it would be wrong to send her back down to Earth to attend their schools. The best instructors are here at the academy as well as on Ceres."

Jason looked at Ariel and slowly nodded his head. "You're right, but I don't know if Greg and Elizabeth would agree to allow Katie to attend the academy full time. It has never been done before with someone so young, and how would Katie adjust to having no students her own age around? As far as attending school on Ceres, that has never been done before either."

"But Katie is a special case," argued Ariel, allowing a little emotion to creep into her voice. "She is one of those rare individuals that only comes along once in a hundred years. If she were to attend school on Ceres, she would be around students her own age."

Jason was silent for a moment. He noticed that several members of the command crew were listening and nodding their heads. Several of them were from Ceres and were permanently stationed on the Avenger. Ariel had given him a lot to think about. He knew that Katie was special; all of her instructors had told him that. Letting out a deep breath, he turned to leave the Command Center. It might be a good idea for him to go and talk to Commandant Everson about this. With what lay ahead in Earth's future, they needed every advantage they could get. If Katie was as special as she seemed to be, perhaps Ariel was right in suggesting she attend the academy full time. As for going to school on Ceres with their advanced education system, that was another matter.

Ariel watched Jason leave, and a gentle smile spread across her face. It would be wonderful if Katie could attend the academy full time. They had become very close, and Ariel didn't want to lose her newfound friend.

Chapter Six

Colonel Sheen smiled as the WarStorm dropped out of hyperspace and exited the spatial vortex. On the main viewscreen, the stars made an appearance and seemed to beckon to her with their unblinking light. Her blue eyes swept across the Command Center, and she was satisfied to see that everyone was busy performing their jobs. The crew had really come together and melded as one. Another few weeks of tests in the New Tellus system, particularly weapons, and they would be on their way.

"Status," she spoke, looking over at the sensors and Lieutenant Stalls. It made Amanda feel confident seeing a few familiar faces in the Command Center from her days back on the StarStrike.

"Sensors coming on line and beginning sweep," Stalls reported as information began appearing on his screens.

The new sensors were capable of showing much more detail than the old ones he had used on the StarStrike so long ago. It had taken a little bit of getting used to, but he had mastered the new systems very quickly.

"I have an incoming communication from the light cruiser Raven," Lieutenant Trask reported, glancing over at Colonel Sheen as she listened to the message using the mini-com in her right ear. "They are requesting our ship ID."

"Send it," Amanda replied with a satisfied nod. This was now standard procedure for all Federation ships. Every safety precaution possible was being taken to ensure that a Hocklyn ship didn't sneak into the New Tellus system and discover the Federation base and inhabited planet.

"Reminds me of our return to New Providence after we destroyed the Hocklyn support ship over the moon of Stalor Four," Richard spoke from where he was standing slightly behind her.

"That was over one hundred years ago," Amanda reminded him, turning her head and smiling at her husband.

"What do you think about these Earth humans?" Richard asked as his eyes moved to the main viewscreen that still showed nothing but an ocean of stars.

"We have a few on board in our marine detachment," replied Amanda, evenly. "They are extremely well trained and competent. I met their commanding admiral recently. He seems like a very able man. In some ways, he reminds me of Admiral Streth. He will have his people ready when the time comes. It's up to us now to find out what the Hocklyns have been up to all these years and how far advanced their technology has become."

"Are we going to Aquaria?" Richard asked quietly, knowing the fate of Amanda's parents still haunted her even after all of these years.

"I want to," Amanda confessed, her eyes taking on a distant look. "But I won't endanger this mission for personal reasons."

"I know," replied Richard softly, putting his right hand on Amanda's shoulder and squeezing it gently. He then removed it and stepped back.

There was a reason why married couples were not allowed to serve together on warships. This was one of them. An exception had been made for this mission since they were both so familiar with Federation space. Richard moved off to speak with Lieutenant Trask so as not to distract Amanda from her duties.

"The Raven has given us permission to move in system," Major Fields reported as he listened to Lieutenant Trask's conversation with the Raven over his mini-com.

"I have a number of ships on the sensors," Lieutenant Stalls reported as his screen began lighting up with multiple friendly green icons. "We have four light cruisers, a battle cruiser, and a battle carrier showing up on the sensors. I am also getting readings on a number of freighters, as well as a number of orbital constructs around New Tellus."

"Those would be the new defense platforms and the shipyard," Major Fields spoke from his position at the holographic plotting table, which was now beginning to display the space around New Tellus. "Those freighters will be from the numerous mining operations we have in the system."

Amanda looked over at the holographic display and was surprised to see all the green icons around New Tellus. If those were defense platforms, then New Tellus was more heavily defended than even Tellus had been back in the Federation. She knew that New Tellus was to serve as a blocking point for any Hocklyn excursions into Earth space. If the Hocklyns made an early appearance in this sector of space, the plans were to lead them to New Tellus where the planet's defenses would annihilate them.

"How many people are currently living on New Tellus?" Amanda asked curiously. She knew that she would prefer the open space of a planet rather than the closed environment of Ceres. However, she also knew that if the Hocklyns were ever led to New Tellus, the surface might not be too safe a place to be with the Hocklyns propensity to use nuclear weapons against their enemies.

"Slightly over 6,500," replied Major Fields, looking over at Colonel Sheen. "There are another 4,000 working and living on the shipyard, as well as several thousand more scattered about at different mining sites throughout the system."

"How many of them are from Earth?" asked Amanda, recalling the massive shipyard that had once orbited New Providence. She still found it difficult at times to accept that was over one hundred years ago.

"Nearly 400 currently," Major Fields responded. "Most are graduates from the academy, and a few are from some of the elite military forces on Earth. From my understanding, that number will be growing rapidly in the coming years."

Amanda sighed deeply. This was a reminder that the population of the Federation survivors was still low. Fewer than 200,000 from what Admiral Anlon had told her. They would need the people of Earth to fight this war. That was one of the primary reasons they had journeyed to Earth's solar system in the first place.

"The people on New Tellus live in one small town," Major Fields continued. "It has a spaceport as well as entertainment facilities for the shipyard and ship crews. They have even set up several resorts along the ocean and a couple more up in the mountains."

"All the comforts of home," Amanda commented with a nod. She knew how important it was to keep up morale.

"Lieutenant Ashton, plot a micro-jump to just outside of New Tellus's gravity well. Lieutenant Trask, inform the shipyard we will be micro-jumping shortly."

Amanda leaned back in her command chair and gazed at the numerous screens on the front wall. Looking around the Command Center, it was as if she were back on the StarStrike. She felt a chill rush down her back as she remembered the last battle in the home system. So many people had died, and a civilization had been destroyed. Now they were rebuilding and preparing for a future war against their enemy.

"Jump plotted and entered into the navigation computer," Lieutenant Ashton reported as she finished entering the last coordinates.

"Initiate jump," ordered Amanda, looking over at Major Fields. "Let's go to New Tellus."

In front of the WarStorm, a blue-white vortex formed, and the helm officer guided the WarStorm smoothly into the vortex. Moments later, the WarStorm and the vortex vanished.

Amanda felt the familiar queasiness associated with entry into hyperspace, and moments later it came again as they exited the vortex. Looking up at the main viewscreen, she watched as it cleared and a blue-white planet appeared in its center.

"I have a view of New Tellus up on the screen, Commander," Lieutenant Stalls reported.

Amanda gazed at the jewel of a planet on the screen. It was so similar to Tellus back in the Federation. Large oceans, landmasses partially obscured by clouds, big areas of green and brown on the continents, and even small white ice caps at the poles.

"Take us in at ten percent sublight and place us 100 kilometers above the shipyard," Amanda ordered. "Put up a view of the shipyard on the screen."

Instantly, the shipyard appeared. It was massive and had been rapidly expanded over the last twenty years. It wasn't as large as the one that had orbited New Providence, but it was still very respectable.

"It contains four construction bays and two repair bays," Major Fields informed Colonel Sheen. He had spent quite some time on his last tour in the New Tellus system as well as on the shipyard. "It has a tremendous amount of manufacturing capacity. It can construct nearly everything the fleet may need. It also processes all the raw material being brought in by the freighters from the mines."

"What about defenses?" Amanda asked as she gazed at the main viewscreen. She could see what were obviously weapon turrets, as well as possible missile launching platforms on the hull.

"There are eight heavy laser turrets, thirty-six HG turrets, and ninety-six defensive turrets. There are also eight Shrike Two missile pods."

"Pretty strong defenses," replied Amanda, impressed. "What about fighters and bombers?"

"There are four twenty ship squadrons of fighters, as well as two ten ship squadrons of bombers," replied Fields, recalling the numbers. "There are plans for more later as trained pilots become available."

"Colonel, I have an Admiral Barnes on the com. She is requesting that we go ahead and dock at docking port four," Lieutenant Trask interrupted. "She says she would like a tour of the WarStorm, and would be glad to show you around the shipyard in return."

Amanda looked over at Major Fields. "Who is this Admiral Barnes?" Admiral Anlon had informed her before the WarStorm departed for New Tellus that an Admiral Barnes was in charge of the New Tellus system and its defenses.

Major Fields smiled. "Do you remember two of your former officers on the Avenger, a Lieutenant Jacen Barnes and Lieutenant Teena Arcles?"

"Yes, I do," replied Amanda, recalling the two. She had spoken to them on several occasions and even approved their transfer. "They were both very competent officers and were transferred to the colony ship Explorer prior to the outbreak of the flu. They both survived the outbreak and went on to start a family on Ceres."

"Admiral Nicole Barnes is their great-granddaughter," replied Major Fields, knowing this would please the colonel.

"Really?" responded Amanda, looking over at Richard.

Richard and she had also discussed settling down to raise a family and leaving the war to future generations once the base on Ceres was livable. However, Amanda was haunted by her memories of the war and not knowing what had happened to her parents. After a few years of living as husband and wife, they had decided to go into cryosleep and someday return to the Federation to find out the fate of those they had left behind. She knew that Jacen Barnes and Teena Arcles had opted to live out their lives on Ceres and raise a family.

"I think she would really like to meet you and hear from someone who knew her great-grandparents back in those days."

"Then let's not disappoint her. Helm, take us in to the shipyard, docking port four. Check with shipyard traffic control for docking instructions." Amanda leaned back in her chair and thought about the decision that Teena and Jacen had made. For them, it had obviously been the right one; she just hoped that Richard and she had made the correct one by electing to go into cryosleep.

A few hours later, the WarStorm was docked to the shipyard. Admiral Barnes came on board, and Amanda and Major Fields took her on a tour of the warship.

"This is a beautiful and powerful ship you have, Colonel Sheen," Admiral Barnes commented as they stood in main Engineering, gazing at all the consoles and screens that controlled the ship. Admiral Barnes was forty-two years old with brunette hair. It was cut short as military regs required, but it was still slightly longer than a man's was.

"The WarStorm needs to be for the mission we have planned," Amanda responded pleased with the admiral's compliment.

"Yes, your trip to our old home worlds," the admiral commented, nodding her head. Admiral Anlon had briefed her in detail about the WarStorm's mission. She watched as the chief engineer instructed several subordinates about readjusting part of the ship's power system. The man seemed very competent and knowledgeable in what he wanted done. "Are there any plans for additional ships of this class? It would be nice to have several assigned to the New Tellus system."

Amanda smiled. Admiral Barnes sounded just like other admirals she had gotten to know back in the Federation. They all wanted more and bigger ships.

"Not at the moment," she replied. "Admiral Anlon says that several additional ships of this class may be constructed later when sufficient crews become available."

"Crews," commented Admiral Barnes, sounding disappointed. "We have the capacity to build the ships, but until the Fleet Academy on Earth's moon starts producing more candidates, our hands are tied."

"I believe plans are already in the works to increase the size of the academy, as well as the classes," Major Fields responded. "Admiral Anlon mentioned that, in just a few more years, we will be seeing some much larger graduation classes. There are also plans for Earth to construct ten destroyers to help protect the new colonies they will soon be establishing."

"There will be more crews available, but for quite some time they will be used to crew the ships that Earth will be building," explained Richard, knowing it would be a while before crews would be available for the Federation's larger ships.

"Perhaps it's for the best," Admiral Barnes spoke with a sigh. "We are still several hundred years away from our new war with the

Hocklyns. I understand the reasoning for bringing Earth's technology up slowly to what we consider Federation norm. I just hope the Hocklyns don't show up ahead of schedule."

"Hopefully our mission will help to confirm that date," Amanda said completely in agreement. "Now, how about that tour of your shipyard? It looks quite impressive from space."

Jeremy let out deep sigh of relief. They had just finished their last FTL jump and hit the mark dead center. They were a considerable distance outside of the Moon and Earth's gravity well. Kelsey had plotted the jump under the careful eyes of Lieutenant Nelson.

"Excellent, Ensign Grainger," Commander Tellson commented with a satisfied nod. "We will make a navigation officer out of you yet if you continue to do this type of work."

"I couldn't have plotted it any better myself," Lieutenant Nelson added with a smile.

"It looks as if we're good to go to Tau Ceti," Major Maher added from where he was standing at the plotting table. "The ship has performed flawlessly."

"Yes, it has," responded Tellson with a nod of his head. "We shall return to the spacedock and if everything checks out, we can depart on our mission in a few more weeks." Tellson then turned toward Lieutenant Nelson. "You have the watch, Lieutenant."

"Yes, sir," Nelson replied as he stood up from his seat in front of the navigation console and walked toward the command console in the center of the Command Center.

Commander Tellson and Major Maher exited the room to go to their quarters, as they had gotten very little sleep through all the FTL jumps.

"Cadet Ensign Grainger, plot a course to the spacedock. Helm, once the course is plotted, activate the sublight drive and move us toward the spacedock at ten percent sublight."

"Yes, sir," Kelsey responded as she began inputting information into the navigation computer. In less than a minute, she had the new course and speed plotted.

The helm officer activated the sublight drive and the ship began accelerating until the sublight drive was operating at ten percent power. "We should arrive at the spacedock in six hours and thirty-two minutes," the helm officer reported.

"Excellent," responded Nelson, looking across the Command Center. Everyone was going about their jobs in a routine manner. Even the four cadets seemed to be at ease in their current positions. "Cadet Lieutenant Strong, you have the watch."

Jeremy stood up from his position at the sensor console where he had been working with Ensign Roberts. Lieutenant Nelson had been allowing him to stand watch periodically under his careful guidance. He made his way over to the command console, and Lieutenant Nelson stood up, indicating for Jeremy to take the seat.

"I'm going to step out for a cup of coffee," Nelson said in a calm voice. "I will return shortly." Nelson turned and left the surprised cadet lieutenant standing there.

Nelson smiled inwardly to himself. This was part of Jeremy's training. He needed to be in command of the Command Center with no one looking over his shoulder, even if it was only for a few minutes.

Jeremy sat down and gazed at the command console, which formed a half arc around him. Everything was showing green, and no potential problems were indicated. Looking up, he noticed Kelsey smiling at him; then she turned around and began working on her navigation console.

Several minutes passed, and things continued to run smoothly. They normally did as the ship had experienced a minimal number of problems over the last few days. Needless to say, Jeremy was shocked when a warning alarm went off loudly in the Command Center.

"I have meteors entering our projected flight path," Ensign Roberts reported as a number of red icons started showing up on the scanner screen. He quickly began using the scanners to determine the exact path of the meteors.

"Are they a threat?" Jeremy asked with concern in his voice as he stood up and looked intently at the scanner screen. "Why didn't we pick them up on the long-range sensors?"

"They're too small," Roberts replied as he checked his scanner screen against the New Horizon's plotted course. "I show a sixty percent probability of them crossing our course at the same point we will be at in four point six minutes."

Jeremy studied the scanner screen for a moment. "Helm, reduce speed to five percent sublight. Kelsey plot us a new course around the meteors. Helm, standby for emergency maneuvers if necessary."

The New Horizon reduced speed. Jeremy was hoping this would allow them the necessary time to plot a new course and go around the approaching group of meteors.

"New course plotted," reported Kelsey in an anxious voice.

"Deviating to the new course," the helm officer spoke as he adjusted the ship's flight path.

Jeremy watched the scanning screen, and after a few moments saw with satisfaction that the New Horizon was going to miss the meteors by a safe margin. He let out a sigh of relief and sat back down. "Helm, once we are safely past the meteors, resume course and accelerate back to ten percent sublight."

"What the hell is going on here?" an angry voice echoed across the Command Center.

Jeremy turned toward the hatch that allowed admittance to the Command Center to see a livid Major Maher standing there.

"We had to adjust course to avoid some meteors, sir," Jeremy replied surprised at the major's anger.

"You don't adjust the New Horizon's course without the approval of a command officer," snarled Maher, striding up to Jeremy and looking down at him. "Where's Lieutenant Nelson? You could have put this entire ship in jeopardy."

"I'm right here," answered Nelson as he entered the Command Center with a look of concern on his face. "What seems to be the problem?"

"Your pet cadet officer here changed the course of the New Horizon without permission and endangered the ship!"

"What happened, Cadet Lieutenant Strong?" Lieutenant Nelson asked, his eyes narrowing.

Jeremy explained in detail what had happened with the meteors and the actions he had taken.

Lieutenant Nelson walked over to the scanning and sensor console and replayed everything back so he could see with his own eyes exactly what had occurred. He then went over and spoke briefly with Kelsey as well as the helm officer.

Major Maher was watching and wondering how he could use this unexpected incident to his advantage. He didn't want to get Jeremy thrown off the ship. He might make a useful hostage later if his plans went awry. Lieutenant Nelson was another matter. The lieutenant had been a problem to his plans from day one, but Maher had not been able to do anything to shake Commander Tellson's confidence in the man. This incident might just be the leverage Maher needed to do just that.

Lieutenant Nelson returned to Major Maher and spoke in an even voice. "Cadet Lieutenant Strong took the correct actions. While we can't be certain any of the meteors would have collided with the New Horizon, his actions alleviated any possibility of that occurring. He reduced speed, changed course, and then after the danger was over put the New Horizon back on her original course and speed."

Major Maher stared coldly at Lieutenant Nelson before speaking. "You both will be going on report," he retorted. "The commander and I will review this incident closely to see if any disciplinary action will be needed."

"There won't be," a stern voice commented from the doorway of the Command Center. Commander Tellson was standing there gazing at his two officers. "I have been standing here for several moments, and from what I have overheard, Cadet Lieutenant Strong acted properly."

"Yes, sir," replied Major Maher, gazing at the commander. He had not noticed Commander Tellson's arrival in the Command Center. He could still use this incident against Lieutenant Nelson, but Strong was still out of his reach, at least for the moment. "I will be putting this in my incident report, Commander," Maher stated. "Lieutenant Nelson should not have left the Command Center, and in my opinion Cadet Lieutenant Strong should have called for a qualified officer to come to the Command Center."

"That is your right as executive officer," Tellson replied, not happy that his second in command obviously had a bone to pick with Lieutenant Nelson. "This incident will be reviewed, but I don't see anything to be concerned with."

"Not even with Lieutenant Nelson leaving the Command Center and placing a cadet in charge in his absence?" Maher pressed.

"It's part of Cadet Lieutenant Strong's training," replied Tellson, his eyes narrowing. "You have done the same thing with Cadet Lieutenant Barr, have you not?"

Maher was silent for a moment. He had allowed Barr to be alone in the Command Center as part of his training on several occasions. "Perhaps I am making too big of an issue out of this," he admitted finally as he realized the commander was correct on this point. "I was just concerned that the New Horizon could have been damaged, and we are so close to starting our mission."

"I can understand that," Tellson replied with a curt nod. "We have a good crew, so let's not do anything to jeopardize that."

"Yes, sir," Maher replied. "I will be returning to my quarters." Maher left the Command Center, keeping his face composed. He would keep an eye on Lieutenant Nelson; the man could still pose a threat to Maher's future plans for the New Horizon.

Commander Tellson turned to face Lieutenant Nelson and Cadet Lieutenant Strong. "I will need an incident report from both of you," he began, his eyes focusing on the two. "I don't believe either of you did anything wrong, but I still wish to review your actions. Cadet Lieutenant Strong, from what I have seen and heard you took the appropriate actions to keep the New Horizon safe. You didn't hesitate, and you were not afraid to make a decision. That's the mark of a good commanding officer. I would expect no less from you."

"Thank you, sir," responded Jeremy, feeling a glow inside at the commander's comments. For several moments, he had been afraid that his days on the New Horizon were numbered.

Major Maher had summoned several of his co-conspirators to his quarters. With the completion of the FTL trials, the rest of the crew and the scientists would be brought on board shortly. Sitting behind his desk, he looked over at Cadet Ensign Trace Rafferty, Lieutenant Reece Sandusky, Cadet Lieutenant Matt Barr, and Ensign Adam Bates.

"We need to keep a close watch on Lieutenant Nelson," Maher began, still smarting from the incident in the Command Center. His eyes narrowed, and he arched his eyebrows. "We should be leaving on our mission to Tau Ceti sometime in the next few weeks. I don't want anyone doing anything to endanger our plans."

"How many of the new people coming up can we count on to side with us in the takeover?" Lieutenant Sandusky asked.

"At least four, possibly six," Maher replied. His group down on Earth had spent a lot of money to arrange for certain people to be included on the mission. "It wasn't easy, but our people down on Earth managed to get four people who are sympathetic to our cause listed as scientists or research assistants and another two that are leaning toward us."

"Any chance the government will find out what we have done?" Sandusky asked. "If anyone talks or someone finds out how much money has changed hands, this whole thing could blow up in our faces."

"It won't happen," replied Maher, shaking his head confidently. "My people down on Earth are watching for this. They will make certain that any mention of what we're planning to do is stopped immediately. We have already had to remove several people who were talking too much. Their deaths were made to look like accidents."

"What about Jeremy Strong?" asked Barr, wanting to get rid of his rival. He had a strong and growing dislike for the admiral's son. "I think he should be taken out along with the command crew."

"Perhaps later," answered Maher, shaking his head in denial. "For now, he will make an excellent hostage if something goes wrong. That's your job. When we launch the takeover, I want you to make sure the cadets are locked in their quarters and well guarded. We may need them later."

"You just need us to keep him alive?" Cadet Ensign Rafferty asked with a gleam in his eyes. "A few broken bones would make him know we mean business."

Maher was silent for a moment. "No, we don't want him hurt. If we need to use him as a hostage, he needs to be unharmed."

"Later, when we don't need him as a hostage, we can dispose of him," Sandusky added, his gaze focusing on Barr. "He could be a trouble maker down the road, and we don't want any of that."

Barr nodded. That would work for him as long as he was the one to dispose of Jeremy. He smiled inwardly to himself; he could see the daddy's boy on his knees begging for his life. It wouldn't be short, and he wanted Jeremy to suffer.

"Now let's discuss our plans in more detail," spoke Maher, wanting to get down to the main reason for this meeting. "Everything has to go down as planned. While we will be outnumbered, we will be the only ones with weapons. Once the command crew and other officers are eliminated, the rest of the crew will fall in line."

"What if they don't?" Ensign Bates asked with a frown on his face. "There may be a few that refuse to follow our orders."

"If they are men, we will dispose of them," Maher spoke, his eyes showing a deadly glint. "However, we will need all of the women. If any of them resist, they can be locked up in their quarters until we arrive at our destination."

"Where is that?" Barr asked. He had been curious for quite some time as to where they were going.

"Somewhere farther in toward the center of our galaxy," Maher replied. "We are going where the stars are denser and where Earth will never find us. If the drive functions properly, we will be going at least ten thousand light years in toward the galactic center. We have chosen several open star clusters that should meet all of our requirements. An area rich in stars and hopefully natural resources where someday we can expand as our population grows."

Barr nodded. This fit in with his plans as well. He wanted to escape Earth with all of its political infighting and corruption. They would begin anew on a new world free of all the hazards of current society. Barr listened as Maher outlined in detail what he foresaw as taking place when they launched their takeover of the New Horizon.

"Won't Admiral Strong come after us?" Bates asked, still showing some concern. "They have four exploration cruisers that could be equipped with FTL drives."

"Not a problem," Maher answered confidently. "It will take several weeks or even a month to equip one of the exploration cruisers with a working FTL drive. By then, we will be long on our way, and they will not be able to follow us."

Jeremy and the other cadets were in the officer's mess eating. They were discussing the exciting events that had occurred in the Command Center and Maher's reaction to what had happened.

"You saved the ship!" exclaimed Angela, allowing some aggravation to show in her voice from Maher's reaction when he had come into the Command Center.

"The meteors may never have even hit us if we had stayed on our original course and maintained our speed," Jeremy reminded her. Changing course and speed had only been a precautionary measure.

The incident with Maher had bothered him immensely, and he didn't understand why the executive officer had been so spiteful. For a moment, it was almost as if he were dealing with Matt Barr. He wondered if the executive officer and Lieutenant Nelson were having problems. If they were, that could very well have been what was behind the incident.

"It's a very good possibility they would have missed us," continued Kevin, nodding his head in agreement. "The scanners only reported that the meteors would be in our general vicinity when we passed through that section of space. The odds are they would have missed us by hundreds of kilometers."

"Perhaps," Kelsey said, looking speculatively at the other three. "But I prefer to play it safe, and that's what we did. Major Maher had no reason to act as he did."

"He's the executive officer," Jeremy pointed out. "He can do what he wants."

Angela took a bite of the stew she was eating and nodded her head. "Perhaps he just overreacted since we are so close to actually launching the mission to Tau Ceti."

"I hope that's what it was," Kevin said, looking down at the hamburger and fries on his plate. The food on the New Horizon was excellent.

"Look at it this way," said Jeremy, trying to put a positive spin on what had happened. "We had our first real emergency situation, and we survived it."

"Yes, we did," responded Kelsey with a smile. "We will soon be on our way to Tau Ceti, and maybe we will find a habitable planet there."

"Can you imagine if we did?" Angela added with excitement in her eyes and her stew momentarily forgotten. "How soon do you think it would be before colonists would arrive?"

Jeremy swallowed the stew he had been eating. It was quite good, and both Angela and he had opted for it. "Possibly a few years," Jeremy pointed out as he thought about what would have to be done before colonists could safely travel to a new world. "The planet will have to be surveyed and the wildlife and plant life categorized. The colonists will have to know what is safe to eat and what isn't. It will take a lot of research and hard work before the planet is deemed safe for colonization."

"Perhaps not as much as you think," Kelsey commented with a faraway look in her eyes. "They may let the colonists do most of the research. Once an Earth like world is discovered there will be a lot of pressure on the governments to begin colonization, particularly with the overcrowding on Earth."

"I agree with Kelsey," Kevin commented. "I think colonization would begin immediately."

"We would have to build some colony ships first," Jeremy reminded them. "That will take some time."

"I think it would be exciting to get to explore a new world similar to Earth," Angela added as she thought about what it would be like.

"Just think of all we could learn. It would be like finding another Avenger."

"I don't know if anything could be like that again," commented Jeremy, recalling his early days of growing up on the crashed spaceship.

Angela was quiet for a moment and then looked over at Jeremy. "I wonder where the Avenger came from? No one has ever said."

"I don't know," replied Jeremy, truthfully. He had asked his dad several times, but each time the answer had been evasive. Sometimes Jeremy had the feeling that his father was hiding something from him. "My mother did manage to recover some of the ship's logs as well as some basic information about the ship in the early days of the Avenger Project, but to the best of my knowledge they never found out where the Avenger came from."

"The ship has supposedly been there for hundreds, if not thousands of years," Kevin added.

It was one of the favorite topics at the academy and students talked constantly about the Avenger and where the ship had come from. The only thing that was common knowledge was that the ship's crew had been human, and the ship had crashed on the Moon hundreds of years in the past. There was a growing group of people on Earth who believed the Avenger came from a previous civilization that had existed on Earth and had been their first attempt at the stars. There was even speculation that the lost civilization of Atlantis had been responsible for building the ship.

"Perhaps we will find out someday," Kelsey said as she took a bite of her salad. She looked at the others for a moment, and then her eyes widened as she saw who had just walked into the room. "Barr just came in; I hope he doesn't say anything."

"After what happened in the Command Center, you know that he will," Kevin said with aggravation in his voice, not wanting to hear Barr's comments about the incident.

Angela watched as Barr picked up his tray and food and took a seat at a table across the room, not even glancing at the four cadets. "Perhaps he hasn't heard," Angela spoke surprised that Barr wasn't going to harass them.

"Maybe after Lieutenant Nelson's last warning, he has decided to leave us alone," uttered Kevin as he reached for a fry and dipped it in ketchup.

"Perhaps," responded Jeremy, glancing over at Barr. He noticed that Barr had been joined by several other people. There was another cadet from his group and several other members of the New Horizon's crew that Jeremy had seen in the Command Center on occasion.

"How soon do you think we will depart for Tau Ceti?" asked Angela, wanting to get her mind off of Barr. She truly enjoyed discussing what they might find in their exploration of the Tau Ceti system.

"Sometime in the next two weeks," replied Jeremy, recalling what Lieutenant Nelson had told him earlier. "The ship will be checked out one more time by the techs, and if everything passes the scientists and their lab technicians will come on board. They will have a week to familiarize themselves with their labs before we depart. From what I understand, the equipment in the labs was picked out by the scientist themselves so it should go rather quickly."

"Are you going to contact Katie when we get to the spacedock?" Angela asked in a teasing voice. "You know she wants to hear from you."

"Katie," repeated Jeremy as he thought about what his parents must be going through.

He was glad that he was on the New Horizon and had managed to avoid seeing Katie, but in hindsight, he knew that he should probably contact the fifteen-year-old and check on her. After all, her parents had put up with him while he was attending school on Earth. The least he could do was speak to Katie.

"Give her a call, Jeremy," Kelsey urged. She could well recall what it had been like to be a teenage girl. "It might do her a lot of good."

"Alright," replied Jeremy, knowing it was the right thing to do.

"Who is this Katie?" asked Kevin, curious to know who this girl was that they were talking about.

"It's a long story," Jeremy began, not really wanting to talk about it.

"We have time," Kevin said as he took another bite of his hamburger.

"Yes," Angela spoke with a big grin. "Tell Kevin about your fifteen-year-old girlfriend."

"She's not my girlfriend," spoke Jeremy, throwing a warning glance at Angela. Then with a sigh, he looked over at Kevin. "It all began years ago. My family's best friends are the Johnsons who live down on Earth."

"Like Greg Johnson, who was with your father when they found the Avenger?" Kevin asked as his curiosity grew.

"Yes, Greg Johnson," Jeremy replied. He then went on to explain his relationship with Katie and how he had spent much of his time on Earth living with the Johnsons and attending school.

Kelsey listened with a gentle smile on her face. She knew that Jeremy would be a good role model for Katie, even though it was obvious he hadn't figured that one out yet. Kelsey had been impressed with the young teenager and was determined that Jeremy would be there to give her needed encouragement.

Angela continued to eat her stew and listen. She had met Katie briefly at the graduation party and had been extremely impressed by the teenager. For some reason, Angela had the feeling that Katie would have a big impact on all of their lives. Sometimes she got these feelings about people she had met. Angela hesitated for a moment and stopped eating her stew as she thought about what this could mean. She had no idea, but she suspected that sometime soon they would all find out.

Chapter Seven

Katie was feeling ecstatic. Jeremy had called her from the spacedock after the New Horizon had returned from its FTL trials. They had talked for nearly twenty minutes with Jeremy asking her how she was doing in her classes and how she liked living at the academy. For the first time in several years, their conversation had been very amiable. It made Katie realize that Jeremy was someone very special and always would be that to her. However, because of the age difference that's all it ever would be.

Tossing her blonde hair back behind her shoulders, she gazed over at the vid screen and Ariel. The two of them talked daily about Katie's experiences at the academy and what she was learning. One thing she had kept secret from Ariel were the special programs she had been working on. Katie was just about finished working on the last program, which was the centerpiece to her being able to sneak on board the New Horizon.

"I am glad that Jeremy called you," Ariel began, her dark eyes watching Katie closely. She had noticed how happy the young teenager had become while she was speaking with Jeremy. Ariel knew that Jeremy could be a very positive influence on Katie if he would just accept the responsibility. She just wished there were someway she could communicate that to Jeremy.

Ariel had noticed that, for the past several weeks, Katie had been working extra hard on her handheld computer on some type of program or programs. Katie wouldn't tell Ariel what she was working on other than it was a surprise and she wanted to keep it secret until it was ready. Ariel accepted this as many humans didn't want to share secrets until they felt satisfied whatever they were working on would work. Ariel suspected it was to eliminate any possibility of embarrassment.

"I'm glad that he called too," Katie replied with a pleased grin breaking out on her face. "It's nice to know that he at least thinks about me every once in a while."

"Jeremy has been busy on the New Horizon," Ariel responded with a nod of her head. Her black hair was slightly curled and lying upon her shoulders. "This mission is extremely important to the Federation survivors as well as Earth. Jeremy and the other cadets are fortunate to be included on the initial exploration trip of the New Horizon."

"Two new planets to colonize," responded Katie, thinking about how exciting it would be to set foot on a new world. Ariel had told Katie all about the Tau Ceti system.

"Both perfectly safe to colonize," Ariel added. "The Federation survivors have surveyed both planets, and they are both excellent colonization candidates."

"Do you ever regret not getting to speak to Jeremy or Mathew like you do me?" Katie asked curiously.

From what she had learned from Ariel, she knew that her older brother was based on the Federation shipyard that orbited New Tellus. It was amazing to her all the secrets that were being kept.

"Yes, I do," responded Ariel slowly. It was something she had always wanted to do. "There was so much that I could have helped them with, and I really would have enjoyed talking to them."

Through the vid screens, she had watched all three children grow up whenever they were on the Moon. However, Jason and Greg had forbid her to speak to Mathew or Jeremy. Ariel understood why, she just wished things had been different. She could speak to Mathew now since he knew about the Federation survivors and what was in Earth's future. However, Mathew had been assigned to the shipyard, and it would be a while before Ariel saw him again. When she did, she planned to have a long talk with the young man.

"I really miss Mathew," commented Katie, wishing she could talk to him.

It had been months since he had started his new assignment. She was also still amazed at what all her parents had managed to keep secret from the two of them all these years. It explained why a lot of times when she or her brother had walked in on their parents, they had stopped talking or changed the subject.

"He is your brother," Ariel replied in understanding. "You should miss him."

Ariel had long conversations with Clarissa on occasion as they were still the only two functioning AIs on Federation ships. There had been some discussion amongst the Federation scientists about creating additional AIs, but nothing had been decided.

"Ariel?" asked Katie, looking over at the vid screen. "How often do shuttles go up to the spacedock?"

"Every day," Ariel replied, mystified as to why Katie would ask this question. "If you want to visit the spacedock there are occasional tours scheduled for some of the students who are attending the summer session. As a matter of fact, I believe there is a special tour scheduled for the same time the New Horizon leaves for Tau Ceti."

"I think Lisa mentioned something about that," commented Katie, trying to sound only slightly interested. "I wonder if there is any chance that I could go up to the spacedock? I would love to see the New Horizon depart, especially since Jeremy and Kelsey are on board."

Ariel was silent for a moment. She had kept her relationship with Katie a secret from Lisa and Jason. She knew they both would be highly upset with her if they knew she was talking to Katie and all she had told her.

"I don't know," replied Ariel, her eyes narrowing as she thought about it. "This special tour is by invitation only, and it is for seniors. The other tours wouldn't be so hard for you to get on."

"Can you talk to Lisa and mention the possibility of my being there?" Katie asked in a pleading voice. "I would really like to say goodbye to Jeremy and Kelsey."

Ariel thought about the possibilities. She didn't want to disappoint Katie. She also didn't want to speak to Lisa about this; it might make her suspicious. "I could add your name to the list of attendees at the last minute. You have to be recommended by one of your instructors. I could arrange it so it will look as if an instructor recommended you."

"Ariel, that would be great!" Katie said, her eyes lighting up. "Can you do it, please?"

"We shall see," replied Ariel, knowing this would be a little bit risky. If Lisa found out that the senior list had been manipulated to add Katie's name, it wouldn't take her long to figure out who had been responsible.

Later, Katie was lying on her bed with the lights out. She allowed a pleased smile to cross her face; so far, her plan was working. She only needed one more bit of information from Ariel, then she would be ready to sneak aboard the New Horizon. Letting out a deep breath, she wondered just how much trouble she would be in when she was finally discovered. Surely, with Jeremy and Kelsey on board it wouldn't be too bad.

Colonel Sheen was sitting behind the command console in the Command Center of the WarStorm. Admiral Barnes was standing next to her, watching intently as the warship closed on its intended target.

"Twenty thousand kilometers to target," Lieutenant Stalls called out as he watched his sensors and close in scanners.

"We have target lock with the forward laser batteries," Lieutenant Mason reported from Tactical.

"How close do you have to get to be in effective range?" Admiral Barnes asked as she watched the main viewscreen, which showed a small asteroid in its center. The asteroid looked dark and gray and was pockmarked from numerous small meteor strikes.

"Minimal effective range is one thousand kilometers," Amanda replied. "However, the closer we get the more damage the lasers can cause. There is some dispersion of the beams the farther away we are. The experts back on Ceres recommend an engagement range of two hundred kilometers or less against a heavily shielded opponent if we want the lasers to inflict the maximum amount of damage."

"Admiral Anlon sent me the specs on the WarStorm," continued Admiral Barnes, turning her head to look at Colonel Sheen. "I was amazed to find out that your energy screen is twice as powerful as the ones currently in use on our battle cruisers."

"Yes," replied Amanda, glancing over at the admiral with a nod. She was extremely pleased with some of the advances in technology that had been implemented on the WarStorm. "The WarStorm has an extra fusion generator that is used primarily to power the energy screen. It would take multiple nuclear strikes in the megaton range to knock it down."

Admiral Barnes nodded her head and shifted her gaze back to the asteroid on the viewscreen. "The Hocklyn's favorite weapons are nukes, even though they never deployed any that powerful in the war. It wasn't necessary, but against a warship such as yours, they might."

"Hopefully we won't give them that chance," replied Amanda, evenly. That was the one part of the mission that still made her feel nervous. Finding a Hocklyn ship and engaging it to see if there had been any technological advances could be extremely dangerous.

"One thousand kilometers," Lieutenant Stalls called out as the WarStorm continued do close on its target.

"Standby to fire lasers," ordered Amanda, looking over at Tactical. She was particularly interested in seeing how much damage the new lasers would cause to the asteroid.

"Ready to fire," Tactical responded. The officer's finger was hovering over the button that would initiate the firing of the lasers.

"Fire!" Amanda ordered, her eyes now focused on the main viewscreen.

Instantly, four orange-red lances of light speared forth from the WarStorm, striking the kilometer thick asteroid. Immediately upon impact, the surface of the asteroid erupted in bright explosions as its surface became superheated. Several moments later, the asteroid erupted in a bright explosion as it tore itself apart.

"Target destroyed," Lieutenant Stalls reported as the asteroid changed from one target to several hundred smaller ones on his screens.

"Excellent," Amanda replied satisfied with the performance of the lasers. "Helm, take us in closer and then turn us broadside to the smaller asteroids. Tactical, once we turn activate our point defense weapons and take out the remaining pieces of that asteroid."

"Very impressive," Admiral Barnes commented. She would have to speak to Admiral Anlon about upgrading the laser batteries on the shipyard as well as installing this new and more powerful energy screen that the WarStorm was equipped with.

For the next several hours, the WarStorm engaged and destroyed numerous small asteroids in the asteroid field as they tested the ship's different weapon systems. At the end of the day's tests there was only one weapon system that remained to be tested.

"Standby to launch Devastator missile," ordered Amanda, taking a deep breath. She had saved this until last since it was the most powerful weapon the WarStorm was equipped with. As soon as she said those words, she could sense an increased aura of anticipation in the Command Center.

This was the test Amanda was most curious about. The new Devastator missile was armed with a ten-megaton nuclear warhead mounted on a special missile that had a miniature sublight drive installed. It was capable of reaching a top speed of one thousand kilometers per second five seconds after launch. To reach such a speed, the small drive unit and inertia dampening system would burn themselves out seven seconds after being activated.

On the main viewscreen, a large asteroid five kilometers in diameter was centered. Its dark gray surface seemed to be waiting for the inferno that was soon to come.

"Major Fields, will you please enter your code for the nuclear weapon's release."

Major Fields stepped over to the command console and entered his command code. As soon as he was finished, Amanda entered hers.

"Use of nuclear weapons has been authorized," she communicated to Tactical.

Admiral Barnes was quite interested in this test. The shipyard was armed with Devastator missiles as offensive weapons, but none of the missiles on the shipyard had warheads in the megaton range or were equipped with a sublight drive. She was highly curious to see this new missile in operation.

"Nuclear weapons release has been authorized," Lieutenant Mason repeated as he pressed several buttons on his weapons console. Two ensigns sat next to him in front of similar weapons consoles. Any of the three could control any of the weapon systems on the ship.

On the outside of the WarStorm, a small metal hatch slid open. Inside the Command Center, a warning alarm began sounding indicating that a nuclear weapon was about to be launched.

"Devastator missile is armed and ready to launch," Mason reported as his finger hovered over the missile release button. "Missile is locked on target. Current range to target is five hundred kilometers."

"Launch," Amanda ordered, her eyes glued to the viewscreen. She was anxious to see the damage this warhead would cause. She could feel her heart racing, this weapon was their ace in the hole against the Hocklyns and the AIs.

"Missile launched," reported Mason as he pressed the button.

On one of the large side viewscreens, the missile made a brief appearance as it erupted from its missile silo, then it seemed to vanish. Almost immediately, a brilliant explosion lit up the asteroid on the viewscreen. The entire asteroid vanished as nuclear fire seemed to consume the material the asteroid was comprised of.

"The missile seemed to vanish as it left its silo," Admiral Barnes uttered amazed at how quickly the missile had struck the asteroid. "It would be almost impossible to shoot something like this down with defensive weapons."

With a slight shudder, Admiral Barnes knew that a weapon like this would make the defensive batteries on the shipyard obsolete. One strike from a missile of this type would probably bring down the shipyard's energy shield and leave the armored hull unprotected from attack. After seeing what this new weapon could do, Barnes felt it was even more important to upgrade the shipyard's energy screen to the same level as the WarStorm's screen.

"Even the WarStorm could not shoot down a missile equipped with a sublight drive like the Devastator is," replied Amanda, nodding her head in agreement. "These missiles are extremely expensive to build. The WarStorm only has four more remaining. Those we will save for the mission. We only had the one to practice with."

"Hopefully, this is a technology the Hocklyns will never develop," Barnes added as she continued to gaze at the screen and the burning asteroid. It was frightening to realize the destructive power of this missile.

After a few more minutes, the nuclear fire was gone, and all that was left was a smoldering asteroid with a huge kilometer deep hole blasted in its center.

"What are the plans for these missiles?" asked Admiral Barnes, turning to face Colonel Sheen. "They are obviously too expensive to build for general deployment to the fleet."

"From what Admiral Anlon told me, they are to be used against the AIs," replied Amanda, hoping she didn't have to use one of the missiles on her mission. If she did, then they had run into some serious trouble. "It's hoped that multiple hits from weapons like the Devastator will knock down their shields, allowing us to destroy their ships."

"I've seen some of the vids from the war," Admiral Barnes spoke in a more subdued voice. "Even from multiple nuclear strikes, the AI's shields never wavered. It might take a weapon even more powerful than the Devastator to take them down."

"Perhaps," replied Amanda, knowing the admiral was correct. "But we still have a lot of time to develop weapons to do so. At least with the new Devastator warhead, we might have a chance if they find us earlier than anticipated."

Or if your mission leads them back to us, Admiral Barnes thought worriedly. She knew this mission was important to check on the current movement of the Hocklyn fleet as well as to determine if they had deployed any new technology. However, there was some risk involved if the WarStorm were detected. She wanted to make sure the shipyard and New Tellus were as strongly defended as possible in case this scouting mission brought the Hocklyns down upon them.

"There will be a supply ship arriving the day after tomorrow with ammunition to replenish what we have been using in our weapon tests," commented Amanda, turning her gaze toward the viewscreen. She wondered herself what the result would be in using one of the new missiles against the AIs. For now, it was the only weapon they had that had any possibility of knocking down those powerful energy screens. "After we are finished with our weapon tests, I would like to give my crew some leave time on New Tellus for a few days before we set out on our mission. Would that be possible?"

"I think it can be arranged," Admiral Barnes replied. She knew that if she were setting off on a mission that would mean months cooped up in a ship with the same people, a few days leave would sound great. "I will make arrangements for one of the seaside resorts as well as one of the mountain ones to be made available."

Later that day, the WarStorm was once more docked at the shipyard above New Tellus. Amanda and Richard were in their quarters discussing the upcoming mission.

"I'm looking forward to going to one of the resorts," Richard commented from his position on the sofa where he was relaxing. "It will be good for us to get away from the ship for a few days before the mission starts."

"I talked to Admiral Anlon earlier and told him how the weapon tests had gone," Amanda said as she came over and sat down next to Richard. She reached out, took his hand, and let out a deep breath. "He was extremely pleased with the report on the Devastator missile."

"That's one hell of a weapon," commented Richard, nodding his head. "If we had those when the Hocklyns attacked New Providence, we might just have managed to hold the planet."

"But we still don't know how effective the new missile would be against the AIs," Amanda reminded him as she laid her head against his shoulder and closed her eyes. Sometimes all she wanted to do was forget that there was a war waiting in their future if they decided to return to cryosleep.

"I know," replied Richard, taking his hand and placing it upon hers. "I just worry that if we use bigger and more powerful weapons how the AIs will respond. They have the knowledge and power from thousands of worlds. Who knows what kind of weapons they may have at their disposal?"

Amanda opened her eyes and looked across the room. Hanging on the wall was a picture of her parents standing on the porch of their house on Krall Island. She felt her eyes moisten. She missed her parents so much. The not knowing what happened to them after the

Hocklyn attack still haunted her dreams. Perhaps on this mission, if things worked out right, she would have the opportunity to find out the answer to that distressing question. If the Hocklyns no longer occupied the home worlds of the Federation, their orders were to scan each one for possible survivors, particularly New Providence.

Amanda knew that General Allister had made plans to survive underground if necessary. She wondered if it were possible for them to have survived in their underground bases after all of these years. Then she thought about Ceres and the world the Federation survivors had built in the asteroid's heart. There was air, plants, animals, lakes, and even moving streams in the new larger cavern that had been built. It was like its own little world. If the people on Ceres could build something like that, what would have stopped General Allister and his people from doing the same thing? Scanning New Providence and trying to make contact with any possible survivors was an extremely high priority on their mission list.

"I wonder what we will find back on the Federation worlds?" asked Amanda, turning her head to look at her husband. "Do you think anyone could have survived?"

Richard hesitated for a moment. He knew that all six worlds had been heavily nuked, but by all indications the half-lives of the radioactive isotopes were very short lived. Almost as if the Hocklyns wanted to wipe out the inhabitants but not seriously damage the ecospheres of the planets.

"I don't know," replied Richard, his eyes narrowing. "We know from what we observed on New Providence, Tellus, and Maken that there were large numbers of survivors fighting against the Hocklyn protectors. On New Providence, all the survivors went underground after we wiped out the Hocklyn forces. I suspect the Hocklyns returned in force, but who knows what might have happened after that."

"General Allister planned on not engaging anymore of the Hocklyn protectors in the hope the Hocklyns would assume the human population had been wiped out," Amanda reminded Richard.

"It might have worked," admitted Richard, recalling those last conversations with the general. "But we won't know until we go there. On Tellus and Maken, the marines were still fighting savagely against the Hocklyns when we left the system. They were still using nukes against each other. After all the fighting, it might have been difficult for anyone to survive as badly damaged as the two planet's ecospheres would have been in the months following. Once again, we won't know until we get there."

Amanda stood up and walked over to the wall, gazing at the picture of her parents. "Richard, do you ever regret our decision to go into cryosleep and not start a family of our own?"

Richard stood up and walked over to Amanda, putting his arm around her. "If we don't win this war, there is no future for humanity. We both decided we didn't want our descendants fighting a war we had fled from. With our medical science, we have years ahead of us yet to raise a family. When we return from this mission, we can talk about returning to cryosleep. I still think it's the wise thing to do. Before we start a family of our own, I want to be sure that humanity will survive. Our experience against the Hocklyns might play an important role in that happening."

Amanda sighed and turned to face Richard. "You're right of course," she spoke, her eyes meeting his. "It's just that sometimes I really want a family. I feel as if I owe it to my parents."

"Don't worry, Amanda," spoke Richard, leaning forward and gently kissing her on the lips. "Someday we will have that family; it might just be a few centuries yet."

Jason was in the Command Center of the Avenger talking to Commander Tellson over the com system. "From all the reports, I gather that the New Horizon is ready to go on her mission."

"Yes, sir," Commander Tellson replied with confidence in his voice. "We have adjusted our FTL equations to give us pinpoint accuracy. I think we can hit our destination coordinates dead on. All the systems in the ship check out, and we can depart whenever you give the word."

"Have all the scientists and their assistants reported on board?"

"Yes, sir," Tellson replied. "They have been on board for several days and seem quite satisfied with their research labs. If we find a habitable world, we can use the shuttles to explore it."

"Just be careful with those shuttles," Jason reminded the commander. "You only have two."

"We will, sir," Tellson responded. "The pilots have been very well trained."

Jason was silent for a moment as he thought about what all needed to be done to get the ship ready for departure. "Let's set a mission start date of four days from today. Departure time will be 1400 on Wednesday."

"That sounds great, sir," replied Tellson, allowing some excitement to enter his voice. "I will tell the crew and begin getting everything ready."

"Keep in mind there will be some dignitaries from Earth coming up to watch the launch from the spacedock," Jason reminded the commander. "We want everything to go smoothly."

"It will, Admiral," Tellson promised confidently. "We will make you proud."

Jason leaned back in his command chair after he finished speaking to Tellson, thinking about all that had been done to reach this point. The careful introduction of Federation technology, the placing of key Federation people in Earth companies to spur research along specific lines, and the slow release of technology supposedly reverse engineered from the Avenger.

Less than fifty people on Earth knew the full secret behind the Avenger Project. Most of those were in the highest government levels of Earth's most powerful countries. There were another one hundred or so that were aware of the Federation survivors on Ceres but didn't know about the Hocklyns. These numbers didn't include people teaching at the academy or working on the Avenger. It also didn't include a handful of graduates from the academy that had been let in on the full secret and assigned to Federation facilities or ships. There were also a few more in the military as several elite military units had been assigned to work with the Federation survivors. Jason knew that nearly two hundred marines had been chosen to provide security on some of the Federation ships.

"Are we ready to launch the New Horizon?" Lisa asked.

Jason turned around. He hadn't noticed that Lisa had entered the Command Center. There were two marine guards constantly on duty, but certain individuals were allowed in the Command Center without question. Lisa was one of them.

"On Wednesday," replied Jason, letting out a deep breath. He knew this would be a major step for Earth.

"What do you think the reaction will be on Earth when the New Horizon returns and announces that they have discovered two habitable worlds in the Tau Ceti system?"

"Excitement," replied Jason, trying to imagine the effect it would have on the people of Earth. "I suspect there will be an instant demand to begin colonization."

"We will have to build some colony ships," Lisa pointed out. "Technically the only FTL capable ship the Earth has is the New Horizon."

"We already have the designs for the first colony ship loaded into the computers in the spacedock," Jason replied with a smile. "Working around the clock, we can have the first ship ready in four months. It will be an exact duplicate of the New Horizon, without the labs. It will be able to handle four hundred colonists on each trip. The second ship will be a supply ship capable of carrying needed materials to the first colony. Then later, when the second construction bay is completed, we will start building larger colony ships capable of carrying over one thousand colonists on each trip. With luck, the new ships should be able to make a trip back and forth between Earth and Tau Ceti once each week. In a few years, we will have an entire fleet of colony and supply ships."

"What about the destroyers you plan on building to protect the new colonies?" Lisa asked. She knew that shortly things would start moving extremely rapidly. They had waited for years for this moment to arrive. It felt strange to realize that it was nearly here.

"Once the new construction bay is built, we will build two destroyers a year at first," replied Jason, recalling all of the careful plans they had made. "In time, we will add a third and fourth construction bay to the spacedock."

Lisa stepped over next to Jason and placed her hand on his shoulder. "We have worked so hard to reach this point, Jason," commented Lisa, gently squeezing his shoulder. "When are we going to tell Jeremy the rest of the truth? He deserves to know."

Ariel was listening, and her avatar was visible on the main viewscreen. If Jason and Lisa told Jeremy the truth, then she would finally be able to speak to him. It sounded too good to be true. She would be able to talk to all three of the special children. She waited curious to hear what Jason would say.

"After he returns from the mission, I will tell him," Jason said, wondering how Jeremy would take the news. He would undoubtedly be aggravated about all the secrets that had been kept from him. Jason knew that he would be if he were in Jeremy's shoes.

"Are Greg and Elizabeth coming up for the launch?" asked Lisa, wondering if she should get the guest quarters on the Avenger ready.

It would be good to see Elizabeth again, and she knew Elizabeth really wanted to see Katie. Lisa made it a point each evening to talk to Elizabeth and give her a report on Katie's progress and activities. She also knew that Katie called home at least once per week.

"No," replied Jason, sounding disappointed. "Greg will be with a number of people at Houston watching the launch from the ground. There will be quite a few important people in the group. Part of this group's from companies that will be highly interested if we find worlds that can be colonized. It will also give us an excuse to introduce even more Federation technology."

Lisa was quiet for a moment, then her eyes turned to look seriously at her husband. "Jason, when this is all over we need to take a nice long vacation. You need to see if you can talk Greg and Elizabeth into going to New Tellus with us. I understand the new resorts they have built are fabulous."

"Greg won't be a problem," Jason smiled completely in agreement about going on a vacation. He would also like to visit New Tellus again just to see all the changes since he had visited that world with Admiral Streth years ago. "Elizabeth is another matter. You may have to work your charms on her. You know she doesn't like space travel. It's all that Greg can do to get her up here to the Moon."

Lisa was silent for a moment. She was well aware of Elizabeth's fear of space travel. "Leave it to me, Jason. I think I know how to talk her into it."

"Then do it and I will set up the trip for sometime after the New Horizon returns. You're right; a week or two away from this job will be good for both of us."

Katie was finally finished with the intricate computer program she had been working on. She had a series of programs loaded onto her handheld computer that should allow her to get on board the New Horizon and safely hide until the ship reached Tau Ceti. Once at Tau Ceti, it wouldn't be practical for them to turn around and bring her back.

"What have you been working on?" Ariel asked curiously. She spent a lot of time watching the spirited teenager. It amazed her to see all of the energy possessed by young people. They never seemed to get tired.

"I'm writing a paper on the New Horizon mission," Katie answered nonchalantly. She actually had started a paper so she could show it to Ariel. "This is what I have so far." She touched an icon on her computer screen, and the half-complete paper was transmitted to Ariel. "I just need some additional information on the shuttles they will be using to explore those two planets with."

Ariel quickly read over Katie's paper and finding several errors she had made pointed them out to Katie. "The New Horizon is equipped with two shuttles capable of landing upon either of the two habitable planets in the system," began Ariel, wanting Katie to do well on her report.

Katie smiled as she listened to the AI. While Ariel was extremely smart and human in many ways, the AI was way too trusting. The entire key to Katie sneaking on board the New Horizon and staying undetected until they reached Tau Ceti lay in the two small shuttles. Now Aerial was giving her the last bit of information that she needed to make her plan work. It made Katie feel guilty at using Ariel this way, but she had to have the information on the shuttles. She just hoped that later, Ariel would forgive her.

Jeremy and Kelsey were in the officer's mess eating a snack before reporting to duty. Jeremy was polishing off his last bite of watermelon while Kelsey was savoring the sweet cantaloupe she was slowly eating.

"We leave on Wednesday," spoke Jeremy, enjoying the alone time with Kelsey. Normally, Angela or Kevin were with them. They had become a close foursome since their arrival on the New Horizon. Kevin had fit right in with the small group.

Kelsey nodded and grinned widely. "Just think, Jeremy. By this time next week we will be at Tau Ceti and exploring the system for new worlds for Earth to colonize."

"I hope we find one," Jeremy replied but knew the odds were not great. "More than likely the planets will not be capable of supporting life."

"But we know from astronomical scans of the system that there are at least five planets there," Kelsey responded, her blue eyes focusing on Jeremy.

She reached up and brushed her blonde hair back unconsciously before recalling that it was cut short in regulation fleet style. She missed her shoulder length hair. The short hair had taken some getting used to.

"I guess it's possible," Jeremy admitted. Looking around, Jeremy spotted Ensign Trace Rafferty watching them from a table across the room.

"I notice one of Barr's friends is in here," commented Jeremy, turning his head back toward Kelsey.

It was hard to take his eyes off of Kelsey sometimes. She was so beautiful, and at times Jeremy regretted not pursuing their relationship further while they were at the academy. However, they had both agreed to put things on hold until after graduation and now until the New Horizon mission was over. Sometimes Jeremy had the strange feeling that there was something mysterious about Kelsey. There was something about her that didn't quite fit. It was as if she were keeping a secret from him. It was the same feeling he got around his parents sometimes when they talked about the Avenger.

"I almost feel as if they are keeping an eye on us," responded Kelsey, using her fork to stab the last bite of her cantaloupe. "It seems so spooky at times. What do you think they could be up to? I've noticed several other members of the ship's crew that sit with them at times."

"I don't think they are up to anything except harassing us," Jeremy responded with a sigh. He too had noticed the company that Barr and Rafferty had been keeping. "We just need to remember not to respond to their barbs or comments, and there is nothing they can do."

Kelsey was silent for a long moment as she finished eating her last piece of cantaloupe before speaking. "Jeremy, what are your plans after we return from the mission?"

"I hope to stay on the New Horizon," Jeremy replied, his hazel eyes taking on a thoughtful look. "Once we get back, the ship will probably be sent out on further exploratory missions. I would like to be a part of that. What about you, don't you want the same?"

"Of course," Kelsey replied with a smile. "I just wonder if they will allow us to since we're cadets."

"I guess it depends on how well we do on the mission," answered Jeremy, then looking down at his watch he added, "It's time for us to report to the Command Center, Kelsey."

Kelsey nodded as she stood up. She really enjoyed the time she spent with Jeremy. But there were things about her that Jeremy didn't know. Things that could seriously impact their relationship later.

Letting out a deep sigh, Kelsey followed Jeremy out of the officer's mess.

Trace Rafferty watched them leave. His eyes focused on Kelsey, admiring the fine figure the young woman had. If they were successful in their takeover of the New Horizon, all of the women would be kept alive for breeding purposes. Kelsey would be quite a catch. As part of the takeover group, Rafferty would have his pick of the available women. Kelsey was at the top of his list.

Major Maher stepped into the officer's mess and, spotting Rafferty, he strolled over. "There will be a meeting in my quarters the morning we depart at 0800. Don't be late, I want to finalize our plans to make sure there are no mistakes. We will only get one shot at this. Make sure you tell Barr about the meeting."

"I won't, sir, and I will tell Matt," Rafferty replied.

"I noticed Strong and Grainger leaving as I came in," Maher continued, his eyes gazing hard at Rafferty. "Don't get any ideas about Kelsey Grainger. I believe your buddy Matt Barr already has his sights set on her."

Rafferty nodded. He had forgotten about Matt. He watched as Maher left and his thoughts wandered to Angela. If he couldn't have Kelsey, Angela would be a suitable replacement.

Jeremy and Kelsey reported in to the Command Center, relieving their counterparts. Jeremy was now serving as Lieutenant Nelson's second officer and took his place at the plotting table. Kelsey was over at the navigation console, already beginning to run simulations on the jump to Proxima Centauri even though Jeremy strongly suspected that Lieutenant Nelson would be the one plotting that particular jump.

"Are you ready for the mission to begin, Cadet Lieutenant Strong?" Lieutenant Nelson asked from his seat behind the command console.

Jeremy hesitated for a moment and then replied. "Yes, sir. I just hope we find something at Tau Ceti."

"I do too," Nelson replied, his confident eyes looking across the Command Center. "If we don't find a suitable planet at Tau Ceti there are a lot more possibilities close by. There could be dozens of suitable planets out there waiting for us to find."

"I hope so," Jeremy responded. Evidently, Lieutenant Nelson was one of those that believed that Earth type planets were quite common, just as Angela did.

"Your father and some other dignitaries will be coming up to the spacedock to see us off," continued Lieutenant Nelson, looking over at Kelsey who was busy with the navigation computer.

He allowed a smile to break out on his face. Cadet Ensign Grainger was committed to becoming a navigation officer. From what he had seen so far, she would probably succeed. The same went for Cadet Lieutenant Strong. He was as dedicated and determined as his father. Nelson knew that if he didn't watch it, someday he would be calling Jeremy "sir." He shook his head as he realized that neither cadet could have a clue as to what was in their future.

"Your father will be coming on board early Wednesday for a final inspection," Nelson continued. "Commander Tellson has given permission for you to go on the tour with your father if you wish."

Jeremy was silent for a moment. He would like to speak to his father before they left, but he also knew that if he were to go on this tour it wouldn't look good to the other crewmembers of the New Horizon. It would make it look as if his father were responsible for Jeremy being on the ship.

"If you don't mind, sir, I think it would be best if I passed on that," Jeremy replied in a steady voice.

"I understand," replied Nelson, nodding his head in approval. Nelson knew this was the correct decision for Jeremy to make and he was pleased the young man had declined the offer.

"We have a number of shuttles coming up from Earth tonight," continued Lieutenant Nelson, falling into the normal Command Center routine. "Make sure we track them from the time they leave Earth until they arrive at the spacedock."

"Yes, sir," Jeremy replied as he stepped over towards the sensor and scanner console where Ensign Roberts was watching the screens. Jeremy would make sure the data was transferred over to the plotting table so he could keep track of the shuttles from there.

Lieutenant Nelson leaned back in his chair. They were at spacedock, and the duty shift should be quite routine.

Chapter Eight

Commodore Rateif stared moodily out the thick reinforced window of his office at the bustling spaceport below him. His office was in a tall tower that jutted high above the spaceport, giving him a grandiose view. The spaceport was located on a desert planet, and looking out over the countryside, everything was the same. Flat ground with sparse plants and very little water. The Hocklyns had chosen this planet as a forward base for this section of space. For ten years, Commodore Rateif had been in charge of this base and the ships that left weekly on exploration missions. In ten years, they had only found three inhabited worlds to bring into the Hocklyn Slave Empire. New honor and advancement had been slow for his family and himself. Recently the Hocklyn High Council had sent a message implying that if more worlds were not found soon to add to the empire, changes would be forth coming.

"You summoned me, sir?" a grating voice spoke behind him.

Commodore Rateif turned and saw First Leader Shrea of the war cruiser Vengeance. Shrea was dressed in simple dark body armor, which was standard attire for a First Leader of a Hocklyn warship. The skin of the First Leader was a light green, and he had a short darker green crest made of bone cartilage going from the top of his head to the back. His body was powerfully built, and his large, powerful hands were held at his side.

"I have a new mission for you, First Leader," Rateif spoke, his cold eyes gazing at Shrea. "This area of space seems to be devoid of civilizations for us to add to our empire. We have searched for ten years and found little. Perhaps some stellar incident millennia ago wiped this area of space clean of life." He knew such things were not unheard of.

"It has been slim pickings," agreed Shrea, clenching his fist and feeling the short claws on the tips of his fingers bite into his hand. "We have not been given the opportunity to bring as much honor to our families as I had hoped since my task group was assigned to this base."

"I agree," Commodore Rateif replied with a slight tilt of his head. "Only three small civilizations and none of them worthy of combat. Honor has been slow to come. However, I have a plan that may change that."

"What is your plan, Commodore?" Shrea asked with interest, his cold gaze meeting the commodore's narrow eyes. "We must find honor soon, or we will suffer the consequences for failure."

"I propose to send your task group on a long distance exploratory mission to the extreme edge of our sector," explained Rateif, walking over to his desk and pointing at a star map that was spread out. "I want you to take your fleet to this section and begin the search for more worlds to add to the empire."

"That's nearly two thousand light years," commented Shrea, feeling appalled at the distance the commodore was suggesting.

They would be completely out of touch with the base at that range. It would take weeks for a message to reach the base. It would almost be quicker to send a ship back rather than an FTL message.

"That should get you out past this dead area we have been searching," Rateif responded evenly, his eyes unblinking. "Your ships will be well provisioned and armed. In addition, two supply ships will be going with you. Between your war cruiser and the six escort ships that will be at your disposal, I hope you will find new worlds to bring into our empire and more honor to be had by all of us. If you send word back that you have discovered new worlds for our empire, I will make arrangements for this base to be moved to the far edge of our sector."

Shrea was silent for a long moment as he gazed intently at the star map, visualizing the long journey his ships would be making. "You are correct that there is little for us here," Shrea said finally as he thought over the proposal. "Perhaps we may find honor in what you have suggested. When would we leave?"

"In two days," Rateif replied. "The supply ships are ready. All we need to do is resupply your task group and you can go."

"Two days," Shrea nodded. "That is good. My crews need action, and the possibility of new honor will spur them to find new worlds for the empire if there are any in that area of space."

"You must succeed, Shrea," Rateif spoke in a hard and cold voice. "If we don't find new worlds for the empire soon, we could face a reduction in the honor of our two families. The High Council is already applying pressure."

"I will not allow that to happen," Shrea replied as he turned to leave the room. "I will bring honor when I return."

Rateif watched him go. This was a desperate move he was taking by sending Shrea and his fleet so far. He walked back to the window and gazed down. Numerous slaves from different races toiled across the shipyard. There were several thousand slaves assigned to this world. Rateif looked out across the distant desert and at the emptiness. It was time to leave this world and this section of space; it had so little to offer.

Katie was waiting for the shuttle to take her up to the spacedock. She had a small, inconspicuous backpack that contained a few clothes and other items she thought might be useful on board the New Horizon. However, the most important item of all was her small handheld computer, which was nestled securely inside.

"Cadet Johnson, I am surprised to see your name on this list," Professor Styles commented as he looked down the list and located Katie's name. "This flight was supposed to be for seniors only, but I suppose since your father is Greg Johnson, it's not too surprising to find that your name has been added."

"I could have gone up with Admiral Strong," replied Katie, keeping her voice calm. "But I prefer to take the tour with the other students from the academy."

"A good decision, young lady," commented Professor Styles, nodding his head. "You have done very well in the advanced computer classes, and if you were a senior, there is no doubt in my mind that you would have been nominated for this tour. Take your place on the shuttle; we will be leaving shortly."

Katie quickly boarded the shuttle. So far, neither Jason nor Lisa had spotted her. Both assumed she was still in her dorm room at the academy being watched over by Ariel.

Finding her assigned seat, Katie stowed her backpack. Then, sitting down, she buckled herself in. Looking around, she watched as the other cadets found their seats. Several frowned at seeing Katie on the shuttle. Katie only nodded and tried to relax. The first part of her plan was working flawlessly. In a few more minutes, they would be leaving the surface of the Moon and flying up to the spacedock. After that, everything would be more difficult, but Katie was confident she could make her plan work.

Jason and Lisa were boarding their own shuttle to fly up to the spacedock. Jason planned on a quick tour with Commander Tellson if the commander was available, and then he would leave the commander alone. Then it would be back to the spacedock to entertain the dignitaries that were flying up from Earth. All the tours of the ship would be completed four hours prior to the ship leaving the spacedock. There were only three small tours planned. The one Lisa and he were taking with Commander Tellson, several dignitaries that Lieutenant Nelson was scheduled to show around, and then finally a small group of senior cadets that Lieutenant Nelson would take on a quick tour of the New Horizon after he was through with the dignitaries.

"This isn't like the old days," Lisa commented as she buckled herself in and leaned back in the comfortable acceleration couch.

She watched as the flight attendant came by, checking on all the passengers. Lisa could well remember her first trip to the Moon with the research team after learning what Jason and Greg had discovered. Those few days crowded together on the Command Module as it neared the Moon and then the frightening descent to the lunar surface were forever implanted in her memories. Now flying to and from the Moon was almost like being on board a jet liner down on Earth.

"I can still remember the look on your face the first time you spoke to Ariel," replied Jason, smiling. "You were nearly speechless."

"She still surprises me sometimes," admitted Lisa as she looked out the viewport at several of the other shuttles that were waiting to go up to the spacedock. "It's hard to believe that here we are today, getting ready to launch an interstellar ship built by Earth to the stars."

"Built with very little help from Ceres," Jason reminded Lisa. "This is an important first step that we need to take on our own."

"A pretty big step flying all the way to Tau Ceti," said Lisa, turning her head to look at Jason. "I just hope everything goes as planned."

"It will," promised Jason. "We have a Federation light cruiser that will be shadowing the New Horizon just in case of an emergency. But I don't foresee there being any problems."

"What will happen to Jeremy after he returns from the New Horizon mission and you tell him the truth about the Avenger and the Federation survivors?"

"Mathew accepted everything pretty well when Greg told him," replied Jason, recalling what Greg had told him about that conversation. "I think Jeremy will understand. I would like to send him to Ceres for a few months, perhaps even let him serve on board a Federation ship for a time."

Lisa was silent for a moment. It would be hard on her not being able to see or talk to Jeremy if he were on board a Federation ship. She knew that Elizabeth was struggling with Mathew being on the shipyard at New Tellus and Katie up on the Moon.

"I spoke to Elizabeth about going to New Tellus last night," Lisa spoke, her eyes looking back out the viewport. She noticed the shuttle the senior cadets were on had just closed its hatch; they would be taking off shortly. "She said she would consider it. I think she is going to take a little bit more convincing, though."

"I will speak to Greg. Perhaps between the two of you she can be convinced to go. I think once we reach the resort on New Tellus and she can see Mathew, everything will be fine."

"I think so too," Lisa responded. She reached out and took Jason's hand. "You know, Jason, I'm surprised that Katie didn't ask to go up to the spacedock with us. I would have thought she would have wanted to say goodbye to Jeremy and Kelsey."

"She's been extremely busy with her classes," Jason answered. He had also been surprised she hadn't asked. "Ariel keeps a pretty good watch on her through the security cameras, and Katie spends most of her time working on homework or on her handheld computer."

"She's doing surprisingly well at the academy," admitted Lisa glad that she had suggested that Katie be allowed to attend the summer session. "We've had no problems, and she has been a model student."

"I spoke to Commandant Everson the other day about Katie," Jason ventured. This was something he hadn't mentioned to Lisa. "He is going to offer her the option of attending as a full time student."

"Will Greg and Elizabeth go for that?" Lisa asked, her eyes widening at the thought. It would be nice having Katie around with Jeremy gone.

"I spoke to Greg, and he thinks it would be a great idea. Katie is bored with the classes down on Earth. He is going to talk it over with Elizabeth."

They both became quiet as they saw the hatch close and the flight attendant sit down. The attendant made a short announcement that they would be taking off shortly, and everyone should be buckled in for safety reasons.

A few minutes later, the massive doors to the flight bay slid open, and the shuttles began to depart. There were four of them going up to the spacedock carrying passengers to watch the New Horizon embark on her historic mission.

Katie let out a sigh of relief as the shuttle left the flight bay. She was on her way up to the spacedock and the New Horizon. Trying to relax, she ran through her mind what she needed to do once the shuttle reached the spacedock. She hoped she wouldn't regret it later, but how often was she going to get the opportunity to stowaway on Earth's first interstellar mission?

Jeremy was in his quarters on the New Horizon with a confused look on his face. Kelsey was sitting at the desk, watching him. For the last few minutes, he had been trying to get hold of Katie and tell her goodbye.

"She's not in her room," Jeremy commented after his last attempt. "I would have thought she would be glued to the vid screen like everyone else. Coverage of the New Horizon's departure is on every news channel."

"Perhaps she just stepped out to eat," Kelsey spoke, her blue eyes watching Jeremy. She had suggested that he give Katie a call before they left. "It's early, and it's still nearly six hours before we depart."

Kelsey looked around the small quarters. They were identical to the one that Angela and she shared. Angela and Kevin had gone on to eat breakfast and were waiting on them. Knowing Angela, she probably thought something else was going on. Angela had a tendency sometimes to let her imagination get the best of her.

"Let's go eat breakfast, Jeremy," suggested Kelsey, standing up. "You can try to contact Katie later. Did you talk to your father last night?"

"I talked to Mom," responded Jeremy, getting up from his bunk where he had been sitting. "She's a little nervous about the mission and really wants to see me today, but she understands the reasons why she shouldn't."

"She's your mother," stated Kelsey, shaking her head. "I think most of the crew would understand."

"Perhaps," answered Jeremy, walking over to the door with Kelsey following. "But there are people on this ship who wouldn't. Let's go eat breakfast before Angela gets anymore perverse thoughts in her mind."

Kelsey laughed and then hesitated at the door, smiling flirtingly at Jeremy. "When we get back from this mission, perhaps we should give Angela a reason to have those ideas."

Jeremy didn't know what to say. He had strong feelings for Kelsey, but had decided to wait until they returned from the mission to explore them further. It made him feel warm inside knowing that Kelsey was feeling the same thing.

Major Maher looked around the group he had gathered in his quarters. There were eight people waiting to hear what he had to say.

"Today, our mission begins," he stated, looking around the diverse group. There were five men and three women listening to him. "You all know the plan. If we do precisely as we've discussed, the New Horizon will be ours. There will be a number of visitors on board the ship this morning, including Admiral Strong, so be extra careful in what you say and what you are doing. I don't want anything to look suspicious."

"Do you think they suspect anything?" one of the women asked. Her name was Cynthia Pierce and she worked as a medical assistant.

"No, they do not," Maher spoke in a cold voice. "And they are not going to. We depart later today, and will perform our FTL jump to Proxima Centauri after we clear the Earth and Moon's gravity well. We will spend a few hours in the Proxima system doing routine scans and allowing the drive core to cool down."

"That should take about six hours," Ensign Bates commented.

"Sometime after that we will be making our jump to Tau Ceti," Maher added. "Once we reach Tau Ceti we will pass out the weapons and then take over the ship."

"Do we have to kill all the Command Center officers?" Cynthia asked. She believed in what they were doing, but she didn't feel comfortable with cold-blooded murder.

"We have no choice," Maher responded, his eyes cutting into Cynthia. "We don't want to leave the crew anyone to rally around. The only exception will be Lieutenant Nelson. We may need him to plot some of our jumps, at least initially. Once we're satisfied we don't need him any longer, he too will be eliminated. Do you have a problem with that?"

"No, sir," Cynthia replied, her eyes meeting Maher's without blinking. "I believe in what we're doing. If some have to die, then so be it."

The meeting lasted for another thirty minutes as Maher outlined in detail what was expected of everyone when it came time for the takeover. "Let's get this done. I don't want any hesitation on anyone's part, or you will have to deal with me."

Katie exited the shuttle, sliding her small backpack on over her shoulders.

"What's in the backpack?" Professor Styles asked as they walked down the ramp of the shuttle.

"My computer and a couple of notebooks," Katie replied easily. "I am doing a report on the New Horizon mission, and I may need them to take some notes."

"I would like to read it when you're finished writing it," Professor Styles commented. "I would be interested in seeing your take on Earth's first interstellar expedition."

Katie nodded and walked on down the ramp. She saw several other shuttles unloading and tried her best to blend in with the other students. It wouldn't be good if Lisa or Jason saw her. She would also have to be careful on the New Horizon. She knew that Jeremy, Kelsey, and Angela would spot her instantly if they saw her.

Professor Styles gathered all the cadets together. There were eight of them total, including Katie. "We will be going on a quick tour of the spacedock first before we tour the New Horizon. Both tours will be short since the ship is preparing to depart later today. We will observe the departure from the observation lounge on the top level of the spacedock. It will give all of us a good view of the New Horizon as she leaves on her mission."

"Will we get to see the Command Center on the New Horizon?" asked one of the female cadets.

"No, not today," Professor Styles replied. "The Command Center as well as the Engineering decks are off limits. Maybe once the New Horizon returns, we can make arrangements for a more thorough tour."

In the Command Center, Commander Tellson was going through the pre-departure checklist with the command crew. He had spoken to Admiral Strong briefly as he had stopped by the Command Center. The admiral had gone on, not wanting to interfere with the commander's preparations.

"Navigation, do we have the first jump coordinates for Proxima Centauri plotted in?"

"Yes, sir," the navigation officer replied. "Lieutenant Nelson loaded the coordinates into the navigation computer on his duty shift. They have been checked and confirmed. We should jump into the system 2.4 billion kilometers from the system's sun."

Commander Tellson nodded. He pressed a button on his mini-com, which would put him in contact with Engineering. "Lieutenant Jackson, are we ready to activate the subspace drive and then later the FTL drive?"

"Both have been checked, sir," replied Jackson. "Sublight is standing by at your command."

"Very well, we have a few hours yet; we want everything to function normally as we leave the spacedock. There will be a lot of people watching us today."

Commander Tellson finished talking to the various stations confirming their readiness. He could feel a little tension mounting in the ship as the crew knew today was the big day. He leaned back in his command chair and let out a deep breath. In the back of his mind, he allowed himself to wonder what they would find. This voyage would go down in history. He hoped it would be remembered as a huge success.

Katie's tour was almost over and her group was standing in the New Horizon's flight bay. The group had divided into two separate groups as they were looking at the two small shuttles in the bay. Professor Styles was with the second group along with Lieutenant Nelson, pointing out some details on the other shuttle.

"I just saw the admiral and Lisa pass by in the outside corridor," Katie casually mentioned to one of the girls in her group when she noticed that Lieutenant Nelson and Professor Styles had their backs turned. "Lisa said I could join them if I wanted. Maybe this way I can see the Command Center. Tell Professor Styles I went with Lisa and Admiral Strong and will be taking their shuttle back to the academy. Katie turned and rushed out of the open hatch that led to the corridor and quickly disappeared from sight.

The young senior cadet only shook her head in exasperation. It wasn't her job to keep up with Katie. Katie should have been the one to tell Professor Styles. Turning back around, she joined the other two cadets as they looked over the shuttle.

Katie managed to slip back out into the corridor with no one noticing except the senior cadet she had talked to. She hoped that by invoking Admiral Strong and Lisa's names there would be no questions as to where she had gone. Also, by indicating that she would be returning on the admiral's shuttle, no one would be looking for her until after the New Horizon had jumped to Proxima Centauri, and by then it would be too late.

Katie walked a few quick steps down the corridor and opened a hatch on her right side. It was a small storage room, and she stepped inside and shut the hatch behind her. She would wait here until she felt the tour was over, and then go to her planned hiding place. A place she didn't think anyone would look.

For what seemed like an eternity Katie waited, hoping no one would open the hatch and find her. If they did, then her plan to sneak aboard the New Horizon would fail. She tried to control her breathing and she could feel her heart pounding. Looking around the small room, she noticed that it contained spare parts for the flight bay.

There was no reason for anyone to check this room unless they had determined that she was missing. The only way that would happen would be if Professor Styles checked with Admiral Strong, and Katie doubted that the professor would do that. After all, she was Katie Johnson, and her family and the admiral's were closely connected. Her leaving to join the admiral's group probably wouldn't come as a surprise to the professor.

After what Katie deemed was a sufficient amount of time, she slowly opened the hatch to the small storage room, only to hear voices in the corridor. She quickly shut the hatch and waited another few minutes. Cautiously opening the hatch again, she saw the corridor was empty. Hurrying down the corridor, she slipped back into the empty flight bay and ran across the deck to one of the waiting shuttles. She quickly took off her backpack and pulled out her computer. Activating a program, she attached a connecting wire to the port on the shuttle's hatch and the door slid open. Disconnecting the wire, she crawled inside and shut the hatch after her. Once inside, she leaned against the hull of the shuttle, trying to catch her breath. She could feel her heart racing, and she was breathing rapidly.

After a few moments, she felt calmer and made her way to a viewport to look out. There was no one else in the flight bay; she had made it into the shuttle undetected. Reaching into her backpack, she pulled out a diagram of the shuttle and its control systems. Ariel had helped her get this information so she could write in more detail about how the shuttles would be used to explore any habitable worlds the New Horizon might discover.

Ariel had never suspected the real reason Katie wanted the schematic. Katie did feel extremely guilty about deceiving Ariel, but she had to get aboard the New Horizon. She didn't know how long she would have to be in the shuttle, and she wanted an idea of what was going on around her.

Going into the small cockpit, she sat down in the pilot's seat and using her computer ran several wires to the connecting ports on the shuttle's main computer. Activating several more programs she had written, she activated the shuttle's life support systems and locked the hatch so no one could get in. She also used another program she had written to tap into the New Horizon's communication systems and viewscreens so she could listen and watch what was going on. Now all she had to do was wait.

Jason was in the Command Center of the spacedock with a number of important people from Earth. There were representatives from all five of the countries that knew about the Avenger Project and what lay in Earth's future. All had their eyes focused on the main viewscreen, which was focused on the New Horizon.

"The ship will be departing in ten more minutes," Jason informed the small group. "Once the ship has safely maneuvered away from the spacedock, the New Horizon will activate its sublight drive to move away from the Earth and the Moon's gravity well. Mission specifics call for the ship to place a distance of four million kilometers between it and the Moon before activating the ship's FTL drive for its jump to Proxima Centauri."

"Why not just do one jump straight to Tau Ceti? Why jump to Proxima Centauri first?" The delegate from the United States asked. "Isn't the ship capable of jumping that far in one jump?"

"The ship is capable of making the jump," Jason confirmed with a nod of his head. "However, due to the distance of 11.9 light years it would put some stress on the FTL core by generating a tremendous amount of heat."

"Why does the FTL drive generate so much heat?" asked the British delegate, focusing his attention on Jason.

"It's a byproduct of being in hyperspace," Jason answered. "Hyperspace is not a natural state, so it is continuously trying to eject a ship traveling in it. The constant pressure on the drive to remain in hyperspace is what generates the heat. It takes a tremendous amount of power to travel in hyperspace, and one of the byproducts of the energy used is heat. It is contained in the drive core and then the core is cooled down after the jump. We estimate it will take six hours for the drive core to cool down sufficiently from a long FTL jump before it can make another. Even on the shorter jumps the New Horizon made on her FTL trials here in our solar system, we allowed the drive core to cool down for six hours as a safety precaution."

Lisa listened to Jason explain in general detail how the New Horizon's FTL drive functioned. Looking at the viewscreen, she wondered if they had made a mistake not inviting Katie to come up to the spacedock with them. Jason had been concerned that it might look as if they were showing favoritism to the fifteen-year-old, but Lisa wasn't so sure about that. Katie was like family, and sometimes you had to place family first over everything else. Lisa knew that Katie would have really enjoyed watching the New Horizon leave to go on its mission.

Gazing at the New Horizon, Lisa wondered what Jeremy was doing. She knew that since he was still technically a cadet, he wouldn't be involved with this part of the mission. More than likely he was in his quarters watching the vid screen like so many others on the Moon as well as down on Earth.

Lisa was correct in what Jeremy was doing. Kevin, Angela, Kelsey, and Jeremy were all in the quarters that Jeremy shared with Kevin, watching the vid screen. They had decided to stay together until after the New Horizon made its first jump to Proxima Centauri.

"This is so exciting," Angela said breathlessly as she watched the vid screen, which was showing a close up of the New Horizon. "We are going to be a part of making history!"

"I'm just nervous about the FTL jump," Kelsey mumbled. "This one will last much longer than the short ones we did earlier when we were testing the drive."

"You're just afraid of getting sick," Kevin teased with a big grin. "I understand you got sick on three of the jumps."

Kelsey felt her face grow warm. "I know now not to eat before a jump," Kelsey replied defensively, glaring at Kevin. "I will be fine on this one."

Jeremy chuckled and looked over at Kelsey. Kelsey and Angela were sitting on his bunk, and Kevin was sprawled out on his. Jeremy was sitting in the chair at the computer desk closer to the girls and watching the vid screen. "I'm sure you will, Kelsey," spoke Jeremy, smiling. "The FTL jumps are something we are all going to have to get used to."

"Proxima Centauri," spoke Kevin, looking curiously over at Jeremy. "It's a red dwarf star 4.2 light years away. I wonder if we will find anything there?"

"The astronomers have never spotted a planet," Jeremy responded. He had read up extensively on Proxima Centauri. "It doesn't mean there are not any, but if there are they're probably on the small side as far as planets are concerned."

"But we know there are planets at Tau Ceti," Angela added, her eyes taking on an excited glint. "That's why we're going there. We know that at least one of the larger planets is in the liquid water zone."

"The Goldilocks zone," Kelsey added with a nod. "Not too hot and not too cold, but maybe just right."

"Wouldn't that be great to discover a habitable planet on our first time out?" Kevin said, sitting up and looking at the other three. "I wonder if we would get to name it?"

"I guess we will find out," Jeremy spoke, his eyes turning back to the vid screen. "If we did discover a planet, I suspect Commander Tellson would be the one to pick out an appropriate name."

"Yeah," added Angela, grinning at Kevin. "I don't think he will name it planet Kevin."

Kevin tossed a pillow at Angela and then focused his attention back on the vid screen. It was time for the ship to depart the spacedock.

Commander Tellson was sitting behind the command console watching his crew. Everyone was working smoothly as they checked to ensure the New Horizon was ready to depart.

"All stations report ready," Major Maher confirmed from his position at the plotting table. "We are prepared to depart the spacedock upon your command."

"Release docking clamps and move us away from the spacedock," ordered Commander Tellson, taking a deep breath. It was time for their journey to begin.

The New Horizon moved slowly away from the spacedock and began a slow turn. Shortly the ship was over one thousand meters away. It was slowly moving away on its station keeping thrusters.

"Activate sublight drive at five percent power," Tellson ordered, once he was satisfied that they had put a safe distance between the ship and the spacedock.

Major Maher passed the order over his mini-com to the helm officer.

A light blue glow appeared behind the New Horizon as it quickly accelerated away from the spacedock.

"Go to twenty percent power on the sublight drive and maintain it until we are clear of the Moon and Earth's gravity well," Commander Tellson ordered. He knew that back on the spacedock as well as on the Earth and Moon, all eyes would be on his ship. Everything needed to go smoothly and efficiently to ensure that future missions would be approved.

The ship continued to accelerate and soon was eating up the distance between the Moon and the border of where the Moon and Earth's gravity well could affect the FTL drive the New Horizon was equipped with. Playing it on the safe side, Commander Tellson allowed the ship to continue on its sublight drive at twenty percent power until they reached the planned distance of four million kilometers from the Moon, safely outside of the Moon and the Earth's gravity well.

"Standby to initiate FTL jump to Proxima Centauri," ordered Commander Tellson, looking toward Navigation and the Helm. He knew that the jump coordinates had already been loaded into the navigation computer.

"Ready to jump," Major Maher reported. He smiled inwardly to himself. Once they were out of the solar system, there would be nothing anyone could do to prevent him and his people from taking over the New Horizon.

"Initiate jump," Commander Tellson ordered.

Major Maher instantly passed on the order.

On the main viewscreen, a blue-white vortex of swirling light appeared. The helm officer maneuvered the New Horizon into its center. The ship vanished and the vortex collapsed in on itself, disappearing. The ship entered hyperspace and was on its way to Proxima Centauri.

Jeremy felt a sudden queasiness, slightly more severe than the previous FTL jumps he had experienced. Looking over at Kelsey, he saw her face was extremely pale. He reached out, took her hand, and smiled in understanding. "I don't feel too hot myself."

"Thanks," Kelsey replied with a weak smile. "I guess this is just going to take some getting used to."

"Look at the vid screen," spoke Kevin, excitedly.

All four looked at the vid screen and were surprised to see the screen covered in deep purple as well as numerous other dark colors that seemed to be in a constant state of flux.

"Hyperspace," Kelsey uttered, her blue eyes glued to the vid screen. "This is what hyperspace looks like."

"How long will we be in hyperspace?" Angela asked intrigued by what was on the vid screen.

Kelsey recalled the calculations that she had helped Lieutenant Nelson with for this jump. "Nearly forty-five minutes. Then we should arrive at Proxima Centauri."

"We're on our way," Angela spoke, her eyes wide. "The Earth's first interstellar mission has begun."

On the spacedock, Jason nodded his head in satisfaction. Everything had gone off without a hitch. He breathed a sigh of relief. Everyone in the delegation from Earth had been quite impressed with what they had witnessed. Jason and Lisa had then escorted the Earth delegates back to their waiting shuttle, wished them a safe trip, and promised to keep them informed as soon as anything was heard from the New Horizon.

As Lisa and Jason entered their own shuttle and took their respective seats, they both could feel the tension of the last few hours evaporate. Talking to the delegates, explaining what was going on and what they hoped to accomplish with the mission, had been trying at times.

"They're on their way," Lisa spoke evenly, her eyes looking over at her husband. "Once they arrive at Tau Ceti and find the two habitable planets in orbit around that gas giant in the liquid water zone, a new era will dawn on Earth."

"This should be an exciting time for Jeremy and Kelsey," responded Jason, reaching out and taking his wife's hand.

Jason allowed himself to relax and think about all that had been done to reach this point. Once he reached the Avenger, the first thing he needed to do was contact Greg. But for now, he just wanted to relax and enjoy the ride back down to the Moon.

On board the small shuttle on the New Horizon, Katie staggered out of the compact restroom in the back of the shuttle. She closed her eyes and shook her head. The jump into hyperspace had made her sick. It wasn't a good feeling to see your lunch make a reappearance. Walking back into the small cockpit, she sat down and looked at the largest viewscreen on the instrument panel. It was now showing the same view as the one in the Command Center of the New Horizon.

Katie was ninety percent certain that no one would be able to detect the program she was using to tap into the ship's systems. She rotated through a number of the viewscreens, but nowhere did she see Jeremy or Kelsey. Katie assumed they must still be in their quarters, and that was one of the few areas that she couldn't see into.

Leaning back in the pilot's seat, she prepared herself for a long wait. Ariel had furnished Katie with the flight plan for the New Horizon, and she knew it would be a while before she dared to reveal herself. Once the ship arrived at Proxima Centauri, there would be a six to ten hour wait for the drive core to cool down and for the crew to take detailed scans of the system. After that, they would make the longer jump to Tau Ceti where the actual mission would begin. Katie knew that it would be wise on her part to wait until the crew was highly involved in their research before she made an appearance.

It also worried her that on the Moon, Ariel would soon realize that something was wrong when she didn't return on any of the shuttles. It would only be a short matter of time before Jason and Lisa realized what she had done. There was no doubt in Katie's mind that shortly after that her parents would know.

A blue-white vortex formed in the outskirts of the Proxima Centauri system, and the New Horizon suddenly made an appearance. The vortex vanished, leaving the ship alone.

"We're at Proxima Centauri," spoke Jeremy, seeing the red dwarf appear in the center of the vid screen. The screen color enhanced everything to show it as it should look.

"We made it," Angela breathed with an excited smile upon her face. "We're the first humans that have ever been here."

"Don't forget that the Avenger came from somewhere." Kelsey reminded Angela, looking over at her close friend.

"We don't know where though," said Angela, shaking her head in denial. "For all we know, the Avenger came from Atlantis and crashed on her first flight. That's something that's still a mystery."

"Next stop will be Tau Ceti," commented Kevin, gazing with interest at the screen. "I wish we could go to the Command Center."

"The command crew will be doing everything today," said Jeremy, also wishing he were in the Command Center so he could experience all of this first hand.

"I think watching everything from here for now will be just fine," added Angela, sliding back on the bunk and leaning against the wall to get more comfortable.

Jason and Lisa had made it back to the Moon and were on their way to the Command Center on the Avenger. They wanted to check on the current status of the mission. A Federation light cruiser was stationed in the Proxima Centauri system and would report to Ceres as soon as it detected the New Horizon exiting hyperspace.

Entering the Command Center, the first thing Jason noticed was Ariel's avatar on the main viewscreen. Ariel had a look about her like nothing Jason had ever seen before. It was as if her best friend had just died. He knew with a sinking feeling in his stomach that something was horribly wrong.

"What's wrong, Ariel?" asked Jason, growing concerned. "Has something happened to the New Horizon?" Jason felt ill and was almost afraid to hear Ariel's reply. Had something disastrous befallen the mission?

"No, Jason," responded Ariel, lifting her dark eyes to gaze at Jason and Lisa. "The light cruiser StarFury has reported that the New Horizon has safely arrived in the Proxima Centauri system."

"Then why the forlorn look on your face?" asked Jason, feeling confused. "Is there something else wrong?"

"Yes," confessed Ariel, knowing she was about to get into a world of trouble. "There is a stowaway on board the New Horizon."

"A stowaway!" Lisa cried her face turning pale. "How can that be possible?"

"The stowaway had help to get on board," Ariel said slowly. If she were human, Ariel knew she would be crying. "It's all my fault. I wanted a real friend, and I let my guard down."

"Who is the stowaway?" Lisa demanded, a growing suspicion forming in the back of her mind. She prayed that she was wrong.

"It's Katie," confessed Ariel, trying to meet Lisa's eyes. "Katie is on board the New Horizon."

"Katie!" Jason exclaimed with anger crossing his face as he stared in shock at the AI. "How is that possible?"

Ariel was silent for a moment, and then began explaining her relationship with Katie. Ariel spent several long minutes covering how they had met and everything she had told the young teenager. When she was finished, both Jason and Lisa were looking at Ariel as if they couldn't believe what they had just heard.

"You told her everything?" spoke Jason, trying to keep his voice calm. He couldn't believe all of this had gone on underneath his nose. Not even Lisa had suspected.

"Yes," Ariel confessed, her voice quivering. "She knows about Ceres, the Hocklyns, the Federation, everything."

Lisa sat down in the command chair. She felt faint as she wondered how she was going to explain to Elizabeth that Katie was no longer in the solar system.

"Where is she on the New Horizon?" demanded Jason not ready to forgive Ariel for this unbelievable indiscretion. "Do you know where she's hiding?"

"I believe she is hiding in one of the two shuttles in the flight bay," responded Ariel, knowing that Jason and Lisa were both extremely upset and disappointed in her. "From some of the questions she has asked me recently, I now believe she intends to stay in one of the shuttles until the New Horizon arrives in the Tau Ceti system. At that point, she will reveal herself to the crew."

"How could she do something like this?" Lisa spoke, feeling stunned at what had happened. She had thought that she was keeping a good watch on the young teenager. How could something like this happen?

"Who knows," replied Jason, looking over at his distressed wife. "She's a teenager and probably looks at this as a big adventure. She also probably feels that since she is Greg's daughter and close friends with Jeremy and us, she can get away with it. I know one thing, when Commander Tellson finds out he is going to be one extremely upset commander."

"Will he end the mission and bring her back?" asked Lisa, looking up at Jason.

"No, I don't believe he will. Katie will be safe on the New Horizon. I imagine he will give her to Jeremy to worry about and tell Jeremy to keep her out of his sight. That young girl is going to spend the majority of this trip locked in Jeremy's quarters and not allowed to roam around the New Horizon. This isn't going to work out as she had hoped."

"Jeremy's not going to like this," added Lisa, knowing how her son would feel. She knew he would be livid when he found out what Katie had done. Gazing at Jason, she continued. "We need to contact Greg and Elizabeth and tell them what's happened."

Jason nodded his head in agreement. This was one call he was not looking forward to. How was he going to tell his best friend that Katie had managed to stowaway on Earth's first interstellar mission? Shaking his head, he walked slowly over to the com station, thinking about what he was going to say.

Ariel watched Jason and Lisa, not knowing what to say or do. She hadn't felt this way since she had watched the majority of the Avenger's crew die from the flu and the crash over a hundred years ago. What Jason and Lisa would do to her was also worrying her. She knew that she deserved to be punished. But even more importantly, Ariel just hoped that Katie would be okay.

On the New Horizon, Commander Tellson gazed around the Command Center. A little over six hours had passed, and the FTL drive core was completely cooled back down. They were finally ready to make the jump to Tau Ceti.

"Coordinates are loaded into the navigation computer," Lieutenant Nelson reported. He had come into the Command Center and taken over at Navigation for this important jump.

"Very well," replied Commander Tellson, gazing at the large viewscreen on the front wall.

"Major Maher, take us to Tau Ceti."

Major Maher nodded and gave the order. Almost instantly on the main viewscreen, a swirling blue-white vortex appeared. It grew closer as the helm officer used the ship's thrusters to maneuver the New Horizon into its center. A few moments later, everyone felt the familiar queasiness as the New Horizon entered hyperspace.

At the plotting table, Major Maher stood with his hands clasped behind his back with a pleased look upon his face. In just another few hours, he would launch his plan to take over the New Horizon. With the weapons he had hidden, there was nothing anyone could do now to stop him. Very soon, the New Horizon would be his.

Chapter Nine

In the Tau Ceti system, a blue-white vortex of swirling light suddenly formed. From the vortex, a 400-meter spaceship appeared. The New Horizon had made it to the Tau Ceti system, completing the longest FTL jump of an Earth built spaceship. As soon as the ship cleared the vortex, the swirling blue-white space anomaly vanished, leaving the New Horizon floating alone in empty space.

"Status," barked Commander Tellson as he waited tensely for the sensors and viewscreens to clear of static. It always took a few moments for the systems to come back on line after a jump. For those few precious seconds, the ship was completely blind.

"All departments are reporting that all systems are functioning normally," Major Maher replied as he listened to the reports coming in over his mini-com in his right ear. "Engineering states the FTL core is hot and will require six to eight hours to cool back down before we can make another jump."

The main viewscreen suddenly cleared, and numerous stars appeared. The scanner and sensors screens started receiving data at the same time.

"Not picking up anything in the initial scans," the sensor operator reported as he watched the data come in over his screens.

Commander Tellson nodded his head as he listened to the report. They were pretty far out, and he hadn't expected to detect anything initially.

"Navigation, plot us a course inward toward the liquid water zone," ordered Tellson, wanting to get the exploration part of the mission started. "Helm, as soon as Navigation has a course, activate the sublight drive and move us in system at a speed of ten percent sublight. Once we're satisfied that there are no navigational dangers, we will increase our speed to thirty per cent sublight. As hot as the drive core is, we won't be using a micro-jump to take us in closer."

Major Maher could feel the excitement in the Command Center as he looked over the crew. They had arrived safely at Tau Ceti. He had expected no less. In another few hours, he would launch his takeover attempt and the New Horizon would be his. Then it would be time to launch the mission that his handpicked group had planned.

"We made it, Major," Commander Tellson spoke with a satisfied smile on his face, glancing over at his second in command. "Now let's find out what's in this system."

Jeremy and the other three cadets stared at the vid screen in rapt excitement. They were in the Tau Ceti system. The com system sounded, and Jeremy reached over and picked up the phone from the computer desk. He listened for a moment and then put it back down. With a big smile, he turned to face the others.

"That was Lieutenant Nelson. We're to report to the Command Center in two hours to relieve the command crew so they can get some rest."

"Fantastic," Kevin uttered, his eyes glinting with excitement. "I can't wait to report for duty today."

"Who knows what we may find," Angela added with an excited look on her face. "We're going to see things no one from Earth has ever seen before. This is history! We will all be remembered as being on Earth's first interstellar mission."

Kelsey smiled at seeing everyone's excitement, and then passed on a warning. "Just remember, everything we do will be scrutinized by the commander, and particularly by Major Maher."

The group calmed down as they all realized they had jobs to do. Jobs that would be extremely important to the mission as the planets in the Tau Ceti system were explored.

"We have two hours before we need to report to the Command Center," spoke Jeremy, realizing that Kelsey was right, particularly about Major Maher. The executive officer had really been keeping an eye on them recently. "Let's go get something to eat and then return to our quarters to get ready for our duty shift."

"We're going to make history," Angela commented with a big grin. "Maybe we will find a habitable planet on our shift, and it will be named after one of us."

"Planet Angela," uttered Kevin, shaking his head in disbelief. "I don't think so. That sounds worse than planet Kevin."

"We'll see," replied Jeremy, shaking his head at Angela's enthusiasm. She was so certain they were going to find a world that could be colonized. He hoped she wouldn't be too disappointed if the system was a bust.

Katie was staring at the small viewscreen on the instrument panel of the shuttle. That had been the second jump, and from what she could overhear on the com channel, the New Horizon had arrived safely at Tau Ceti. She breathed a deep sigh of relief knowing that she had successfully stowed away on Earth's first interstellar mission without being caught. Now all she had to do was stay hidden for another day or so, and then she would reveal herself.

She felt nervous and a little frightened about what Jeremy would say when he discovered what she had done. Katie also wondered if there was any way she could find Jeremy or Kelsey first before any of the other crewmembers found her. Taking a deep breath, she knew there would be trouble and anger when it was discovered what she had done. Thinking everything over now, Katie realized that she might have made a big mistake in stowing away on the New Horizon.

Before she had done it, the idea had sounded like a big adventure and extremely exciting. Now that she had succeeded in stowing away, she was starting to realize just how upset the ship's commander was going to be. She was worried about what they would do to her. She just hoped that considering who her father was and knowing Jeremy's parents would be enough to prevent her from being thrown in the brig. She didn't know if the New Horizon had an actual brig, but she knew that on the vid shows she had watched that was what was done to people who committed crimes on spaceships.

Getting up, she went back into the main cabin of the small shuttle. Rummaging through a small storage compartment on one of the walls, she looked for something to eat. From what Ariel had told her, the shuttles had enough food and water to last six people for two weeks. Therefore, food and water shouldn't be a problem if she had to stay in the shuttle longer than she planned. The only bad thing was the food was more like emergency rations and wasn't particularly tasty. At least most of it wasn't. She had found some chocolate bars in the emergency rations. Picking a self-heating meal, she sat down and pulled out the small table set into the wall. Once she was finished eating she would return to the cockpit so she could see more of what was going on. Perhaps now that they were at Tau Ceti, she would be able to see Jeremy or Kelsey on the viewscreen.

On the Moon, Jason had just finished talking to Greg. To say that Greg had been upset was an understatement. How do you tell your best friend that his daughter had stowed away on Earth's first interstellar mission?

"How did it go?" asked Lisa, knowing that Elizabeth was probably in shock right now. Lisa felt terrible over what had happened. She was supposed to be in charge of Katie. How would she ever get Elizabeth to forgive her? Katie hadn't just managed to sneak off, she had stowed away on a spaceship!

"Not good," answered Jason, coming over to stand next to her. Lisa was still sitting down. "Greg is going to catch a shuttle and come up to the Moon. He wants to talk to Ariel."

Ariel face blanched at hearing Jason's words. Greg was coming to speak to her. It was only now beginning to dawn on her just how much trouble she was in. What if they decided to wipe her program because of this? Her actions had endangered one of their children. As she was thinking about what could happen to her, she received a message from Clarissa. Clarissa was the AI on the Vindication, which was still docked in one of the large bays on Ceres.

"I just received a message from Clarissa, and she reports that the StarFury has jumped to Tau Ceti. The New Horizon is already inbound toward the liquid water zone. The ship seems to be functioning normally, and they are proceeding on their mission."

Jason stared at Ariel for a moment without answering. He didn't know what to do with Ariel. The mere fact that she could disobey his orders or ignore them had come as a major shock. It made him wonder just what else she was capable of. Were there other things she had done over the years that he wasn't aware of?

"That's good, Ariel," Jason responded in a voice still tinged with agitation. "Keep us informed. You also had better start thinking about how you're going to explain your actions to Greg and what's been going on between you and Katie. The fact that you revealed classified information to a fifteen-year-old is not going to go over very well either."

Lisa looked up at Ariel, still finding it hard to accept what had happened. She was surprised to see what looked like tears in Ariel's eyes. "Why did you do it?" she asked, trying to understand the AI's reasoning. She thought she had known Ariel and what the AI was capable of."

Ariel looked at Lisa; she had modified her program over the years so it better reflected her innermost thoughts or feelings. She had wanted to look more human, to feel more human. "I wanted a close friend, someone I could confide in," confessed Ariel, looking down and away from Lisa. "I was never allowed to speak to Mathew or Jeremy, and I didn't want to miss out on the opportunity to become friends with Katie."

Lisa and Jason were silent as they looked at each other. Perhaps it had been a mistake to keep Ariel away from Mathew and Jeremy. Now look at what it had led to.

"You can speak to them now," Lisa reminded Ariel. "Mathew knows the truth, and soon so will Jeremy."

"But it won't be the same," Ariel spoke with sadness in her voice. "I wanted to experience them growing up, to be a part of their lives. I guess I was just lonely."

Jason nodded his head, knowing that part of the guilt for what had happened also lay upon him. Sometimes it was difficult to remember just how advanced Ariel's AI program was. Even the scientists on Ceres were amazed at how human Ariel and even Clarissa seemed at times.

"When all of this is over Ariel, we will have a long talk. Perhaps we were wrong to keep you out of our children's lives, but that still doesn't excuse you for what has happened with Katie."

"I understand, Jason," replied Ariel, raising her dark eyes and using her Avatar's hand to wipe the tears from her eyes.

Lisa gazed at Ariel, her mind a turmoil of conflicting emotions. What Ariel was displaying and what she had done clearly demonstrated that the AI on the Avenger had evolved into a real life form. She wasn't a computer program any longer. Lisa couldn't believe that she hadn't realized what was happening over the years. Perhaps she had been so wrapped up in studying and working with Ariel that she hadn't realized that the AI was still evolving and becoming more human every day.

Jeremy entered the Command Center and saw that Lieutenant Nelson was already there. Commander Tellson and Major Maher had already left to go get some rest. The other members of the duty shift that normally worked with Lieutenant Nelson were also reporting for duty.

"Lieutenant Strong, take the executive officer's post at the plotting table," Nelson ordered. He had dropped the cadet part of Jeremy's rank once he was satisfied the young man could perform all the jobs in the Command Center with a reasonable amount of competence.

Nelson waited until the duty shift had been changed and his people were all at their stations before continuing. "As all of you know, we have successfully jumped into the Tau Ceti system. We are currently 300 million kilometers from the system's primary, and we are moving in system at thirty percent power on our sublight drive. Tau Ceti Five is 142 million kilometers from our current position and will be the first world we investigate. At our current speed, we will arrive in extreme sensor range in 2.4 hours."

Everyone was paying attention to Lieutenant Nelson. The crew knew that long-range observations of Tau Ceti had indicated that there were five planets in the system. All of the planets were orbiting within 205 million kilometers of the star. Tau Ceti Four and Tau Ceti Five were both in the liquid water zone. Tau Ceti Four was over four times the mass of Earth and Tau Ceti Five was nearly seven times the mass of the Earth. There was speculation that more planets lay farther out from the star, but Earth and space based telescopes had not been able to detect any.

Jeremy gazed speculatively at the plotting table. It showed the New Horizon's current position as a green icon and the five known planets in the Tau Ceti system as blue circles. The smallest was Tau Ceti One, which orbited extremely close to the star at a little less than 16 million kilometers. However, planets four and five were what held Jeremy's attention. While they were both much larger than Earth, they could potentially have liquid water and a breathable atmosphere. However, Jeremy couldn't see how someone could live on either because of the higher gravity.

Time passed as the New Horizon moved farther in system. Occasionally a wayward asteroid or what might be a comet would show up on Ensign Robert's long-range sensors. These Ensign Roberts carefully logged and put into the ship's records. While the system might not be suitable for colonizing, it might be rich in natural resources.

At last, the long-range sensors began picking up Tau Ceti Five. Lieutenant Nelson had the sensor scans put up on the main viewscreen so everyone could see what Ensign Roberts was recording.

Kelsey looked up at the viewscreen and smiled. Tau Ceti Five had a large number of moons in orbit. Several of them seemed to be quite large.

Jeremy looked in surprise at the sensor screen as more detailed information started to come in from the scans. "Are those moons that are showing up?" he asked looking over at Ensign Roberts. There must be a dozen or more.

"Yeah, and several are quite large," Roberts replied as he entered more commands on his console. After several moments of intensely scrutinizing the data, he turned around to face Lieutenant Nelson. "Sir, two of those moons in orbit of Tau Ceti Five are nearly Earth size."

"Earth size," said Lieutenant Nelson, standing up and walking around the command console to come and stand behind Ensign Roberts. "What are their orbits?"

"The closest one to Tau Ceti Five is 1.2 million kilometers from the planet; the second one is nearly 2 million kilometers away."

"Are you sure they are orbiting the planet?" asked Nelson gazing intently at Ensign Roberts.

"Yes, sir, and because they are both orbiting Tau Ceti Five, they are in the liquid water zone."

Nelson could feel the excitement suddenly rising in the Command Center. "Calm down, people," he ordered in an even voice. "We don't know yet if they are capable of supporting life. All we know at the moment is that we have two Earth size planets in the liquid water zone."

"But they could be habitable," Angela burst out, feeling the excitement. "If they have a suitable atmosphere we could colonize them."

Lieutenant Nelson shook his head. "Perhaps," he replied not wanting anyone jumping to conclusions before they had more conclusive data. "But let's not jump to any conclusions. We will know what we have as we get closer to Tau Ceti Five."

Jeremy watched for the next hour as the New Horizon moved closer to Tau Ceti Five. The closer they got the more promising the two orbiting planets looked. Everyone was watching Ensign Roberts as the latest sensor scans were analyzed.

"Well?" asked Lieutenant Nelson, waiting for Ensign Roberts to report the latest findings.

"Sensor scans are showing large amounts of liquid water on both planets," Roberts confirmed with excitement in his voice. "If there is liquid water, there has to be oxygen as well."

Nelson leaned back in the command chair and smiled. "I think it's time we called Commander Tellson to come to the Command Center. He will want to see this."

A few minutes later, Commander Tellson was in the Command Center, staring with stunned amazement at what the long-range sensors were showing. He spent some time reviewing the data and then looked over at Lieutenant Nelson, allowing a huge grin to break out across his face.

"If these readings are correct, we have two possible Earth type planets on our sensors."

"Yes, sir," replied Nelson, nodding his head in agreement. Looking over at the commander, he added. "We will soon be entering Tau Ceti Five's gravity well. Should we reduce speed?"

"Yes. Reduce speed to ten percent sublight. Let's take our time and do this right. I want the entire space around Tau Ceti five scanned thoroughly. This is too important to screw up."

For the next hour, the ship moved closer to Tau Ceti Five at a reduced speed. Major Maher came to the Command Center and watched quietly as the ship neared scanner range. Everyone waited tensely as the first close in scans of the two Earth size planets were run and analyzed.

Several scientists had appeared in the Command Center and were looking excitedly at the data as the information appeared on the computer screens. "This is amazing," Marcus Lynch commented as he gazed at the data. "Both planets are very Earth like. The planet nearest Tau Ceti Five is comprised of forty percent water with an atmosphere very similar to Earth. There are obvious signs of plant life on its surface. The second planet has a larger amount of liquid water. Nearly sixty percent of its surface seems to be covered with it. Its atmosphere is also similar to Earth. I don't see any reason why people couldn't live on either planet. We will have to run some more tests, but these two planets are exactly what we were looking for!"

Several crewmembers broke out in cheers. A quick, irritated glance from Major Maher calmed them back down.

Commander Tellson nodded his head in satisfaction. "Major Maher, recall the first duty shift. They should be rested enough by now. We will go into orbit around the outer Earth type planet first and begin taking more thorough readings. If they are satisfactory, we will send down some atmospheric probes for further tests." Looking around the Command Center, he smiled at the crew. He couldn't blame some of them for cheering earlier. This was a fantastic discovery. "You have all done an excellent job. Go get some rest and we will keep you informed over the vid screens as more information becomes available."

Major Maher came over to the plotting table and gestured for Jeremy to leave. A few minutes later, the entire duty shift that normally worked with Lieutenant Nelson had been replaced.

"I told you!" Angela spoke jubilantly, gazing at Jeremy with an I told you so look as they walked down the corridor toward their quarters. "We did find Earth type planets."

"So you did," Jeremy responded, also feeling Angela's excitement. This was one time he didn't mind her teasing.

"Two new worlds," Kevin continued, his eyes wide feeling the thrill of discovery. "Do you think Commander Tellson will allow any of us to go down to the planets on the exploratory missions?"

"I doubt it," responded Kelsey, shaking her head negatively. "The scientists will be handling that. We will be here in the ship monitoring everything."

"Let's go get something to eat," suggested Kevin, feeling some hunger pangs. "After all the excitement, I could use a good meal."

"You mean a hamburger and fries," teased Angela, knowing that was Kevin's favorite shipboard meal.

"Hey, they make excellent hamburgers on this ship," spoke Kevin, defending his favorite food and patting his stomach.

"I'm hungry also," ventured Kelsey, smiling. "Let's eat a quick meal and then go to our quarters so we can see what's going on over the vid screen."

Lieutenant Sandusky, Adam Bates, and Trace Rafferty were all in the small storage room that held the weapons Major Maher had brought up from Earth. Over the last few minutes, they had been handing out pistols to selected crewmembers to use in the takeover. More time passed as weapons were passed out to the rest of the conspirators. There were eighteen members of the crew and four of the civilians that had come on board that were part of the plan to take over the New Horizon. Most of the weapons being passed out were pistols, since they could be hidden rather easily.

As time passed, the entire group was armed. Sandusky had chosen six that were to accompany him to the Command Center. Four of them were armed with pistols and two others with assault rifles.

Sandusky had chosen a pistol for his own use. Reaching back into the large box, Sandusky pocketed several stun grenades.

He looked around his group of fellow conspirators who were waiting for his orders. "We need to move quickly," he stated in an even voice. "If anyone gets in our way, kill them! I don't want to see any hesitation or you will answer to me. Is that understood?"

Bates smiled and nodded. "Let's go take over the ship."

Sandusky indicated for everyone to follow him as he glanced at his watch. They had fifteen minutes to reach the Command Center before the other members of their group began taking action in other areas of the ship. There were twelve officers that would be targeted. All had to be eliminated quickly. In addition, another fifteen crewmembers would be taken into custody as they could be expected to cause problems later on.

"We'll take the smaller corridors as few people should be in them," Sandusky commented as he opened a hatch to an auxiliary access corridor.

The small group moved quickly through the ship taking small access corridors, which took them around most of the heavy traffic areas. They finally reached the main corridor that led to the Command Center. It was in this corridor that they could expect to possibly encounter a few crewmembers. Opening the hatch carefully, Sandusky glanced down the large corridor that led to the Command Center. He could see two civilian scientists going into the open hatch, but other than that, the corridor seemed clear.

"Let's go," ordered Sandusky, flinging the hatch open and running toward the open hatch to the Command Center.

Looking down at his watch, he saw that he had less than five minutes before others in the group took action across the ship. Coming to a stop just outside the hatch, he reached into his pocket and took out one of the two stun grenades he was carrying. Looking at the others, he nodded his head, pulled the pin, and tossed the stun grenade into the Command Center.

Inside the Command Center, both Major Maher and Lieutenant Barr had been expecting this. They were both standing behind the plotting table, and as soon as they saw the stun grenade, they ducked behind the table, using it to give them some protection. There was a loud bang and a brilliant flash of light. Maher could hear screams and people falling to the floor. Standing back up he reached under the plotting table and pulled out two pistols, one of which he handed to Barr. He had hidden these earlier hoping no one would discover them.

"Let's make this quick," he ordered as the ventilation system struggled to clear the smoke in the room from the stun grenade. Looking at the hatch to the Command Center, he saw Sandusky and the others come into the room. "Eliminate your targets!"

Maher walked over to the command console. Commander Tellson was struggling to stand up, and there was a large cut that was bleeding profusely across his forehead. He had struck the command console when the stun grenade had gone off, knocking him off his feet.

"What's going on?" Tellson managed to mumble weakly, looking at Maher in confusion. He was still suffering from the blow to the head and the after effects of the stun grenade.

"We're taking over the ship," Maher replied as he pointed his pistol at the commander's head and calmly pulled the trigger.

He felt the pistol buck in his hand and watched with satisfaction as Commander Tellson fell to the floor, dead. There were screams and other shots now ringing out in the Command Center as his people carried out their orders.

In moments, it was over. Looking around, he saw that all the intended targets were down. The entire command crew had been eliminated except for two frightened women who were under guard by one of Maher's men.

"Get these bodies out of here," Maher ordered as he reached down and dragged the commander's body away from the command console. He then returned and sat down, gazing across the Command Center as his orders were rapidly carried out. Reaching up, he activated the mini-com in his right ear so he could hear what was going on in the rest of the ship. He sent four of his people to help with the takeover in other areas of the ship. Over the next few minutes, his fellow conspirators reported in as each section of the ship was taken over. Twenty-three crewmembers, including the command crew, were reported killed. That was a few more than Maher had expected, but within twenty minutes the ship was fully under his control.

"What the hell's going on here?" a loud voice spoke from the hatch to the Command Center as Lieutenant Nelson strolled in, looking about in confusion.

Rafferty and Barr instantly pointed their pistols at the lieutenant. Nelson was the only surviving officer that was not a member of Maher's group.

"Take it easy, Lieutenant," warned Maher, standing up and striding over to stand in front of the stunned officer. "The ship is mine now, if you do exactly as I say your life will be spared. He had left Lieutenant Nelson alone because he was the best navigator on the ship and might be needed in order for the New Horizon to make it to its ultimate destination.

Inside the officer's mess, Jeremy, Kelsey, Kevin, and Angela were all sitting at their table under guard. There were two armed men in the room keeping a careful watch on the people inside. Occasionally, others would be brought in and ordered to take a seat. They were told that if anyone stood up they would be killed.

"What's going on?" Angela asked with a frightened and confused look in her eyes. "Why do they have guns?"

"They're taking over the ship," Kelsey spoke quietly, keeping her eyes on the two armed men at the door to the officer's mess.

"This is bad," Jeremy said as he watched another woman crewmember being shoved into the room. She had several bruises on her face, and it was obvious she had resisted the takeover.

"What are we going to do?" asked Angela, looking expectantly over at Jeremy. "We can't just sit here and do nothing."

"I don't think we have any choice at the moment," Jeremy replied as he saw Matt Barr come into the room. It didn't surprise him to see Barr holding a pistol. Rafferty was right behind him.

"We have taken over the ship," Barr announced, his eyes looking over the room. He noticed there were about twenty crewmembers sitting at the tables, many in shock over what was happening. With a wolfish grin, he looked over at Jeremy and the other three cadets sitting with him. "If you do exactly as we say, no one else will get hurt. Major Maher is now in charge of the New Horizon, and we are going on a different mission. If you refuse to obey us, you will either be shot or tossed out the airlock. The choice is yours."

Barr looked over at Jeremy and walked toward him with a purpose. "What do you think now, daddy's boy?" sneered Matt, gazing down at Jeremy. "You will obey me now or you and your friends will end up dead!"

Jeremy said nothing. There was nothing he could say, and he didn't want to make the situation even worse.

Barr looked over at Rafferty, who was standing behind him. "Take these four to their quarters and lock them in. I don't want them wandering around the ship."

"With pleasure," replied Rafferty, gesturing for the four to stand up.

All four cadets stood up and started walking toward the door. Rafferty shoved Jeremy in the back, nearly knocking him down. "Come on Strong, you don't want to get hurt do you?"

They walked to their quarters in silence. Even Rafferty was silent. Reaching their quarters, Jeremy and Kevin went inside and heard the door lock behind them.

"Now what?" asked Kevin, whirling around and trying to open the door. It was locked securely and wouldn't budge.

"We wait," replied Jeremy, going over to his bunk and sitting down. His mind was racing as he thought about the ramifications of what was happening. "They have all the weapons and control of the ship. We don't know what has happened to the ship's officers. I doubt if the majority of the crew is involved in this."

"We're helpless," Kevin muttered as he came over and sat down on his bunk and looked over at Jeremy. "How could they do something like this?"

"I don't know," answered Jeremy, feeling anxious for the girls. He hoped they would be okay.

Kelsey and Angela were standing in front of their quarters preparing to go inside. Kelsey was worried about Lieutenant Nelson and what had happened to him. If there were any way possible, she needed to talk to him.

"You know Angela, you have a cute ass," commented Rafferty, gazing at the young brunette. "If you're nice to me this whole thing could go a lot easier on you."

"If by being nice means what I think it does, you can forget it," Angela responded defiantly, her face taking on a deep flush. "You're the last person on this ship I would ever consider sleeping with!"

"We shall see," Rafferty commented with a leering grin. "I might look a lot better in a few days when you get hungry enough."

Kelsey grabbed Angela's hand and pulled her into their quarters, hitting the button on the wall to shut the door. Behind them, she could hear Rafferty laughing. Then she heard a loud clicking noise as the door was locked from the outside.

"What now?" Amanda wailed in fright as she walked over to her bunk and collapsed upon it.

"We wait," replied Kelsey, wondering how they could get in contact with Lieutenant Nelson.

She knew that he would not have been a part of this takeover plot. Kelsey just hoped he was still alive. If Nelson were alive, then there was a good chance they could still get out of this mess. There were things about Nelson that no one else on the ship except Kelsey was aware of. Kelsey went over and sat down next to Angela. Taking a deep breath, she looked around their quarters; she had a sinking suspicion they were going to spend a lot of time in this room.

Lieutenant Nelson was sitting in front of the navigation console. Major Maher stood above him with his pistol pointed at Nelson's back. "It's very simple, Lieutenant," Maher spoke in a cold and deadly voice. "Do what I say and you will live. If you disobey me one time, then I will start killing your little cadets. Or maybe I will turn Kelsey and Angela over to my people. Several of the men have already indicated an interest in the two. If you want them to remain unharmed, you will follow my orders."

Nelson drew in a sharp breath. He had been stunned when he had entered the Command Center to find most of the command crew dead and Major Maher holding a pistol. Maher in a cold and commanding voice had told him that his group was taking over the New Horizon.

"What do you want?" asked Nelson, knowing he needed to be careful and not antagonize Maher. He needed to bide his time. There were a few things about the New Horizon that not even Maher knew about.

"Plot a jump to these coordinates," ordered Maher, placing a piece of paper in front of Nelson with some numbers on it. "We're leaving this section of space so Admiral Strong will never be able to find us."

Nelson looked at the coordinates. "That's a jump of nearly ten light years, I'm not sure the FTL drive will handle that without overheating the core."

"It will handle it," Maher replied confidently. "We will be making four jumps in rapid succession, allowing just enough time for the core to cool. After the fourth jump, we will be making some adjustments to the drive core."

"What type of adjustments?" Nelson demanded. He knew how important the drive core was as it held all the excess heat generated from the FTL drive.

"Don't worry about that; just get us to where I want to go."

Maher turned and looked over at the Helm where one of Barr's fellow cadets was sitting. "Turn us around and accelerate to forty percent sublight. I want to get out of this system as soon as possible."

"Yes, sir," the ensign replied without hesitation.

The New Horizon slowed to a stop, turned around 180 degrees and began accelerating away from the two Earth like planets. The ship's engines glowed a bright blue as the ship rapidly accelerated to forty percent power on the sublight drive.

Maher returned to the command console and sat down, feeling satisfied with how everything had gone down. Looking around the floor of the Command Center, he realized he needed someone to clean up all the blood on the deck. He dispatched one of his trusted people to fetch a couple of crewmembers to take care of that. Leaning back, he knew that the next order of business was to select several command crews that he could depend on.

He thought the different duty shifts could be handled by Rafferty, Barr, and himself. As long as the only armed members of the crew were in the Command Center and Engineering, he could easily maintain control of the ship. His gaze wandered back to Lieutenant Nelson. Nelson was the only ship officer that was not in his group that had been spared. If not for Nelson's navigation skills, he too would have been eliminated as being too dangerous to keep around.

Lieutenant Nelson carefully plotted the next jump as he thought about his options. He wasn't sure how many of the crew were involved in this takeover. It had to be a quite a few, or it wouldn't have worked. Letting out a deep breath, he knew his best bet was to bide his time. At some time, Maher would make a mistake, and that was when he would make his move to retake the ship. He had a secret ace that no one knew about. He would just have to be careful about when and how he played it.

Katie was in the shuttle, literally shaking in fear. Her face was white, and she felt terrified over what she had witnessed on the shuttle's small viewscreen and heard over the com system. There had been a mutiny on the New Horizon and a group of armed terrorists had taken over the ship. She had searched frantically, switching the viewscreen, trying to spot Jeremy or Kelsey. Katie had been relieved when she had spotted them being led down one of the corridors that led to their quarters. At least they were safe for the moment.

There was now no doubt that she would have to remain hidden. There were enough supplies in the shuttle to last for several months, but she couldn't imagine staying in the small shuttle for that length of time. They would surely find her if she was forced to stay in the shuttle. There was a com system in the shuttle, but she knew that it couldn't reach Earth. It would take years for a message traveling at the speed of light to reach home.

Getting up, she walked back into the shuttle's main compartment, making sure once more that the hatch was securely locked and secured from the inside. Opening a small storage locker, she took out a bottle of drinking water. Stepping over to one of the small viewports, she gazed speculatively over at the other shuttle.

Should she move the supplies from the other shuttle into this one while the terrorists were still organizing themselves? She shuddered knowing that if she were caught, Jeremy and Kelsey would not be able to protect her. She could end up killed or thrown out of the nearest airlock. No, it was better to stay hidden in this shuttle for the time being. She could use the shuttle's systems to keep track of what was happening on the New Horizon. It was fortunate for her that she had created all the programs on her handheld computer that allowed her to tap into the New Horizon's systems. She just hoped no one detected what she was doing.

Going back into the cockpit, she sat back down in the pilot's seat still holding the bottle of water. She intended to keep a careful watch on what was happening on the New Horizon. Her future, as well as Jeremy and Kelsey's, might very well depend on it.

Jason was in the Command Center listening to an angry Greg berate Ariel over the transgressions she had taken with Katie and the security of the Avenger Project. Listening to Greg, Jason almost felt sorry for Ariel.

Ariel was doing her best to keep her eyes up and focused on Greg. The words coming out of his mouth were something she had hoped never to hear. What was even worse was the fact that she knew she deserved it.

"I thought we were friends," Greg was saying in an irritated voice, his eyes looking sharply at Ariel. "I told you explicitly that you were not to ever speak to Mathew without my permission. How could you possibly think that it was okay for you to speak to Katie? She's only fifteen and highly impressionable. An AI with your abilities would be like a dream come true to her, as fascinated as she is with computers."

"I'm sorry," Ariel said in a pleading voice, sounding almost like a child. "I made a serious error in judgment. I promise it won't happen again."

Greg strolled over to the main computer console and gazed down at it. He glanced back at Ariel. "I am almost tempted to open up this panel and jerk out all of your processors. How can we ever trust you after this?"

"Please, Greg," begged Ariel, starting to feel frightened. "I just wanted a friend."

"What are we?" asked Greg, gesturing toward Jason and Lisa. "I thought we were your friends."

Ariel was silent for a moment. "You are," she said, knowing that Greg was extremely upset. If he opened up that panel, she wasn't sure that Jason or Lisa would stop him. "But over the years, we have all grown apart. You had your children and all three of you were talking to me less and less. I needed a friend and Katie was my last and best hope."

Greg strolled back to stand in front of the main viewscreen where Ariel's avatar was prominently displayed. "You saved my life once," commented Greg, recalling the time that Lisa and he had become trapped behind a sealed hatch on the Avenger. "I owe you that. Once Katie is safely back we will discuss this, but I will not be talking to you again until the New Horizon returns safely and I have my daughter back in my arms."

Greg turned to leave the Command Center, knowing that if he didn't he might say or do something he would regret later.

"Stop, Greg," Ariel suddenly said her face turning pale. "I am getting an emergency message from Clarissa."

"What is it?" demanded Jason, taking several stepped closer to the main viewscreen. "Does it concern the New Horizon?"

"Yes," Ariel replied with a look of confusion on her face and in her dark eyes. "The StarFury is reporting that the New Horizon has jumped out of the Tau Ceti system."

"What!" uttered Greg, turning around and gazing at Jason in surprise. "Could they have discovered Katie and are bringing her back?"

"I can't imagine Commander Tellson scrubbing the entire mission over a stowaway," Jason replied, doubtfully. "Ariel, contact

Admiral Anlon and ask him to send a scout or a light cruiser to the Proxima System and see if they jumped back into that system. Something is going on, and I don't like the feeling I'm getting."

Ariel passed on the orders and then looked back at Jason. "Clarissa reports that both light cruisers are being dispatched to the Proxima Centauri system in case something has gone wrong on the New Horizon. Admiral Anlon wants to know if they should contact the New Horizon if they find her there."

Jason hesitated for a moment. If either of the light cruisers contacted the New Horizon, the cat would be out of the bag as far as Ceres and the Federation survivors were concerned. But he knew there was another reason that Admiral Anlon had asked that question. His daughter was on board the New Horizon. She was one of the ten cadets that had been chosen to go on the mission.

"Yes," Jason finally said. "With Katie, Jeremy, and Admiral Anlon's daughter all on the New Horizon, we can't take the risk of any of them being harmed. The cruisers have permission to make contact with the New Horizon."

Greg walked back over to stand next to Jason. "Jason, I'm sorry, but it's the right decision. If something has happened on that ship, we need to find out what it is."

"This could change everything," added Lisa, reaching out and taking Jason's hand. "Earth isn't ready to find out about Ceres and the people living there."

"It was going to happen eventually," said Jason, letting out a sharp breath. "It may just have to happen much sooner than we had planned."

-

In the Proxima Centauri system, two blue-white vortexes of swirling light formed. Out of each, a Federation light cruiser appeared. Each cruiser was 600 meters in length and heavily armed. As soon as they arrived in the system, the two cruisers began using their long-range sensors to search for the New Horizon. If the ship was in the system, the two cruisers would find it.

After nearly two hours, the commanders of the two cruisers were stone faced as they realized the simple truth. There was no sign of the New Horizon. Wherever she had jumped to, it was not into the Proxima Centauri system. They both communicated that disappointing information to Ceres.

-

"There is no sign of the New Horizon in the Proxima Centauri system," Ariel reported, her face taking on a look of deep concern. "Clarissa says the two light cruisers are being directed to check out Alpha Centauri A and Alpha Centauri B." Ariel was silent as she received another message from Clarissa. "Admiral Anlon is also sending orders to Admiral Barnes at New Tellus. Two of the system's light cruisers are being directed to join the search effort as well as the Battle Carrier Tellus. They will be deploying ten stealth scouts to jump to all the nearby systems."

"There are fifty-six star systems within sixteen light years of Earth, and nearly 200 within twenty-five light years," commented Jason, knowing it was going to take a while to search all of those star systems.

"Jason, what do you think happened?" asked Lisa, worried about Jeremy. If there had been an accident on the New Horizon, she hoped and prayed that no one had gotten hurt.

"This doesn't make any sense," Greg spoke with a growing frown on his face. "I'm going to contact General Greene down on Earth. This threat we had to the New Horizon mission several months ago may have been more serious than we had thought."

"You think the ship might have been sabotaged?" Lisa spoke, her hand going to her mouth.

"I'm starting to wonder," replied Greg, hoping that Katie was still okay. "We had a few names to go on, but all the rumors vanished several months ago. General Greene felt that it didn't need to be followed up. Now I'm wondering if we didn't make a big mistake."

"Make your call," said Jason, indicating the com console where an ensign from Ceres was sitting. "We need to get to the bottom of this as quickly as possible. We need to find the New Horizon."

Chapter Ten

For the next forty-eight hours, Jason literally lived in the Command Center of the Avenger, waiting for news on the New Horizon. Federation scout ships and warships were searching all of the nearby stars for any sign of the missing ship. Time after time, they came up empty. After each report, Jason's confusion grew. Where were the New Horizon and Jeremy?

"That's it," Ariel spoke as the Battle Carrier Tellus sent in its latest report. "All the star systems within twenty-five light years of Earth have been scanned. There is no sign of the New Horizon. Wherever they have gone, it's nowhere close by."

"How can that be?" Lisa asked, her eyes showing a lack of sleep and her face showing her frustration. It had been a rough forty-eight hours as the reports had slowly come in. It was as if the New Horizon had vanished.

"It means they made at least two additional jumps after leaving Tau Ceti," Jason surmised, not understanding why Commander Tellson would do such a thing. "Lisa, why don't you go get some rest? I will let you know if we hear anything." Jason could tell this was really taking a toll on her. She blamed herself for Katie stowing away on the ship, and now Jeremy was missing as well.

"I may have the answer," Greg said, striding into the Command Center with an extremely worrisome look upon his face. "I just finished talking to General Greene. He had his people pick up several of those individuals that were rumored to be threatening the New Horizon mission several months ago."

"Did they find out anything?" asked Jason, turning around to face Greg. He had been standing next to the com console listening as each ship reported in on their search results.

"It's bad, Jason," answered Greg, letting out a sharp breath. "Greene managed to get one of the people they picked up to talk. It seems there was a plan to hijack the New Horizon."

"To hijack the ship!" Lisa cried, her eyes growing wide in shock. "Why?"

"It seems they wanted to set up a colony far away from Earth. Their leader was Major Maher."

"Maher," repeated Jason, shaking his head in disbelief. "He's the executive officer on the New Horizon."

"Yeah," responded Greg, knowing his daughter was on board that ship somewhere. He didn't know what Maher would do when he found her. "It seems the group had a lot of money behind them, and they managed to get a number of their people through the screening process. Several very large bribes were paid, and it looks as if a few people may have been killed to keep the plan a secret."

Jason stepped over and put his arm around Lisa. He didn't know what to say.

"But how could they take over the New Horizon?" asked Lisa, feeling disbelief at what she had just heard. "Surely most of the crew would have been loyal to Commander Tellson?"

"They had weapons," Greg replied, his eyes focusing on Lisa and Jason. "Evidently they managed to ship a crate of armaments up to the New Horizon for Major Maher and his group to use in hijacking the ship."

"Do we know where they were headed?" asked Jason, wondering if they could use a Federation warship to catch up to the New Horizon before it got out of range. The jump drives on the Federation ships were more efficient and had a longer range. If they knew where the New Horizon was heading, they just might be able to catch up with her.

"That's the bad news," Greg replied with a grimace splitting his face. "Our informant says that Major Maher had picked out two open star clusters farther in toward the center of the galaxy. He plans on going coreward about eight to ten thousand light years before finding a world to set up a colony on."

"Toward Hocklyn controlled space," Jason said in a stunned voice. "If they head in that direction, they could well stumble across a Hocklyn support ship or a conquered world."

"That's what General Greene is worried about," responded Greg, nodding his head in agreement. "We don't know how far the Hocklyns have expanded their empire, but the New Horizon's eventual destination could well lie within Hocklyn controlled space."

"Can they go that far?" asked Lisa, fearing for Jeremy, Kelsey, and Katie's safety. "The New Horizon is a new ship; the first FTL capable ship Earth has ever built. Surely the ship isn't capable of going on such a long journey."

"That's the problem," Jason confessed in a troubled voice as he thought about the design of the ship. "Even though the New Horizon is Earth's first starship, we based her on Federation science. I don't know if the ship would be capable of going eight to ten thousand light years, but the New Horizon could manage at least a big part of that."

"What are we going to do?" asked Greg, fearing for Katie's safety. "We can't let them make it to Hocklyn space."

He also didn't know how he was going to explain this most recent bad news to his wife. Elizabeth had been very distraught when he had told her about Katie stowing away on the New Horizon. This was going to be much worse.

"We won't," answered Jason determinedly, thinking about their options and what they could do. Turning around, he looked over at the com officer. "Contact the flight bay and have my shuttle prepped. I'm going to Ceres. I need to speak in private to Admiral Anlon."

"What do you have in mind?" asked Lisa, wondering what Admiral Anlon could do. "Have you thought of a way to track the New Horizon and rescue Jeremy and Katie?"

"The WarStorm is scheduled to start her mission next week," responded Jason, thinking about the powerful Monarch Two cruiser under Colonel Sheen's command. "Her primary mission may have just changed."

On board the New Horizon, Lieutenant Nelson was gazing with shock and worried concern at the work being done on the drive core of the ship. A group of technicians and engineers were greatly expanding the core and the cooling system.

"Why are you doing this?" demanded Nelson, looking over at Major Maher. He was well aware of the two armed guards standing directly behind him. "This could be extremely dangerous. You shouldn't be trying to modify the drive core."

"We're going on a long trip," Maher replied as he watched the work being done. "We can't get there if it takes six hours or more for the drive core to cool back down after each jump. These modifications will allow the core to cool down in about three hours. That will greatly increase the amount of jumps we can do per day."

"The core wasn't built to be modified," Nelson responded as he looked over the modifications being made. "You could seriously endanger the ship or the FTL drive."

"I don't think so," replied Maher, turning to look at Nelson with a smug look upon his face. "I managed to sneak out the drive core design to some friends down on Earth. After a lot of study, they concluded that it wasn't built quite as efficiently as everyone had thought. These changes will bring it up to speed. All you have to worry about is getting us where I want to go. If you don't, or refuse to cooperate, you know what will happen to your little cadets."

Nelson was silent for a moment. They had jumped three additional times since leaving the Tau Ceti system. Major Maher had picked out the destination for each jump and then had double-checked the coordinates after they had been transferred into the navigation computer. "Where are we going?"

"You will know in good time," replied Maher, watching the engineers working on the core. As long as he had the cadets to threaten Nelson with, he figured the man would obey him.

"This ship wasn't designed for a long journey," continued Nelson, hoping to instill some doubt in Maher. He was worried that if they got too far from Earth, they would never be found.

"I just wanted to show you this," spoke Maher, turning to face Nelson directly. "If my people's calculations are correct, we can jump ten to twelve light years with each jump. I will give you the destination each time. Your job is to make sure we get there, and you know the penalty for failure."

"I will do your navigation calculations," responded Nelson, knowing at least for now he had no other choice. He couldn't let any harm come to those cadets. "You just make sure those cadets are left alone."

"Very well," replied Maher, feeling satisfied with Nelson's answer. "Guards, take Lieutenant Nelson back to his quarters."

Maher watched as the guards ushered Nelson out of Engineering. Then, walking over to one of the engineers who was working on the drive core, he asked, "How much longer until the core is ready?" He was growing impatient to be on their way.

"Another four hours," replied Ensign Treadwell, standing up and stretching. He had been working on a console that controlled the drive core. "Some of these adjustments are very delicate."

"I don't care how delicate they are!" Maher roared in a loud voice, drawing the attention of most of the personnel working on the core. "I just want it done, and done right!"

"We can't rush it," Treadwell responded nervously, his eyes focused on the floor. He didn't want to say or do anything to aggravate Maher. He had witnessed how failing to do as Maher ordered could result in a beating or worse. One of the engineering technicians had been shot earlier in the day for refusing to work on the drive core. "Some of these adjustments take time, particularly with the expanded cooling system we are installing. I can't guarantee how long it will last. We are also using a lot of our spare parts up building this. If something goes wrong, we may not be able to repair it."

"Just so it lasts long enough," Maher warned, his eyes gazing piercingly at Treadwell. "If it fails, I will hold you personally responsible."

Treadwell's face turned pale as he nodded his head in understanding. "I will make sure it won't fail," he stammered.

Maher nodded and then turning, left Engineering. Ensign Bates could oversee the rest. Bates had already loaded his computer program into the engineering system so no one could activate the ship's FTL drive without first inputting Maher's own password.

Jeremy and Kevin were sitting in their quarters watching the vid screen. At least they were allowed to access the ship's entertainment library. The library contained thousands of movies and other forms of entertainment to watch. Their door suddenly sliding open caused both of them to take notice.

"Hello, daddy's boy," Matt Barr spoke from where he was standing just outside the door. He stepped inside and tossed two loosely wrapped sandwiches and two bottles of water onto one of the bunks. Behind him, Ensign Rafferty watched with a smirk on his face. "There are your rations for the day. Enjoy."

"Why did you side with them, Matt?" Kevin asked, his eyes focusing on Barr. "These people are killers. Do you really want to be a part of what they're doing?"

"Yeah, so they are," commented Barr with little concern. "Certain individuals on the New Horizon had to be removed. For your information, I have been a part of this plan from the very beginning."

"What plan?" demanded Kevin, wanting to understand what was going on.

"It's quite simple really, freckles," Barr spoke contemptuously "We're taking the New Horizon and leaving this section of the galaxy. Earth can have this section of space; we're going on a long trip and will be setting up our own colony away from all of Earth's prejudices and misguided government policies."

Kevin became silent; he didn't know what else to say. If Maher succeeded, they might never see Earth again.

Jeremy had been quiet, not wanting to provoke Barr. However, he couldn't help asking. "What about the command crew and Commander Tellson, what happened to them?"

"They won't be a problem," Rafferty said, running his finger across his throat. "You just need to worry about yourself and when it will be your turn."

"What do you mean, our turn?" Kevin demanded, his eyes widening at the implication of what had happened to the command crew.

"It's simple," replied Barr coldly, his eyes focusing on Jeremy. "Major Maher promised that I would be the one to get rid of you. You're probably safe, Walters, but daddy's boy here is all mine. As soon as Major Maher feels the admiral can't come after us then I get the pleasure of disposing of daddy's boy here. Maybe I'll just shoot you, or perhaps I will place you in one of the airlocks and slowly bleed out all of the air. Either way, I'll make sure you suffer."

"Let's go check on the girls," Rafferty commented with a leer on his face. "Kelsey and Amanda are waiting."

"Stay away from them," warned Jeremy, standing up, his hand closing in a fist.

"Screw you, Jeremy," Barr laughed as he stepped back outside the door. "The girls are ours now, and there's nothing you can do about it." Barr reached forward and shut the door.

"Do you think Angela and Kelsey are in trouble?" Kevin asked worriedly, looking over at Jeremy.

"I hope not," replied Jeremy, feeling anger running through him. He felt so helpless locked here in these quarters. He hadn't liked the look on either Rafferty or Barr's faces. "The girls can handle themselves for now." Jeremy sat back down on his bunk, thinking about Kelsey and Angela. He just hoped he was right, and the girls would be okay.

Jason had reached Ceres and was on his way to the admiral's office. Admiral Anlon's office was deep inside the asteroid and heavily shielded. In case of a Hocklyn attack, it and the area around it were nearly impervious to nuclear bombardment. This area deep inside of Ceres contained the defense headquarters for the Federation survivors.

Reaching the admiral's office, a marine guard opened the door, allowing Jason to enter. Stepping inside, Jason saw that Admiral Anlon was talking to several fleet officers who were sitting in front of his desk.

"Admiral Strong, I'm glad you could join us. We were just making plans to increase the size of our search radius. Commander Krill has suggested we expand the radius to fifty light years."

"That's about as far as we can expand it, I'm afraid," Commander Krill spoke, turning his head toward Jason. "Any larger than that and it will involve too many stars to search. It could take years."

"That's not the problem, I'm afraid," Jason spoke, his eyes focusing on Admiral Anlon. He had not yet told the admiral what General Greene had found out down on Earth. "The New Horizon has been hijacked and is currently on its way core ward toward Hocklyn controlled space."

All three of the Federation officers looked at Jason, stunned by his announcement. "Hijacked, on its way toward Hocklyn space?" Admiral Anlon stammered, his face turning pale. "How do you know all of this?"

Jason sat down in one of the empty chairs in front of the admiral's desk and began explaining where he had gotten his information. Admiral Anlon asked several questions, as did the other two fleet officers. Jason tried to answer them as best as he could.

"If I understand you correctly, Admiral, a terrorist group managed to infiltrate the crew of the New Horizon, then hijack it at Tau Ceti and are even now jumping toward Hocklyn controlled space?" asked Commander Krill.

"That's correct," Jason replied with a heavy sigh. "It was very well orchestrated, and they managed to sneak their people through all of our security screenings. We only learned recently that several of the screeners have met mysterious deaths over the last few months. There were also some very hefty deposits made into their bank accounts just before they died."

Anlon leaned back in his chair and closed his eyes in disbelief. This could ruin everything. Then, opening his eyes, he gazed back at Jason. "We have three Federation people on board the New Horizon. What do you think the hijackers have done to the crew?" He didn't need to add that one of those three Federation people was his daughter.

"They will need the majority of the crew to help operate the ship," Jason replied. He had already thought about this. "They will need the scientists to help evaluate whatever planet they eventually find to settle on." Jason then hesitated for a moment, this was the part he didn't like and knew that Admiral Anlon wouldn't want to hear. "They will also undoubtedly save all the women crewmembers for breeding purposes when they reach their new world."

Admiral Anlon let out a sharp breath. He slowly shook his head. If anyone of them touched his daughter, he would make sure they suffered for it. "What can we do? This is a big galaxy to search for one spaceship."

Jason looked at the other three officers. "We put some failsafes on board the New Horizon in case something went wrong. One of those failsafes is an FTL communicator that is only known to the two Federation officers on board the New Horizon. It's my hope that, at some point in time, they will try to contact us."

Admiral Anlon nodded. He had forgotten about that. "The only problem is that the FTL communicator only has a range of several hundred light years, once they're past that point they won't be able to contact us."

"That's why we need to send the WarStorm after them," Jason said, gazing intently at Admiral Anlon. "We know the general direction they're heading. If the WarStorm was to follow, there is a chance they might be able to pick up that transmission."

Admiral Anlon reached out and pressed a com button on his desk. "Get me Admiral Barnes on New Tellus right now. I have a new mission for the WarStorm." Admiral Anlon was glad that one of their recent technological advances allowed them to communicate almost instantaneously with New Tellus. A series of FTL signal boosting satellites had been placed in a direct line between Ceres and New Tellus.

"We won't just be sending the WarStorm," Admiral Anlon commented as he reached an important decision. "We will be sending a fleet!"

Colonel Sheen was listening to her new orders with shock. Admiral Barnes had requested her presence on board the shipyard for an emergency meeting. She could scarcely believe what she was hearing.

"How could terrorists hijack the New Horizon?" she asked still trying to fathom how this could possibly have occurred. It sounded like a nightmare.

"We're not completely sure yet, but Admiral Anlon's daughter is on board as well as Admiral Strong's son," Admiral Barnes replied in a serious and concerned tone. Her eyes took on a grave look. "From what Admiral Strong's people have been able to find out, the New Horizon is heading toward Hocklyn space."

"Can they reach it?" asked Amanda, feeling doubtful that a ship built by Earth could make it that far. Particularly since this was their first working starship.

"Possibly," Admiral Barnes replied. "Since the ship is partially of Federation design and is based on Federation science, it does have the potential to make it to the outskirts of what we believe is Hocklyn controlled space."

"What are we going to do?" Amanda asked with growing concern. She knew that neither the Federation survivors nor Earth were ready for a conflict with the Hocklyns. It would be years yet before they were ready for that war.

"Fortunately, there are two Federation officers in the New Horizon's crew. There is also an emergency FTL transmitter hidden on board. It is our hope that, at some point in time, one of the two officers will manage to get off a message."

"What's the range of the transmitter?"

"Only two hundred light years," admitted Admiral Barnes, shaking her head. "We need to have a ship in position to receive that message."

Amanda nodded her head in agreement as she realized what was at stake. The New Horizon must be found before it reached Hocklyn space. "What are my orders?"

"We are activating a number of ships on Ceres as well as several that are docked in the construction bays here. It will stretch us to find the crews, but it has to be done. The Battle Carrier New Tellus will be going with you as well, as four light cruisers. The Tellus is being equipped with twenty additional stealth scouts that can be used to form a net around the main fleet to help detect any incoming signal. The ships we are activating will serve as their security replacements until you return."

"This is a tall order, Admiral," commented Amanda, knowing the odds of finding the New Horizon were not good. "What are my orders if we reach Hocklyn space without finding the ship?"

"The New Tellus and the four light cruisers will stay just outside of Hocklyn space and continue to monitor the FTL communication frequencies, while you continue on to complete your original mission. Once that is complete, you will return to the waiting fleet and return home."

Colonel Sheen stood up. "We will do our best, Admiral."

"I know you will," Admiral Barnes replied. "I have already given orders to have your ships loaded with the necessary supplies and spare parts. Just bring that ship back home safely if it's possible."

A few hours later, Amanda was back on board the WarStorm. The crew was still busy stowing all the supplies that had been brought hurriedly on board. As soon as she arrived, she ordered the ship to move away from the shipyard, but then had to belay that order as Admiral Barnes contacted her and informed her that additional marines were being assigned to the WarStorm.

They waited as the detachment of heavily armed marines boarded the ship. There were already one hundred marines on board; this would bring the marine complement up to two hundred and twenty. All of the marines were highly trained and from Earth special forces. Amanda knew they might be needed to retake the New Horizon or fend off Hocklyn protectors if the WarStorm were boarded.

As soon as the marines were safely on board, she gave the order for the WarStorm to move away from the shipyard. Once they were a safe distance away, she gave the order to activate the ship's sublight drive. In moments, the ship was moving rapidly away from the shipyard. Two light cruisers were following close behind, quickly dropping into formation with the WarStorm.

"So we're going on a rescue mission," Major Fields commented as he stood up and turned the command console over to Colonel Sheen.

"Yes," Amanda replied. "It's going to be like looking for a needle in a haystack, but we need to find the New Horizon before the Hocklyns."

"So we might be going into a war situation."

"It's possible," admitted Amanda, unhappily.

"The New Tellus has jumped back into the system, along with two additional light cruisers," Lieutenant Stalls reported as three green icons blossomed on his long-range sensor screen. "I am picking up two fleet supply ships leaving the shipyard."

"Those will be additional supplies for the New Tellus and the two light cruisers," Amanda commented. "There will also be some stealth scouts that will be rendezvousing with the New Tellus shortly. As soon as all ships are adequately provisioned, we will be jumping out. Lieutenant Ashton, plot three jumps of ten light years each inward toward the galactic core. Once we reach that point, we will begin deploying the fleet to detect any incoming messages."

"Do you think we will hear from them?" Major Fields asked with doubt on his face. It was going to be a big area they were going to have to cover.

"I hope so," Amanda replied with a worried look upon her face. "From what Admiral Barnes said there are two Federation officers in the New Horizon's crew. Both men are supposed to be very dependable. If there is any way they can get a message to us, Admiral Anlon feels confident they will do so."

Major Fields looked out over the Command Center. He had confidence in the crew, but detecting this message and being in the right spot at the right time was something else.

On board the New Horizon, the modifications to the FTL drive core were complete. Major Maher had called his new command crew into the Command Center. Lieutenant Sandusky would be handling the second duty crew, and Lieutenant Barr would be responsible for the third.

Looking over at Navigation, he saw with satisfaction that Lieutenant Nelson was working on the FTL coordinates for the first jump. An armed guard stood watchfully behind him. While most of the crew didn't like what was happening, they had been reluctant to resist. This was what Maher had expected. His people controlled the only weapons on board. The only officer left to rally around was Lieutenant Nelson, and he was being kept under heavy guard with little or no contact with the other crewmembers.

"Ship is ready to jump, sir," the helm officer reported as Lieutenant Nelson finished loading the jump coordinates.

Major Maher quickly called up the jump coordinates on the command console and looked closely at them. They looked right, and he nodded at the ensign sitting at the Helm. "Engage the FTL drive and let's begin our journey."

In front of the New Horizon, a swirling blue-white vortex formed. The helm officer carefully maneuvered the ship into the center of the vortex, and the New Horizon jumped into hyperspace.

Kelsey felt the sudden queasiness she associated with an FTL jump and knew the New Horizon had jumped again. At least her stomach was empty, so she didn't feel that nauseous.

"Where are they taking us?" asked Angela, her face turning pale. "How is anyone ever going to find us?"

"Just have faith, Angela," Kelsey replied as she walked into the small bathroom at the back of their quarters and ran a little water. She used a wet washcloth to wipe across her face. It helped to relieve the queasiness. Just as she stepped back into the main part of their quarters, the door slid open. With unease, Kelsey saw a grinning Ensign Rafferty standing there.

"Hello, girls," he said, allowing his eyes to roam leeringly up and down Angela's body. "I don't suppose you have thought about my offer?" he asked.

"Forget it," Angela spoke with distaste in her voice. "You're not my type."

"As I said, you might change your mind when you get hungry enough," replied Rafferty, tossing one sandwich and a bottle of water on Kelsey's bunk. "I'm on my way to eat a steak. You could be too if you were to reconsider my offer. Come with me right now if you like."

"Never!" Angela cried, her heart beating wildly in her chest, as she grew angry at the mere thought of what Rafferty was suggesting. "Leave us alone!"

Rafferty laughed and shook his head. "We have plenty of time. Eventually, you will take me up on my offer." Rafferty stepped back and closed the door. Turning, he started walking back down the corridor with a contented smile on his face. He had already talked to Barr and, once they arrived at their destination, Angela was his.

"Kelsey, what are we going to do?" Angela wailed as her pent up emotions burst forth.

"I don't know," answered Kelsey, worriedly. She wished there were someway to get out of their quarters. She needed to know if Lieutenant Nelson was still alive. Picking up the sandwich, she passed Angela half of it. "Eat this; it will make you feel better."

"I just wish we knew how Jeremy and Kevin are doing," Angela said as she took a small bite of the sandwich. "We don't even know if they're still okay."

Kelsey nodded. That really concerned her also. She suspected that since Jeremy was Admiral Strong's son, he was probably being kept as a hostage in case the admiral managed to catch up to them. Kelsey knew that they were in a bad situation, but what worried Kelsey the most was how much longer Jeremy would be worth keeping alive, particularly considering how Barr felt about him.

In the small shuttle in the flight bay, Katie was feeling very frightened at her current situation. She didn't see any way out of her predicament. If she revealed herself, the terrorists might very well kill her. There was no way she could free any of the others, and even if she did what could they do? They had no weapons and no way to take over the New Horizon.

Leaning back in the pilot's seat, Katie started thinking really hard about what she could do. The ship was run by computers, and Katie was a computer genius. Looking at her handheld computer, an idea began to form in her mind. What if there was a way she could take control of the ship, maybe not for a long amount of time, but just long enough to free Jeremy and Kelsey? If they were in a system with a suitable planet, they could use the shuttle to escape.

Taking a deep breath, she knew it wasn't the best escape plan. It would leave them marooned in deep space, but it was better than dying on the New Horizon. Looking at her computer, Katie began writing a new program. She already had access to some of the ship's systems. She had an idea that would give her access to all the rest.

Back in the New Tellus system, Colonel Sheen was finally ready for the first jump. The fleet ships had taken up their escorting positions with the New Tellus in the center and the WarStorm slightly above and to one side. At an order from Amanda, blue-white vortexes began to form in front of the fleet.

"Do you think we will find them?" Richard asked from where he was standing behind her.

"I hope so," Amanda replied as the WarStorm moved toward the swirling vortex in front of it. "A lot of people are counting on us."

"Light cruisers are jumping," Major Fields reported as the light cruisers began disappearing from the holographic plotting table. "The battle carrier is jumping next." Moments later, its large green icon vanished. "We're next."

Moments later, Amanda felt the familiar jump into hyperspace. Their mission had begun, and she wondered just what they would find. Somewhere in their future, she hoped the New Horizon waited. She just prayed that they found the hijacked ship before the Hocklyns did, or the war of the future might start very shortly.

Chapter Eleven

First Leader Shrea stared moodily at the viewscreens across the front wall of the War Room. They were covered with stars and little else. The Vengeance, her six escort cruisers, and the two supply ships had arrived in this far off section of space two days ago and had only recently started their search for inhabited worlds. They were over two thousand light years from Rateif's base, which was responsible for exploring this entire sector. Never before had he been so far away from Hocklyn controlled space. If anything went wrong, they would be on their own. At least they had the two supply ships that had been sent with them that were packed to the brim with supplies and spare parts.

Shrea allowed his large dark eyes to gaze with scrutiny around the War Room of his war cruiser. The crew was busy using the ship's sensors to finish the detailed scans of the system they had chosen to use as their forward base. They were working efficiently and quickly as expected of them. The 1000-meter Vengeance and the two supply ships would be staying in this system, while the six support ships began searching the nearby stars for civilizations to add to the Hocklyn Slave Empire. Shrea was impatient to get the search started. It had taken seventy long days to reach this point in space. He could have gotten the fleet here quicker by using longer jumps, but he had seen no reason to stress their drive systems. Repairs would be difficult this far from a properly equipped fleet base.

"The Anvil and StarSeeker have left to go to their assigned search quadrant," Second Leader Vrill reported as he approached the command pedestal. "The other four support ships will be receiving their assigned search quadrants shortly."

"Very well," Shrea replied in his rasping voice. His large, cold eyes gazed sharply at his second in command. "What do you think of this plan to search for new worlds to add to our empire?"

Vrill was silent for a moment. It was very seldom that the First Leader asked for his opinion. "We must find honor," replied Vrill, choosing his words carefully. "We were finding no honor where we were searching. Perhaps this area will be rich in worlds to add to the empire."

"I hope that you are correct," replied Shrea, his eyes drilling into his second in command. "If not, then I fear our families will suffer a significant loss of honor and prestige. Make sure the First Leaders of our support ships understand that. We must not fail!"

Shrea's large eyes returned to the main viewscreen. A blue-green planet was now visible. This planet was one of the reasons they had chosen this particular system as a base. It had a habitable world that could be used to furnish fresh water as well as food for the fleet. It would be necessary to send a complement of protectors and engineers down to the planet's surface to build a small processing facility. However, once the food and water processing facility was complete, it would allow them to stay in this sector for an extended period of time.

Shrea took in a deep and long breath. Now the waiting game began. Each day, the support cruisers were scheduled to report in on their findings. Each ship had been assigned two systems per day to search. It wouldn't take long to discover if this section of space contained the inhabited worlds that Commodore Rateif was counting on.

Gazing at the blue-green world on the viewscreen, Shrea wished sometimes that the Hocklyn High Council would allow additional colonization. The home systems were becoming extremely over crowded. Additional space habitats were constantly being built to contain the ever-growing populations in the home systems. It was even reported that the sunlight on several worlds had been reduced because of all of the habitats in orbit. The problem was the AIs. They had made it extremely plain that no new worlds could be colonized by the Hocklyns. Looking at the blue-green world on the viewscreen, he wondered how the AIs would ever know if the Hocklyns established a new colony if it was this far out.

Shrea let out a deep breath. It was useless and counter productive to have such dangerous thoughts. The consequences of the AIs finding an unauthorized colony were too terrifying to even contemplate. No, the Hocklyn race would have to find another solution to their growing population problem.

Jeremy was feeling bored. For over two months, Kevin and he had been cooped up in their quarters. They had spent most of their time watching the vid screen and talking. However, after two long months of not being allowed out of their quarters, they were rapidly running out of things to say to each other. They also hadn't seen or heard from the girls in that time. Jeremy was deeply concerned for the girl's safety, particularly with Matt Barr and Rafferty on board the New

Horizon. Jeremy found that he was spending a lot of time thinking about Kelsey. Every day they were locked here in their quarters, the greater his concern for her grew.

"I've been thinking," said Kevin sitting up, sliding his legs off his bunk, and looking despairingly over at Jeremy. "We have been jumping five times per day now for over sixty days. We must be thousands of light years from Earth. Unless we can think of someway soon to retake this ship, we won't ever be able to go home again."

Jeremy sat up and gazed over at Kevin. He had been thinking about the same thing. If they were jumping ten light years during each jump, they had come at least 3,000 light years. Even if his father equipped all four of the smaller exploration cruisers with FTL drives, they would never be able to find the New Horizon. It would be like searching for a needle in a haystack, and the galaxy was an extremely large haystack. He also could tell that Kevin was becoming more depressed with each passing day of inaction.

"I don't know what we can do," spoke Jeremy, allowing his frustration with their situation to show. "They control all the weapons, and from what we have been able to get Barr and Rafferty to tell us, all the command crew except Lieutenant Nelson were killed in the takeover."

"Major Maher is a cold-blooded murderer," Kevin said passionately with anger in his eyes. He had become extremely close to some of those that Maher had ordered killed over the long months of training.

"It's best we remember that," Jeremy reminded Kevin, his eyes narrowing. "We need to watch what we say and do around them, or we could be next."

"Lieutenant Nelson is our only chance," responded Kevin, wondering why Nelson hadn't done anything. "The loyal part of the crew would follow his lead if he tried to retake the ship."

"But how many would die?" asked Jeremy, pointedly. He too felt the crew would rally around Nelson. "We know these people are ruthless and won't hesitate to kill when pushed."

Their talking was interrupted as their door opened. Ensign Rafferty was standing there with two armed guards. "All right you two, come with us. Major Maher wants to speak with you."

"What about?" Jeremy asked as he stood up. He wondered what Maher could want. This would be the first time since the takeover that they had been allowed out of their quarters.

"Don't ask any stupid questions!" Rafferty spoke in a harsh voice, looking irritated. "The major will tell you what you need to know when we get there."

They were escorted in silence to the officer's mess and were surprised to find Kelsey and Angela sitting at a table. Rafferty indicated for Jeremy and Kevin to join them. "Sit down and be quiet."

"Jeremy!" spoke Kelsey, jumping up and hugging him tightly. Her eyes showing intense relief at seeing him unharmed. "We were so worried about you and Kevin."

"We're fine," answered Jeremy as he held on to Kelsey. Letting her go, he looked her over and noticed with relief that she looked unharmed. A little thin, but otherwise she looked okay. "We haven't been allowed to leave our quarters since the takeover."

"Us either," commented Angela as she looked over with obvious distaste at Rafferty.

"Sit down!" Rafferty ordered with a scowl on his face. He didn't like the way Kelsey had jumped up and hugged Jeremy. This was something he would have to mention to Barr later.

The three cadets sat down, with Kelsey sitting next to Jeremy and Kevin next to Angela. All four wondered what was going on. Why had they been brought to the officer's mess?

"Enjoy yourselves for now," Rafferty commented snidely as one of the guards brought over a tray of freshly made sandwiches and tea. "It might be a while before we allow you out of your cages again."

"We'd better eat," spoke Jeremy, reaching for a sandwich and keeping a wary eye on Rafferty. He didn't know what was going on, and he was even more surprised that they were being allowed to eat a decent meal.

The girls nodded, reaching for sandwiches. Jeremy could see by the way the two girls were eating that they seemed to be extremely hungry. He wondered if food was being withheld from them. What kind of game were Barr and Rafferty playing with the two girls?

"These are better than what we normally get," Kevin spoke quietly as he reached for a second sandwich.

"Much better," Angela agreed as she swallowed the last bite of her ham sandwich and reached for another.

Jeremy's eyes were suddenly drawn to the open doorway as Maher stepped in. What does he want, Jeremy wondered? His eyes focused on the former executive officer with distaste. He knew that, under this man's orders, a lot of good people had died. People he had known and became friends with.

Maher walked over to the table and looked down at the four cadets. "As you know, the New Horizon is now under my command. We have another sixty days to go before we reach the destination I have chosen to establish our colony. You two girls are being kept alive for obvious reasons; we will need all the females on this ship to help expand our population once we reach our new world. As for you, Cadet Strong and your friend Cadet Walters, there is no real reason to keep you alive. We are far out of range of any possibility of your father ever finding us."

Jeremy felt an icy hand grip his heart. Looking over at Kevin, Jeremy could see that Kevin's face had turned extremely pale. Forcing himself to look up, he gazed at Maher. "What do you want?"

Maher allowed a fleeting smile to cross his face. "It's very simple, Cadet Strong; I want the four of you back in the Command Center. You have all been trained to operate the various Command Center stations and at the moment, we are slightly shorthanded in that department. If the four of you agree to return and obey my orders, I will spare you and Cadet Walters from being executed. If not, then consider this your final meal."

"You wouldn't dare harm them," Angela broke in, her face in shock at hearing Maher's words. "Admiral Strong would kill you when he catches up to you."

"I have already killed a number of people on this ship who stood in my way, what's a few more?" responded Maher, looking unconcerned. 'Besides, Admiral Strong will never be able to find us. You can kiss Earth and your former lives goodbye. You will never be going back!"

Angela looked over at Kelsey and said nothing. It was hard to imagine she would never see her family or friends back on Earth again. The reality of that was starting to set in. She could feel her hands start to tremble as she realized what might be in store for Kelsey and her.

Jeremy was silent as he looked over at Kevin. He knew they had no choice. It would also at least get them out of their quarters and around more of the crew. It might also give them an opportunity to speak to Lieutenant Nelson. "Okay, we will do it," Jeremy said in an even voice. "But Barr and Rafferty have to leave the girls alone."

Maher laughed derisively and glanced over knowingly at the two girls. "For now that's acceptable, but once we reach our destination the girls are on their own."

Jeremy nodded. He knew that, for now, there was nothing else they could do.

-

Katie had been watching over the small viewscreen in the shuttle. She had been excited and relieved to see Jeremy and Kelsey brought into the officer's mess. They both looked okay but a little thin. It was a shame that the surveillance cameras throughout the ship, except those in the Command Center, didn't allow sound. She really wanted to hear Jeremy or Kelsey's voice.

Leaning back in the pilot's seat, Katie thought about her current deplorable situation. She really missed her parents. Her mother would be frantic over Katie's continued absence. It had been a serious mistake to sneak aboard the New Horizon, Katie now realized. However, she also knew that she might be Jeremy and Kelsey's only real hope of escaping. From what she had seen over the viewscreen in the past two months, she guessed that nearly a quarter of the crew were now actively supporting Major Maher.

Getting up, she walked the few steps back into the shuttle's main compartment. Getting a bottle of water out of a storage compartment, she sat down and looked speculatively at her computer. The program she had been working on was finally complete. All she needed now was for the New Horizon to come close enough to a habitable world so she could set her plan into motion. If everything worked out right, she might just be able to work out an escape.

-

Colonel Sheen gazed down at the latest reports. There had still been no sign of the New Horizon. "It's as if they've vanished," she said with a frown, looking over at Richard. He was standing next to her in the Command Center, reading the various reports as she did.

"They could have changed directions, we could have passed them, or they could still be ahead of us," responded Richard, feeling the anxiety. Everyone was worried about what would happen if the New Horizon stumbled across a Hocklyn controlled world or ship.

"We have to find them before the Hocklyns do!" Amanda said, passionately. "Our entire future civilization depends on it. All the information the Hocklyns will need to find Earth is in that ship's navigation computer and on their star maps."

Getting up, Amanda walked over to the large holographic plotting table. Pressing a few buttons, a view of the surrounding stars appeared above the table. The four light cruisers were spread out in a circle fifty light years from the WarStorm. Fifty light years beyond them, there were twenty scout ships. Only the New Tellus remained with the WarStorm.

"We have an area of space two hundred light years across covered with our ships," spoke Amanda, gazing intently at the holographic image and wondering if there were anything else she could do. "If they are even close to their estimated course, we should intercept any message sent from that ship."

"If the two Federation officers on the New Horizon can get to the FTL transmitter and send a message," Richard reminded her. "For all we know, they both could have been killed in the hijacking."

"Let's hope not," said Amanda, feeling her heart pounding at that worrisome thought. "If they were killed, then we might not be able to find the New Horizon before they stumble into the Hocklyns." That was Amanda's biggest fear. The Hocklyns couldn't be allowed to discover the location of Earth. If they did, then the future for the human race was over.

Richard was quiet as he knew that Amanda was right. He understood his wife was extremely worried about the New Horizon and what could happen if the Hocklyns found the ship before they did. Everything that Admiral Streth had worked for could be lost if the Hocklyns learned of Earth's location prematurely. Amanda wasn't sleeping well at nights, and several times he had woken up in the middle of the night to find her missing from their bed. Getting up, he had found her sitting at her desk poring over star maps. Letting out a deep breath, Richard knew that all they could do was hope.

Jeremy looked pensively around the Command Center. Kelsey was at Navigation, Angela at Communications, and Kevin was at the ship's sensor console. Jeremy was standing at the plotting table waiting for Major Maher's next order. Letting out a deep breath, he thought about the last several weeks since they had been allowed to return to the Command Center. Only once had he seen Lieutenant Nelson, and that had been only briefly. Nelson had said hello as they passed in one of the corridors. One thing that Jeremy had taken note of was how heavily guarded Nelson was. From the reports that he had heard, Nelson always had two heavily armed guards with him wherever he went. No wonder the lieutenant had not been able to do anything about the hijacking.

"Lieutenant Strong, commence the next jump," ordered Maher, looking over at Jeremy.

"Are the coordinates in the navigation computer?" Jeremy asked Kelsey over his mini-com. At least since they had returned to the Command Center, Kevin and he had been allowed to eat with the girls. He also knew that Kelsey and Lieutenant Nelson were the only two that Maher trusted to plot the jumps. Jeremy suspected that had played a big part in why they had been allowed back into the Command Center.

"They're in," affirmed Kelsey, looking back at Jeremy with a weak smile. "The jump will be 10.2 light years."

"Helm, activate the FTL drive and commence jump," Jeremy ordered.

Instantly in front of the New Horizon, a blue-white vortex of swirling light formed. The helm officer maneuvered the ship into it, and the New Horizon jumped into hyperspace.

Jeremy felt the ship make the transition and, looking over at Kelsey, saw the pale look on her face. Even after all of these jumps, she still felt queasy each time the ship entered and left hyperspace. He was beginning to doubt if she would ever get used to it.

For over an hour, the ship remained in hyperspace. Occasionally Major Maher would contact Engineering and ask about the heat buildup in the core. Jeremy knew that the core had been modified. He also knew from overhearing several of the ship's engineers talk that the core was beginning to fail. The ship had not been designed to make the lengthy jumps that Maher was insisting on. The engineers had begged him repeatedly to reduce the jumps to six light years or less to reduce the strain on the drive core, but Maher had stubbornly refused to lessen the length of the jumps.

Listening closely over his mini-com, Jeremy could hear Maher even now talking to one of the ship's engineers.

"I don't care what it takes, you keep that core functioning," Maher threatened, his voice rising in anger. "If it fails I will personally push the button on the airlock sending you out into space."

"Yes, sir," the engineer stammered. "We will do everything we can."

"See to it," Maher spoke. He turned to glare at Jeremy. "Your father should have constructed a better ship. If this ship fails before we reach our destination, I will turn you over to Lieutenant Barr. He is still highly upset that I allowed you back into the Command Center as it is."

"I'm sure the ship will make it," replied Jeremy, attempting to placate Maher. The man seemed to have an extremely short temper. "The engineers will keep the drive core functioning."

"They better," warned Maher, turning his attention back to the command console.

Katie waited pensively for the New Horizon to drop out of hyperspace. Being alone for such a long time with no one to talk to was starting to get on her nerves. She really missed the long talks with Ariel and even those with her mother. This lengthy time alone had made her realize just how big a pain she had been to those she loved and at times had taken for granted.

For several weeks now she had been ready to implement her plan, all she needed was a habitable world to escape to. However, each time the New Horizon completed a jump, the ship did a minimum amount of scans and then, as soon as the drive core cooled down sufficiently, jumped again. Katie was beginning to fear that her escape attempt might have to wait until they arrived at their eventual destination. She was also deeply concerned that, at some point in time, someone would come into the flight bay to check on the shuttles. On several occasions, members of the ship's crew had come into the flight bay for quick inspections, but they hadn't done anything more than glance at the shuttles and go on.

Katie stood up and stretched. Walking back into the main cabin, she pulled down one of the small bunks on the wall and lay down. It was becoming increasingly difficult to fall asleep. If the New Horizon didn't reach its destination soon, Katie didn't know what she would do. Closing her eyes, she thought about Jeremy and Kelsey. She would really like to talk to either of them.

More time passed, and Jeremy fell back into a normal routine in the Command Center. Days passed by, and the days became weeks. They were making fewer jumps each day as the engineers were beginning to have some serious cooling problems with the drive core. On the last jump, it had taken nearly six hours for the core to cool back down, and Major Maher had been livid. He had left Jeremy in charge of the Command Center, informing the two armed guards that were always present to keep on eye him. Maher had then marched down to

Engineering to speak to the ship's engineers. Jeremy wasn't sure what happened in Engineering, but when Maher returned, his face was dark and covered with a scowl.

Walking over to the plotting table, Maher almost shoved Jeremy out of the way. He entered some commands and called up a detailed star map of their current location. Carefully examining the map, he chose three G type stars similar in size and age to Earth's sun.

"Ensign Grainger," he grated out. "Come over here!"

Kelsey stood up and walked over to the plotting table, not sure what Maher could want.

Pointing to the three stars he had chosen, he said, "Plot jump coordinates to this first star here. Thanks to those incompetent engineers, our drive core is about to fail. We will search all three of these stars for a habitable world to settle."

Jeremy was silent as he gazed at Kelsey. Their journey was almost over. When they reached Maher's new world, what would that mean for the crew of the New Horizon that hadn't as of yet sided with Maher? More than that, Jeremy wondered what it might mean for Kelsey, Angela, Kevin, and him.

Later, the four of them were in the officer's mess eating under guard. They had made the first jump and the system had not possessed any planets in the liquid water zone. This had infuriated Maher, he had ordered the cadets out and called Lieutenant Nelson to the Command Center.

"What's going to happen to us?" asked Angela deeply concerned and frightened that their journey might nearly be over. Several times recently, Ensign Rafferty had commented snidely that she would be his when they finally arrived at their new world. Angela had already decided that she would rather die than submit to Rafferty.

"I don't know," Jeremy responded. He tried to think of what his father would do in this situation. His dad was one of the bravest men he knew. He had to be after what he had faced upon first finding the Avenger. One thing he knew about his dad; he would never give up, no matter what the odds. "We just need to play it by ear, and if we get an opportunity to escape, we need to take it."

"That means we may have to wait until we get down to the planet Maher intends to colonize," spoke Kevin, knowing that might be their only hope of survival and keeping the four of them safe and together." Living on a new planet with very few supplies might be nearly impossible. But it would be significantly better than submitting to Maher's group and their plans.

"Barr and Rafferty just walked in," warned Kelsey, seeing the two enter the officer's mess. "Be careful what you say."

"Hello, daddy's boy," Barr spoke arrogantly, striding over to stand next to Jeremy. "I hear our trip is about over. That means in a few more days, you're all mine. Should I shoot you, or just blow you out of one of the airlocks?"

Jeremy said nothing; he just took another bite of his food. Right now, Barr held the upper hand. With the armed guards watching, there was nothing Jeremy could do. Sometimes he felt so powerless due to the situation he was in. He would like nothing better than to stand up and knock that smug look off Barr's face.

"You shouldn't say things like that, Matt," Kelsey spoke, her face flushed red with anger. She hated when Matt came in and threatened Jeremy as he did at every opportunity.

Barr hesitated for a moment as he looked thoughtfully at Kelsey, and then spoke. "We might be able to work out an agreement if you want daddy's boy here to live."

"What sort of agreement?" Kelsey asked, already suspecting where Barr was going with this.

"It's really quite simple," Barr said with a conniving grin. "When we reach the planet, you're going to live with me and Angela with Rafferty. If the two of you agree to that, then Jeremy and Kevin might live a little longer. There will be a lot of hard work to be done once we arrive at our destination, and I might be able to find something for them to do. What do the two of you say?"

"Forget it, Barr," Jeremy spoke, his eyes rising and locking unflinchingly with Matt's eyes. "I would rather die than see you humiliate either of the girls."

Barr laughed. He patted the pistol at his waist. "It really doesn't matter," he said taking a step back. "The girls will be ours anyway, and it's only a short matter of time before Major Maher turns you and Kevin over to me. Enjoy your meal; there probably won't be too many more of them."

Barr turned and gestured to Rafferty, they left the officer's mess without saying anything else.

"What are we going to do, Jeremy?" asked Kevin, worriedly. He knew their time was getting very short.

"Be ready," replied Jeremy, thinking feverishly about possibilities. He knew their options were extremely limited. "If we see an opportunity, we need to seize it."

Katie had watched the entire exchange from the cockpit of the shuttle. She had just gotten up from her bed to go to the bathroom and had checked the viewscreen out of curiosity. Seeing Jeremy and Kelsey in the officer's mess had drawn her instant attention. From the way that Kelsey and Jeremy had looked at the other two cadets, it was obvious there was some bad blood there. It was something she had noticed increasingly over the last several months. There was no doubt in Katie's mind that she had to be ready to launch her rescue and escape attempt at a moments notice.

Sitting down, she wondered if she should attempt to move the supplies from the other shuttle over into this one. If she did manage to rescue Jeremy, Kelsey, and their two friends, they might need them. Taking a deep breath, she leaned back in the pilot's seat and thought it over. It might be dangerous, but they could really use those extra supplies. She had nearly eaten and drank the majority of the supplies that this shuttle had originally been stocked with.

Jeremy and Kevin were in their quarters when they completed the second jump. The ship shuddered and seemed to leap to one side knocking Kevin off of his bunk. At the same time, emergency alarms began sounding.

"What the hell was that?" blurted Kevin, picking himself up off the floor and looking over at Jeremy.

"Sounded like some type of explosion," Jeremy said worriedly, rising to his feet and walking to the door. Checking it, he found it was still locked.

"What do you think happened?"

"The drive core overheated," answered Jeremy, wondering how badly the ship was damaged. "The chief engineer was worried about that and has been trying to warn Maher what might happen if he didn't reduce the distance of the FTL jumps. Maher has refused to listen to reason."

"Crap!" Kevin muttered, his eyes focusing on Jeremy, realizing the enormity of what this meant. "If the drive core is damaged, that means we're stranded with no way home."

"I don't think we were going home anyway," replied Jeremy, returning to his bunk and sitting down. They were trapped in their quarters until someone unlocked the door.

Kevin remained standing for a few moments longer and then sat down also. "Do you think the girls are okay?"

"They should be," Jeremy responded. "Their quarters are on this level, and we're quite a ways from Engineering."

In the Command Center, Major Maher was fuming. He could barely contain his rage. He had just finished speaking to the chief engineer; the drive core was irreparably damaged. Even after being threatened, the chief engineer had reported that they just didn't have the parts to completely rebuild the drive core. Maher had demanded to talk to Ensign Bates, and Bates had reported the same. Whatever star system they had jumped into on this last jump was where they were going to remain.

At least from the last report, the fires in Engineering were out and the sublight drive was still on line. Looking across the Command Center, Maher let out a sharp breath, and then his eyes focused on Lieutenant Nelson. There was no longer any point in keeping the lieutenant alive. If they couldn't jump any more, then he was useless. Maher had only kept him alive for his navigation abilities. Nelson was also the only real threat that Maher had to his command. Once Nelson was eliminated, those members of the crew that were still against his plans to colonize another world would fall into line.

"Guards, take Lieutenant Nelson back to his quarters," Maher ordered, his eyes turning dark. He would order Nelson's demise later, once things calmed back down.

"Helm, take us in system toward the liquid water zone. If we're stranded here, let's hope there's a world we can settle on."

The helm officer nodded and began turning the ship inward toward the central part of the system. Activating the sublight drive, he began accelerating the ship. The helm officer felt nervous as he could feel the ship vibrating slightly, and he even thought he could hear the hull groaning. The explosion in the drive core might have comprised the integrity of the ship's hull.

Maher flinched as he heard the groaning noise coming from the ship. If this system didn't have a habitable world, then all of his careful planning and taking over of the New Horizon would have been for nothing.

The Hocklyn support cruiser Arkon was just finishing its scans of this new star system when a red icon suddenly appeared on one of the ship's sensor screens. The sensor operator looked at it in surprise, and then turned to notify the First Leader.

"First Leader, there is an unidentified spacecraft that has just jumped into the system."

First Leader Makill looked at the sensor operator in surprise. There should be no other Hocklyn ships in this area. "Is it one of ours?"

"No, First Leader," the sensor operator replied. "It is much smaller than one of our support cruisers."

"What is its current range?" Makill asked with growing curiosity. Could it be an exploration craft from a nearby star system? Perhaps honor was closer than they had thought.

The sensor operator was quiet for a moment as he checked the information coming across his data screens. "Three hundred and sixty million kilometers. They have activated their sublight drive and are now moving in system."

Makill was quiet for a moment as he thought over his options. "Send a message to the Vengeance and inform them of what we have found. Inform First Leader Shrea that we will attempt contact in the guise of a trading vessel to see if we can learn of their point of origin."

"Yes, sir," the com operator replied.

Makill gazed thoughtfully at the main sensor screen and the red icon it was displaying. In their search of this region of space, three possible worlds had already been found to add to the empire. Two were rather primitive and had just begun their industrial age, another had already placed satellites in orbit and was experimenting with nuclear energy. Those three alone had already made this distant journey the fleet had taken worthwhile. If they could discover where this spacecraft had come from, everyone in the fleet might well receive an increase in their honor as well as their status within the empire.

"Move us to within two hundred million kilometers of the unknown ship and follow it. If it is on an exploratory mission, it will be inbound toward the liquid water zone. We will make contact after they discover the fourth planet. It is marginally habitable, and they will undoubtedly enter its gravity well to study it in detail. That is when we will use a micro-jump and close the range."

The helm operator nodded and made the necessary adjustments to the Arkon's course.

Major Maher gazed with jubilation at the main viewscreen. It was showing a world with traces of blue and green and some white clouds drifting in the atmosphere. Two of the scientists had been called to the Command Center to offer their evaluation of the world the New Horizon had found.

After some careful examination of the sensor data, the senior of the two scientists turned to face Major Maher. His face looked relieved, but also concerned.

"Well, speak up," demanded Maher impatient to find out about this new world. This world would be their future home there was no other choice. The chief engineer had made it very plain that the drive core could not be repaired.

"The planet is marginally habitable," the older man replied cautiously.

"What do you mean, marginally?" Maher demanded, his eyes cutting sharply into the scientist. "Can we live there or not?"

"We can live there," the scientist replied. "From the sensor readings, the areas in the equatorial regions of the planet are habitable, but if you move away from those regions the planet becomes very inhospitable to human life."

"How's that?" Maher asked, not liking the sound of this. "How large is this area that is habitable?"

"We will have to wait until we can use the close in scanners, but we estimate there is an area five-hundred kilometers across that extends completely around the planet that is easily habitable for human life. You can go out an additional five-hundred kilometers north or south of that and humans could probably survive. Outside of that and the temperature extremes would make survival extremely doubtful."

"What about water?" Maher demanded. He knew they needed plentiful amounts to water to establish a colony. "Are there sufficient supplies of fresh water?"

"In the equatorial regions, yes," responded the scientist, glancing back at some of the data on one of the sensor screens. "There are even several small oceans."

Maher nodded, satisfied with the answer. The equatorial region would work just fine. It would allow sufficient room for future growth and someday allow them to leave this world and find one more suitable.

"Take us into the planet's gravity well," Maher ordered the helm officer, satisfied that they had finally reached their destination. "Let's go look at our new world."

Maher watched over the next few hours as the New Horizon entered the planet's gravity well. "Does the planet have any moons?" he asked as the planet grew larger on the main viewscreen.

"One small one around three hundred kilometers in diameter," the scientist replied as he studied the data coming in on the short-range scanners.

"Sir, I have an unidentified contact showing up on the long-range sensors," the sensor operator suddenly reported. "It's a spaceship, and it just jumped in. It's less than two million kilometers away from us."

"Admiral Strong," Maher grated in sudden anger, seeing his plans crashing down in front of him. "How the hell did he find us?"

"It's not an Earth ship," the sensor operator replied uneasily. "It's too large."

"How big is it?" demanded Maher, striding over to the sensor screen and shoving one of the scientists out of the way. He wanted to see this for himself.

"It's at least eight hundred meters," replied the sensor operator nervously. "It's also wedge shaped. Earth never built anything like that."

"Put us into orbit around the planet," Maher ordered the helm officer as he weighed his options. Encountering an alien ship had never been in his plans. With the drive core damaged and this far into the planet's gravity well, they couldn't flee even if they wanted to. They would have to wait and see what the alien wanted.

For the next four hours, Maher watched as the alien ship drew nearer. That it had detected the New Horizon's presence was obvious.

"Put it up on the main viewscreen," Maher ordered when he deemed the alien was close enough so they could get a good look at it.

On the main viewscreen, the large wedge shaped ship appeared. Even from this distance, it was obvious that the alien ship was heavily armed. Maher leaned back in the command chair with deep concern on his face. What did the alien want? He knew the only real choice he had was to wait and see if they attempted to make contact. The New Horizon was unarmed and couldn't attempt to escape with the drive core damaged. Maher felt frustrated at this new development, letting out a deep breath, he continued to watch the viewscreen as the alien ship continued to come closer.

Inside the shuttle in the flight bay, Katie was gazing fearfully at the viewscreen on the instrument panel. She had it set to show the same view as the main viewscreen in the Command Center. From her talks with Ariel, she knew whose ship that was. It was a Hocklyn support cruiser, and it had found the New Horizon. Katie knew this was a disaster. If the Hocklyns took over the New Horizon, they would find the coordinates to Earth.

From what Ariel had revealed to Katie, she knew it would be several centuries yet before Earth and the Federation survivors were ready to face the Hocklyns. She had to do something. She knew she had no other choice. She had to launch her rescue attempt now to free Jeremy and Kelsey. Maybe one of them would know what to do.

Reaching forward, she pressed several icons on her small computer, which was sitting on a console next to her. Instantly several programs she had designed were transmitted into the New Horizon's computer core. It was time to go and get Jeremy.

Chapter Twelve

Major Maher was standing in the Command Center watching the main viewscreen pensively. The alien ship was about to enter the planet's gravity well and was still on a direct course for the New Horizon. The short-range scanners had given additional information on the alien. It was 800 meters long with its widest width at 250 meters. It was even more heavily armed than had been originally thought, with numerous weapon turrets and what looked like missile launching tubes embedded in the hull.

His thoughts were interrupted as numerous emergency alarms suddenly began sounding on the damage control console. He hurried quickly over to it swearing under his breath. Was the entire damn ship falling apart? What was going on now? Glancing at the console, he felt an icy chill across his back. Red warning lights were blinking on showing ongoing damage in various compartments. There were numerous uncontrolled fires breaking out in the forward area of the ship on three separate levels.

He instantly tapped his mini-com trying to contact those areas to see how bad the fires were. Fires on board a spaceship were bad. They ate through a ship's limited oxygen supply quickly. He wondered if there had been some type of electrical overload from the damage to the drive core that could have caused all of this. All he received on his mini-com was silence.

"What's wrong with the damn mini-coms?" he roared, looking over at Communications. They had to get a handle on those fires and quickly.

"They're down in the forward sections, sir," the communications officer reported as she pressed various buttons on her console, and then tapped in additional commands on her computer. "I can't get them to come up."

"Crap!" uttered Maher, feeling frustrated. The drive core, the damn alien ship, and now this! What else could go wrong? He went back to his command console and jabbed his finger down on a button, activating the ship wide address system. "All personnel, report to your emergency stations. Damage control teams are to report to," he paused and checked on a location near the worst of the fires, "Level ten, section fourteen. We have several fires burning that are in danger of getting out of control and causing serious damage to the ship. Get them out quickly!"

Sitting down, he gazed frustratingly at the viewscreen. The alien ship was still approaching, and Maher had a feeling, as heavily armed as that ship was, that nothing good was going to come out of this first contact.

Jeremy and Kevin were staring at each other with deep concern listening to the ship alarms that had just started blaring. There was something seriously wrong with the ship, and then they heard Major Maher ordering everyone to their emergency stations and all damage control teams to the front of the ship to combat some spreading fires.

"What's happened now?" uttered Kevin, growing extremely worried.

They were trapped in their quarters, and if the fires spread to this part of the ship, they couldn't get out. He didn't know what they could do. Suddenly the door to their quarters slid open and a young girl he had never seen before was standing there with a frightened and hopeful look upon her face. She had long blonde hair and captivating green eyes.

"Who are you?" Kevin asked, stunned by this apparition. She didn't look as if she could be much over sixteen.

"Katie!" cried Jeremy, recognizing who was standing there and rushing over to the door in confusion. Where had she come from?

"We don't have a lot of time," spoke Katie, looking intensely at Jeremy. "Those fires don't exist. They're part of a computer program I put into the New Horizon's systems. We need to get to the flight bay and leave in one of the shuttles. We're orbiting a planet that is habitable."

Jeremy nodded. He had a million questions to ask Katie, but he recognized that now was not the time, explanations could come later. He didn't know where Katie had come from, but this might be their best opportunity to escape. "We need to get Kelsey and Angela."

"No problem," replied Katie, looking down the corridor and making sure no one was in sight. "We need to hurry."

Jeremy and Kevin quickly led Katie to the girl's quarters, and they watched amazed as Katie hooked up a wire from the small computer she was carrying to a port on the control panel next to the door. The door instantly slid open, and the girls came hurrying out.

"Katie!" Kelsey spoke in a stunned voice, seeing the young teenager standing there. "Where did you come from?"

"I don't have time to explain now," replied Katie, knowing they needed to hurry. "There is an alien ship about to rendezvous with the New Horizon. We have to go now!"

"An alien ship?" Kelsey said, her face turning pale. She had a sinking feeling in the pit of her stomach that one of her worst fears was about to be realized. "What does it look like?"

Katie looked at Kelsey, wondering why she was asking such a question. "It's wedge shape and heavily armed."

"A Hocklyn support cruiser!" Kelsey said with fear showing in her eyes.

"Yes," replied Katie, gazing in surprise at Kelsey. "How did you know?"

"How close is it?" Kelsey demanded, her eyes drilling into Katie's eyes.

"It's just now entering the planet's gravity well," Katie replied.

"We need to find Lieutenant Nelson," Kelsey said, looking decisively at the others. "We can't let the New Horizon fall into Hocklyn hands."

"Who are these Hocklyns?"' asked Jeremy, feeling confused. What was going on here?

Katie looked at Kelsey with dawning comprehension. There was only one way Kelsey could know about the Hocklyns. "You're from Ceres aren't you?"

Kelsey was silent for a second, looking at Katie. Who had Katie learned all of this from? "Yes," she replied without hesitation. "And so is Lieutenant Nelson. He will know what to do."

"Nelson's quarters are this way," spoke Jeremy, growing more confused by the minute. What did Kelsey mean when she said she was from Ceres? Ceres was an asteroid.

"We need to hurry," Kelsey said in a deadly serious voice. "I will explain everything later."

Jeremy nodded and led the small group down the corridor and up a small stairwell to the next level. Reaching that level, Jeremy carefully glanced down the corridor and saw Ensign Rafferty standing guard in front of Lieutenant Nelson's quarters. Rafferty had a pistol in his belt.

"Damn, Rafferty is standing guard," Jeremy said in a quiet voice looking back at Kelsey. "He's armed, too."

"What now?" Kevin asked. "Rafferty won't hesitate to shoot, particularly if he sees you or me."

"Not necessarily," spoke Angela taking a deep breath. She carefully unbuttoned the top two buttons on her uniform, allowing a large amount of cleavage to show. "Put your eyes back in your heads, guys," Angela said, feeling her face flush. "I'll distract Rafferty. You two just make sure you disarm him before he goes too far." Stepping out into the corridor, she began walking casually toward Rafferty.

Hearing a peculiar noise, Rafferty glanced down the corridor and his eyes widened upon seeing Angela. "What are you doing out of your quarters?" he demanded, his eyes dropping down to gaze at her exposed cleavage. He could feel his heart start to beat faster.

Angela walked just past Rafferty and then turned to face him so he would be facing away from where the others were waiting. "Your friend Barr let me out," she replied in her best flirting voice. "I told him that I would agree to your terms."

"Really?" Rafferty spoke in disbelief, forcing his eyes up to gaze into Angela's eyes. "What made you change your mind?"

Angela only smiled. She leaned forward and kissed Rafferty on the lips. Out of the corner of her eyes, she could see Jeremy and Kevin coming up behind Rafferty, trying to be quiet.

"You did," she replied, leaning back and running her hands suggestively across his chest. Just as Rafferty started to reach for her, Jeremy and Kevin grabbed him, throwing him roughly down to the deck.

Katie came running down the corridor with Kelsey and in just a few seconds had the door to Lieutenant Nelson's quarters open.

Lieutenant Nelson stepped out, seeing Rafferty pinned to the floor by Jeremy and Kevin and Kelsey standing there. He didn't recognize the young green-eyed blonde who had evidently opened his door.

"What's going on?" demanded Nelson, knowing the cadets had to have been desperate to try to free him. He could see the frightened and worried look on Kelsey's face.

"There's a Hocklyn ship inbound," Kelsey informed Nelson, hoping he would know what to do. "It's already detected the New Horizon and is on an intercept course."

"What type?" Nelson demanded as he helped Jeremy and Kevin disarm Rafferty, tossing him into his former quarters and shutting the door. Using the pistol, he smashed the console, which allowed entry to his former quarters. That would keep Rafferty trapped inside. The com system had already been disabled so Rafferty couldn't call for help.

"Katie says it's an escort cruiser," replied Kelsey, looking over at the nervous teenager.

Looking at Katie, Nelson asked her. "Where have you been hiding? You're obviously not a member of this crew."

"I'm Katie Johnson, Greg Johnson's daughter. I stowed away when the ship left the spacedock. I've been hiding in one of the shuttles."

Nelson nodded as he took it all in. He checked Rafferty's pistol and pocketed the two extra clips they had taken from him. "Let's get back to the flight bay. We need to try to contact a Federation ship."

"What Federation ship?" asked Kelsey, shaking her head. "We're thousands of light years from Earth. We also don't have an FTL transmitter."

"Yes, we do," Nelson spoke as he led the small group down the corridor. "One of the shuttles has an FTL transmitter on board, and there is a chance, even though it's a small one, that the WarStorm may be in range."

"The WarStorm," Kelsey said, her eyes growing wide. She had heard her father mention the new warship. It was supposedly the most powerful ship the Federation survivors had ever built.

"Yes, it was due to leave on its mission and should be close by. I just don't know if it will be close enough to receive our transmission."

Jeremy was listening to all of this and growing more confused with every word. There was something going on here that he had no clue about. What was this Federation and what was the WarStorm? He had never heard of either.

It took them a few minutes to reach the flight bay using the auxiliary corridors. Once inside the flight bay, Katie led them to the shuttle she had been staying on and showed Lieutenant Nelson the Hocklyn ship on the small viewscreen.

"Kelsey, do you remember how to fly a shuttle?" Nelson asked as he thought about his options. He knew they had less than an hour before the Hocklyn ship reached them.

"Yes, sir," replied Kelsey, uneasily. "My father made me learn last summer when I returned home. He thought it might be useful. I'm not the greatest pilot, though."

"He was right, and you will do fine," Nelson replied satisfied with her answer. "We can't let that Hocklyn ship take the New Horizon. I have to destroy the ship."

"What!" cried Angela, realizing what Nelson had just said. "What about the crew? You can't just let them all die! Most of them are not part of Major Maher's group."

Nelson shook his head sadly. "There is a lot going on here that you cadets don't understand. Jeremy, your father knows everything, and I hope someday you will understand why this had to be done. If these Hocklyns discover Earth, years of careful planning by your father and others will be destroyed. I can't let that happen"

Jeremy only nodded his head; he didn't know what to say. Angela and Kevin were equally confused as they stared at each other in shock over Nelson's words.

"I have to get to Engineering and set the self-destruct," Nelson said, his face pale. "There is no other choice."

"What self-destruct?" asked Kelsey, drawing in a sharp breath. "I thought only warships were equipped with those."

"All FTL equipped ships have them now," Nelson replied as he glanced at the confused cadets. "Even the New Horizon. The device is hidden in Engineering, and Ensign Treadwell will help me. He is also from Ceres."

"What do we need to do?" Kelsey asked. She knew Nelson was serious about the self-destruct. It was something that everyone on Ceres was well aware of. No ship could be allowed to be taken that would lead the Hocklyns back to Earth and Ceres. That was why the self-destructs had been added to all Federation ships. She was just stunned to learn that there was one on the New Horizon.

"Get all these supplies moved over to the other shuttle. It's the one with the FTL transmitter." Nelson took a pen out of his pocket and found a piece of paper. He quickly wrote down a series of numbers. "This is the code to enter into the com system to activate the FTL transmitter. Give me twenty minutes, and if I haven't returned by then get this shuttle out of the flight bay. Once outside the flight bay start transmitting, and then get this shuttle down on the planet. Do whatever you have to in order to destroy the shuttle's computer, and then hide. Hopefully the WarStorm will eventually find you."

Kelsey nodded as Lieutenant Nelson turned and exited the shuttle, running toward the exit. "Let's get the supplies moved," Kelsey said, opening a storage compartment and grabbing some containers of food.

"He's going to destroy the ship and kill everyone," said Kevin, feeling confused. "Why is that necessary?"

"The aliens in that ship will destroy Earth if they learn of it," explained Katie with dread in her eyes at what Lieutenant Nelson was about to do. "They will send word back to their empire and come for us."

"Katie's right," Kelsey said, nodding her head and trying not to think about all the innocent people that were about to die. "Lieutenant Nelson has no other choice. This has to be done."

"I think you have a lot of explaining to do," Jeremy said to Kelsey as he loaded his arms up with bottles of water. Then, turning to Katie, he added. "And so do you, young lady."

"Yes, Jeremy," replied Katie, meekly. She reached into a storage compartment and grabbed more supplies. She had just moved all of this over from the other shuttle.

It took nearly the entire twenty minutes to get everything moved. As soon as the supplies were moved, Kelsey sat down in the pilot's seat in the cockpit of the shuttle, hoping she remembered how to fly it. Taking a deep breath, she reached forward and began activating the shuttle's flight systems. Jeremy was sitting next to her watching in amazement as she entered commands on the touch screens and flipped switches. He was learning very rapidly that there was a lot about Kelsey he didn't know.

"So what is this Ceres stuff?" asked Jeremy, knowing there wasn't a lot he could do to help Kelsey. He also didn't understand how she knew how to fly a shuttle. He had heard her mention something about learning it the previous summer when she had returned home.

"We're originally from the Human Federation of Worlds," Kelsey replied as she finished activating all the shuttle's systems. "The Hocklyns destroyed our worlds over one hundred years ago, and the survivors of my people fled to Earth. The Avenger was one of our ships that crashed on your moon. Because of a deadly disease on your world, we were forced to settle inside the asteroid Ceres. This all remained a secret until your father discovered the Avenger on his moon mission."

"So my father knows about all of this?" asked Jeremy, feeling perplexed. His father had never mentioned anything about this.

"Yes, your father has been to Ceres numerous times. Your father and my father are trying to get Earth ready for when the Hocklyns arrive several centuries from now."

"Just who is your father?" asked Jeremy, curiously.

"My father is Admiral Anlon; he is in charge of all the Federation survivors. I just changed my last name so none of the Federation instructors at the academy would know who I was."

"There are Federation instructors at the academy?" repeated Jeremy, taking a deep breath. He was still struggling to understand everything he had heard since Katie had freed them. It was starting to sound as if a lot had been going on that had been kept secret from him.

Their conversation was interrupted as Lieutenant Nelson staggered back into the bay carrying an assault rifle. One look told them that he was seriously injured.

Jeremy yelled at Kevin, pointing at Lieutenant Nelson, and they hurriedly left the safety of the shuttle to help the lieutenant. He motioned for them to stop as he leaned weakly against the wall.

"Jeremy, take this assault rifle, I got it off one of Maher's men down in Engineering. Take these extra clips and these two pistols also."

"I don't understand," spoke Jeremy, taking the weapons and handing the two pistols to Kevin. "Aren't you coming with us?"

Nelson smiled and then grimaced in pain. There was blood flowing from his side. "No, someone has to open the flight bay doors. Tell Kelsey to tell her father I'm sorry. I did my best." He coughed and nearly fell.

Jeremy reached forward to help steady him.

"Get back inside the shuttle and seal it up. The self-destruct will go off in ten minutes. Ensign Treadwell is dead. He was killed when we jumped Maher's two guards in Engineering. I'm not going; I have to open the flight bay doors."

"Isn't there any other way to open the doors?" asked Kevin, wanting Nelson to go with them. He seemed to know what was going on, and they could really use him. Their chances of surviving on the planet would be greatly increased by his presence.

"Only from the Command Center, and I don't think Maher will agree to do that. I can override the system from the control panel outside the hatch. Get in the shuttle; we don't have a lot of time. They're bound to be looking for me."

Jeremy and Kevin turned to leave and Nelson added, "Jeremy, you're a lot like your father. You will make a good commander someday."

Jeremy turned back to Nelson and nodded, finding it hard to reply. "Thank you, sir."

"Now get going," Nelson ordered as he turned and staggered out the open hatch, shutting it behind him.

A few moments later, Jeremy and Kevin were back inside the shuttle and had sealed the hatch. Jeremy went into the cockpit and sat down in the copilot's seat. "Lieutenant Nelson isn't coming," he said to Kelsey. "He has to override the flight bay door controls from the corridor."

Kelsey only nodded, struggling to keep her emotions under control. She had been counting on Lieutenant Nelson coming with them and helping to fly the shuttle. She had wondered how they would get the doors open, and now she knew. Even as she nodded her head in acceptance, the doors slid open and red warning lights began flashing in the flight bay. Reaching forward, she activated the flight controls and using the shuttle's engines, flew the small shuttle smoothly out of the open doors.

In the Command Center, a livid Major Maher had just received the report that all the fires were unreal. Somehow or another the damage control console had been made to show fires that were not there. Then came the stunning news that Lieutenant Nelson had appeared in Engineering and he and one of the assistant engineers had managed to kill both of his guards. The assistant engineer had been killed, but Nelson had managed to escape. Maher wondered if Nelson had been responsible for putting the fake information in the damage control computer. Also, why the hell had he gone to Engineering?

Barr had made his way to the Command Center to find out what was going on. He had just been told about Lieutenant Nelson killing the two guards in Engineering. As he entered, he heard the sensor operator announce to Major Maher that the flight bay doors were opening, and one of the shuttles was being flown out. Turning around, Barr made a mad dash to Jeremy and Kevin's quarters, angrily knowing what he was going to find. Reaching them, he found the quarters empty. He knew if he checked the girl's quarters, he would find the same thing. Somehow or another Lieutenant Nelson must have freed all four of them. What really concerned Barr was what Lieutenant Nelson had been doing in Engineering? Also, where was Rafferty?

Reaching Lieutenant Nelson's quarters, he had to go get some tools to pry the door open, only to find Rafferty standing inside with a frustrated look upon his face. "What the hell happened to you?" demanded Barr, angrily.

"It was Strong and the others; they have some young girl with them I've never seen before. They managed to get the jump on me and locked me in here."

"Fool!" roared Barr, shaking his head in disbelief. "Follow me. Someone launched one of the shuttles, and the only way to do it outside of the Command Center is through the override panel in the outside corridor of the flight bay. I want to find out who did it."

The two hurried through the ship, arriving in the indicated corridor. To their surprise, they found Lieutenant Nelson sitting on the floor and leaning against the wall in a growing pool of blood.

"Where are they, Nelson?" screamed Barr, seeing that Nelson was still alive. He reached down and grabbed Nelson's shoulders, jerking him roughly to his feet.

Nelson moaned loudly at the sudden pain, looking at Barr. Then his eyes focused on his watch. "Did you know this ship came with a self-destruct?" he asked weakly with satisfaction in his voice. He allowed a smile to spread across his face. "You and your hijacking friends are about to die." The biggest regret that Nelson had were the numerous innocents among the crew that would have to die to keep Earth and Ceres safe.

"A self-destruct!" Barr spoke, his eyes growing wide in fear. Now he knew what Nelson had been doing down in Engineering. Even as he turned to race to Engineering a brilliant flash lit up his eyes.

Jeremy covered his eyes as the New Horizon exploded in a raging, all consuming, ball of nuclear fire. He felt sick inside knowing how many innocent people had just died, and there had been nothing he could do to prevent it.

Kelsey reached forward on the com panel and carefully punched in the code that Lieutenant Nelson had given her. Listening on the com, all she could hear was static. She would have to wait a few minutes until the aftermath of the nuclear explosion cleared.

"She's gone," Jeremy said as he looked out the cockpit window at the fading nuclear explosion. Then turning to look at Kelsey, he asked. "Now what?"

"We send out our signal and then find a safe place to hide on the planet. Hopefully we will be rescued before the Hocklyns can find us."

"You think they will come after us?" Jeremy asked. He saw that all the flight instruments, including the shuttle's short-range scanners were coming back on line.

"They're Hocklyns," said Kelsey, knowing Jeremy didn't understand. How could he? All his life this horrendous secret had been kept from him. "They will want to find us and this shuttle to learn where Earth is so it can either be destroyed or added to their slave empire."

"Slave empire," repeated Jeremy, incredulously. Leaning back in the copilot's chair, Jeremy was beginning to have some serious questions about what all his father had kept secret from him. He also wondered how much of this his mother knew.

"Yes, a slave empire," Kelsey explained. "They conquer every world they come across, and if they find out about Earth or Ceres, we will be next."

"I guess there's a lot I don't know," admitted Jeremy, letting out a deep breath.

"When we get somewhere safe I will explain it all," Kelsey promised as she checked the com once more. "Right now, we need to worry about getting this FTL message off, and then finding a safe place on the planet to hide."

"So your people have a method of faster than light communication?" asked Jeremy, wondering if Kelsey were completely human. Were there other things she was hiding from him? He had known Kelsey for over four years now, and he was just realizing that he didn't really know her at all.

"Yes," replied Kelsey, glancing over at Jeremy. She knew he had a lot of questions. It had always bothered her that it was necessary to keep so much a secret from him, but that was one of the conditions her father had made if she wanted to attend the academy on the Moon. "There is even an FTL communications system on the Avenger."

Jeremy only shook his head. Now he was beginning to understand why so much of the Avenger had always been off limits. Evidently, the ship was much more functional than his father and others had let on.

Kelsey checked the com system once again and, with relief, she found the interference from the nuclear explosion was gone. She hurriedly sent out a broad beam broadcast in the direction of Earth giving their situation and their coordinates. She boosted the signal as far as possible, burning out the com system. If the WarStorm wasn't within three hundred light years, the signal would never be heard.

"Jeremy, tell everyone in back to buckle up. This descent is going to be fast and rough. We need to get down and hidden as quickly as possible."

In the Arkon, First Leader Makill looked on in anger as the nuclear explosion dissipated. All that remained of the alien ship was some glowing wreckage and expanding gases.

"What happened?" demanded Makill, looking over at his Second Leader.

"It looks like a self-destruct was activated or the ship's drive detonated," replied the Second Leader, studying some sensor data. "I have replayed the explosion in slow motion, and the nuclear explosion originated in the Engineering section of the ship."

"Sensors, are you detecting anything else?" First Leader Makill demanded. He was fearful of contacting the Vengeance and informing First Leader Shrea of what had just happened. He knew Shrea would hold him personally reasonable for this. It could result in a loss of honor for him and his family.

"I have a small shuttle on the sensors," replied the sensor operator, gazing intently at his screen. "It is making for the planet."

"I have an outgoing com message," the communications operator reported. "It was very brief and not in any known language in our data banks."

"Perhaps it was an accident," commented Makill, nodding his head as he thought about what had just happened. "Launch two of our fighters to follow that shuttle. I want to know where it lands. Can we tell what direction that com message was sent?"

"The dispersion was set to wide," the com operator replied, shaking his head. "We know the general direction, but we will not be able to narrow it down to do us any good."

Makill nodded his head in disappointment and then turned back to the Second Leader. "Get those fighters launched now; I don't want to lose that shuttle!"

"Yes, sir," the Second Leader responded. He moved hastily to obey First Leader Makill's orders.

Downward the small shuttle flew as Kelsey fought to keep it under control. She knew her entry into the atmosphere was too fast and too steep, but it was expedient that they get down and hidden quickly. Already the scout's short-range scanners had detected two small vessels leaving the Hocklyn ship. Kelsey had a sinking feeling that those were Hocklyn fighters. They were faster than the shuttle, but she had a good head start.

"They're coming after us," Kelsey said, pointing toward the scanner screen.

"I see them," Jeremy replied as he did some quick calculations on the shuttle's computer. "They can't catch us before we reach the surface. I figure we will have about ten minutes to find someplace to land before they can detect us on their scanners."

The shuttle continued to arrow downward, leaving a glowing trail behind it in the atmosphere. Kelsey fought to maintain control as the shuttle shook from the results of their sharp reentry profile. She just prayed that the shuttle didn't come apart around them. It hadn't been built to handle the stresses she was putting it through. Already, several red warning lights were flashing on the instrument panel.

"The hull's overheating," Jeremy warned Kelsey as he read one of the readouts. "You need to reduce the angle of our reentry, or we're going to burn up."

"I know," Kelsey responded in a strained voice as she adjusted their downward course slightly to take some pressure off the hull. She also fired the forward jets and began braking the shuttle, slowing its rapid rush through the atmosphere.

"Jeremy, see those two levers on your right side?" she asked, tilting her head in that direction. She didn't dare take her hands off of the controls.

"Yes," responded Jeremy, looking down and spotting the two levers.

"Pull both of them all the way back. I need the flaps fully extended so we can level out our flight path."

Jeremy pulled them both back and felt the shuttle reduce its shaking.

Kelsey fought the controls and finally got the shuttle's nose to start to pull up. It finally leveled out and they were flying parallel to the surface, heading toward some small mountains in the distance.

"If we can reach those mountains, we can hide the shuttle," Kelsey said, her hands shaking. "The mountains should shield the shuttle from their scanners."

It was taking all of her concentration and effort to keep the shuttle under control. When she had been learning to fly a shuttle the previous summer, she had never attempted something like what she was doing now. If her father could only see her, he would be amazed.

Reaching the mountains, Kelsey and Jeremy gazed out of the cockpit windows, looking for a good place to hide the shuttle. The area they were flying over was heavily forested, and they could see a few small streams and mountain lakes. It looked similar to some of the mountainous regions back on Earth.

"That cliff over there," Jeremy said, pointing downward and to the right. "It has a slight overhang, and there are several trees next to it. Can you set the shuttle down between those trees? Between the overhang and the trees, it will be hard to see."

"I'll try," Kelsey replied as she turned the shuttle.

Carefully working the shuttle's engine and maneuvering thrusters, she managed to get the shuttle where Jeremy had indicated. Setting it down, she turned off the engine and then leaned back in her seat. She started shaking, realizing how lucky she had been to be able to get the shuttle down safely with no one getting hurt.

"You did fine, Kelsey," Jeremy said, reaching over and taking her hand. "No one else on the shuttle but you could have done this."

"I don't think the Hocklyn fighters will be able to spot us now," Kelsey spoke with obvious relief in her voice.

"What now?" asked Kevin, coming into the cockpit. "Where are we?"

"We need to go outside and try to cover the shuttle with whatever we can find. Also, if there are any burn marks from our landing, we need to cover those up too," Jeremy answered. "Kelsey says that alien ship we saw will come looking for us. No matter what happens, we can't let them take us or capture this shuttle intact."

For the next several hours, the five of them covered the burn marks left by the shuttle's descent. They gathered large amounts of brush and tree limbs, which they laid up against the shuttle's hull, making it difficult so see.

Kelsey and Jeremy looked critically over what had been done to conceal the shuttle, knowing it was the best they could do, but it probably wouldn't be good enough.

"It will be night soon," commented Jeremy, seeing the dark shadows slowly descending down the mountain slopes. They were in a small valley, and the sun was already behind the mountain peaks.

"We need to get as far away from the shuttle as we can," Kelsey stated with her hands on her hips. "Jeremy, what are we going to do if the Hocklyns find us?"

Jeremy reached over and put his arm around Kelsey, pulling her close. "Don't worry, we will get through this."

For a moment, Kelsey felt safe in Jeremy's arms, and then she stepped back. "We can spend the night in the shuttle and get some packs ready. In the morning, we need to find a safer place to hide. It probably won't take the Hocklyns long to find the shuttle, and then they will send their protectors after us."

"Protectors?" Jeremy asked, arching his eyebrows. "What are those?"

Kelsey took a deep breath. "Let's get everything ready for in the morning, and then I guess I owe everyone a big explanation."

"I would say so," spoke Angela, walking up to the two. "I think you and Katie both have a lot of explaining to do."

Kelsey nodded. If they were going to survive, everyone needed to know what was at stake and why Lieutenant Nelson had destroyed the New Horizon.

Jeremy looked around in the fading light. It was time to get inside the shuttle. He had a suspicion that the nights up in these mountains would be cold. "Everyone in the shuttle," he ordered. Taking Kelsey's hand, he turned and led her back inside. Once everyone was safely in the shuttle, he shut and secured the hatch. They should be safe here for the night, at least.

Kelsey sat down with Jeremy beside her on one of the bunks that had been pulled down. "It all started over one hundred years ago back in the Human Federation of Worlds," she began. For the next two hours, she described the Federation's encounter with the Hocklyns, the destruction of their worlds, the desperate flight to Earth, the fleet coming down with the Spanish Flu, and finally settling in Ceres. When she was through, she looked expectantly around the small group.

"So you're an alien," Kevin said, looking at Kelsey. She looked human enough.

Kelsey allowed herself to laugh. "No, I'm just as human as you are. The remote ancestors of the people of the Human Federation of Worlds were actually taken from Earth thousands of years ago, but that's another story."

Jeremy had listened to Kelsey's explanations, shaking his head in disbelief at what all his father had kept a secret from him. He wondered if Greg's son Mathew knew the truth. Turning his head he looked over at Katie, who had remained quiet throughout Kelsey's explanations.

"Alright, Katie," spoke Jeremy, looking straight at the teenager. "I want to know your part in all of this, and how you know abut Ceres and the Hocklyns. Also, how in the hell did you sneak aboard the New Horizon?"

Katie looked over at Jeremy. She knew he wasn't happy with her being here. She couldn't blame him, there were so many things she had done wrong. Taking a deep breath, she began telling the small group about her first contact with Ariel and how it had grown into a friendship. She finally explained how she had used that friendship to sneak on board the New Horizon.

"I can tell you one thing," admonished Kelsey, shaking her head in amazement when Katie was finished. "Ariel is going to be quite upset with you if we ever get back home. If you think the lecture that Jeremy is probably going to give you is bad, just wait until Ariel gets a hold of you. I've spoken to Clarissa on the Vindication, and both AIs are very human."

"I know," Katie replied in a regretful and hurt voice. "But if I hadn't stowed away on board the New Horizon, you all might have died on the ship."

"There is that," admitted Kelsey, looking over at Jeremy.

"What you did was wrong," began Jeremy, seeing the frightened and lonely look in Katie's eyes. "But I think we can wait until we get home to talk this over." He patted the bunk next to him. "Come sit over here by me."

Katie stood up, walked over, and sat down next to Jeremy. Then losing control, she started crying uncontrollably and buried her face in Jeremy's shoulder. Jeremy put his arms around the fifteen-year-old, knowing she had been through a lot. Kelsey stood up and came and sat down on the other side of Katie, reaching out and patting Katie on the back.

"You will be fine," Kelsey said soothingly to the young girl. "You saved all of our lives. When we get back home, we will make sure everyone knows that."

"I'll be grounded forever," sobbed Katie.

"Perhaps," Kelsey said, letting a fleeting smile cross her face. "We will talk to your parents and Admiral Strong."

"Will you?" asked Katie, sitting back up and wiping the tears from her eyes.

"Yes," spoke Jeremy, nodding his head. "After all, you're just like a member of my family."

Katie smiled at this. She felt safe with Jeremy and Kelsey here. She knew they wouldn't let anything happen to her.

The small group of close friends continued to talk as darkness covered the small valley. In the morning, they would have to destroy the computers on the shuttle and then find a safe place to hide.

On board the Arkon, First Leader Makill gazed angrily at the reports coming in from the two fighters. The small shuttle had managed to land before the fighters had gotten into range. All they had was a general area of where the shuttle had landed, and darkness was already falling on that section of the planet.

Letting out a sharp, frustrated breath, he turned his dark eyes toward his Second Leader. "Contact the Vengeance and tell them the alien ship exploded due to unknown reasons. However, a shuttle escaped the destruction of the ship and managed to land upon the planet. We may need their contingent of protectors to help search the area the shuttle landed in. It is mountainous and will not be easy to search."

"Yes, First Leader," the Second Leader responded. He then turned to the communications operator to ensure the message was sent.

Makill walked to the front of the War Room and gazed speculatively at the large viewscreen, which was now covered with an image of the planet. They were orbiting at ten thousand kilometers using the ship's sensors to try to pick up the shuttle, but because of the numerous ore deposits in the mountainous region in which the shuttle had landed, the scans were coming back negative.

On board the war cruiser Vengeance, First Leader Shrea read the communication from the Arkon. He stared angrily at the viewscreen in front of him where the planet they were orbiting was being displayed. Already a large amount of material and personnel, including some of his protectors, were being used to build the food and water processing facility.

He turned and looked at Second Leader Vrill. "Contact all of our support cruisers and have them rendezvous in the system the Arkon is currently in. We must find that shuttle and its crew. There is much honor at stake here if we can find their world of origin."

"Yes, First Leader," replied Vrill, hurrying to follow the order.

Shrea then turned to the helm operator. "Take us out of this planet's gravity well and prepare to jump to the Arkon's location. I want to get there as rapidly as possible."

Shrea walked back to the command pedestal and saw with satisfaction that the Vengeance was already breaking orbit. If they could find this missing shuttle and alien crew, he would send a support cruiser back to Commodore Rateif. He would request that the forward base be moved to this section of their search area. It would take a while, but it could be done. Yes, if things worked out, there would be much honor and advancement for all of them.

Two days later, Amanda was busy working out in the WarStorm's weight room. It had been a disappointing four months as there had been no trace of the New Horizon. She stepped back and swung at the punching bag in front of her feeling the satisfaction of contact. This was a good way to let out her pent up frustrations. She knew with growing concern that they must be nearing Hocklyn space.

"Colonel Sheen, please report to the Command Center," a voice announced suddenly over the ship's internal com system.

Amanda stepped over to the unit on the wall and touched it. "This is Colonel Sheen," she said simply.

"Colonel, the light cruiser StarFury is reporting that they have picked up an emergency signal from the New Horizon."

Amanda froze upon hearing the words she had been waiting on for so long. "I'm on my way," she said.

A few moments later, she hurried into the Command Center. No one said a word about the fact she had obviously been working out and wasn't in her full uniform. "What do we have, Major Fields?" asked Amanda, stepping behind the command console.

"It's not good," Major Fields replied from where he was standing at the holographic plotting table, entering some coordinates.

"What's happened?" demanded Richard as he charged into the Command Center.

"The Hocklyns have found the New Horizon," Fields answered.

"Crap," uttered Richard, feeling that their world had just crashed in around them.

"Fortunately, Lieutenant Nelson managed to activate the ship's self-destruct and destroyed the ship before the Hocklyns could board her."

"So everyone's dead," said Amanda, trying to control her emotions. Admiral Strong's son and Admiral Anlon's daughter were gone. How was she going to explain that to them?

"No," replied Major Fields, shaking his head. "Evidently one of the shuttles managed to escape the destruction and landed on the planet they were orbiting. It's habitable and the crew is going to attempt to hide until we can reach them."

"Do we know who is on the shuttle?" Richard broke in. He prayed it was Jeremy Strong and Kelsey Anlon. Lieutenant Nelson would have made sure of that if at all possible.

"Yes, we do," replied Fields. "Cadet Lieutenant Jeremy Strong, Cadet Ensign Kelsey Anlon, Cadet Ensign Kevin Walters, Cadet Ensign Angela DeSota, and Katie Johnson."

"The stowaway," spoke Amanda, thoughtfully. She knew that Nelson had made sure that these five survived. "What type of Hocklyn ship did they encounter, and how far away are they?"

"It was an escort cruiser of the standard type from the information that Ensign Anlon sent. However, they are over two hundred and seventy light years away, and this message was sent two days ago."

Amanda looked over at her husband. Two days were a long time for four cadets and a teenager to survive on a planet being searched by Hocklyn protectors. Amanda walked over to the plotting table and gazed at the glowing star that designated their destination. "Major Fields, order the light cruisers to meet us here," she said, pointing to a set of coordinates that would put them on the extreme outer edge of the star system. "We will go on ahead and see what the situation is."

Amanda then contacted the New Tellus. The battle carrier would have to gather up all the outlying stealth scouts and then follow. Hopefully, all the WarStorm would have to deal with was the one Hocklyn support cruiser. If that was the only Hocklyn ship that was in the system when the WarStorm arrived, Amanda intended to engage it immediately and destroy it. She would then send the marines on the WarStorm down to rescue the cadets.

"Navigation, plot a series of long-range jumps to the coordinates Major fields has up on the plotting table. Helm, as soon as you have the first set of jump coordinates, initiate the jump. I want to get to that system yesterday, am I clear?"

"Yes, Colonel," Lieutenant Ashton and the helm officer replied.

For several minutes, Amanda waited impatiently. For every minute of delay, she knew the risk rose of the Hocklyns finding those cadets. She just hoped they could survive until she could get there. Watching the main viewscreen, she saw the familiar blue-white vortex form. Moments later, she felt the ship jump into hyperspace.

Richard reached out and took Amanda's hand. "Don't worry, we will get there in time."

"I hope so. I'm not leaving those cadets behind, not like I did my parents," Amanda replied softly.

Leaving her parents behind on Aquaria had always haunted her dreams. She knew there had been nothing else she could have done but in this instance, she was determined to rescue those cadets. Nothing the Hocklyns could throw at her would deter her from that goal. I'm coming, she thought to herself, wishing those cadets could know that their message had gotten through. She let out a deep breath, using maximum jumps it would still take them a little over eighty hours to reach that system. She just hoped those cadets could survive until she got there with the WarStorm.

Chapter Thirteen

Jeremy gazed intently through the small pair of binoculars at the small valley below. The four cadets and Katie had taken refuge in a small cave up on the side of the mountain, shielded by several very large boulders. The cave was invisible from the valley floor, where a number of Hocklyn protectors could be seen methodically searching for signs of the small group.

Sliding back down out of sight, Jeremy walked back into the cave. It extended back about fifteen meters into the side of the mountain. "I can see about eight Hocklyn protectors in the valley," reported Jeremy, reaching the back of the cave where the others were waiting. He was still feeling the shock from his first sight of a Hocklyn. The protectors were over two meters tall, light green in color, and very obviously of reptilian descent. All of the Hocklyns wore some type of dark colored body armor and were heavily armed.

"That's more than yesterday," Kevin spoke with worry in his eyes. He was sitting down against the back wall of the cave with the assault rifle leaning against the wall next to him. "Eventually they're going to start searching the slopes of these mountains."

"I was hoping someone would have come for us by now," Angela said. She was sitting next to Katie, and the two had been talking about Ariel. Angela had been sitting captivated as Katie had described the Avenger's AI.

"It's been almost six days now since we landed," Kelsey said, coming to stand next to Jeremy. They had managed to move quite a few of the shuttle's supplies into the cave. The cave was a little over three kilometers from their landing site. Kelsey estimated that they had enough food and water to last at least another week. "If the WarStorm received our transmission, they should be here any time."

"That's a big if," Jeremy spoke quietly so no one else could overhear him. "What if they didn't, Kelsey? Then what are we going to do?"

Kelsey motioned to Jeremy, and they stepped back outside the cave to where the large boulders were. All of her life she had been brought up with the full knowledge of the Hocklyns and the horrific danger they represented to humanity. She could well remember her childhood classes on Ceres where the teachers had repeatedly hammered into all the children's heads the danger the Hocklyns represented and why they must not find Earth or Ceres until the time was right.

The teachers had shown the children pictures of the Hocklyns and what they had done to the Federation worlds. Even as she had gotten older, the teachings had been the same. The Hocklyns and their AI masters were a scourge that wanted to control the galaxy. The only hope the Federation survivors and Earth had was to remain hidden until they could build up the necessary strength to stand up to the Hocklyns and the AIs and say, no more!

She looked deeply into Jeremy's hazel eyes. She hadn't realized until this very moment what color Jeremy's eyes were. Letting out a deep breath, she reached out and took Jeremy's hands.

"Jeremy, we can't let the Hocklyns take us," she spoke in an even voice.

Kelsey had been putting off this conversation for as long as possible, but each day the Hocklyns were getting closer. Closing her eyes, she knew what she had to say. Opening them, she looked at Jeremy wishing that they could have had more time together. She would have really liked to have been able to show Jeremy the wonders of the Federation world inside of Ceres.

"I don't understand," replied Jeremy, his eyes focusing on Kelsey. "If the WarStorm doesn't arrive they're going to find us eventually. I don't think there's anything we can do to prevent that."

He knew that, with the supplies they had remaining, they couldn't survive more than another seven to ten days without going out and foraging. Once they had to resort to leaving the cave, the likelihood of the Hocklyns finding them went up exponentially. He didn't know how the Hocklyns would treat prisoners, and he didn't want to find out.

"Jeremy, we can't let the Hocklyns interrogate us," Kelsey continued in a strained voice. She squeezed his hands tighter. "If they find out where Earth is, they will go there and either conquer or destroy it. It's better if that secret dies here with us."

"Dies here with us," Jeremy repeated, his eyes growing wide as he finally realized what Kelsey was alluding to.

"Yes," Kelsey said, her gaze dropping down to the pistol in Jeremy's belt. "If the Hocklyns find us, save enough rounds to make sure they learn nothing of Earth."

Jeremy swallowed and felt slightly faint as he fully understood what Kelsey was saying. Their lives were not as important as keeping

Earth's location a secret. "I understand, Kelsey," responded Jeremy, letting out a sharp breath. "I will make sure the Hocklyns don't capture us."

"Thanks, Jeremy," Kelsey said, leaning forward and kissing him gently on the lips. Leaning back, she added. "I just wish things could have been different. There is so much I would have liked to have been able show you. I think you would like my parents, they are a lot like yours, and of course there is Ceres." For the next few minutes, Kelsey described to Jeremy what living on Ceres was like.

Katie was watching the two from the back of the cave and could tell they had been talking about something serious. She had no idea what they had been discussing. She did feel better and allowed herself to smile when she saw Kelsey lean forward and kiss Jeremy. Leaning back against the cool wall of the cave, she glanced down at her handheld computer. Fortunately, she had several extra batteries for it, and one battery was good for nearly twenty hours of continuous use. She was currently writing a program she hoped would aid in their rescue. She hadn't mentioned what she was doing to anyone else in case it didn't work, but she had no interest in dying on this world or allowing the Hocklyns to find them.

Kevin walked back out to where Kelsey and Jeremy were standing. Carefully glancing out over one of the boulders, he looked down at the small valley. It was covered in trees, and the tree line actually went up a little past where they were hiding. Seeing some movement down below, he squinted his eyes and could barely make out a Hocklyn protector moving through the trees holding what looked like an assault rifle in his hands.

"Do you think they have found the shuttle yet?" asked Kevin, looking over at Jeremy.

"Probably," replied Jeremy, walking the few short steps over to Kevin with Kelsey following.

Kevin was holding the assault rifle Lieutenant Nelson had given them. He was the only one of them that had a lot of hunting experience in his background. He had learned to use a rifle when he was ten years old when his father had begun taking him deer hunting.

"I hope you don't have to use that," Kelsey said, looking at the rifle Kevin was holding loosely in his hands.

"Me too," Kevin said in a serious tone. "We don't have a lot of ammunition. We have the clip in the rifle plus two spares. That's less than sixty rounds."

"We just have to hope they don't find us," spoke Jeremy, looking down into the valley. Taking his binoculars, he slowly scanned the visible part of the valley once more. He thought he could see at least six Hocklyn protectors. If he could see six, there were probably others he couldn't see.

"What will they do to us if they find us?" asked Angela, walking up to the other three and looking at Kelsey.

Kelsey didn't answer, she only shook her head. Looking up into the light blue sky, she just prayed that the WarStorm would find them.

Up in orbit, First Leader Shrea was pacing back and forth in the War Room, listening impatiently as report after report came in from the protectors and shuttles searching on the ground. All six escort cruisers and the Vengeance were currently in low orbits, scanning the planet for any trace of the survivors from that shuttle. The shuttle had been found two days previously, but its computer system had been destroyed. He had sent several engineers to the shuttle to investigate its systems, but they had found nothing that could indicate where the shuttle had been built or the type of race it belonged to, other than they were slightly smaller in stature than a Hocklyn.

"Where are they?" Shrea roared in anger as he listened to another negative report. He turned on Second Leader Vrill with a heavy scowl on his face. "They can't just have vanished!"

"We have two hundred protectors and six shuttles searching for them," Vrill replied, his large, cold eyes looking over at First Leader Shrea. "We will find them; they can't have gone too far. Those mountains are heavily forested, and there are a lot of places the survivors of the shuttle can be hiding. It may take time, but eventually we will find them."

"Were we able to recover anything useful from the wreck of their ship?" demanded Shrea, wanting to hear something positive. They had managed to find several small pieces of wreckage, which had been brought inside the Vengeance for study.

"Nothing, First Leader," Vrill responded, his eyes looking down. "The small pieces we have found were too badly damaged from the nuclear explosion to be of any use."

Shrea said nothing, only turned to look coldly at the main viewscreen, which was focused on the planet below. No matter how long it took, he would not leave this planet until those survivors were found.

Colonel Sheen gazed worriedly at the large sensor screen above the plotting table. With a heavy sigh, she walked over closer to it and then gazed at the holographic image the plotting table was generating. It showed the fourth planet of the system where the message had originated from with seven deadly red threat icons in orbit.

"Six escort cruisers and a war cruiser," Major Fields reported as he studied the information carefully. "They are in low orbits, obviously scanning the surface. We have detected numerous shuttles going back and forth between the ships and the planet."

"They're searching for the cadets," commented Amanda, feeling frustrated. She had not expected to find an entire Hocklyn war fleet waiting for her. The message from the cadets had indicated that only one Hocklyn ship had been detected approaching the New Horizon. The war cruiser was what concerned her. It was larger than the WarStorm and packed a hell of a lot of firepower in its weapons. It would have powerful shields as well as those deadly energy beams.

"It will be another sixteen hours before our light cruisers reach us and another twenty hours after that before the New Tellus can get here," added Richard, coming to stand next to his wife.

"We have six stealth scout ships on board," Amanda said, reaching a decision. "I want two of them made ready to micro-jump into the system. She touched the controls of the holographic imager and the planet and the Hocklyns ships swelled, appearing much closer. "Find Captain Gaines and tell him to have two squads of his marines ready to deploy. If we get any hint of the location of those cadets, I want those two scout ships ready to go in for a rescue. Make sure both scouts are equipped with self-destruct charges. They can't be captured."

Major Fields nodded and began passing on the orders. Captain Gaines was in charge of the marine contingent on the WarStorm.

"What are you going to do, Amanda?" Richard asked. He knew they were in a bad situation.

"I don't think we can wait on the New Tellus," Amanda said, turning to look with deep concern at her husband. "The Hocklyns evidently have a pretty good idea where the cadets are hiding. I think we have to attack as soon as the light cruisers get here. But if we get an opportunity to rescue those cadets, I want the marines in a position to do so."

"That's a war cruiser," Richard reminded his wife, nodding at the holographic image above the plotting table. "It will be heavily armed. The mission profile originally called for us to engage an escort cruiser. Against a fleet of this size, we could take some losses. We also don't know if our new shields will stand up to a war cruiser's energy beams."

"I know," Amanda replied evenly, turning to gaze into her husband's eyes. "But I don't think we have a choice. We have to rescue those kids and destroy this fleet before the Hocklyns can send word back to their base."

"If they haven't already," Richard spoke in a soft voice, his eyes focusing on the holographic display. "They may have sent a message by now."

It was early the next morning, and Jeremy and Kevin were watching the Hocklyns below them. Over a dozen protectors were slowly working their way up the side of the mountain.

"Another hour or two at the most and they will make it up here," Kevin muttered, his eyes focused on the protectors below.

"Looks like it," replied Jeremy, knowing Kevin was right. "Kelsey said their body armor is pretty tough, so you may need to make head shots." Jeremy wished they had another rifle. The single assault rifle they had and the two pistols would not hold the Hocklyns off for long.

Kevin nodded; he had never killed anyone before. He steadied his breathing and continued to watch the advancing Hocklyns.

Katie was in the back of the cave fooling around with the small emergency FTL transmitter they had brought from the shuttle. It had been hidden in an emergency pack, which had contained a first aid kit, several small packs of emergency rations, fire making tools, the binoculars, and several small flashlights. Kelsey had recognized it for what it was, but had told the group it wouldn't reach outside of the solar system they were in. It was for short-range communication only.

Getting up, Katie carried the small transmitter and her computer to the edge of the cave. She had hardwired her computer to the transmitter in the hopes of boosting its range.

"What are you doing, Katie?" asked Kelsey, coming to stand next to the young teenager. She noticed with surprise that Katie had modified the emergency transmitter.

"The Hocklyns will be here shortly," replied Katie, her eyes showing fear at facing the aliens. "I've set my computer to send out a quick pulse signal which your Federation ship might be able to receive if it's within range. The pulse will continue once every thirty seconds for ten minutes. Then the power will be exhausted."

Kelsey looked at Katie. The teenager had held up remarkably well in this situation. Kelsey knew they didn't have much more time before the Hocklyns found them. She also knew that there was a good chance the Hocklyns would pick up the signal.

Letting out a deep breath, she looked at Katie. "Do it."

"I've got a signal!" Lieutenant Trask screamed excitedly as a short-pulsed message was intercepted by her com system. She quickly read the short message, her face turning pale.

"It's the cadets. The Hocklyns are getting close. They estimate they have another hour or two at the most before they're found."

"Do you have a location?" demanded Amada, striding over to stand above Trask.

"Yes, the signal is repeating every thirty seconds. I'm sending the coordinates over to Major Fields."

Amanda turned and rushed to the plotting table as a map of the distant planet appeared. Over the last day, the two stealth scouts with the marines on board had made a detailed scan of the planet.

"They're right here," Fields said, pointing his finger part way up a small mountain.

"Is there anywhere we can land the scouts?" asked Amanda, looking at the topography in that area. She had to get her marines to the cadets before the Hocklyns reached them.

"There's a small plateau right here, slightly above the cadets. We can have the scouts there in less than forty minutes." Major Fields looked questionably at Colonel Sheen, waiting on his orders. "It will be a dangerous operation, Colonel."

"Send the scouts in," ordered Amanda, decisively. "If they can't get the cadets safely back to the stealth scouts, the marines are to destroy them and then set up a defensive perimeter around where the cadets are hiding. They will have to hold it until we can get there with reinforcements."

Amanda turned and went back to the command console. "Lieutenant Ashton, plot a micro-jump to just outside the fourth planet's gravity well. Transmit it to the four light cruisers as well. We're going in." Amanda was glad she had the four light cruisers. They had only arrived four hours back. She had already briefed their commanding officers on the situation. Activating the ship-to-ship communications on her mini-com, she addressed all the warships. "All ships go to Condition One. We will shortly be engaging the Hocklyns."

On the Vengeance, First Leader Shrea had smiled when the com operator reported that they had picked up what seemed to be a distress beacon from the planet. He had already sent the location of the beacon to his protectors down on the ground. Shortly, the survivors from the shuttle would be captured and then they would be brought up to the Vengeance for interrogation. He doubted if they would survive it very few did.

"They're nearly here," reported Kevin, peeking back over the boulder at the Hocklyns working their way up the steep slope. His palms felt sweaty, and he was feeling scared.

Jeremy nodded his head. This was it. They had run out of time. He glanced down at the pistol in his belt. It had a full clip in it and he had two more if needed. It was hard to believe that everything was going to end this way. He wished he could have spoken to his father and mother one last time. There were so many things he would have liked to have said to them.

"Kevin, I need you to take out one or two of them with the rifle. That might buy us some more time."

"Okay," Kevin said as he laid the rifle on the boulder and took aim at a Hocklyn several hundred meters down the slope. Then, glancing over at Jeremy, "I just don't think anyone is coming, Jeremy. I know what Kelsey told you. If you have to use that pistol, make it quick. Start with Katie so she won't have to see the rest of us die."

Jeremy nodded. He didn't know what else to say.

Kevin took careful aim and steadied his breathing. He tried to remember everything his father had taught him about hunting. Sighting in his target, he carefully squeezed the trigger, hearing the sharp report of the assault rifle. He let out a deep breath as he saw his target fall.

The other Hocklyns yelled and pointed up the slope toward the cave. They instantly started scrambling over the rough terrain. Kevin fired several more rounds, striking another Hocklyn who fell wounded to the ground.

Jeremy and Kevin both ducked as a fusillade of return fire struck the boulders and the surrounding Cliffside. They hunkered down behind the boulders, knowing it was over. The Hocklyns now knew exactly where they were and were rushing up the slope. They would reach the cave shortly. Jeremy pulled the pistol out of his belt and clicked the safety off. He looked over at Katie, who was standing just inside the cave entrance. He hadn't known she was standing there, and she was staring at him with sudden understanding in her eyes.

"I'm sorry, Katie," Jeremy said softly as he raised the pistol.

"I love you, Jeremy," replied Katie, closing her eyes as a tear rolled down her cheek.

"Hold your fire!" a strange voice yelled from above them.

Jeremy looked up, shocked to see four heavily armed marines descending rapidly on ropes to land just behind the boulders. At the same time, he heard additional weapons open up from above. Jeremy let the pistol drop from his hand as he gazed in astonishment at the marine who was coming toward him.

"I'm Corporal William Sanders from the WarStorm. I take it you must be Jeremy Strong?"

"Yes, sir," replied Jeremy, feeling stunned. The other marines had taken up positions behind the boulders and, along with Kevin, were laying down a withering fire at the Hocklyns below.

Katie opened her eyes and upon seeing the marines, started crying.

Kelsey hurried over and put her arms protectively around the teenager. She looked questionably at the marine corporal. "Did you say the WarStorm is here?"

"It will be shortly," replied the corporal as more heavily armed marines rappelled down into the cave. "Our mission is to hold this position until the WarStorm can send reinforcements."

Angela walked over to Kelsey, gazing in disbelief at the marines. She suddenly threw herself at Corporal Sanders, hugging him and sobbing uncontrollably.

"You're safe," Sanders said, knowing all five of these young people had been through a horrendous ordeal. "It's not over yet, but my marines and I will make sure the Hocklyns never make it up here." He looked over the cave and nodded in satisfaction. This was a good defensive location, particularly with the large boulders concealing the entrance.

"Corporal Sanders, what's your situation?" a tense voice asked over Sanders mini-com.

"We're in a small cave with good cover, Captain Gaines," Sanders reported as four more marines made it down to the cave and took up firing positions at the boulders.

"It's not so good up here," Gaines replied. "We have some inbound fighters closing in on us. I'm going to blow the scouts and then we will be coming down to you."

Jeremy looked at Sanders questionably. Were they destroying their ships?

"We thought we might have to destroy our scout ships," explained Sanders, looking back over at Jeremy. "We can't let them fall into Hocklyn hands, so we rigged them with self-destruct charges."

Sanders had scarcely gotten the words out when two dull explosions rattled the cave, sending some loose dirt cascading down from the ceiling.

Sanders smiled at Jeremy and said, "You know, you look a lot like your father."

Jeremy only nodded as more marines rappelled down into the cave. The last one was a captain, and he instantly took charge of the situation as he walked up to Corporal Sanders.

"Corporal Sanders, set up some of our heavy weapons to cover the entire slope leading up to this cave. If we can hold out for two hours this should be over."

Sanders nodded and hurried over to the other marines. He tapped Kevin on his shoulder and indicated he should move back to the other cadets. There were fourteen marines now in the cave, counting Captain Gaines.

Gaines looked thoughtfully at the four cadets and Katie. He shook his head, amazed that they had managed to survive this long with the Hocklyns searching for them. But then again he also realized who Kelsey and Jeremy's parents were.

"You five get to the back of the cave where it's safer," he ordered. "It will take the Hocklyn protectors a few minutes to get reorganized before they can launch a new attack."

"Yes, sir," Jeremy replied, then he added. "Thank you, sir; you have no idea how glad I was to see Corporal Sanders."

"I can imagine," Gaines replied as he turned to go check on his marines.

In the war cruiser Vengeance, First Leader Shrea was livid with rage. "What do you mean a military force has landed and engaged our protectors?"

"That's what's being reported," Second Leader Vrill replied as he listened to the frantic reports coming in from the ground. "A military force of unknown size landed in two large shuttles on a small plateau on the mountain. They engaged our forces that were coming up the slope, wiping them out. They then destroyed their shuttles and took up a defensive position where we think the survivors from the destroyed ship are."

"They're waiting for retrieval," Shrea said, his mind racing. "Order all of our ships to form up on us; we need to get out of this planet's gravity well. We can expect inbound warships at any moment."

"Too late," the sensor operator reported as red threat icons began blossoming on his screen. "They're already here."

"Scan them and see if you can identify what race they belong to," Shrea ordered in a shrill voice. "We need to know if one of our subject races has built a fleet in secret, or if we are dealing with a new group of aliens."

"We have one capital ship and four escorts inbound," the sensor operator reported as he ran the ships profiles through the database of the Vengeance. Then the sensor operator turned pale as he read the results of the search. "First Leader, these are warships from the Human Federation of Worlds."

"Impossible!" Shrea spoke, his voice radiating anger. "All the human worlds and their fleet were wiped out years ago."

"Evidently not," Second Leader Vrill replied as he studied the information coming in over the sensors and scanners. "We have a 900-meter Monarch heavy cruiser coming in, as well as four 600-meter light cruisers of human Federation design. Some of the humans must have escaped the destruction and settled elsewhere."

Shrea stood on the command pedestal looking with deep concern at his Second Leader. "The AIs will be extremely upset about this. The families responsible for allowing these humans to escape and become a threat to us once again will lose all of their honor and family holdings. There has been treachery on the part of at least one Hocklyn family if humans managed to escape the destruction of their worlds. Someone high up in the attack fleet back then had to know some of the humans escaped."

"No one will know if we can't defeat this human fleet," stated Vrill, wondering just how powerful the human capital ship was.

"Move all of our ships into a screening formation and standby to launch our war wing," First Leader Shrea spoke as he prepared for battle. "Today we have an opportunity to earn honor for ourselves and our families. We will not fail!"

Amanda gazed with cool detachment at the main viewscreen. It showed a close-up of the war cruiser as it began to pull away from the planet with its escort cruisers forming up in a defensive formation around it. The Hocklyns were already launching their fighters.

She tapped the mini-com in her right ear, activating ship-to-ship communications. "All ships, launch fighters and engage incoming enemy craft."

On the main sensor screen, it showed thirty-four inbound Hocklyn fighters. Her own fighters would be outnumbered almost three to one. It was evident that the fighter wing on the WarStorm was far too small for this type of battle. Of course, if the New Tellus were here she would have an advantage in fighters. At the moment, she couldn't take the risk of the inbound Hocklyn fighters closing the range and damaging any of her warships until she knew if there had been any new developments in Hocklyn ship weaponry. Her fighters would have to engage them first and keep them away from the warships.

"Helm, continue to move us in on an intercept course, I want to engage their warships within the gravity well of the planet so they can't escape."

"Communications, contact our other four stealth scouts and tell them to begin jamming all FTL communication frequencies."

The stealth scouts had been launched earlier and taken up positions far outside of the gravity well of the planet to jam all FTL transmissions. Amanda knew this would stop any FTL transmissions from leaving the system, but all the ships on both sides would still be able to use their short-range communications to talk to one another.

"Combat range in twenty minutes," Major Fields reported as he studied the information that was constantly being updated on his plotting board and entered into the holographic imager above the table. "Fighters will enter combat range of each other in seven minutes."

Amanda nodded as she took her seat behind the command console and buckled herself in. Across the Command Center, everyone was doing the same. This was a change from the old ships. Too many crewmembers had been injured in Command Centers when they had been thrown off their feet or knocked into consoles. Richard had gone to auxiliary control, ready to take over if the Command Center were knocked out.

"Tactical, when we get within range, I want all the forward lasers locked onto that war cruiser."

"What about the Devastator Two missiles?" Major Fields asked. He knew they were the most powerful weapons they had and could probably easily destroy the war cruiser.

"Have them ready, but we won't use them unless we absolutely have to," Amanda answered. She preferred to save them in case they ran across an AI ship. This was going to be an old-fashioned slugging match. Besides, she had orders to evaluate the Hocklyn's current weapons development.

She watched the sensor screens as the red icons representing the thirty-four Hocklyn fighters and the fourteen green icons indicating her own fighters suddenly became intermixed.

"Fighters engaged," Major Fields reported.

"Stand by on Hunter missiles," Amanda ordered. Once they got within range, she would use the hunters to try to even the odds for her fighters. But for a few minutes, they would be on their own as they tried to turn the Hocklyn fighters away from the Federation warships.

In space, the fighters were involved in a wild dogfight as they darted and turned trying to avoid incoming missiles and cannon fire. Both sides were using small interceptor missiles, and occasionally a missile would find its mark and a fighter would explode in a bright fireball as its fuel ignited and tore the fighter apart. Both sides were losing fighters. The Hocklyns died at a two to one ratio, but there were far more Hocklyn than human fighters.

"Extreme hunter missile range," Tactical reported. "Missiles are locking on targets."

"Fire," Amanda grated out as another human fighter vanished off the sensor screen.

From the WarStorm, forty-eight missiles blasted out of their missile ports and flew unerringly toward the targeted Hocklyn fighters. The Hocklyns instantly went evasive and managed to shoot a few down with their cannons, but sixteen Hocklyn fighters exploded in bright fireballs as the hunter missiles salvo found their targets.

"Thirty-three percent hits," reported Tactical as another wave of hunters was prepared. The closer they got the more accurate the missiles would be.

"Hocklyn warships are firing missiles at our fighters," Lieutenant Stalls reported as his sensor screens lit up with red threat warnings.

"Pull our fighters back," ordered Amanda, sitting up straighter. "Retask our hunters to take out those missiles and fire!" She could feel the adrenaline rushing through her. She had forgotten what combat was like. Amanda felt intensely alive, her senses heightened as she became immersed in the battle.

More missiles erupted from the WarStorm and quickly began intercepting the deadly missiles aimed at the human fighters. Several fighters were unlucky and vanished in bright fireballs as the deadly ship launched missiles struck them.

The Hocklyn fighters suddenly turned and returned to their warships, taking up a defensive position around them. Only twelve Hocklyn fighters remained. The six remaining human fighters retreated to the safety of the fleet, which was now beginning to enter weapon's range of the Hocklyn warships.

"Laser lock on war cruiser," Tactical reported.

"Fire lasers," Amanda ordered, her eyes now focused on the viewscreen, which was showing the massive 1,000-meter war cruiser. She could see the weapon turrets and missile tubes. All of those weapons would soon be focused on the WarStorm. Amanda just hoped the new energy screen would hold.

Four bright orange-red beams of light jumped from the bow of the WarStorm, striking the shields of the Hocklyn war cruiser. The shields wavered briefly and then two of the beams penetrated striking the war cruiser's hull, cutting deep inside.

First Leader Shrea felt his ship cry out in pain as its shields were ravaged and two of those deadly beams cut deep into the hull. On the damage control board, a number of red lights started flashing. He frowned to himself. Those lasers were much more powerful than the ones the humans had reportedly used in the original war. Even so, his own energy weapons were now locked on.

"Fire!" he ordered, his cold eyes locked on the viewscreen. He had the humans outnumbered, and he planned to make short work of this human fleet. If he could capture one of their smaller vessels, then his honor would be greatly enhanced.

Two light blue energy beams reached out and slapped the protective shield of the WarStorm. The shield wavered but did not go down.

"Shields holding," Fields reported as he checked the power readings on the WarStorm's energy shield. "But just barely."

"All ships engage!" Amanda ordered as the WarStorm and her four escorting light cruisers reached optimum firing range.

Orange-red and light blue beams played back and forth between the two fleets. Occasionally a beam would penetrate an energy screen, causing major damage to the unlucky ship.

"Hocklyns are launching missiles," Lieutenant Stalls reported over his mini-com. "Some are armed with nukes."

"Turn us broadside and bring the HG turrets on line. Fire when we have a target lock. All defensive turrets fire and bring those incoming missiles down."

The WarStorm turned rapidly and the HG turrets began firing on the Hocklyn war cruiser. One-meter shells traveling at 10,000 kilometers per second struck the war cruiser's shields, delivering a one-kiloton blow with each exploding shell. Defensive fire began bringing down the inbound Hocklyn missiles in bright explosive bursts. The WarStorm's screen lit up as numerous missiles and cannon fire began to rake her energy screen. Then a Hocklyn nuclear missile detonated against the screen, causing it to waver and allowing several rounds to impact the hull.

"Minor damage to section seven," the damage control officer called out. "We have lost hull integrity there, and we're venting atmosphere. Damage control teams are en route."

"Light cruiser Raven has been hit by several nukes and has lost her shields," reported Major Fields, his face turning pale. "She is trying to withdraw."

The Hocklyns, seeing that the Raven had lost her energy shielding, redoubled their efforts to destroy it as three Hocklyn support cruisers poured everything they had into her. Moments later, a series of powerful explosions blew the Federation cruiser apart.

"Raven is down," reported Lieutenant Stalls, trying to keep his voice calm.

"Shields are starting to fail on the war cruiser," Major Fields reported as he studied the inbound tactical data. "Our shells are starting to get through."

Amanda watched as massive explosions covered the war cruiser's hull, blasting huge jagged rents in the ship. It was starting to suffer some major damage.

Inside the War Room of the Vengeance, First Leader Shrea was picking himself up off the floor. Looking over at the damage control board, he saw it was covered in red warning lights. The Vengeance continued to shudder as it was pounded by the human weapons. This human warship was much more powerful than those of the past. This didn't bode well for the Hocklyn Slave Empire in the future. The AIs kept the Hocklyn's weapon development to a minimum. If there were more of these human ships out there, the Hocklyn fleet could some day be facing a very dangerous opponent. He needed to get word back to Commodore Rateif.

"Communications, can we get out an FTL message?"

"No, First Leader, all FTL frequencies are being jammed."

Shrea looked at the sensor screen and felt dread. They were too far inside the planet's gravity well to escape into hyperspace. They had to defeat the human fleet. Even as his thoughts turned to what needed to be done an HG shell penetrated deep into the heart of the war cruiser, detonating and taking the War Room with it. Moments later, the Vengeance exploded as its self-destructs engaged automatically.

Amanda instinctively covered her eyes as the war cruiser on the viewscreen vanished in nuclear fire. As she looked back at the screen, all she could see were burning remains and expanding gases.

"The war cruiser is down," reported Lieutenant Stalls, letting out a sharp sigh of relief.

"The StarFury is being hard pressed by the Hocklyn support cruisers," Major Fields informed Colonel Sheen. "They are requesting assistance."

"Move us closer and begin targeting the support cruisers," Amanda ordered, determined to destroy all of the Hocklyn ships. Now that the war cruiser was gone, the surviving Hocklyn ships didn't have the heavy weapons needed to endanger the WarStorm.

The WarStorm moved closer, and the Hocklyn support ships began to suffer heavy damage. Unlike the more powerful energy screen of the war cruiser, the WarStorm's lasers tore completely through the lesser-shielded support cruisers. The HG turrets were devastating as they blasted down the Hocklyn's shields and then ripped massive holes in the hulls. In another ten minutes, it was over as the last Hocklyn ship exploded in nuclear fire when its self-destruct activated.

Amanda let out a deep breath. She looked over at the damage control board and was surprised to see over a dozen red lights glowing. She hadn't even been aware that the WarStorm had taken that much damage.

"How are the cruisers?" asked Amanda, feeling her adrenaline starting to subside.

"We lost the Raven. The StarFury is reporting heavy damage and her FTL core has been destroyed," reported Major Fields as he listened to the incoming damage reports over his mini-com. "The Far Reach and Distant Star are reporting only light damage. They will be back to full operational status within the hour."

"Send some engineers and repair crews from the WarStorm to the StarFury to evaluate their FTL core damage. If we can't repair it, the StarFury will have to be abandoned."

"Yes, Colonel," Major Fields replied. It only took him a few moments to pass on the orders and make the necessary arrangements to assist the StarFury.

Satisfied that everything possible was being done to repair the damage to her wounded ships, she passed on some additional orders. "Recall the stealth scouts," ordered Amanda. She needed to get her marines and the cadets off the planet. "Once the scouts are back, load them up with marines and let's get our people off of that planet."

Six hours later, Amanda watched as the last scout came up from the planet's surface. The cadets and her marines had been rescued and were being brought back to the WarStorm. Even as she watched, two large nuclear detonations occurred on the planet's surface. There would be no trace that anyone had ever been down on the planet. The nukes would erase all of the evidence. They would also eliminate any surviving Hocklyn protectors that were still down on the surface that the marines might have missed.

"Major Fields, scan the battle zone for any wreckage from our ships and fighters. I don't want to leave anything behind that can be attributed to a Federation warship. If the Hocklyns ever come back to this system, I don't want them to be able to find anything."

"Yes, Colonel," Major Fields replied. "We have also just received a com message from the New Tellus. The battle carrier has arrived on the outskirts of the system."

"They're ahead of schedule," responded Amanda, looking at the long-range sensors, which were now showing a friendly green icon on the far edge of the system. "When their drive core has cooled down sufficiently have them micro-jump in. We can certainly use their shuttles to help scan the wreckage."

On the stealth scout ship, Jeremy gazed out one of the small viewports at the massive ship they were flying toward. Jeremy guessed it must be over eight or nine hundred meters at least.

"That ship's huge," uttered Jeremy, glancing over at a smiling Kelsey. Jeremy had thought the New Horizon had been a large ship.

"Just wait until you see a battle carrier," Kelsey commented knowingly. "One of those comes in at over 1,500 meters."

Jeremy took Kelsey's hand and shook his head. "I guess I have a lot to learn."

Kelsey nodded and looked around at all of her friends. "I think we all do. After this our lives will never be the same again."

She didn't say it, but she knew that none of her friends would ever be able to return home to Earth again. The secrets they now knew were too dangerous to risk being accidentally revealed. She thought she could arrange for Katie to be transferred to the schools in Ceres. She would fit right in with their modern curriculum.

As for Kevin and Angela, they could join the fleet and would probably be stationed at New Tellus. Then, of course, there was Jeremy. Kelsey had already decided that she and Jeremy were going to be a team. One day they would have a ship of their own to command. She leaned back against Jeremy and felt him slide his arm protectively around her. Smiling to herself, she relaxed. The WarStorm was here, and she knew they were going to be safe. Very shortly, they would be returning home.

Katie looked across the small scout ship with a pleased smile. Kelsey and Jeremy were cozy, and Angela and Kevin were still talking. Looking down, she gazed at her small handheld computer. She turned it over and could tell that it was irreparable. Transmitting the signal had burned out its processor. Leaning back, she thought about Ariel. Only now did she truly realize just how important friends were. She knew that this group of five she was a part of would always be special. When she returned to the Moon, she knew she had a lot of serious apologizing to do. She just hoped that Ariel would forgive her.

Chapter Fourteen

Amanda gazed at the large viewscreen on the front wall of the Command Center. The WarStorm was currently in a high orbit around the former Federation world of New Providence. It was extremely evident that the planet's ecosphere had recovered from the war of over one hundred and twenty-five years ago. The planet was green and blue, with scattered white clouds covering large areas of the surface.

Close scans had revealed the remains of former cities, but the planet was rapidly removing any signs that humanity had ever lived there in large numbers. It was also very evident that there were no signs of human life.

"It's the same as New Eden, everything is returning to how it was before the war and before the planet was colonized," spoke Amanda, recalling the last time she had been to New Providence. That was when the StarStrike and First Fleet had returned from their scouting mission deep into Hocklyn space, only to find the Human Federation of Worlds destroyed.

"We're not picking up any obvious power sources or any indications that anyone survived the Hocklyn occupation," Richard spoke from where he was standing behind Lieutenant Stalls as they studied the data being recorded by the sensors and scanners.

"What about the hidden marine bases?" asked Amanda, letting out a deep sigh. She had hoped that a few people might have survived up in the mountains where it was more isolated and there were more places to hide. But so far, they had found nothing.

"We have sent signals down to where the underground marine installations are supposed to be, but there have been no responses to our hails," replied Richard, shaking his head in disappointment. "I don't think they made it. After we left, the Hocklyns must have returned and overrun the bases. General Allister's plan must have failed."

"What I don't understand is why there are no signs of battle damage at any of the sites," commented Amanda, feeling confused. "As heavily armed as General Allister's people were it should have been one hell of a battle, but there are no signs of anything."

The viewscreen changed to show a view of the former planetary capital of New Ashton. At one time, over six million people had made

231

the city their home. Now the countryside was encroaching back into the shattered ruins. Already, overgrowth was hiding much of what had once been one of the largest cities in the Federation.

"I don't think there is anything here for us," Richard said finally after looking at the latest scans.

"Let's go on to Aquaria," Amanda said with a heavy sigh.

She had really hoped to find a few survivors on New Providence. The home system had been a surprise. Two Hocklyn support cruisers were still patrolling the system. Amanda had sent in the stealth scouts, but they had found very little. Both Tellus and Maken were rapidly recovering from the war, but there were no signs of human life.

As the WarStorm accelerated away from the planet, Amanda wondered how the rest of the fleet was doing. The battle carrier and the two surviving light cruisers had been sent back to New Tellus after the battle to rescue the cadets. The StarFury had to be scuttled because of the severe damage to her FTL drive. They had lost two valuable ships in the battle with the Hocklyns, which should serve as a reminder to the people back home of just how dangerous the Hocklyns were, even when faced with superior weapons and shields.

Once the fleet was ready to return to New Tellus, the WarStorm had continued on to complete her mission. They had used the stealth scouts to scan numerous worlds to see how far the Hocklyn Slave Empire had expanded. From what Amanda could tell, the Hocklyns were slightly ahead of their predicted schedule.

"As soon as we have cleared New Providence's gravity well, plot a jump to Aquaria." Amanda ordered. She felt her hands shaking and had to concentrate to steady them. Perhaps soon she would know the fate of her parents.

Down on the planet of New Providence, passive sensors continued to track the departing ship. Deep beneath the ground in the planetary defense center, General Craig Parr watched the departing Federation ship.

"We don't know if it was a trick or not," Colonel Adamson spoke, his eyes focused on one of the large viewscreens which was showing the warship.

"It's a modified Monarch heavy cruiser," General Parr spoke, still aggravated that his superiors had refused to allow contact. "Admiral Streth must have escaped and built a new colony far away from Federation space. That ship is the proof of that."

"Perhaps," Adamson admitted with a nod of his head. "But what good could have come from contacting them, other than revealing our presence? Our greatest defense all of these years has been the fact that the Hocklyns don't know we're here."

"You're right," replied Parr, looking over at Adamson. "At least we know they're out there. Perhaps someday we will be strong enough to go looking for them."

"We have ten million people to protect," Colonel Adamson commented. "Ten million people we need to keep hidden from the Hocklyns."

"I don't think we have seen the last of them," General Parr said, indicating the large viewscreen. I have a feeling that someday they will return. When they do, we need to be ready." Reaching forward, he turned the large viewscreen off. They had other work to take care of. However, it was still comforting to know that somewhere out in the galaxy other Federation people had survived.

Amanda stepped out of the stealth scout surrounded by half a dozen heavily armed marines. Looking down the beach, she felt a chill run down her back.

"How's that possible?" asked Richard, gazing at the same sight she was. Amanda's parent's small white beach house still stood. It looked just as pristine as it had the day the two of them had left it after coming to Aquaria to go scuba diving and to spend some time with Amanda's parents.

"Only one way to find out," Amanda replied as she began walking down the beach. The sand was just as beautiful and white as she remembered it. Out over the blue ocean waves, white sea birds floated gracefully. Occasionally one would dive into the water, searching for fish.

"It's as if the war never touched this place," spoke Richard, walking next to his wife.

They were nearly to the house when the front door opened and an old woman stepped out onto the porch. She looked at Amanda and the marines with a look of surprise. Then she walked down the steps and started coming toward them.

"Hello," Amanda said, finding it hard to believe they had found a living human.

The woman was silent for a moment gazing at Amanda as if she were seeing a ghost. "You're Amanda Sheen," the woman spoke. "You look so much like your mother."

"How do you know my mother?" stammered Amanda, feeling her heart fluttering in her chest.

The old woman smiled. "My name is Janice Brennon, Avery Brennon's great granddaughter. My great grandparents took shelter here in the basement of this house with your parents when the Hocklyns attacked. We have lived here ever since."

"So my parents survived the attack?" asked Amanda, feeling her heart racing.

"Oh yes," Janice replied with a gentle smile. "A number of people on the island survived."

"Are there other survivors on the island now?" asked Richard, looking around. It was obvious someone had been helping to maintain the place.

"A few," Janice replied with a nod of her head. "Most of us stay to ourselves now. There are fewer every year. I fear that, in a few more years, there will be no one left."

Richard nodded his head in understanding. The surviving population on the island after the war must have been too low to sustain itself. Due to a lack of births, the few surviving humans were dying out.

"Why don't you and your husband come inside for some tea?" Janice asked. "I have a letter for you."

"A letter?" Amanda replied, her eyes growing wide. She almost felt as if this were a dream.

"Yes, from your mother. She said you would return some day."

Amanda and Richard followed Janice into the house. Going inside, it was like returning home. Much of the furniture was the same and, if Amanda closed her eyes, she could imagine her mother and father walking in from the kitchen at any moment.

Janice reached up on a shelf filled with old books and took one down. Opening it, she removed a faded letter and handed it to Amanda.

With shaking hands, Amanda gently unfolded it and looked down at her mother's writing. She read the half dozen short paragraphs and then handed the letter to Richard to read. Somehow, her mother had known that Amanda and Richard had survived. Her parents had lived out their lives here in this house on the island that had meant so much to them.

"Your parents are buried out by the great oak on the hill," Janice said as she poured each of them a small cup of tea.

Amanda nodded and slowly sipped her tea. She asked Janice about her life here on the island and the other survivors. From what Janice was telling her there were still around a dozen people living on Krall Island. After drinking her tea, she went outside and walked up the hill to where the great oak stood watch over the house. There were two headstones there.

For several long minutes, Amanda gazed at her parent's final resting place. She felt at peace knowing that her parents had lived out a good life here on the island they loved so much.

She watched as Richard walked up the hill to join her. Taking his hand, she looked out over the house and the blue ocean beyond.

"This war is still in the future, Richard," Amanda said, her eyes thoughtful. "Someday all of the Federation worlds will be free again. I think I want to see that happen."

"So, when we get back we return to cryosleep," he said, not surprised. He to would like to see their former worlds free from the Hocklyns.

"Yes," responded Amanda, squeezing Richard's hand. "There is a war to be fought in the future. The Hocklyns drove us from our homes, but someday we will return, and I want to be a part of that."

Richard nodded. In the distance, he could see colorful sea birds circling lazily in the clear blue sky. Up above in space, he knew the WarStorm waited. Very shortly, they would be starting their long journey back to New Tellus, and then Ceres to return to cryosleep. Sometime in the distant future, the next war was waiting for them.

Several months later, Admiral Jason Strong was out on the surface of the Moon. He didn't know when the last time was he had put on a spacesuit and gone for a walk. It took some time, but he finally made it to the top of the ridge that over looked the crater that held the Avenger and the Fleet Academy.

Stopping at the top, he took a few minutes to look around at how everything had changed in the last twenty-five years. He could still remember the stunned feeling of amazement that had swept over him the first time he had stepped upon this ridge that day so long ago. Greg and he had been looking for the source of the signal that had caused their lunar lander to crash on the Moon. Instead, they found the Avenger.

Looking down at the foot of the ridge, Jason noticed another spacesuited figure slowly climbing up. It only took Jason a moment to figure out who it was. He waited patiently as Greg finally made it to the top.

"I didn't realize how out of shape I am," puffed Greg, coming to stand next to Jason.

"We're just getting older," Jason replied with a chuckle. "I guess you heard that the New Tellus will be arriving tomorrow."

"Yes, Elizabeth is ecstatic," replied Greg, taking several deep breaths. "She can't wait to see Katie."

"Have the two of you decided what you're going to do?"

"Elizabeth and I have had several long talks about this. The officials down on Earth don't want Katie around. They say she's too big of a security risk, particularly with her computer skills. So in order to keep the three of us together, we will be moving to Ceres until Katie finishes her education. I've shown Elizabeth some photos of what the Federation survivors have built inside the asteroid, and she is willing to give it a try."

"I'm glad you were able to talk her into it. I think once she gets there and the two of you get settled in, she will love it. The Federation survivors have a lot to offer."

"General Greene will be taking over my job down on Earth," Greg added as he looked out over the crater and at the Avenger. "What are you going to do about Jeremy?"

"Jeremy is being reassigned to a Federation light cruiser to finish his officer's training; after that we'll see."

"What about the other cadets?"

"Same thing, except for Kelsey. Her father wants her to stay on Ceres for a while before she is reassigned. I suspect she is going to demand to be close to Jeremy."

"Those two make a fine couple," Greg responded with a knowing laugh.

"They will also both make a fine pair of officers," Jason calmly pointed out.

"What are you going to do, Jason?" Greg asked in a more serious tone. "I understand Admiral Anlon has offered to allow both Lisa and you to go into cryosleep and be part of the future war against the Hocklyns."

Jason was silent for a long moment, then turning he looked over at his best friend. "My job is here, Greg," he said in a somber voice. "The Columbia only returned last week from Tau Ceti bringing the news about the two habitable planets. I've already received numerous demands from Earth wanting to know when we can start building colony ships."

"I saw the report about the Columbia not finding any trace of the New Horizon."

"Yes, we're telling everyone she is missing and may have suffered a catastrophic failure of her FTL drive core."

"It looks as if you're going to have a lot to do the next few years."

Jason nodded as he looked back out over the crater with his eyes focusing on the Avenger. "We have to expand the spacedock and drastically increase the size of the academy. We're also discussing moving up the timeline to reveal the presence of the Federation survivors and the Hocklyn menace. That may very well happen in the next ten to fifteen years."

"Things are changing," responded Greg, knowing how those revelations would affect everyone.

"Yes," Jason replied as his eyes looked up to gaze at the unblinking stars. "The Hocklyns are still out there, and someday we will be facing their warships. Our job is to make sure we're ready for that day."

The two stood there for quite sometime in silence. They had been best friends since before the New Beginning's mission and would continue to be for the rest of their lives.

In the Command Center of the Avenger, Ariel turned off the main viewscreen, which had been focused on the two men on top of the distant ridge. She had been listening to their conversation with interest.

Katie would be returning shortly, and while Ariel wouldn't be able to talk to her on the Avenger, she had already made some special arrangements with Clarissa on Ceres. The two AIs were going to set up a communication line for Ariel to talk to the young teenager on a regular basis.

For some time now, Ariel hadn't felt so alone. Lisa and she had discussed her future role with the children, and Lisa had agreed that from now on Ariel would be a part of all of the children's lives. This particularly pleased Ariel as she had secretly looked at Lisa's latest doctor's report. Lisa was three months pregnant and had not told anyone yet. Ariel smiled to herself. She was already making plans on how she would introduce herself to this next special child.

The End

If you enjoyed Moon Wreck: Fleet Academy and want the series to continue in the Slaver Wars, please post a review with some stars. Good reviews encourage an author to write and help books to sell. Reviews can be just a few short sentences describing what you liked about the book. If you have suggestions, please contact me at my website listed on the following page. Thank you for reading Fleet Academy and being so supportive. Current plans call for the Slaver Wars series to be a total of six books. The next full-length novel in the Slaver Wars series will deal with Earth's first contact with the Hocklyns. It will be action packed and fast moving.

The Slaver Wars: First Strike

The cryosleep chambers are beginning to fail. Surveillance of Hocklyn space has revealed that the Hocklyns are thirty years ahead of their projected schedule and will soon reach human occupied space. War could break out any day if something isn't done. The human leaders suggest a daring plan to buy them additional time to strengthen the Fleet, as well as the defenses guarding their worlds. A First Strike deep into Hocklyn space might just buy the human worlds the extra time they need to finish their preparations for all out war against the Hocklyn Slave Empire.

Books in the series should be read in the following order.

Moon Wreck
The Slaver Wars: Alien Contact
Moon Wreck: Fleet Academy
The Slaver Wars: First Strike
The Slaver Wars: Retaliation
The Slaver Wars: The AI War

For updates on current writing projects and future publications go to my author website. Sign up for future notifications when new books come out on Amazon.

Website: http://raymondlweil.com/

Other Books by Raymond L. Weil
Available at Amazon
-

Dragon Dreams: Dragon Wars
Dragon Dreams: Gilmreth the Awakening
Dragon Dreams: Snowden the White Dragon
-

Star One: Tycho City: Discovery
Star One: Neutron Star
Star One: Dark Star
-

Moon Wreck
The Slaver Wars: Alien Contact
Moon Wreck: Fleet Academy
The Slaver Wars: First Strike
The story continues in
The Slaver Wars: Retaliation
Coming January 2014
-

Star One: Tycho City: Survival
Coming December 2013
-

Dragon Dreams: Firestorm Mount
Coming 2014

Turn the page for a quick description of Star One: Neutron Star

Star One: Neutron Star

It is the year 2044 on Earth. At the Farside observatory complex on the Moon, a startling astronomical discovery has been made. A survey for pulsars has found an x-ray source in a region of space where none has been detected before.

Upon further investigation, they find that this x-ray source is just outside of the solar system. The astronomers are paralyzed by what they have found knowing what its disastrous ramifications might be.

A neutron star is approaching the solar system. It appeared out of a small dust cloud that was shielding its approach. Armageddon has arrived; the star is on a trajectory that will take it through the center of the solar system. Life on Earth will not survive its passing.

The only hope for survival will be on the massive Star One space station at the Earth-Moon Lagrange point or possibly in Tycho City deep beneath the Moon's surface. It will be a race against time to save a fraction of the Earth's frightened population.

A power struggle will erupt on Earth over who is to survive. On Star One and at Tycho City they prepare for the worst, unfortunately, the threat from Earth might be just as dangerous as the approaching neutron star.

http://www.amazon.com/gp/product/B00860XMVU/ref=cm_cd_asin_lnk

Raymond L. Weil

Made in the USA
Middletown, DE
18 June 2018